Y0-BRG-640

# The Last Summoner

## A Novel

## By

## Nina Munteanu

**Starfire World Syndicate**

# The Last Summoner

Copyright © 2012 Nina Munteanu

All rights reserved. No part of this book may be reproduced or transmitted in any form or by any means, electronic or mechanical, including photocopying, or recording, or by any information storage and retrieval system, without permission in writing from the publisher, except by a reviewer or academic who may quote brief passages in a review or critical study.

Cover Illustration: Tomislav Tikulin
Cover Design and Typography: Costi Gurgu
Interior Design: Nina Munteanu

Published in United States by:

Starfire World Syndicate
2132 Cherokee Pkwy
Suite 2
Louisville, 40204, KY, United States
www.thepassionatewriter.com

ISBN 978-1-938658-99-0  Trade paperback (alk. paper)
ISBN 978-1-938658-00-6 Digital

Library of Congress Control Number: 2012943249

Printed in the United States of America on acid-free paper

For Karen, with gratitude

# Acknowledgements

I consulted many resources and historical authorities in the areas of medieval customs, battle, historical events, and "what if" scenarios; far too many to mention here. I thank them all and provide a selected bibliography at the back for a few. Any mistakes are mine, not theirs. My sincere gratitude goes to Craig Bowlsby, expert swordsman, for his consultation on all aspects of medieval combat and to Vanessa Rottner and Doina Maria Munteanu for superb research. I thank Margaret Ross, Vanessa Rottner and Craig Bowlsby for inciteful comments on the manuscript and fun discussions on story, character, altruism, and multi-dimensional travel. I owe my thanks to Tomislav Tikulin for a magical cover that evoked a dream, not only for my characters but for me. Thank you, Costi Gurgu, for a stellar cover design.

Heartfelt thanks go to my publisher Karen Mason whose faith and hand of genius have kept this dream alive. You are my Aeon.

# Praise for Munteanu's Previous Works:

*"Angel of Chaos* is a gripping blend of big scientific ideas, cutthroat politics and complex yet sympathetic characters that will engage readers from its thrilling opening to its surprising and satisfying conclusion."
> — **Hayden Trenholm**, Aurora-winning author of *The Steele Chronicles*

*Darwin's Paradox* is "a thill ride that makes us think and tugs the heart."
> — **Robert J. Sawyer**, Hugo-Award author of *Wake*

*Angel's Promises* is "a stunning example of good storytelling with an excellent setting and cast of characters."
> — **Tangent Online**

*Collision with Paradise* is "a very intelligent story, with fantastic world-building."
> — **Romantic Times**

"Munteanu asserts her mastery of the sensual SF romantic thriller. [*Collision with Paradise* is] an unforgettable read that's immensely alluring, surprising, and heart-throbbing."
> — **Yet Another Book Review**

"A master of metaphor, Munteanu turns an adventure story into a wonderland of alien rabbit holes…[*Outer Diverse* is] a fascinating and enthralling read."
> — **Craig Bowlsby, author of Commander's Log**

"Those who do not remember the past are condemned to relive it."

— Santavana

## *Dramatis Personae: Book One (Prussia, 1410)*
## Members of the von Grunwald Household:

- ✠ (Lord) *Herr* Ulrich (Ulreeh) Schoen, Baron von Grunwald: Vivianne's father
- ✠ (Lady) *Frau* Rosamund Schoen, Baronin von Grunwald: first wife of the baron (*deceased*)
- ✠ (Lady) *Frau* Dianne (Dee-ànne) Schoen, Baronin von Grunwald: second wife of the baron; Vivianne's mother (*deceased*)
- ✠ (Lady) *Herrin* Vivianne (Vee-viànne) Schoen, Baronesse von Grunwald: only daughter of the baron; later to become the Comptesse d'Anjou
- ✠ *Herr* Wolfgang (Volfgang) von Eisenreich: young squire under the baron's tutelage.
- ✠ Uta Wolkenstein: Vivianne's old nursemaid and current chambermaid
- ✠ *Père* Daniel Auger: the chaplain of the castle and pastor of Grunwald village
- ✠ Doctor Baldung Grien: castle and village physician
- ✠ Gertrude Schwartzburg: the new dairymaid
- ✠ Berthold Kramer: the castle seneschal
- ✠ Frieda Kramer: Berthold's wife, head housekeeper
- ✠ Theobald Bikenbach: the head cook
- ✠ Georg Sachsenhausen: one of Theobald's scullions
- ✠ Warner Seinsjein: the gatekeeper
- ✠ Milda: a Lithuanian slave
- ✠ Tancred Frosch: a young footman of the castle
- ✠ Reinmar Vogt: an older footman of the castle
- ✠ Walther Meissen and Nerdhart Burdach: two of the baron's young footmen and guard, and friends of Wolfgang
- ✠ Gunter: one of the baron's pages
- ✠ Sigmund Haupt: a young peasant village boy

## Brethren Knights and guest Knights of the Teutonic Order:

- ✠ Ulrich von Jungingen: *Hochmeister* (Grand Master) of the Teutonic Order
- ✠ Kuno von Lichtenstein: Teutonic Knight, *Großkomtur* of the Order
- ✠ Markward von Salzbach: Teutonic Knight, *Komtur* of Brandenburg
- ✠ Konrad *der Weis* VII of Schweidnitz: Polish Duke of Oels (Olesnica), allied with the Order
- ✠ Heinrich Schaumburg: Voigt bailiff (mayor) of Sambia Burgemeister??
- ✠ Friedrich von Wallenrode: Teutonic Knight, Grand Marshal of the Order
- ✠ Casimir V: Polish duke of Stettin, allied with the Order
- ✠ Werner von Tettingen: Teutonic Knight, Hospital *Großmeister* and *Komtur* of Elbing
- ✠ Heinrich von Schwelborn: Teutonic Knight, *Komtur* of Tuchel
- ✠ Jan Grabie, Count von Wendem: Teutonic Knight, *Komtur* of Gniew
- ✠ Albrecht von Schwartzburg: Teutonic Knight, commander of supply for the Order
- ✠ Nicholas von Renys (Mikolaj Rynski of the clan Rogala): Polish secular knight, leading the banner of Kulm and joint founder of the Lizard League
- ✠ Siegfried von Heidelberg: German Knight Templar
- ✠ Holbracht Ekdahl: Livonian Teutonic Knight, friend and former colleague of the baron

## Others:

- ✠ Leduc Mortameur: mysterious visitor from France, betrothed to Vivianne

## Dramatis Personae: Book Two (Paris, 2010)

- ✠ François Rabelais: common thief and sometime anarchist
- ✠ Antoine Rabelais: François's destitute uncle and anarchist member of the *Résistance*, the SSLF
- ✠ Marcel Rabelais: François's father (deceased), former member of the *Résistance*
- ✠ Angeline Rabelais: François's mother (deceased), former founder of the *Résistance*
- ✠ Dietmar von Eisenreich: Grand Marshal of the First Nazi Reich Empire, descendant of Wolfgang von Eisenreich
- ✠ Lizette von Eisenreich: the third wife of the Grand Marshal Eisenreich and one of François's patrons
- ✠ Julien Boulanger: a prominent Nazi officer but secret member of the SSLF; Dianne's lover
- ✠ Sabine and Etienn Escoffier: waitress and owner/chef at *le Coude Foux* and member of the SSLF
- ✠ Vincent Rouard: a former drug dealer, slum neighbour of François and descendant of Baldung Grien
- ✠ Sylvie: one of François's girlfriends

## Dramatis Personae: Book Three (Rest of the World, 1410 to present-day)

- ✠ Konrad Frankl; Baron von Grunwald's lawyer in the Rhineland in 1447
- ✠ Doctor Eduard Albert Martin: the chief of obstetrics at the University of Berlin in 1861
- ✠ Oskar: a coachman of the Crown Prince Friedrich and Princess Victoria
- ✠ Jurgen von Eisenreich: descendant of Wolfgang von Eisenreich, in the service of the impetuous Kaiser Wilhelm II in 1889
- ✠ Count Alfred von Waldersee: Aides-de-Camp of the Kaiser in 1889

- ✠ Crown Prince Wilhelm II in 1889
- ✠ Annie Oakley: an American sharp shooter with Buffalo Bill's Wild West Show in 1889
- ✠ Nikola Tesla: Serbian scientist and visionary in 1905
- ✠ Wolfgang von Eisenreich: son of Jurgen, in the service of Kaiser Wilhelm II during the Great War of 1914
- ✠ Claus Schoen, Baron von Grunwald: descendent of Ulrich Schoen; in the service of Hitler I in the late 1930s and 1940s
- ✠ Otto von Heidelberg: descendent of Siegfried von Heidelberg
- ✠ Vivian von Heidelberg: grand-daughter of Siegfried von Heidelberg, headed women's and minority rights movement in England during the Renaissance
- ✠ Vincent Rouard: CEO of *Aeonic Visions* in 2025
- ✠ Helena von Heidelberg: descendant of Siegried von Heidelberg; Director of Education with Worldwide Classroom, an arm of *Aeonic Visions* and Head or Metatron University in 2025
- ✠ Dr. David Suzuki, co-founder of Suzuki Foundation, broadcaster and environmentalist in 2025

✠

# Prologue
*Prussia, 1395*

Ulrich Schoen stumbled into the oily swamp and seized in a breath as bracing cold water rose to his waist. He thrashed out, gasping, and leaned a hand against one of the trees of the drowned forest. He wasn't going to surprise a boar this way. He surveyed the thick forest mist. No matter. His heart wasn't in the hunt today.

"Let Ekdahl get the first kill," he muttered to himself. "I'm drunk." He belched loudly. "I don't care. She's gone, my love is gone." Today was the anniversary of her death six years ago. "The love of my life, the reason for living..." he blathered on to himself and leaned his forehead on the tree then closed his eyes.

"Schoen!" he heard his friend shout. "You bastard! Where've you gone!" Ekdahl was closer than he thought. Desperate to be alone, Ulrich scrambled behind the large tree and leaned against it to make himself invisible. It was drizzling. The sun hadn't yet risen. His dark hose and cotehardie blended in with the dim light of the forest, especially this early in the morning. Ekdahl came into view, muttering to himself, and trudged right past him.

"That pathetic drunk," Ekdahl went on, making Ulrich wonder if Ekdahl really knew he was there and was speaking for his benefit. "Each year he does this...He should have become a monk, like me. Smitten by love only to lose it to the holy fire. She was a fine woman that Rosamund but you'll find another, Schoen...you always do. Damn it, Schoen!" he shouted practically into Ulrich's ear. "It's been six years, for God's sake! And you're driving your whole household mad with all this dark brooding and nasty glowering. Your shouting's got little Gretel crying in her bed. You have to get over it, Schoen...or you'll drown...in your own SHIT!" he ended so loudly, Ulrich winced. He heard a quick shuffle and a splash then a curse as Ekdahl obviously slid into the mire. "*Verdammt*! I hate this swamp!" Ekdahl muttered. "Why he insists on hunting in here, where you could...DROWN!" he turned it into a shout as if making a point to the forest. "Or break your neck on these roots and things...Bah!" he ended in disgust and Ulrich heard the harsh rustle and clink of Ekdahl's trappings as he marched back toward the clearing with determined steps. Ekdahl turned his head and said over his shoulder, "Go to Hell!"

Ekdahl eventually disappeared and Ulrich stumbled out from behind the water-logged tree. "He's right," Ulrich admitted darkly as he straightened his *balderich*. "I'm a rightful mess. But I can't help it. Rosamund...my Rosamund...you were so beautiful...and soft...and kind..." Then he glowered. "Kindness killed you..."

He stumbled aimlessly through the drowned forest of Grunwald and cast a cursory glance about. It was all his—this forest and the grounds beyond to the castle. He was its lord, the Baron von Grunwald...He'd have given it all away to have her back, he thought with a hiccup and a sigh. After a long moment Ulrich decided to return; his good friend, his only friend, would be impatient for his safe return. He owed Ekdahl that much. They'd been inseparable comrades at arms on campaigns off the coast of northern Prussia, Samogitia and Lithuania. They'd watched each other's back, saved the other from a treacherous death, on many occasions.

Ulrich wiped his runny nose and realized that he was a bit lost. Just as he was making his bearings to return he heard a light splash then a gasp and more splashes. Then more sounds of distress. It was a woman!

Ulrich instantly sobered and scrambled over the uneven turf toward the desperate sounds. He came upon a large dark pond and at its center, thrashing in the water, was a young woman. Without thinking he dove into the deep water and swam toward her. Within moments he'd retrieved her. She did not struggle and he brought her easily to shore.

She lay on her back, staring past Ulrich with wild unfocused eyes, coughing and seizing in gasping breathes. Ulrich stared, mesmerized. Even wet and bedraggled, she was the most beautiful woman he'd set his eyes on. She was dressed in strange clothes, men's Hussars: dark loose breeches and a short tight-fitting coat. She wore a large backpack made of curious smooth and resilient material. She stared straight at him yet through him, as if she didn't see him at all, and murmured in some other language: "*où est que je suis…c'est quand…Cher Dieu! Sauvez-moi!*"

He boldly touched her arm to get her attention. She winced and cried out in pain. She was hurt! Then he noticed a small hole in her sleeve, wet and shiny with oozing blood. Some projectile had passed through and embedded in her flesh. The wound bled profusely and her face blazed with a fever. Who would hurt this woman with the face of an angel?

In sudden determination, Ulrich gently but firmly pulled her up over his shoulder and hushed her sounds of terrified pain with soft murmurs. "It's all right, *mein schatz*…I'll take care of you…don't be afraid…"

When he got to the forest-edge, his loyal friend was there, waiting for him, along with a few other members of his hunting party.

"Holbracht!" Ulrich shouted, crashing out of the trees with his injured charge. "Fetch a horse! She's hurt. I must get her to the castle at once!"

The hunting party hastened back to the castle and Ulrich, carrying the injured woman in his arms, shouted for the castle physician and barged into his small office. Grien came rushing out of his bedchamber, still in his nightshirt. Ulrich laid the half-conscious woman onto the doctor's examination table and Grien proceeded to remove her outer clothing.

"What happened to her? Who is she?"

"I don't know," Ulrich returned, still breathless from the incident.

"Not a Polish peasant? Or an escaped Lithuanian slave?"

"No, no," Ulrich insisted nervously. "She looks like a lady." He didn't tell Grien that she spoke some foreign language; he wanted the good doctor to do his best. Ulrich pointed. "She has a puncture on the left arm. It's bleeding." He pointed to the obvious.

"I see it. Help me get these wet clothes off her." Grien instructed him. Then Grien turned to the footmen, crowding the doorway, the same ones who had accompanied Ulrich and Holbracht on the hunt, "Be off—except you, Reinmar. Fetch my tools from the shelf there. That's it. Now go get some hot water, boy! Now! And my leeches—"

The woman suddenly grew delirious and Grien and Ulrich had to hold her down. Grien struck her hard in the face. The shock made Ulrich wince but it stilled the woman. She'd cried out and her eyes flew open wide. But she ceased to struggle. Ulrich watched her cheek go from livid white to deep crimson where Grien had struck her.

"Did you really have to do that?" he turned on the doctor.

"She was flying into hysterics," Grien said off-handedly. "I've seen it before. Women aren't stable. Not like men. Their bodies are ruled by imperfection. This makes them generally unruly. They must be controlled, particularly when in shock from an injury. Now hold her down while I undress her," he commanded the baron. Although the woman had ceased to struggle and had closed her eyes as if to shut out the harsh world, Ulrich kept his hands on her and told himself he was doing something useful.

He watched Grien gruffly undress the woman and lay her on her right side, treating Ulrich to the splendor of her naked body. As his eyes traced her torso from elegant neck, firm breasts, flat stomach and Venus triangle to slender legs, he concluded that her smooth alabaster body was the image of perfection: a roman goddess.

"Look at this," the doctor said, pointing to the woman's back.

Ulrich moved around to see and felt a surge of alarm. Dark purple marks dotted her entire back from buttocks close to her neck. "What is it? Surely not…the plague?"

"No, no," the doctor reassured him. "But passing strange. Looks natural, though I've never seen such markings on a person before…"

The boy returned with a pail of hot water, a cloth and some leeches in a bowl.

"Good, Reinmar," Grien said then added gruffly to the staring boy, "Be off with you!"

Grien rolled up his nightshirt sleeves and grabbed a bottle of spirits. "Hold her firm now," he said to Ulrich. Then he seized the woman's face gruffly to force the alcohol down her throat. As she struggled, coughed and spluttered and involuntarily drank, the doctor explained, "It'll deaden the pain. I'll have to cut through her flesh to get the metal object out. It must come out or the fever will take her." Then he shoved the bottle into Ulrich's hand. "Keep pouring more into her mouth as she cries out."

Grien took a pair of forceps in one hand and a scalpel, stained with old blood from its last use, in the other. Then he proceeded to cut. The woman screamed. Holding down her stiff arching body with one arm, Ulrich poured the alcohol with a shaky hand into her mouth. With surprising strength—and still screaming—the woman abruptly seized his hand and forcefully directed the bottle to her wound. Alcohol spilled over the doctor's hands, his forceps, the scalpel and her wound.

Then, with a visible sigh, she let her head fall back and passed out.

Grien snorted. "Shame. Waste of good alcohol," he quipped then continued his work as Ulrich shivered. Somehow, this was worse than any of the battles he'd been in; worse than witnessing boys bleeding from severed limbs or deep gashes with entrails spilling out or damaged faces covered in blood. She was a lady.

Grien removed the metal object from her arm and bandaged her up.

"Let's get her to a bed," he said, eying the cylindrical object with curiosity. "My work is done. Have Uta come by when she awakes with some warm broth and a bath for the fever, if necessary. Uta should watch over her for the next few days to ensure she does not succumb to the fever. I wager she'll be fine eventually, though. She's a fighter, that one."

Yes, Ulrich thought, staring down at the limp beauty. Her fair hair radiated around her flushed face like a halo. She'd fought like Boadicea earlier, but she looked so peaceful now.

Ulrich ordered Frieda to open up the Solar and make up the bed for the lady. He carried her there and gently laid her in the bed then gruffly dismissed the head housekeeper with instructions to have Uta attend. He took a chair to sit next to the beautiful stranger and quietly watched her sleep.

He was there when she awoke many hours later with a long sigh. She turned large but lucid eyes toward him. They were the color of the sky after a rainstorm. She stared at him with quiet trepidation.

"You're safe," Ulrich said softly and gently touched her small hand. It was delicate and so soft to touch. He hadn't touched a woman's hand in so long! To her look of inquiry, he nodded slightly and blinked in reassurance. "You're safe now...here with me. You're in my castle."

She seemed to understand what he said, at least she understood their soothing nature, because the fear in her eyes melted into pools of gratitude and she gave him a small smile. "*Merci*," she sighed out, squeezing his hand in return. It sent a flush of pleasure through him that made him tremble. "*Merci...vous m'avez sauvé.*"

Ulrich tapped his chest. "I'm Ulrich Schoen, Baron von Grunwald." Then he pointed to her with an inquiring smile.

"Dianne." She pronounced it *Dee-anne*. "*Je m'appelle Dianne.*"

Uta arrived with some broth and sat down on the bedside to feed the lady. But Dianne's gaze drifted to the baron.

"I think she wants you to feed her, my Lord," Uta said, getting up off the bed and handing him the bowl. Ulrich nodded to Uta and took her place with an inward smile.

It was only much later, after Dianne lay back and closed her eyes, falling almost instantly into an exhausted sleep, and Ulrich sat by the fire with his friend Holbracht in the withdraw room when he noticed that he'd totally forgotten about Rosamund. Then Ulrich smiled with unrestrained pleasure for the first time in six years. Who had saved whom?

✠

# Book One: Emanation

"To see a world in a grain of sand
And Heaven in a wild flower,
Hold infinity in the palm of your hand
And eternity in an hour."

—William Blake (*Auguries of Innocence*)

## ...1

*Von Grunwald Castle, Prussia, 1410*

VIVIANNE bolted awake and flushed despite the coolness of the room. Her head swam in the daze of a disquieting dream. Fritz, the large tabby cat curled at her feet, stretched out a forepaw to her and began to purr loudly. She sat up in her bed and rubbed the sleep out of her eyes with the palms of her hands.

The dawn had just broken. Shafts of sunlight blazed a flaming cross in the shape of her window on the floor beside her. It was as though the burning villages to the southwest had set the sky on fire. Vivianne craned to catch the blood-red sun aching over the horizon. It cast a molten glow over the corn and rye fields and traced long shadowy fingers wherever an obstruction, like a tree or windmill, intersected its flaming path.

Vivianne raked the rumpled hair off her face and raised her knees to hug them. She stared out at the breaking dawn. Her mind lingered on her dream, her recurring nightmare.

In it she was fleeing. She ran along a strangely lit tunnel, tightly clasping the hand of a boy her age, a special friend—her *ritter* perhaps. The tunnel was man-made, like the castle halls but wider and smoother with flat simple paintings on the walls. Through the center of the tunnel ran a chasm with tracks. A strange snake-like machine resembling several rooms with open doors, sat on the track. A familiar and disturbingly handsome man—the devil himself—burst out of one of the doors and chased them. She shrieked with surprise and bolted, clutching the boy's hand in a steely grip. Sparks flew out of the devil and burned her. They coursed through her body and flamed her belly. Her face blazed with a feverish heat as the devil caught up, flames licking her thighs. The boy's hand slipped out of hers and disappeared as the man with the frighteningly beautiful face reached her...*Mary, mother of Jesus*! NO! She knew that if he touched her she'd become his slave. Feeling powerless, her sluggish feet dug deep like in quicksand....Laughing, the devil reached out for her. She felt his scorching touch and screamed—

Vivianne always woke in a cold sweat, perversely aroused. This morning, her belly also ached with a dull throb.

She shook her head to clear it and seized Fritz in an embrace. He reacted by licking her nose. She endured the rasp and fishy smell of his tongue for a few licks then buried her face in his fur. She forced the disturbing images from her mind by contemplating the coming day. But that only crowded her brain with new terrifying thoughts and the thrill of tense excitement stirred in her belly like an animal awakening.

"It's my birthday today, Fritz," she announced to the cat after pulling back. July 14, 1410. She was fourteen years old. Her father and now deceased mother had pledged her since her birth to a stranger from a foreign land on her fourteenth birthday. *Today*—if the rumor was true, that is. Though she'd overheard the entire von Grunwald *Ordensburgen* gossip of it for years, her father had never mentioned it to her. Surely, he would have told her of such an important thing in her life if he'd meant it in earnest. Vivianne sighed and stroked Fritz. Then again, perhaps not, she reflected, summoning the stern image of her taciturn father. He never told her anything. If her mother was alive it might have been different....

Besides, of late her father had much more important things on his mind; like the recent surprise attack on the Teutonic State by the combined Polish-Lithuanian-Masovian forces. They'd crossed the Vistula River and intended to traverse the Dwerca River to take Marienburg Castle, the Teutonic Order's Capital. A few days ago they'd crossed into Prussia and assaulted the border village of Lautenburg, looting and desecrating the church there; but *Hochmeister* Ulrich von Jungingen and his Teutonic Knights held them off at the fords of Kurzetnik on the Dwerca River.

Late yesterday more dreadful news had come to the baron: the enemy had outflanked von Jungingen's defense; they'd moved northeast and sacked Gilgenburg and were heading straight for Grunwald. Today was the eve of a battle amassing in the fields between Grunwald, Tannenberg and Ludwigsdorf. The Teutonic Knights and their troops were marching the twenty-kilometers from the Dwerca River to cut off the Slavs. They intended to camp later today just a few kilometers from the castle. There they would await the Polish-Lithuanian army who were languishing near Gilgenburg after committing atrocities to the villagers then looting and burning it to the ground. Although von Jungingen had sent some of his commanding knights ahead to von Grunwald castle, the sharp-eyed fifty-year old had stubbornly refused the baron's hospitality in order to stay with the bulk of his troops. Vivianne knew it was more than that. But that was the official story. He and his Hospital *Großmeister*, Werner von Tettingen, would oversee the establishment of their military camp and tabor for horse drawn wagons outside Grunwald. She knew it was really something personal between her father and the *Hochmeister*.

Despite the sudden descent upon the castle of several dozen weary Teutonic Knights, the imminent arrival of a special guest today and the long-arranged feast seemed to confirm Vivianne's suspicions that something was indeed afoot here besides war. Dreaded thoughts of her strange suitor resurfaced. It occurred to her that the very idea of a pre-nuptial feast was discordant with preparations for battle. Then again, perhaps it would help raise their spirits and boost morale if not distraction—even if at her expense.

In any case, the castle household had for days been bustling with the intense urgency of the feast: sweeping the floors and replacing the old mats in the Great Hall with new sweet-smelling ones of grass, flowers and herbs; dusting off the tapestries and decorating the Great Hall; cleaning out the lavatories, stocking and preparing fresh meat and spices from the village farms; baking bread; making new candles and flower arrangements.

As if the battlefield had come to the castle, the whole household rushed about, ill-tempered and nervous. The old cook and his scullions, usually kind-hearted with Vivianne, had become downright cantankerous with her lately whenever she sauntered in to steal an apple or sweet tart. Vivianne had heard from Gunter, one of the baron's young pages that her father had even sent for a band of *minnesängers* from Gilgenburg to attend and entertain at the coming feast. They'd just made it out of there in time now that Gilgenburg had fallen to the Slavs and was burned to the ground.

Vivianne shifted in her bed with flushed thoughts. Did the baron really mean to give her away at this ill time to some old stranger she'd never met? This foreign suitor had to be at least two dozen years her senior if a promise had been made directly to him before Vivianne was even born! Surely, the baron had taken his promise to the realm of the ridiculous. Or was there more to it, she thought, and felt renewed dread chill her. As if sensing her disturbed mood, Fritz meowed and sprang out of her arms.

Vivianne watched her cat leave the room and let her mind cloud with absent thoughts. She hardly knew her father, the baron. She didn't recall ever seeing him when she was a small child. Her earliest memory of him was when she was almost five years old: his sudden appearance in her outer bed-chamber had caught her in mid-speech as she was relating to Uta some made-up story of a heroic knight. The baron had just returned from a two-year campaign in Gotland.

Soiled and stained with fresh blood, he'd burst into the room with his face exhausted but glowing from his victory. She remembered thinking, as he swept in like a manic wave, that he was a splendid though terrifying sight. Piercing azure eyes flashed with elation beneath a wilderness of tawny brown hair. A true heroic knight like those she fantasized over and Uta told stories about.

✠

He looked the epitome of a warrior, feather-crested *bascinet* helm tucked carelessly under his arm and dressed in plate armor and chain mail from head to toe. His armor was mostly covered by a knee-length white tunic of the Teutonic Knight, belted at the waist by a soft leather girdle from which hung a dagger. The Greek letter 'tau', shaped like a 'T', emblazoned in the front, identified him as a secular member of the Teutonic Order; one who had not taken the three vows of chastity, poverty and obedience to God. The mantle was hardly white now; it was smeared and spattered with old and fresh blood and rubbed-in dirt. A leather backhanger *balderich* hung across his chest and the hilt of his splendid longsword was visible behind his shoulder, poking out of a calf-length white cape that flowed recklessly over his great shoulders. The cape was fastened in front with a black enameled silver *ritterkreuz*, the symbol of the Knights of the Teutonic Order; a personal gift from the *Hochmeister* to the baron for his valiant loyalty during the Gotland campaign.

He was truly magnificent, Vivianne had thought. Then he fixed on her a fearsome look and corrected her speech in a deep basso voice that reverberated in her gut like a meal gone awry.

Uta, the only servant who ever stood up to him, scolded, "*Herr* Baron! Look how you've frightened the poor child, your own daughter. And blood from those you've killed still on you! For shame!"

He'd laughed with spiteful amusement. In truth, the fresh blood would have been from a deer hunt in the local forest he'd embarked on immediately upon his return; her father was passionate about hunting and would have missed that more than anything. But Vivianne didn't know this at the time.

Out of mischievous ill-temper and perhaps mostly to annoy Uta, the baron leaned close to Vivianne and reached a filthy blood-smeared hand to touch her face. Even then he drank; his breath reeked with it, though Vivianne didn't know then what it was. Full of frightful heroic stories and Uta's reprove, Vivianne shrank back in fear and might have cried out in fright. The baron straightened with a forced exhale and frowned at Vivianne.

Uta scooped her up into her arms then shoved the baron out with another rebuke as he gruffly handed her the one thing he ever gave Vivianne—a silver jeweled-studded *ritterkreuz* pendant on a gold chain—with a terse instruction that it was a present for the child. Uta commanded him to return only when he was presentable and less forbidding looking.

✠

He never did, Vivianne reflected in bed as she fingered the silver cross that hung around her neck. As if that event had been a test that she'd failed miserably, Vivianne saw him no more until she was old enough to sit at the dinner table beside him in the Great Hall. By then she'd heard the other stories, the vicious gossip about his drunken stupors and temper tantrums, and her ache for his attention and love had lost their way.

These days, when he wasn't glowering at her for doing something wrong, her father ignored her as though she didn't exist. They seldom exchanged any words at the high table of the Great Hall when he was there. He never responded to her feckless attempts at conversation—as though she wasn't sitting right there beside him. The only time he acknowledged her presence was to correct her eating habits in a gruff rebuke; it always silenced her like a bear's harsh cuff to its cub.

In truth, she seldom saw him. Most of the time he was away on campaigns; often for months, sometimes years, coordinating a raid or skirmish deep in Lithuanian territory. When he was home he spent most of the day behind the great doors of his council room with his war masters and monk warrior colleagues or in meetings with his seneschal, the wiry old Berthold. In the evening he rode to the village just outside the castle to drink and bicker with the gentry and vassal knights of his fief until late at night. Vivianne knew because sometimes he came home with several of them and they would continue their drunken carousing into the early morning. It made her wish her bedroom in the keep, which used to be her mother's solar, lay farther away from the Great Hall.

On days when he held his long war-meetings with Brethren Knight guests visiting from the various nearby convents, they'd finally emerge from the council room into the Great Hall late at night and drink hard; the Teutonic monks liked their wine and ale. Amidst the lively sounds of late-night feasting, she heard desultory shouts of war against the Slavs, "those damned filthy pagans", impassioned calls for the Holy Roman Crusade of the "*Drang nach Osten*" the "*Ostsiedlung*" and the need for a growing "*Ordenstaat*".

Driven by curiosity, Vivianne often slipped out of bed and crept down the hall to park herself behind the thick curtains and eves-drop. She learned a lot about military affairs of the Order as a result, and suspected that this was where many of the real decisions were finalized.

Vivianne recalled such a gathering just two weeks ago; she'd been specifically mentioned. Her father was entertaining an eclectic group of vassal and *Knechten* knights, as well as several Brethren of the Order. Rife with tension since rumors of a Polish-Lithuanian build up, late-night drinking in the Great Hall had ignited some blistering quarrels.

✠

"It's not enough that *Hochmeister* von Jungingen has concentrated his forces in Schwetz—"

"He's left the largest part of the Order in Ragneta, Rhein and Memel," her father cut in with a condescending voice. She pictured him glowering with cerulean eyes and his sensual lips held in their usual purse. "It's a good plan, Sigiswald, considering what those infidels are up to in the east."

"The Poles aren't that stupid, Ulrich. They've got some other plan with Lithuania. Those two cousins—"

"*Are* that stupid!" her father shouted back in a strident voice slurred with liquor. Vivianne imagined his thick lips pouting. "They're so busy fighting each other they haven't the time or ability to fight us. They're pagan idiots, Sigiswald!"

"Jagiello got himself baptized, didn't you hear?" a new tenor voice Vivianne didn't recognize piped up. "When he married Jagwida, the Polish heiress, and made himself King of Poland. He's been a Roman Catholic for over twenty years; they *all* are. Poles and Lithuanians. Both you and von Jungingen underestimate them. They're *not* pagan idiots—"

"What are you saying, Count von Wendem! Are you demented?" Someone mocked loudly. Vivianne recognized the impassioned basso voice of Heinrich von Plauen the Elder, one of her father's Brethren guests from Schwetz. The forty year old was one of her father's more vociferous and opinionated colleagues: "You dare challenge our *Ordenstaat*! The Duke of Masovia summoned our Order here two hundred years ago to subdue the Prussian pagans. *Reichsfürst* Hermann von Salza had a commission authorized by the pope to Christianize the pagan lands of the Baltic Region. He took it as a sign to bring the fear of God to these wild barbarians."

"Fear indeed," the count said sullenly. "Starting with Truso, I suppose…That's if you call killing all the Prussians and leveling their cities to ash Christianizing…I call it something else…."

"*Meister* Hermann Balk did what needed to be done. He founded Elbing. It became one of the League's greatest seaports for northern trade."

There followed a bitter laugh. "Yes, *after* he 'purged the Vistula spit of the insult of the infidels'."

"It was God's wish. They were barbarians. They refused to be baptized."

"Did they even get a chance?" von Wendem challenged. "And what about Danzig, Chelmno, and Dobrzyn? Were they all God's wish? Massacring most of the Polish citizens then replacing them with German immigrants. Is *that* Christianizing?" After a pause, von Wendem added pointedly, "Now that the Poles and Lithuanians *are* Christians what are we doing?"

"You *are* an infant!" von Plauen scoffed. "Slavs may call themselves Christians but under those official Christian skins breathe healthy Godless heathens. That Lithuanian prince, Jagiello, pretended to become a Christian only so he could marry Jagwida to win the Polish crown. Those mass baptisms he ordered for Lithuanians were a sham. They still pray to their thunderbolt warrior god, *Perkūnas*. And what about those pagan

Tartars from the Golden Horde? Are *they* Christians? Eh?...*eh*?"
he taunted; he was probably poking von Wendem in the chest.
"Bah! Conversion, my ass!" Vivianne pictured him suddenly
leaning back with a conceited scowl. "They're apostates. Let me
remind you, von Wendem, that it wasn't too long ago when they
roasted our captured brethren alive in their armor, like
chestnuts, before the shrine of their evil pagan gods!"

"Hear! Hear!"

"Or shot our brethren full of arrows while bound to one
of their stinking sacred trees!" shouted another.

Several voices rose in a chorus of drunken agreement
followed by a desultory raucous of shouting: "I remember!"
"Yeah, poor Udo."

"Or what about all the desecrations of our churches,
their alters, and crucifixes. They spit on and crushed the conse-
crated wafers of the host...they tortured and killed the village
women and children...."

"As though we didn't do the same—"

"They're the pestilential enemies of Christ!"

"A good Slav is a dead Slav!"

"Vytautus is a devil!"

"The *Hochmeister* is right: we should wipe out all the
infidels!"

Amid the rabble, the count's tenor voice piped up again,
as if he didn't know what was good for him: "I still think the
Order made a mistake taking Pomerelia. Poland was our ally
against the pagan Prussians and Lithuanians—"

"Someone teach this *bauernlümmel* some history!" von
Plauen cut in. Vivianne heard a loud clink of a mug on a table.
"It was a strategic move, you idiot. Just like with Samogitia.
Pomerelia connected our monastic state with the borders of the
Holy Roman Empire of the German Nations. Besides, we
relinquished Kuyavia and Dobrzyń to them in the Treaty of
Kalisz."

"Only to declare war on Jagiello and his cousin,
Vytautas, last year—"

"Who's side are you on, Grabie?" Vivianne's father burst

out.

The count persisted, "I counseled *Hochmeister* von Jungingen against war with Poland. But he let his hatred for them get the better of him—"

The baron cut in, "The *Hochmeister* had no choice after the tribal uprising in Samogitia—"

"After he put an unreasonable embargo in place—"

"Unreasonable!" von Plauen scoffed. "Both Jagiello and Vytautus were secretly helping the rebels, you idiot! It was collusion all along!"

"The *Hochmeister* knows *exactly* what he's doing!" the baron added passionately.

"Ulrich! You sly bastard!" Vivianne heard a loud smack: von Plauen clapping her father on the back, perhaps. "Have you patched things up with the *Hochmeister*?"

"Ulrich von Jungingen never trusted me...especially after...." Her father trailed.

"You were always Conrad's boy, I know; your namesake never trusted you for your loyalties to his older brother, eh? Conrad didn't want the Order to vote his younger brother in as *Hochmeister*...but we did anyway..."

After a slight pause, during which everyone probably recharged their drinks, von Plauen added, "I hear a plan in your confidence, Ulrich. Perhaps it's some new contraption like your wife's crazy plumbing, or that smelly gas you heat your castle with, eh? Does this have to do with your daughter's impending fourteenth birthday, Ulrich? An offering the *Hochmeister* can't refuse, eh? You do have some interesting friends..."

Vivianne felt her heart pound up her throat. Had he meant this stranger, her intended, coming on her birthday?

Her father's voice had a smug ring, "You'll see. There shall be a feast. After this the *Hochmeister* will have to forgive my previous transgression..."

"Very interesting friends..."

The party naturally dissolved into a drunken disorder and the tittering nervous laughter of women filled the halls, as various knights and gentry caught them in eager embraces.

Vivianne recognized several of her father's favorite servant maids. Even a few of the brethren partook to Vivianne's astonishment. They were sworn celibate monks, but not all of them held their vows, she concluded. Vivianne hastily crept back to her bedchamber and tried to sing herself to sleep.

She was still awake, curled in her bed, when her father's clumsy stumbling gait and slurring raucous shouts to himself echoed in the hall near her room. Like every other time, he hesitated by her door. And like every other time she prayed that he wouldn't barge in, stinking of stale beer and old cheese, and touch her like a father should never touch his own child.

He'd only done it once, a month ago, when rumor of the Polish-Lithuanian forces amassing near Danzig and Samogitia had fired his rage and he'd tried to douse it with more ale. He'd roused her out of a deep sleep by throwing off her covers to give her a good look and had remarked on how like a woman she'd become of late, tall and blossoming. Then he'd bent close, rank breath blowing over her face. He mauled her small firm breasts with unseemly eagerness and smacked his wet lips against hers, thrusting his tongue into her mouth. She'd pushed him gruffly off her with a muffled shriek then gasped and involuntarily wiped her mouth as he stumbled back and nearly fell. She thought for a terrified moment that he would be angry and beat her. But his eyes looked suddenly fearful and he shuffled quickly out of her room, closing her door with unexpected gentleness. In truth, he'd never laid an angry hand on her, despite the many times he'd railed at her, consumed by rage for some little thing she did or simply was. She could never please him, it seemed. And had stopped trying to.

✠

Vivianne pulled down the covers and examined her girlish figure, revealed through the flimsy night shift she wore. Despite her not yet having begun to flower with the woman's cycle, her hips and breasts had begun to fill out. But she'd grown overly tall and was still too slim for a decent lady. Succumbing to a wistful moment, Vivianne pushed up her breasts with her hands so that she could see cleavage, then let go with a sigh. Did she remind her father of her dead mother?

She hastily disrobed and before putting on the clothes laid out for her, Vivianne made a swift appraisal of herself in the full-length mirror. She twisted her head to gaze at the reflection of her backside and inhaled sharply. The persistent rash of purple blemishes on her buttocks had increased in size and intensity. They'd migrated up her back! *What is happening to me?* She'd developed the odd purple markings almost a year ago, the same time her disturbing dreams had begun. At first the spots had appeared yellow-green, like a spate of bruises. Then, like ripening fruit, they'd blushed to deep purple and rose up like welts.

Alarmed by the markings, Uta had whispered of the plague. Vivianne knew it wasn't the plague; she knew plague symptoms and suffered none of them. She'd heard a rumor of such markings on her mother's back; pagan markings they'd called them, the mark of God's displeasure with her mother's strange ways. Nevertheless, Vivianne had to assure a frightened Uta that she suffered no ill effects. Uta had interrogated her with a string of symptoms: "Are you sure that you've no chills or fever, child?" And before Vivianne could even respond Uta had clapped her hand against her forehead. "No pains or headaches? No dizziness? No visions?" Vivianne insisted that she didn't and grew more irritated. "You've not coughed up any blood, My Lady..."

"No, no, NO!" Vivianne had finally shouted in exasperation and twitched out of Uta's grasp.

Fearing close examination by the castle physician, Vivianne had insisted that Uta not mention it to the doctor or her father. The doctor would only consult his astrological books, poke her skin for blood and force her to give him her urine and stool only to place leeches on her rash and bleed her until she was giddy. In response, Uta had filled the girl's room with the scent of roses, violets, bay leaves, fennel and mint to ward away the plague. She'd also firmly persevered in her demand that

Vivianne turn to the Penitential Psalms in her Book of Hours during her six prayer times. Vivianne didn't have to consult her Hours; she knew them by heart. She'd uttered them often enough for her many transgressions: *Domine, ne in furore tuo arguas me, neque in ira tua corripias me*—she knew them in Latin and in German—*O Lord, rebuke me not in Thy furor; nor chastise me in Thy wrath. For thy arrows are fastened in me: and Thy hand hath descended upon me....There is no health in my flesh in the face of Thy wrath: there is no peace for my bones in the face of my sins....*

Sadly, she barely got in two prayers in a day, and those only occurred thanks to her morning and afternoon instructions with *Père* Daniel in the chapel library and scriptorium. However, Vivianne surely made up for her lack of prayers with the intensity of her prayers. And she certainly knew them all, every penitential psalm and litany, every invocation and joy of the Virgin. It was a vicious circle, Vivianne reflected sadly: her doubts of God's presence motivated her lapse in prayers; invariably followed by feelings of great shame for such heretical thoughts, which inspired more penitential prayers.

For two weeks, Uta, who was also skilled in the use of natural herbs and medicines, arrived every morning before Vivianne rose from bed with a regular breakfast of smoked herring or rollmops and a roll with butter and whole milk and a steaming hempseed pottage to balance the humors. Vivianne, who normally did not partake in a substantial breakfast, usually gave the cat the herring, drank the milk, and threw the rest down the toilet. Uta also prepared a foul-smelling poultice of mashed nettle leaves and seeds, butterbur, blessed thistle, angelica, mint, treacle and common rue, mixed with egg and urine—probably a dog's. Uta intended to apply it on the infected area each morning, but Vivianne had sternly insisted that Uta just give it to her with instructions on how to apply it herself.

For the first few days Vivianne had loyally applied it. After Uta's repeated inquiries, Vivianne lost her patience and lied: the poultice, combined with the pottage, had worked and the rash had vanished. In truth, it had not abated. The poultice stank and Vivianne, seeing no effect, had abandoned using the herbal remedy and flushed the vile mash down the *garderobe* along with the uneaten food. Because the rash didn't burn or itch, Vivianne decided to just live with it. But she vowed to no longer reveal her naked body to anyone, including Uta, who was like a mother to her. To the old nursemaid's dismay, Vivianne insisted on bathing and changing on her own. Another eccentricity of hers that would displease her father if he cared enough to notice.

The list was endless, Vivianne thought soberly. She poured water from the silver ewer on the small chest into its accompanying basin and dipped her hands and a small washcloth to briskly wash her face. She paused for a moment to gaze through the water at the *repoussé* relief of the basin that showed the young Actaeon bursting in on the bathing Goddess Diana. In the myth, the angry goddess punished the poor boy for his mistake by setting his own dogs to tear him to pieces. Vivianne glanced at the ewer that matched the basin, its relief depicting Jupiter's deceitful seduction of Callisto in the forest. After studying the ewer more carefully, Vivianne decided that it looked more like an abduction than a mutual tryst.

She hastily washed then threw on a cotton shift. Ignoring the bright pink gown laid out for her, she chose out of her wardrobe a plain form-fitting one of dark green brocade with reasonable décolletage then shrugged into it, pulling here and there and fastening the buttons in the back with deft hands. Looking in the full-stand mirror, she adjusted the *cross-pattée* pendant on her gold chain—the only gift her father had ever given her—that hung just over her still small bosom and realized that her hands were trembling. What would today bring? Her father's next and last gift? Her betrothed: an old crusty knight thirty years her senior—

"Hallo, *Hase!*" Uta announced her presence with a trilling singsong then entered Vivianne's room in a bustle of nervous energy. "Ahh!" she expostulated, finding Vivianne up and dressed already, though not in the clothes she'd laid out for the girl. "Happy birthday, *kleine Hase!*"

Uta rushed to Vivianne and gave her a full matronly

squeeze that made Vivianne smile despite the portent of the day. In contrast to all of Vivianne's dresses, Uta's beige kirtle and russet barbet, fastened over the plain wimple that covered her chin and neck, was shapeless and made of rough linen. And it covered every bit of her, except her wrinkled face and hands.

"I saw your father. He's in a fine mood for your birthday and your special handing off. I haven't seen him this merry in ages. He must be proud and happy for you, child."

*He's just glad to see me go*, Vivianne thought to herself. She blurted out morosely, "My father hates me."

"Of course he doesn't, child!" Uta expostulated. Vivianne thought Uta's denial suspiciously exaggerated. "How can you say such a thing! Of course he doesn't hate you," she repeated as if to convince herself.

"I'm of no use to him," Vivianne muttered. She should have been a boy; at least then she could have served as a knight in the baron's castle. Perhaps then he might have liked her a little....

"What ever are you thinking, child! Of course you're useful. You're a lady!" Then she murmured on as if to herself, "Though at times I dare say you don't act like one...As for the baron, it's just that..." She cut herself off and patted Vivianne on the shoulders then pulled fretfully at the sleeves as if to fix them. "Well, just don't you go and let anything ruin this special day for you. You know that your father has a special gift for you—"

"It's just *what*?" Vivianne persisted with an ill-humored frown. She already knew what her father's *special* gift for her was: some querulous smelly warrior, who would haul her to his castle where the kind of freedom she'd enjoyed thanks to her father's neglect would no doubt be severely curtailed. The stranger would have her do his every bidding and surely impose his will upon her in his bed. She felt like throwing up at the thought.

Uta smoothed out Vivianne's dress, eyes flitting over her and unable to keep her gaze. "Well...when your mother—when she—when you were born..." '*When your mother died giving birth to you*', Vivianne knew Uta had started to say. "...that's when

32

your father took to drinking again. He grieved her loss so much, tiny *Hase*."

"I'm not so tiny," Vivianne murmured to her old nursemaid's endearment. She was still mulling over the old ache Uta had brought up. She didn't like that her father drank so much. It made him act foolish. And it made him cruel. Vivianne had ached for his attention since she could remember. Now that he gave it to her, she wished he wouldn't. And felt guilty for being here instead of her mother.

"No, I suppose you aren't, child!" Uta chortled sadly. "But when your mother passed away, it was like a piece of the baron went with her, like he was broken."

*He still blames me*, Vivianne considered.

"I remember what he was like before she died, My Lady," Uta went on. "He stopped drinking." Vivianne appreciated Uta's honesty. Uta sat on the bed and Vivianne saw her eyes glaze with memories. "He was full of life. Like you are, My Lady. He was...happy. Before Lady Dianne came along, your father was a sad drunk. He'd lost his first wife to the *Holy Fire* in eighty-nine. Did you know? Ah, yes...Doctor called it *ignis sacer*. T'was an awful thing to see. She was so young and beautiful, the Lady Rosamund, almost as young as you are now, with round cheeks like roses and a beautiful laugh and so helpful in the village. Then she went mad with visions of evil things attacking her and being burned at the stake. She lost her limbs to *mormal* and died in agony, poor child. Several children and women in the village also got the same sickness..." Uta shook her head in sad remembrance. Vivianne knew that Uta's own husband and two of her children had succumbed to that awful disease. "They say it was witches who called the devil, tormenting their fellow creatures with sores and disease," Uta went on. "I was but a wee child when an angry God—or more of Satan's witchery—visited us with the Black Plague in sixty-three. T'was awful. I lost my whole family to it. My parents, my sister and brother."

"I'm sorry," Vivianne said in a subdued voice. "I didn't know, Uta." Vivianne felt some shame that she hadn't before learned this vital fact about her old nursemaid, who'd brought her up like her own child. Vivianne had known about the old woman losing her husband and two of her children to the *Holy Fire* in eighty-nine; but she'd known nothing of Uta's own childhood family. She silently watched Uta who had gone quiet for a moment and found the old woman staring out past her into space. Into the past, Vivianne supposed, and wondered how many siblings Uta had lost along with her parents. She must have wondered why she alone had survived, Vivianne mused somberly, and suddenly felt very sorry for her old nursemaid whose fate she'd only now discovered. Vivianne remembered Uta telling her of how she'd been taken in by the von Grunwald household when she was thirteen; Vivianne quickly did the math: Uta was sixty years old this year; so, the baron's mother had taken Uta in right after losing her family.

Uta roused. "It took the baron's father too, Konrad von Grunwald, did you know? It happened when your father was a wee boy of four. Left the place to the Lady Baronin." Then Uta fixed on Vivianne a more intense look. "Did you know that your father ran away from home when he was ten?"

Vivianne leaned forward and shook her head, urging Uta on. It was a mystery why Uta was telling her all this now, but she didn't want to spoil Uta's train of thought and listened attentively.

"His uncle Wilhelm, who was a monk knight with the Teutonic Order, wanted your father to take the vows and join too. Even then the baron knew he was meant to love women, child. A life of celibacy would have destroyed him. But the uncle persuaded the mother and they would have forced the boy. So he ran away. He ended up with a secular order under another lord and your father became one of the land's best knights. He became known for his brilliant strategy in warfare and his great sword-fighting skills. When his mother died, the baron returned to his rightful place as lord of the castle. It's passing strange that he is now working for the Teutonic Order anyway, though not as an avowed Brother."

Vivianne had only a moment to reflect on how little her

own father knew his parents, when Uta continued, "Temper and that awful drunken behavior aside, I must say that your father loves the ladies—and they him."

Vivianne could see that in her father. He had a kind of penetrating intensity in his regard and a sensual way of carrying himself that was no doubt attractive to women. And she'd seen him with them; apart from the old crones, any woman was fair game for his charms.

Uta's gaze strayed to the sketch of Vivianne's mother by her bedside. "How you do resemble that exotic French beauty, meine Hase! Your shiny long brown hair, your cheeks and mouth."

Her mother was indeed beautiful, Vivianne thought, staring longingly at the painting of her mother by the bed. If it had been rendered accurately, Vivianne saw why her father had fallen for the Lady Dianne; she was the most beautiful woman Vivianne had ever laid eyes on. Despite what Uta said, Vivianne had no misconceptions of having inherited her mother's beauty, although she decided that her large hazel eyes were earnest—when she wasn't beguiling her staff for favors like sweets from the cook. And her wide mouth was sincere—except when she was tormenting Wolfgang. It seemed that she was destined to be tall like her mother however. *Exotic*, Uta said. Vivianne knew what that meant for *her*; she didn't resemble the full-figured ladies Father kept inviting to the castle. *They* weren't skinny and gawky with unruly hair, big teeth and a grin that looked like two parentheses in an angular face. They weren't still waiting to be women.

Misunderstanding Vivianne's morose thoughts, Uta quickly offered, "You are rather comely for a child. You have a nice complexion and beautiful teeth." Vivianne bit back a wry laugh at Uta's intended compliment. Uta was one to talk of teeth; what teeth she had were rotten, brown and broken. "You still have some filling out to do," Uta went on, peering down the length of Vivianne's torso under thick furry brows. "But you're showing lots of promise, dear. You'll be a beauty when you grow up, you'll see." That was a kind way of saying she didn't measure up, Vivianne thought. "You've also inherited your handsome father's long straight nose and firm chin, my little *Hase*."

"I'm nothing like him!" Vivianne retorted. She hadn't seen any resemblance between herself and her debauched father. Vivianne shared nothing of her father's Germanic nose of aristocratic hubris, his cold and commanding azure eyes or his sensually cruel mouth that he seemed to hold in a permanent pout of disdain. She felt like an orphan and had frequently imagined that she was. "We share nothing," she said.

"Oh, and his stubborn unreasonable temper too, my little scamp!" Uta added with twinkling eyes and a wry tooth-gapped smile. Uta then stared out the window into the past. "As for *Herr* Baron and the Lady Dianne, I'd never seen two people more in love. Then she was pregnant so soon. It was a shame..."

It *was* a shame, Vivianne agreed in morbid silence. A shame the couple hadn't had a chance at a life together before Vivianne came along and ended it all.

She'd wished desperately that she could have known her mother. Vivianne knew very little about her, except that her name was French like Vivianne's. Her mother simply appeared one day. They'd fallen instantly in love and were married right away. She died giving birth to Vivianne a short nine months later. It was only after she died that the rumors began to circulate: of her strange behavior and mysterious identity; of pagan markings on her back, her arcane knowledge of weird things like the revolutionary plumbing system or "biogas" heating system she'd installed in the castle or innovative agricultural practices she'd introduced to the village farmers.

Apparently, she'd also dabbled in alchemy and had earned the disdain of the doctor as a result. It was rumored in turn that her mother was arrogant and did not respect the doctor. The dark castle walls carried whispers that Dianne had been punished by God because she was a heretic and a witch.

When Vivianne was ten years old, Uta had shown her the small decorated leather chest her mother had bequeathed to her. Although she'd kept her thoughts to herself, the strange items and books she'd found inside had compelled Vivianne to wonder if they weren't right about her mother being a witch. The function of some of the items still eluded Vivianne.

Vivianne felt betrayed somehow by the mother she'd never known. A woman who had otherwise flouted convention, who displayed a healthy ego and espoused independence and unconventionality for womankind. Why had she given in to convention on this one account that involved her only daughter, and complied in that unfair promise to give Vivianne away to some strange man from a foreign country?

"Were you there?" Vivianne blurted out her question.

"*What*? When she gave birth to you? Oh, *Guter Gott!*" Uta raised her hands in sad exasperation. "No, child. I wish I'd been there to midwife your poor mother." Before Vivianne had a chance to steer her to her real question, Uta blustered on, "Alas, she went into labor early; I'd given her some cockspurs but I didn't think they'd work so fast. And she had corruption and dropsy and wouldn't let Doctor Grien look at her." Uta shook her head sadly. "Oh, she hated the doctor, child!" Vivianne knew the feeling was mutual. Did the 'good' doctor question the nobility of Vivianne's mother? He probably suspected her of low birth, like himself, and had reason to despise her for that alone. Uta went on, "I was at the town fair in Gilgenburg and no one came to fetch me—I had no idea. When I returned she was already dead and you, child, were born."

Vivianne knew that the castle physician also disliked Uta, the castle midwife and she didn't for a moment doubt that Baldung Grien had made sure Uta was in Gilgenburg when her mother gave birth.

Vivianne knew that the castle physician also disliked Uta, the castle midwife, and she didn't for a moment doubt that Baldung Grien had made sure Uta was in Gilgenburg when her mother gave birth.

"I wish I could have helped the poor woman," Uta lamented. "She already had a bit of a fever and chills and some foul-smelling discharge from the barbolle. I suspected a womb fever. She complained of headache, dizziness and blurry vision, then she had awful pains in the abdomen and started to vomit. I told her to see the physician for the corruption but she refused and said she was taking her own medicine—something called hydrazine and some other thing I can't remember—and she was drinking hibiscus tea. I gave her some chamomile with foxglove and horseradish before I left. But then she went into early labor and Marthe said her contractions wouldn't stop. She fell into a dreadful fever and started to bleed heavily. Marthe said it flowed like a waterfall from her birthing chair and made a great big puddle on the floor. Your mother asked Marthe to give her something from her kit but the poor girl was too frightened. And then the Lady suffered awful seizures. That's when the good doctor came."

Vivianne swallowed convulsively. Part of her desperately wanted Uta to stop. But another part of her was mesmerized with the need to hear all the morbid details. She clung to every word as the cheerfully complying Uta shared on:

"Doctor Grien said later that your mother had *eclampsia*. They feared you would be lost with her seizures. *Gott sei Dank* that *Herr* doctor acted fast! Or we might have lost everyone!" Then she leaned forward and added, as if sharing a conspiracy, "Of course, he had orders from the baron to save *you* no matter what."

Vivianne's mouth went dry and she swallowed involuntarily. Not her mother?

"The chaplain was there too so the Lady Dianne thankfully received *Extreme Unction* before she passed on. But she refused the *Confession*, poor thing; her mind had already gone. Frieda said that your mother yelled profanities at both the priest and the good doctor and wanted some 'anti-beeatic'…or something like that. Frieda didn't understand the words. Neither did the doctor, it seemed, though your mother thought he should. Your mother called him a superstitious charlatan and a butcher and accused him of deliberately killing her. It got really ugly," Uta ended with a sad shake of her head. "She wanted the Doctor to poke a needle with liquid in her, she kept pointing to her kit and shouting for some 'magneeziasuffet' or so. When he finally did get out a needle, she changed her mind, called it coumadin, and said it would kill her. He gave it to her anyway, despite her struggles and screams. I think he thought her mad with the devil by then. According to Frieda, your mother screamed at everyone, calling us all primitive bumpkins and this place a barbaric hinterland. Then the devil took her completely and she had such a fit of convulsions, *Herr* doctor had to cut you out of her before you died too."

Vivianne felt her face and throat tighten and found it hard to breathe.

"*Guter Gott*, even after all that bleeding and in her dying state it took four of them to hold her down as *Herr* Doctor cut her open. I would have given her some dwale at least to dull the pain. They say her death screams rang through the entire castle into the courtyard and beyond the outer bailey as the priest anointed her with unguent."

Vivianne felt ill. *Do I really need to hear this?* But something prevented her from stopping Uta.

"He had to shout out the *Last Rites* over her screams," Uta relentlessly went on. "But your mother refused the *Viaticum*."

Of course she would, Vivianne thought scathingly, picturing her mother screaming in agony as the doctor cut her open. How could they expect her to blithely accept the *Eucharist* as she writhed in excruciating pain?

"Marthe said that at the precise moment your mother ceased to scream you started to cry."

Vivianne shivered. That hadn't been her question and it was far more information than she had wanted to hear just now. "I mean," she said shakily, "were you there when *he* came...and my parents promised me to him."

Uta's face paled. "Ah..." She abruptly stood up, suddenly nervous, and tapped her head as if she'd just remembered an urgent chore. She smoothed out the bed and let her eyes flit only momentarily on Vivianne. "I must see Frieda about the laundry, child!" Then she left in a flurry of nervous motion, leaving Vivianne confused in her wake. Why did this man—her intended—inspire such fear among the castle staff?

✠

# ...2

BOOK of Hours clutched in her hand, Vivianne decided to bypass the Great Hall on her way to the chapel library where she expected to find the chaplain. She headed down the winding staircase through the kitchen on the ground floor. As she approached the kitchen, a wave of hot air stirred her hair and brought with it the delicious scents of roasting meat, stewing vegetables, spices and herbs amidst the sharp undercurrent of smoke and pickled fish. The nervous clanking of pots followed by the bellowing baritone of the cook alerted Vivianne to the anxious nature of the kitchen personnel. Fully prepared for an onslaught of hostility, she passed the doorway and slid anonymously into the mayhem of hustle and bustle of scullions and maidservants as they stirred giant iron-cast cooking pots bubbling with pottage and stews, turned the spit, and prepared pastries at the bidding of Theobald, the cook.

Vivianne immediately spotted Theobald's imposing figure, railing at a young kitchen maid beside the tethered animals by a far wall. Observing that Theobald wasn't looking her way, Vivianne cast her sharp gaze about and instantly caught sight of several dozen sweetmeats arranged like little soldiers on a platter on a side table on the opposite side of the kitchen. She sidled over, intending to snatch one on her way through to the scullery without being seen by the stern cook.

Just as she slipped past a fiercely blushing Georg, to whom she'd raised a finger to her lips to hush him, and had her hand poised over a sweetmeat, Theobald's growling voice boomed, "So, gypsy!" She flinched and retracted her hand with a sharp inhale. Theobald was already towering beside her. "I suppose you expect a cake for your birthday!"

Vivianne inhaled the delicious fragrance of sweet almonds clinging to him like clouds on a craggy mountain. She shrank back with a shaky grin, not sure if he would hug her or clout her for her insolence. In truth, she hadn't yet thought of the celebratory aspect of her birthday; only the part about being given away to some strange man twice her age—who the castle staff feared—to do with her as he pleased. And that part terrified her.

Theobald's craggy grey-stubbled face softened suddenly and his eyes grew lustrous with compassion as he threw his big flower dusted arms around her in a bear hug. "Don't let him scare you, child," the old cook said as if reading her mind. "Grit your teeth and show him you've got spunk. He'll come round soon enough and respect you for the lady you are. Any man should be proud to have you for his wife." He smoothed back the disordered hair away from her face with a gentle sweep of his hands. "Even if you do steal from my pantry all the time!" Then he winked. "Keep them guessing, gypsy!" he added and covertly slipped her a marzipan sweet then pushed her gently away from him to continue his work. "Now, get out of here before you knock something down or make my scullion knock something down!" he added with a harsh glance at Georg, who blushed again.

Vivianne grinned back at Theobald, marzipan clutched in her free hand. Despite her fears she felt better as she scurried out of the kitchen toward the stairs to the library and stopped mid-stair to pop the sweet into her mouth. Something brushed across her legs with a very loud purr and Vivianne crouched down to pat Fritz.

"Are you following me again?" she asked with a full mouth. The cat responded with an insistent meow, which made her grin. "Not now, Fritz," she scolded. "You'll get your milk when I get it. The kitchen's too busy; they'll catch me!"

She'd no sooner finished savoring her almond sweet and was about to run up the stairs when a gruff voice from behind jolted her to a halt: "A word, Your Ladyship!"

Vivianne fought from cringing and turned to face Doctor Grien, approaching her from below. His pasty square face was screwed up into an unnatural smile. Vivianne had never seen a genuine smile on him. He had steely eyes the color of a lake just before a tempest and a thin purplish mouth that looked more like a slash of blood, which he always held in disdain. She thought him cold beneath his lacquer of fawning bedside attendance; he gave her the shivers. It was bad enough that he constantly made disparaging remarks about Uta. But Vivianne didn't see any evidence of Grien liking or respecting anyone, except for the chaplain perhaps. And that might have been more out of political savvy than genuine feeling, she guessed. Aligning with the chaplain, who wielded the power of the Church, was no doubt in the doctor's best interests. Vivianne knew that Grien nursed a burning hatred for all non-Christians: Jews, Gypsies, Saracens, Tartars, witches, heretics, heathens …and women in general. They were all purveyors of the devil to the 'good' doctor.

Vivianne had once witnessed him beat little Sigmund Haupt, one of the peasant village boys who'd entered the castle grounds to beg for food. Vivianne had suspected from his inordinate harshness that the doctor had himself come from peasant stock. She'd overheard some of the older servants discuss how Vivianne's grandmother had paid for Grien's education at the Sorbonne, no doubt with the condition of later serving as the von Grunwald's doctor; something he clearly did grudgingly. It made sense to Vivianne; it explained why he hated Uta—she reminded him of his lowly peasant beginnings of which he was ashamed.

As for his talents in doctoring, Doctor Grien actually performed an admirable job of keeping her healthy, Vivianne supposed; for she made a point of not getting or showing illness to avoid him.

Doctor Grien's calculating eyes flitted up the stairs then back to her with a puzzled frown. "Who were you talking to just now?"

"Just my cat," she said.

"Ah," He looked at her shrewdly. "Your cat, of course. The one I always see you with. You are in the habit of talking to it, eh? Does it talk back to you?"

Vivianne knew it was a trap and barely curbed a frown of disgust. "Of course not! Cats don't talk, *Herr* Doctor. I'm just being friendly." Something he surely wouldn't understand, she thought cynically.

Grien nodded, as if he'd expected that answer from her. "Well, then..." He crossed his arms and fixed piercing pale eyes on her. "I was just wondering when you were ever going to see me for your examination, My Lady."

She stared at him, pretending bemusement.

"You are in need of an examination before your presentation to your betrothed, My Lady," he reminded her sternly. Chastising eyes studied her up and down as if she were naked and ripe with disease.

Vivianne flushed and delivered her words more sharply than she intended, "I am perfectly healthy, Doctor Grien. So I don't require an examination."

He raised his brows and lifted his head to peer down at her in open disdain. "That's for *me* to decide, My Lady," he returned forcefully, pronouncing *My Lady* as though it meant something else. "Just like your mother," he muttered to himself. He then sniffed dismissively. "May your new master have joy of you, then. I promised your father, the baron, that I would examine you before the feast. But I'll tell him you refused."

With that last remark, delivered as an obvious threat, Doctor Grien wheeled and descended the stairway. If he expected her to chase after him, he was mistaken, she thought. She honestly didn't care if her father learned of her refusal. She was beginning to feel downright surly about the whole thing.

Just as she turned to go up the stairs, the doctor stopped and turned. "Oh, that cat used to be your mother's wasn't it?" Before Vivianne had a chance to respond, he added, "They say that witches always keep at least one familiar, a shape-shifting demonic pet. Cats are the favorite, I'm told." Then he turned, but not before giving her a simpering smile and glancing down at her cat.

✠

...3

VIVIANNE found *Père* Daniel Auger in the chapel's library on the first floor above the scullery. The castle chaplain divided his time each day, delivering liturgical services between the castle chapel and the parish church in the village outside the castle. Aside from Sundays, when the village was invited to the castle chapel for devotions, the villagers generally used the parish church and the chapel was generally reserved for the von Grunwald family and their servants.

As usual, the *Père* was taking his breakfast there of black bread, cheese and ale. He sat at the thick oak table beneath her favorite glass-painted window that faced the castle courtyard. He didn't notice she was there at first and Vivianne had a chance to study his square massive face, roughly hewn—as though God had forgotten to finish him. In truth, she thought it more the battered face of a warrior, with widely set keen grey eyes and a nose that looked like he'd broken it a few times or smashed it against a knight's shield. His wispy reddish-brown but mostly grey beard was already covered in bread crumbs. The chaplain was dressed in an old black robe of rough linen, not yet having donned his liturgical vestments—his alb, stole and chasuble, the only richly embroidered piece of clothing he owned. He was chewing with his mouth open.

*Père* Daniel looked up from his meal and flinched in startled surprise. He looked nervous this morning; surely he was expecting her like every other morning? A convulsive shudder rippled in a wave across his face; then he beamed at Vivianne with a mouth full of food. His black four-pointed biretta slid askew on his balding head. He'd acquired a rather alarming nervous twitch lately, Vivianne thought.

"*Ah, bon fête, ma petite!*" he said in lilting French. Pieces of half-chewed bread and cheese spilled out of his mouth. He stood up to bow to her and ale ran down in rivulets, dripping off his unkempt beard. He was a bit of a pig when it came to table manners, Vivianne reflected, but otherwise the most gentle and kind-hearted man she knew.

"*Merci, mon Père,*" she returned and sat down across from him at the hardwood table as he sat heavily down to return to his food. She averted her eyes as he tore at his bread and butter with his teeth then smacked his lips loudly in obvious enjoyment. Vivianne thought it odd that a man who'd been educated in the best university known to her, *le Collège de Sorbonne de l'Université de Paris*, could have such vulgar table manners.

Needing to look elsewhere, she let her gaze drift to the *Glaßmalerei* above the *Père*. It depicted a praying knight kneeling at an alter with an open manuscript resting on it. The glazier had painted the knight in a richly patterned tunic. Shining *vambraces*, *besagew* and *pauldron* covered his arms and *cuisse*, *greaves* and spurred *sabatons* his legs. He was utterly beautiful, she mused. The knight's handsome young face, raised devoutly up to the heavens, reminded her of the innocent Wolfgang with his long chestnut hair flowing behind him in turbulent curls.

*Père* Daniel offered her some of his breakfast but she demurely declined. She seldom ate breakfast and *Père*'s table manners didn't inspire her to eat. In any case, rye bread was not a favorite with her; she clung to her noble right of eating white bread, leaving the black bread for the servants and villagers. Only her father and the priest seemed to prefer the less refined bread.

"*Alors, ma petite,*" he said, nodding to the Book of Hours in Vivianne's hand. She glanced down at the ornamented cover of her prayer book. It held a special place for *Père* Daniel. He'd hand-scripted and beautifully illuminated it himself for

Vivianne's mother. He'd decided to give it to her mother as a birthing present, after hearing that she had no prayer book. She'd died giving birth to Vivianne before he'd finished it, so he gave it to Vivianne instead.

"Let us begin the matins," *Père* Daniel said. They had long ago taken to doing their morning prayers in the library-scriptorium, where they would proceed with her lessons, to leave the chapel free for other household members who wished to pray in its holy silence. "Psalm sixty-three." He let her find her place even though she knew the psalm by heart and as they recited together, "*O, God, you are my God, I seek you...*" her eyes lifted, as always, to her precious knight in the glass-painting. "*My soul thirsts for you; my flesh faints for you, as in a dry and weary land where there is no water. So I have looked upon you in the sanctuary, beholding your power and glory. My soul is satisfied as with a rich feast, and my mouth praises you with joyful lips when I think of you on my bed, and meditate on you in the watches of the night; for you have been my help, and in the shadow of your wings I sing for joy.*" Then, as always, her face heated and her gaze dropped back to her prayer book at having sinfully profaned her Lord with prurient thoughts of her precious knight instead of Him.

Vivianne had inadvertently flipped the pages to a well-worn site and stared at the miniature of King David watching Bathsheba in her bath; the miniature introduced the first of the penitential psalms. As she closed her Book of Hours with cheeks burning, Vivianne's gaze slid to the sloped desk-top on the table, upon which lay a completed illuminated manuscript, the exemplar, and its parchment copy, still in progress; both were held down from curling by several hanging weights. Several ink pots, gold leaf, a pen knife and a quill lay beside the sloped desk-top—the scribe's tools. Vivianne took a closer look and blinked several times, blushing suddenly; the exemplar was a leaf of her own unbound manuscript collection! The chaplain was copying *her* work—without asking her permission.

*Père* Daniel had studied the art of manuscript illumination, scribing, binding and even parchment-making at the *Sorbonne*. Last year he had begun to teach Vivianne the art of creating illuminated manuscripts and she had eagerly begun her own, finding herself a good and steady hand at illumination. *Père* Daniel had shown her how to make parchment from the skins of deer that the baron brought back from his hunts in the Grunwald forest. Despite the availability of paper, parchment was worth it "because it is velvety, folds easily and gives an agreeable flexibility to pen strokes compared with the unyielding flatness of writing on paper," the chaplain reasoned.

He always gave a reason for the painstaking preparation that involved flaying, soaking, stretching and scraping: "Parchment wants to curl onto its darker, grain side; and hastily prepared parchment wants to do it more." Nothing was better than parchment made from game "because the vein marks left from blood in the skin when the animal died is the animal's contribution to the art of illumination," he attested with the fervency of a man with a passion.

*Père* demonstrated with exacting care and infinite patience how to use the illuminator's tools and create a professional-looking manuscript. For instance, she needed parchment, a quill for a right-handed scribe, a penknife to sharpen her quills, a pot of ink and a sloping desktop. He taught her how to make iron-gall ink by mixing a solution of tannic acids and copperas with added gum arabic from the dried-up sap of the acacia tree as thickener. It was important to pick a mature oak-gall, one that bore a hole from the matured wasp that had developed inside and left a juicy concoction of gallic acids. The galls were then crushed up and boiled for as long as it took to recite the *Pater Noster* three times, he'd said. The blackness, he told her, resulted from the chemical reaction of the oak-gall potion when copperas was stirred in. He'd shown her how to create the vermillion color, commonly used in headings, which he made from brazilwood chips infused in urine and stirred with gum arabic. Like with Uta's concoctions, Vivianne never asked *Père* Daniel where he got his urine. She and *Père* had raided Theobald's kitchen to hunt down the outer right wing pinions of a goose for making a quill pen that naturally curved to the left, because she was left-handed.

*Père* then showed Vivianne how the height of the written area should equal the width of the whole page in a well-proportioned manuscript. *Père* also showed her how to rule the guidelines for the script and make the initial under-drawing of her illumination in plummet then in ink after which the gold leaf was applied. Vivianne had become adept at applying the gold leaf over the raised *gesso* that she made of slaked lime and white lead mixed with pink clay, sugar, a dash of gum and egg glair glue. After painstakingly painting the *gesso* where she wanted the gold leaf to remain and letting it dry, Vivianne then carefully lowered the fragile tissue-thin leaf over the *gesso* and pressed down through a piece of silk then buffed the gold to a brilliant finish with a dog's tooth by vigorously rubbing back and forth until it was smooth and the edges where there was no *gesso* crumbled away.

Vivianne had started a collection of her own *minnelieds*: love poems inspired by the tale of *Parzival* written by the impoverished knight, Wolfram von Eschenbach in the early 1200s. Vivianne had sat for many hours in front of the sloped desk-top, facing that same humble knight on the painted glass for inspiration as she scripted her poems. She patiently illuminated them with borders of gilt flowers and leaves and coats of arms scattered with *trompe l'oeil* creatures like jousting frogs and *bas-de-page* scenes of young lovers. A miniature of her shining knight enclosed within the stylized enlarged first letter, "D" introduced her first *minnelied*. She'd painted him with dark wild hair and fierce eyes but a gentle mouth. He resembled no one she knew; a boy of her imaginings. Fierce and honorable. A gallant and terribly charming lad, who could capture her heart as easily as capture a notorious villain.

The knight's image inflamed her heart with fiery thoughts of courtly love; it burned her cheeks as she wrote of a chivalrous knight's honest devotion for his beloved lady, who entrusted him with her noble lands and her heart—but not her bed. He was her shining *ritter*, who whisked her away from the trappings of this place and her awful obligations to some strange old man thirty years her senior whom she'd never met. Taking her cue from von Eschenbach's *Tagenleids*, Vivianne often summoned a glimpse of her own private darkness to dwell on a lover's passionate lament of unconsummated love, like the illuminated poem now displayed on the sloped desk-top:

*"You are mine, I am yours,*
*Of that you may be sure.*
*Deep within my heart*
*You're safely locked away,*
*But I have lost the key*
*And there you'll ever stay!"*

Knowing too well the church's view on carnal or romantic love between a man and a woman, Vivianne had told *Père* Daniel that these were her personalized love poems to God. Overwhelmed, the chaplain had praised her devotion and called her his little Hildegard. Vivianne had initially felt shame at her subterfuge, but then she rationalized that surely *all* love was God's love—even if the Church didn't agree.

Seeing where Vivianne had glanced, *Père* Daniel grinned suddenly like a guilty child and leapt to his feet. Vivianne thought he was going to explain why he was copying her personal poems without consulting her. Instead he scrambled nervously to his ornate gold and enamel reliquary on the floor behind him and stooped to open it, releasing the groaning sigh of a man of more advanced years. The purse-shaped container was gold plate and parcel gilt silver over a wooden core with precious stones, pearls, *cloisonné* enamel and glass. Vivianne had often stared at the beautiful 8th Century container, imagining macabre old holy relics *Père* Daniel might have stashed inside. It looked like she was finally going to find out.

After unlocking it with shaky hands, he pulled out—not a mummified piece of an ancient saint or momento—but several manuscripts Vivianne hadn't seen before. *Père* stacked them in his arms and brought them to the table. The books were quite small and oddly bound, unlike most of the books in the library and in *Père* Daniel's special collection, which were hand bound with leather or metal. These resembled the books her mother had secretly left for Vivianne in a chest in the solar. After Uta had shown the contents of the chest to her, Vivianne had stashed everything inside the rucksack her mother had included and hidden it in her secret passageway. She'd heard of the use of block printing; it was used to print Bibles. But these books, like her mother's, were different again. They were perfect. Too perfect. Feeling her heart race, Vivianne wondered: were these books magical too? *Père* Daniel laid the books on the table in front of her and giggled nervously, scratching himself with an involuntary tremor.

"*C'est pour toi, mon ange*," he stammered, nodding at her eagerly then furiously scratched at his body. Fleas, Vivianne concluded. And lice. Judging from his body odor, she didn't think he bathed very often.

Vivianne stared from the books to the priest's pale face. "For me? I don't understand."

He shoved the books toward her as if they carried a disease. "You were supposed to read them. Before—well, before...." He trailed, eyes blinking rapidly. Vivianne felt sure he was spooked by something, perhaps this imminent guest of theirs...her intended. Frowning in concentration, Vivianne turned back to the stack of books and took the top one in her hand. The book cover was made of what looked like layers of *papiér maché*, glossed with oil and embossed with red lettering and an image of a man. Cruel eyes gravely stared out at her from a rounded face of a man with dark, slicked back hair, clean-shaven except for a small mustache. When she opened the book to look inside, the script was plain black ink, tiny and without any illustrations; definitely produced by some kind of printing machine. It was written in German but in a strange dialect she could barely read:

*Menschlichen Kultur und Zivilisation sind auf diesem Erdteit unzertrennlich gegunden an das Vorhenensein des Ariers. Sein Austerben oder Untergehen wird auf diesem Erdball weider die dunklen Schleier einer kulturlosen Zeit senken....*

She closed the book and read the title: *Mein Kampf* by *Adolf Hitler*.

"What is this?" she asked, putting the book down and looking up at the priest with puzzlement.

"*Je suis désolé...*" He looked afraid now. "I was supposed to have you read all of them. But I didn't. Instead we read Hildegard von Bingen, Thucydides, Dante, and Chaucer." He stuttered out her extensive reading list: Christine de Pisan's histories and poetry; Plato, Homer, Euclid, Virgil, Julian of Norwich; the plays of Hrostwitha, the memoirs of Margery Kempe, the writings of *Meister* Eckhart, Herodotus, Tacitus. "Now with...*him* coming..." *Père* Daniel faltered, visibly trembling. Vivianne recognized fear in his eyes.

"You fear retaliation from my father for not having had me read these?" she offered, glancing down at the pile of books again. This was news indeed: that her father had taken sufficient interest in her education to provide a fixed curriculum. The baron had otherwise neglected her. He'd never sent her to be educated as a lady; Uta had cobbled together an education in simple medicine, embroidery, spinning and sewing. Then Berthold's wife, Frieda, the head housekeeper who fancied herself the lady of the castle, sternly "adopted" Vivianne as her ward to edify her in the responsibilities of being a lady. It had seemed to Vivianne that her father had just left her in the castle to while away her life.

Left to her own devices, Vivianne had gravitated to the old clergyman, who was kind and had agreed to teach her in all manner of things scholarly. While Uta and Frieda had given her some instruction on her duties as a lady, it was left to the chaplain to teach her the truly interesting things like astronomy, history and geography, arithmetic, geometry, reading, music, Latin, French and English. Now Vivianne realized that it had all been by design. It seemed now to her astonishment that she'd been far from neglected; rather it seemed as though everyone had conspired in her education: her dead mother, her father and even *Père* Daniel.

*Père* Daniel nodded, responding to her remark. "Your father, yes—I mean, no!" He shook his head in a fluster, mouth twitching. "Not the baron." the chaplain corrected her.

Vivianne blinked, at a loss. If not her father then... "Who, *mon Père*?"

The chaplain visibly trembled. "He, who's coming for...to claim you...your—eh—betrothed."

Vivianne stiffened but kept her face composed. Even the chaplain was having a hard time admitting to her betrothal. This latest revelation startled Vivianne: her education had been directed not by her father but by the strange man she was promised to! "Why?..."

"Why did I *not* give them to you?" *Père* Daniel said. She'd meant: why had she been given an unconventional education for a lady. But she was also curious about the question he'd posed, so she nodded. The chaplain abruptly straightened and his eyes gleamed with the strength of righteous conviction. "Because they're blasphemous, but mostly because they're heartless. They promote cruelty to 'lesser' people for the so-called betterment of society."

"Like burning villages and taking slaves?" Vivianne raised an eyebrow. "Or removing children from their homes and families to labor for their captors?"

The priest smiled sadly. "You've learned well, *ma petite*. Yes, the Order and its knights are guilty of the same atrocities. These works of heresy give reasons for doing so." He pointed to the stack of books in front of her with a shaky finger. "They justify actions of cruelty and hatred on the basis of societal cleansing. Anything that isn't 'pure' is an abomination, not to be tolerated but to be exterminated: Jews, Poles, Gypsies, homosexuals...any non-Teutonic or non-Aryan. They promote fear and hatred and oppression. It perverts God's will, *mon ange*, and does not follow the true path of the righteous Christian."

Neither did her father or those he served, Vivianne considered, but she kept that to herself. She thought it ironic that the monastic order sanctioned so much brutality and death in its

*Drang nach Osten*. In the name of Christianity, they'd burned and sacked villages of infidels unwilling to convert. It seemed that their answer to the challenge of the heathens was not so much to convince them to convert as to simply eliminate them. How did that differ from what *Père* Daniel had just described?

She picked up *Mein Kampf* again and frowned at it. *My struggle...my battle*. She checked the other titles: *Vom deutschen Nationalgeist*, by Carl von Moser; *Auch eine Philosophie die Geschichte* by Johann Gottfried Herder; *Reden an die deutsche Nation* by Johann Gottlieb Fichte; *The Origin of Species by Means of Natural Selection* by Charles Darwin; *Also sprach Zarathustra* by Friedrich Nietzche; and *Grundlagen des Neunzehnjahrhunderts* by Houston Stewart Chamberlain. What was the motivation in having her read these? It made her very uneasy about her mysterious betrothed.

She picked up Fichte's book, flipped it open to a page and read: *Ein wahrhafter Deutscher nur könne leben wollen, um eben Deutscher zu sein, und zu bleiben, und die Seinigen zu eben solchen zu bilden*. It was an urgent call for a united German nation based on a common identity and common language, something the German dukedoms, states and cities were thoroughly rejecting at the present time. She shrugged and shut the book then picked up Nietzsche's *Also sprach Zarathustra* and flipped the pages. She spotted words like *übermensch* and *üntermensch*, which made her uncomfortable. Further on, she read about *"Gesundung"* of the people to purify them. Vivianne picked up *Grundlagen des Neunzehnjahrhunderts*, eyes darting over words: *Einige Menschen sind von Natur frei, andere Sklaven*. Chamberlain was suggesting that some people were meant to be free and others weren't; he claimed that history played itself out in a racial confict, a *blutigen Kampf zwischen Germanen und Nicht-Germanen*. Vivianne put the book down with a frown. And who were to be the privileged? *Der Germanen*? The Teutonic race? She found herself glaring at the books and pursed her lips with disapproval. Her first thought was that *Père* Daniel was right to have kept them from her.

"But, why all this for *me...now?*" she let the words she

was thinking escape her lips as she closed the book. Why had they all taken such an interest in giving her an extraordinary, highly skewed education?

"*Voyons*! It's so you would—" the chaplain cut himself off with a halting breath and pursed his lips in contemplation then sighed. His shoulders drooped and he shook his head, "*Je ne sais pas....*"

Vivianne let her brows come together. What was he not saying to her? She opened *Mein Kampf* again. She showed *Père* the supposed date of publication and hiked one brow. "How do you explain this, *Père?*"

*Père* Daniel looked nervous again. "I don't know, petite. It is obviously some kind of trickery. I wish your mother was here. She'd know how to instruct you." He shook his head with flustered thoughts and tapped his face nervously with his fingers. "The man...Mortameur...I fear that he uses black magic." His eyes seized hers with alarming intensity. "But you, *mon ange*, have white magic."

What was he saying to her! She must have looked alarmed because he quickly grew flustered and added, "*Tiens.*" He held out the key to his reliquary. "*Prendre. Il appartient maintenant à toi.* You can keep the books safe in there along with the others."

"But..." She hesitated.

"*S'il te plait!*" He looked suddenly desperate and forced the key into her hand. Then his whole body shuddered in a violent convulsion. His nervous tick was turning into something serious, Vivianne thought with growing concern. "I insist, child," he said in close to a shriek. "Let it be a gift for your...eh...coming nuptial with..." He couldn't finish.

Vivianne blushed then conceded with a silent nod and took the key, placing it into the small velvet embroidered purse on her belt. "*Merci, Père,*" she said quietly and felt the silence grow thick with more questions.

She held off her string of inquiries to help the chaplain set up the chess pieces for the game he'd just pulled out. As she made the opening move, the chaplain scratched himself furiously and grabbed a second mug in his shaking hand. Vivianne noticed for the first time that it steamed and caught the acrid aroma of herbs. Surely not ale, then.

Noticing her eyes following his movement, the chaplain scowled down at the mug, "For my headache and the stomach and bowl problems I'm suffering of late..." he explained. "Chamomile and rose-hip tea with coriander. According to Hildegard von Bingen it's very good against headache and cramps. I've added cinnamon, comfrey and dandelion for this awful itch...I think it is all making me a bit melancholy and giving me bad dreams...like your father and some of the servants," he ended, taking a small sip then grimacing. He could cure that itch just as easily by taking a bath, Vivianne thought to herself. "Uta suggested a meal of chicken stewed in hyssop, lemon balm and wine as a treatment for melancholy...another of Hildegard's remedies." He grinned and Vivianne thought that anything with wine or ale in it could cure the chaplain of his depression. "I am preparing my *none* service at the feast and *vespers* Eucharist service for the Teutonic monks; they will be arriving soon," *Père* Daniel continued, after another loud sip of the tea. "They are used to at least eight church services a day."

So that was what was making him nervous, Vivianne concluded. Was he worried that these Teutonic monks would appear more devout than him? *Père* Daniel wasn't exactly the most conservative clergyman in the region, Vivianne reflected. The unconventional education he'd given Vivianne suggested that he was far from a conformist. He didn't waste time lecturing her on the church's dogma nor did he attempt to coerce her into more frequent prayer sessions. He'd long ago acknowledged her wayward nature when it came to religious matters; yet he never forced her to behave.

"There may be a sickness in the castle, child..." *Père* gave her a strange look. "Your father is a bit poorly like me. Complains of fiery bowels and dizziness." If he stopped drinking her father might find his cure too, Vivianne thought cynically. "Your father is also having bad dreams...visions of some evil apparition choking and strangling him...a witch...."

Vivianne swallowed convulsively, not certain why this made her uncomfortable.

"Sometimes it's *you* choking him, *ma petite*..."

Vivianne inhaled her saliva and fell into a sudden coughing spell. The chaplain pretended to study the chessboard but was obviously watching her quietly until she recovered. Then he pursed his lips in thought and looked up at her.

"You know what is inscribed on the temple of Apollo at Delphi, *ma petite*..."

"*'Know thyself'*," she said, moving a pawn forward on the board, then looked up at him with intensity. She wondered why he had brought this up. "But if we're the most complex beings on Earth, *mon Père*, how can we come to know ourselves or our fellow men?"

"Ah...." *Père* Daniel smiled, moving his pawn forward. "You ask the question of questions. And its answer lies partially in the study of your forefathers. In their experiences. Your future lies in your past, *ma petite*."

"But, surely, we can change the future, *mon Père*," she challenged, moving her knight. "My future need not be a slave to my past."

*Père* Daniel threw his head back with a loud snorting laugh. "*Touché, ma petite*! Spoken like a true rebel!" he said with a grin then moved another pawn. "Ah, the fervour of innocent youth. You may yet cure the world of all its ills, *mon ange*!" He laughed heartily. "*Make your world a better world*." He'd repeated a phrase she'd often shared with him: of making a difference; to make her world a better world. No doubt he thought her naïve, but he always indulged her. Vivianne strongly suspected that the chaplain was a genuine heretic and grinned at him through sad eyes. She would miss him terribly. He was more like a father to her than her own father was. And knew her better too, she thought, pushing her pawn forward.

As though he sensed her thoughts, *Père* Daniel took her pawn with his bishop then leaned forward with sad eyes. "I spoke on your behalf, *ma petite*," he suddenly confessed. "I told the baron of your tremendous devoutness, how your love for

God superseded all other love..." He glanced at her *minnelied* beside him. She felt her face heat with the hidden truth and slid her queen forward. He went on, "I told him you have a greater calling than to become someone's wife. To work with your extraordinary gift for learning, reading and writing for God." He meant as a nun in an abbey, Vivianne realized. *"To make this world a better world,"* he repeated her mantra. "I even showed him your love poems, *ma petite,*" he added, pointing to the illuminated manuscript.

Vivianne stared at *Père* Daniel in bewilderment, knight poised in her hand. She wasn't sure if she should thank him for his effort or be angry that he showed something private of hers to her father without asking her. Not to mention his copying it without telling her. But it was hard to be angry at *Père* Daniel, thought Vivianne as she gazed at his rather homely earnest face then placed her knight on the board. He had meant well.

The priest sighed then moved his rook. "The baron wouldn't listen."

The baron never did, Vivianne thought. She curbed her lips from curling in a victorious smile and moved her queen one last time on the board. "Check mate, *mon Père,*" she said, now letting her smug smile loose on him.

He made a sound of exasperation then nodded to her in silent congratulation. *"Eh bien, mon elève.* What will I do without you, *ma petite.* There will be no one to tease me, or challenge me, or make me laugh...or beat me at chess in seven moves!" Then he looked at her with such sad longing in his eyes that she felt a lump of emotion catch in her throat and she reached for the *ritterkreuz* pendant—a small version of the *ritterkreuz* broach her father wore—that hung below her neck. She rubbed her fingers against the wide arms of the cross and concluded that the chaplain was as sad to see her go as she was.

He sighed then shook his head, thinking of something that appeared to disturb him. He put on his lecture face once more. "You must be strong, *ma petite.* Do you remember what Hugh of St. Victor said of woman's creation?"

Vivianne smiled. "That *'woman was created from man's*

57

*side, which shows that she was designed to be his companion.'"*

*Père* Daniel finished for her, " '*She was not made from a man's head, so she would rule, nor from his feet, so she would be his servant.'"*

Suddenly inspired with a wicked thought, Vivianne lifted a brow at *Père* Daniel in challenge. "You met him, didn't you? 'He, who's coming to claim me'," she repeated the chaplain's words. She couldn't bring herself to say 'betrothed'. She imagined an old paunchy man in his forties, scarred and smelling of liquor and old sweat, with cruel eyes and a cynical mouth.

The priest licked his lips nervously. "Yes, I met him, *mon ange*, the man who brings you your destiny," he conceded in a subdued voice. "I met him twice..."

"Is he a knight?" she asked.

"No," he responded. He glanced furtively behind, as though he was worried someone would overhear his admission. Then he placed his arms on the table and leaned toward her conspiratorially, continuing in a hushed voice, "His name is Leduc Mortameur; he's French—"

"Like you."

"*Ah, oui, comme moi*," he hesitatingly agreed, a little flustered by her remark. "*Mais sur tout comme ta mère...*" But mostly like her mother. *Père* Daniel often absently interchanged his French and German, especially when he got nervous or excited; he knew that it didn't matter because Vivianne was fluent in French, English and Latin by now. "*Et toi même.*" And *her* too! The chaplain fixed an intense look on Vivianne and she almost recoiled, nervous of where this conversation was heading. "You are...different from me, *mon ange*," he said, voice rising in pitch. Vivianne felt her heart beating wildly. What did he mean? Did he know about the strange marks on her back? The same ones she was certain her mother had. "Your mother...and he—Mortameur—they come from a different place."

"Yes, France."

"Ah." He sighed. "Yes, but not *my* France," he ended

cryptically. "I know about your...eh..." He nervously waggled his finger at her.

Vivianne swallowed hard. "The marks on my back?"

He nodded vigorously. "The doctor told me about them...Uta told him." So, nothing was sacred, Vivianne concluded. After she'd commanded her not to, Uta had told after all! "I know you didn't have those marks when you were first born when I baptized you, *ma petite*...but you have developed them since, eh?"

The chaplain probably knew about her mother when they'd changed and dressed her to place her in her shroud for the burial rites. Or the doctor had told him about that too. Both graduates from *Sorbonne*, the chaplain and doctor often conferred on matters of mutual responsibility. The church, after all, taught that God often sent illness as a punishment and that repenting would cure all ills. Vivianne knew that the doctor consulted *Père* Daniel on most matters of complicated ailments; the remainder of which he usually prescribed bloodletting from various parts of the body to rectify the balance of humors. Vivianne suspected that the doctor had been the one who had started the rumors of her mother being a witch because of those decidedly pagan markings. And what about Mortameur, *the man who brought her destiny*? Did Mortameur also have those heathen marks? What did it all mean? This revelation fueled her suspicions that her suitor had known her mother...very well, in fact. He was also more than likely linked to her mother's strange and sudden appearance in Grunwald's marsh fourteen years and nine months ago this day.

*Père* Daniel continued, "Always remember, *ma petite*, that whatever happens, you are a child of God; God made you too." His face glowed with warm sincerity as he smiled at her the way Vivianne wished her own father would. *Père's* eyes grew sad as he studied her. "*Meister* Eckhart said, '*suffering is the fleetest animal that bears you to perfection.*'"

*Lieber Gott!* What did he think was in store for her, Vivianne thought with mounting alarm.

*Père* Daniel exhaled with a frown, eyes glazing with a

vision of the past. "I met Leduc Mortameur fourteen years ago when he..." The chaplain hesitated, forming his words carefully, "...first came."

"And extracted my parents' promise to give me to him."

*Père* Daniel nodded sadly. "Yes. You were already inside your mother, *ma petite* when he came to claim...you."

He'd hesitated and Vivianne caught it. Who had he really come to claim? She'd heard an awful rumor and the chaplain had just earlier confirmed that Mortameur knew her mother from before. What had her mother run away from? Had she run away from *him*? And had Mortameur claimed the yet unborn daughter—Vivianne—as ransom? Were they related? Or worse—had they been lovers?

"He returned five years later, though he looked no older than the last time he'd been here. He brought these books for you and instructed the baron on your education." Then *Père* Daniel looked at her gravely and reached out to take one of her hands. He pressed it between his two. "I will miss you terribly, *mon ange*. You were a good student. *Mais*...I fear...I fear for us all, but for you especially. *Ma petite*, your destiny carries a special burden, I believe...*A devenir ce que tu cherches*...To become *that which you seek*...."

Vivianne gave the old chaplain a puzzled half-smile. "I don't understand, *Père*."

He squeezed her hand. "It is a portent. I do not know of what it signifies but I cannot help fear some calamity that involves you."

Vivianne felt her heart suddenly throb in her throat. It was the same feeling she'd had when she'd arisen today, she thought with a convulsive swallow. "What do you mean, *mon Père*? What portent?"

"Have you not wondered at the oddness of it, child...At two o'clock, you will meet your destiny: on the fourteenth hour of the fourteenth day of your fourteenth year in the fourteenth hundred year..." *Père* Daniel whispered in terrified reverence.

*Lieber Gott!* She started back and felt her heart beat like a drum. She'd never considered the oddness of the date and time.

Did she have something to do with that awful war happening out there? Who was this Mortameur that he struck fear in everyone?

✠

# ...4

VIVIANNE knelt in supposed prayer facing the altar and gold cross of the chancel of the castle chapel; but, in fact, was daydreaming while staring in a daze at the north-facing rose window to her left. The window was a mandala of predominantly sapphire blue soda glass and ruby painted-glass that depicted The Creation.

Something stirred beside her and she flinched in surprise and might have even cried out then blushed furiously. A young knight in the full trappings of light mail and armor stood there, looking at her with unabashed curiosity. His white tunic was emblazoned with a plain red cross of the Knights Templar.

He must have silently entered the nave from the south door, through the scriptorium to her right, thought Vivianne.

"Hello." He bowed. "I'm Siegfried von Heidelberg, a Knight Templar from the Rheinland. I've come with my arms bearers to command a large lance of crossbow archers for your father." He was rather handsome and splendid looking in his warrior's garb. She thought him young for someone who already commanded a lance of archers. The knight had swiftly glanced down at the invitation in his hand to get her name, having correctly guessed that she was the baron's daughter. "You must be Lady Vivian—"

"Vee-vianne," she'd tersely corrected him. He'd used the English pronunciation, which she disliked. Then she hastily explained, "It's a French name…We pronounce our i's as ee's, like in German. And the accent is on the last part of the name, not the first." She pushed down on her thighs to stand up quickly without his help and faced him. Her face heated again as she saw that she came up fully to his height; he was short for a knight, she decided. She now also realized just how young he was; not much older than Wolfgang. And already a commander! He betrayed his youth in those large unguarded brown eyes. And together with his long straight nose, this diminutive knight reminded her of Spritz, Berthold's collie; intelligent, loyal and dewy-eyed.

"Ahh…" The knight smiled and repeated, "Vee-vee-anne." Then nodded, pleased with himself. "A pleasure, My Lady. I'm Siegfried von Heidelberg. " He bowed again. "I've just come from England and will return there again, where there are quite a few Vivians. They're both pretty names." He looked a little embarrassed for a moment then added, "I'm sorry if I disturbed you in your prayers…" She hadn't exactly been praying, Vivianne admitted silently to herself, blushing anew. "But I'd been told about the stunning stained-glass rose windows in the chapel and I had to see them. They are remarkable, aren't they? Suspended between floor and vault…" He swept his brown-eyed gaze up to the vaulted clerestory then to the north facing rose window of the apse, then the west window depicting the death of the Virgin and finally to the south window, which showed the Resurrection. "Like beautiful jewels."

"Yes," Vivianne murmured, not knowing what else to say, and let her gaze drift back to the north rose window. Although irrevocably drawn to the west window, Vivianne always preferred the north-facing window.

Von Heidelberg followed her gaze. "It is beautiful, isn't it? A giant web of glass, lead and stone, created with such reverence and artistic skill. Have you seen the old cathedral they built in Paris?"

She'd never been to France. "Do you mean Notre Dame Cathedral? The one dedicated to 'Our Lady'?"

"No," he responded. "It was started first but they finished building it much later in 1345." He rushed into rapt description, "I'm talking about Sainte-Chapelle, the palace chapel built for King Louis IX on the Île-de-la-Cité. The stained glass there is remarkable. Light shines through it like God's grace, creating lanterns of divine light. Your Ladyship must go on a pilgrimage there sometime."

Needing to say something, Vivianne pointed to the north window and blurted out, "This one's my favorite. At the center is Creation." She pointed. "It's surrounded by the four seasons and the twelve months of the year, beyond which are the twelve signs of the Zodiac and the four elements. The blue color symbolizes Divine light. The interlaced squares and circles show the interaction of temporal and earthly things with the eternal and celestial."

Von Heidelberg stroked his smooth chin and eyed her with a quizzical smile of puzzled appreciation. He returned a ponderous gaze to the rose window and they stood in awkward silence for a moment. His eyes lit up suddenly. "I dabble a bit in *Glaßmalerei*. These works were no doubt made in a glass-house in Erfurt, in my part of the world," he blithely announced. "I'd say the glazier was *Herr* Georg von Zaehner."

"Really?" She turned to glance at his smug face with a smile of doubt. "How do you know that? These were made years ago, commissioned by my grandmother." Before he was born.

"Well…" He brushed his face with his hand in contemplation and studied the glass-painted window more earnestly. "First, there's the use of abraded flash-ruby glass with yellow stain and his ample use of green pot metal glass. A telltale moniker of von Zaehner. And look there, how he uses trace-lines and smear-shading on the scorpion or stipple-shading on those fish." He pointed. "But mostly it's that example of painting on the back of the glass. Do you see there, on the archer's headdress? And then finally, it's the design—"

"You mean the Islamic-inspired system of radiating squares and circles?"

He looked at her in puzzled amazement. "You know a

lot about *Glaßmalerei*."

"I read Theophilus and Father Daniel taught me a lot too."

He nodded appreciatively. "You are fortunate to have so erudite an instructor." Then his eyes sparkled and he practically giggled. "Anyway, the real reason I know this is because the *Glaßmaler* left his initials there by the coat of arms of his patron." He pointed.

Vivianne studied the von Grunwald heraldic coat of arms on one of the lancets below the rose window. There, scratched below, lay the initials GZ. So, the knight had led her on with his talk of artistic interpretation, Vivianne thought, not appreciating his little deception at her expense. He'd known all along by one glance at the initials.

"Your grandmother must have visited the *Glaßmaler* in Erfurt," von Heidelberg went on. "And she must have seen examples of his works." Then, as if he suddenly thought he'd stayed too long, he bowed again and said, "But, I've kept you from your prayers long enough. I will leave you to them now. I hear it is your birthday and wish you every happiness."

With that he'd bowed and went on his way, leaving her heart a-flutter in his wake with thoughts far from divine running through her mind.

✠

## …5

ON her way past the Great Hall, Vivianne ran across a young girl about her own age and recognized her as the new dairymaid, Gertrude. She'd just come to the castle yesterday to take over for Hedwig, who'd left to be with her own family.

The girl looked lost; she was absently staring at a sheaf

of papers, plucked brows furrowed, with her tongue sticking out the side of her rosy little mouth. Vivianne realized the girl was trying to read.

"Hello, Gertrude," Vivianne said to the full-figured blonde beauty; the kind her father had trysts with during those drunken late night gatherings. Perhaps the real reason she'd been appointed, Vivianne thought cynically.

Gertrude looked up and jolted, then curtsied with a slight bow. "Oh, My Lady von Grunwald!"

"Can I help you with that?" Vivianne put *Père* Daniel's reliquary full of her new books on the floor and leaned over to see what was written. Most of the servants of von Grunwald *Ordensburgen* couldn't read.

"Can you read?" the girl gushed, hopeful. "I can't read worth a horse's ass!" Then she blushed as Vivianne hid a smile. "Oh, pardon me, Your Ladyship." She hastily shoved the paper into Vivianne's hand. "It's my list of equipment I need for my work, isn't it?"

Vivianne glanced at the paper. "Yes. All listed here." She read out the list to Gertrude, who listened intently with lips absently pursed, obviously in the effort of committing it all to memory.

When Vivianne returned the paper to the new dairymaid, the girl thanked her effusively, grabbed her hand and kissed it then rushed off.

Left alone in the dank hall, Vivianne abruptly felt the flush of febrile heat. A sudden cold chill then swept through her like a winter storm and she caught—or imagined—the faint whiff of a cloyingly sweet fragrance that reminded her of the secret passageways. And she knew: her suitor was here *now*...already! How she knew, Vivianne had no idea. A feeling. A crackling energy of portent surged through her gut that was just shy of palpable and made her shiver to imagine that he could feel her too—

"Ah! There you are!" a familiar basso voice boomed down the dank hallway.

Vivianne flinched and inhaled sharply at the call.

Recognizing the voice, she let her shoulders relax then turned and waited dutifully as her pouting father swaggered toward her with a tankard of ale in his hand. He'd just emerged from the Great Hall.

"Daughter!" He looked rakishly splendid in dark hose and a bright blue damask cotehardie with jagged sleeves of gilded gold embroidery. His black *hoyke,* with the Grunwald coat of arms emblazoned on it—a sable field with green oak tree and a golden unicorn—sat askew over his shoulders as if carelessly thrown on. It was fastened by a gold broach with a large amber stone at its center. Even his seven pointed gold coronet set with amber jewels sat recklessly askew on his head like a boat in a storm. Three years ago, during a heated argument with the *Hochmeister* over some matter of which Vivianne knew nothing, her father had renounced his secular membership in the Teutonic Order. He'd discarded the Order's mantle and re-adopted his own von Grunwald coat of arms. Vivianne noticed that he was wearing earrings and more rings today than usual, including the gold von Grunwald unicorn on his left ring finger.

The baron tamed his wild salt and peppered hair with a brusque sweep of his free hand. He straightened his coronet, then halted, almost stepping on her skirts, with a scowling appraisal of her. A sudden involuntary tremor tightened his face and Vivianne thought he should take some of *Père* Daniel's chamomile tea. They were both suffering from a case of the nerves.

As if to confirm this, her father suddenly jerked as if struck from behind and swiped madly at the air then rubbed his arms briskly. "Be off with you!" he shouted at nothing. Vivianne shrank back involuntarily. She looked around and saw no one in the hall except she and her father. He grimaced at her with sparkling eyes. "Don't be alarmed, daughter. It's only the specters nipping at me…"

The specter of too much morning ale, Vivianne thought and eyed the silver tankard in the baron's hand. He was already drunk.

He righted himself with a sniff and pushed his lips

outward. "You are to be ready for me in the Great Hall at two o'clock to receive a special guest," he imperiously informed her. His whole body shook as if from the palsy. "Do not disappoint me, Vivianne."

"I won't, Father," she murmured, dropping her gaze to the stone floor.

"You will do me proud, child," he said in that deep lyrical voice that she used to long to hear. It made her look up. Hope bloomed on his face and he stroked her hair with sudden gentleness and calm. His breath on her smelled faintly of licorice. Then she noticed his bloodshot eyes assailing her with unseemly longing, and cringed. But the moment was fleeting. He dropped his hand and snapped back to his distant demeanor, then pointed a slender shaking finger at her.

"Wear the dress I left for you. And don't be late, daughter!"

As Vivianne watched him march off in a staggering loping gait, *hoyke* sailing behind him, she had a vision of another man in another time, a man not yet broken, and wished she'd known that man.

Vivianne grabbed the reliquary and hastened down the hall. She wasn't thinking especially of where she was going, except to go in the opposite direction of where her father was going. As a result, she instinctively took herself down the winding staircase toward her secret hiding passageways. The castle was riddled with them. A nexus of secret doorways lay at the end of a lower dark and drafty hall off the pantry and wine cellar, behind a series of bizarre and rather profane *Wilde Leute* tapestries that depicted hairy men-creatures, bare-breasted women, children and fantastical beasts like unicorns, monkeys and colorful birds. Three of them—*Wild Man with the Unicorn*, *Wild Woman with the Unicorn* and *Wild Child with the Unicorn*, each concealed a secret door that led to a different hidden passageway. Vivianne was convinced that she had not yet discovered all the hidden passages that riddled von Grunwald Castle.

She was too busy running to her tapestries at the end of

the sporadically lit hall to notice the sounds until she was almost upon them and skidded to a halt—

A half-naked man, with his backside exposed to her, had pinned a young girl at knifepoint like an insect against the *Wild Man* tapestry! The man wore a stiff black waist-length cotehardie. Hussar's trousers pooled around his shiny boots and he bared his muscular buttocks and legs. He'd ripped off the girl's upper bodice and held his knife poised over her exposed taut breasts. The tapestry behind the girl and the floor were splattered with pottage that had spilled when she'd dropped her cauldron.

The man drawled in a dark husky voice, "*...Laß endlich die Gottesmensch über die Affenmenschen siegen...*" He spoke the strange words with a strong foreign accent.

The girl struggled and murmured, "Please, don't! I'm not—"

"You were a moment ago, slave!" he cut her off with a sharp laugh and then slid the knife point to her alabaster throat. "You're a wicked witch to taunt me with your tempting smile and then to refuse me. '*That which gives light must endure burning*'. Now suffer the consequences of your incredible beauty and teasing looks!"

He hunched over the girl, then gruffly groped at her skirts, raising them as she whimpered and mewled in desperate entreaty. Ignoring her imploring cries for mercy, he thrust into her with a hard jerk, smothering her shriek by plastering his mouth on hers. He followed with a fierce rapid rocking, lifting her up like a rag doll with each grunting effort. His moans chased her muffled cries in a cruel perversion of an antiphonal.

Vivianne recognized the girl as Milda, one of the Lithuanian slaves her father had picked up in one of his raids last year. Alerted by Vivianne's sharp inhale, Milda struggled with new urgency. The brute struck her with the back of his hand then half-turned, still engaged, and stared at Vivianne.

Vivianne gasped before locking her lips shut. The man was disturbingly familiar and stunningly beautiful, like an unsettling work of art that begged scrutiny. Appearing in his early-twenties, his finely chiseled face was lightly dusted with the stubble of a dark beard, framed by thick dark hair, a long straight nose and decisive chin. His sensual mouth was an ode to beauty, parted now with arousal. But his cold blue eyes cut into hers like a blade, finding the heart of her. Vivianne's breast tightened as if squeezed by a fist and her hand strayed to clutch the *ritterkreuz* that hung below her throat. Their eyes locked, trapping her in a fatal gaze. How could God have put the Devil's eyes into the face of an angel? *Lieber Gott*, it was more than that; he looked *into* her as though he knew her! As though he *owned* her....

His potent eyes narrowed slightly. " '*We die only once, and for such a long time*'..."

*Mary, mother of Christ!* He was the man in her awful dream! She broke off her gaze and stumbled back with a moan of horrified fear. She wheeled, then, clutching the reliquary in one hand, grabbed her skirt with the other and ran as fast as she could. She tripped over her skirt once but recovered without falling as her eyes filled with tears of helpless despair.

The echo of his churlish laugh and the girl's renewed sobs—as he must have resumed his assault—chased her down the dark hall, past the kitchen, and toward the scullery. Vivianne fisted away her tears and felt her anger swell. *If only I were a man, a knight, I'd have challenged the brute!* She conjectured that he was one of the baron's new mercenaries—guests of the Order— arrived from Western Europe for the battle tomorrow. Mercenaries had a reputation for debauchery and a noticeable lack of respect for property. She felt suddenly faint and, letting the reliquary drop to the floor, leaned a hand against the cool stone wall to steady herself. The poor girl! It was likely not the first time that would happen to Milda; she was a pretty girl with a body men liked to handle and a mouth they liked to slide their tongues into. She was also a slave, and not much older than herself, Vivianne concluded. She leaned her back against the wall and breathed in deeply, closing her eyes. But the brute had done more than take his man's pleasure of her; he'd hurt her, cut her....

The age of the chivalrous knight was dissolving, Vivianne lamented. Too many lords, like her father, had resorted to hiring mercenaries to battle for them. The plague, incessant war, increasingly inhospitable winters and famine, loss of critical trade routes and great unrest had conspired to reduce the work force and corrupt the joy in the world.

It was an interesting and troubled age she was living in, Vivianne contemplated. A world of great mistrust and growing evil. There was the great war between the French and the English that seemed never to want to end. The Holy Roman Empire of the German Nations was fraught with a morass of disputes and bickering among its Cities, Principalities, Kingdoms, Republics and Episcopal dioceses. Even 'popes' were squabbling among themselves. Alas, amid its own turmoil the church appeared all too eager to hunt down heretics on mere hearsay and ruthlessly subdue them, usually in a permanent way by beheading them or burning them alive. *Père* Daniel was probably right to be fearful of what lay in store for them all—

"My Lady! What are you doing here?"

Vivianne jerked up from the wall, eyes bolting open.

Frieda, the head housekeeper, frowned at her with critical black crow's eyes; she'd just rounded the corner of the hall and stood like a stone, fists planted against her small hips. Vivianne met Frieda's scolding gaze with difficulty. The slim upright woman always managed to make Vivianne feel guilty of something, usually of not being a lady. Spurning Uta's feckless efforts in educating the wayward girl, the exacting housekeeper had taken it upon herself to teach Vivianne all that she needed to know to be a lady, including how to run a castle household, which would be her responsibility once she was married off to that strange man her father had chosen for her.

"The lady of the house must know everything, so she can effectively oversee her staff. Otherwise she is a fool and will be taken for it!" Frieda often said to Vivianne, who always felt like a fool.

Vivianne could not gainsay Frieda's efforts; there was much to learn and much the head housekeeper could teach her.

Vivianne just didn't like the way Frieda demeaned Uta—and herself, come to think of it—in doing so. But it had also given Vivianne the opportunity to escape the castle walls: to forage in the local forest with other maidservants for berries, nuts, mushrooms and wild herbs needed in meals; or visit the village on castle errands.

"What are you doing, gallivanting in the lower halls at this time?" Frieda reproved, now tapping her foot. Vivianne stood easily as tall as the stern housekeeper; yet she always felt like the woman was looking down her long nose at her. "This is not the way a lady behaves. You should be getting ready for dinner, young lady!"

Thinking suddenly that the two of them could take on the brute, Vivianne took in a gulping breath and pointed down the hall from where she'd just come. "There's an awful man violating our Milda! I think he's one of Father's hired mercenaries. Come! You must help me stop him!" She grabbed Frieda's arm and was spinning around to return, when Frieda jerked back and brusquely removed Vivianne's hand.

"What gibberish is this! Milda's gone. She's been missing since April. We think she was just waiting for the weather to improve then escaped and went back to her home northeast of here."

Vivianne stared, bemused. "But..." Surely it was Milda she'd seen. The pretty girl's face was unmistakable. "In any case, *someone* is being ravished by a brutish man!" she stuttered out and aimed pleading eyes at the housekeeper's harsh face. "Oh, *Frau* Frieda! We must do something!"

This time the housekeeper relented—if only mollified by Vivianne's respectful use of her title—and let Vivianne pull her down the hall; although she resisted running the speed at which Vivianne tried to coax them. When they finally reached the tapestry of the *Wild Man with the Unicorn*, there was no one there. In fact, there was no sign of any altercation having taken place. No wet pottage stains on the tapestry or the floor. No blood spatters. Vivianne wandered the area, searching with a puzzled face. She bent over the tapestry and drew her hands over the intricately woven wool, silk, gold and multi-colored thread, as if touching it would give her a sign. Her fingers felt along the long strong hatchings and coarse irregular ribbings of a mosaic of needlework that resembled a textured sea swimming in rich Tyrian purple, woad blue, saffron yellow, green and carmine red.

"What nonsense is this?" the older woman said, steely eyes glowering. "Is this another one of your girlish tricks, young lady?"

"No, *Frau* Frieda—"

"It is not becoming of a lady, *Herrin* Baroness," she scolded harshly, showing anger in her flushed angular cheeks. "Sometimes I think that you haven't listened to a thing I've taught you, *Herrin* Baroness—"

"They were right here, up against this *Fabeltierteppiche*," Vivianne insisted, leaning with her back against the soft tapestry like the young Milda had when the brute had ravished her. He had been swift about it, Vivianne decided. How had it been possible for him to clean up? There would at least be wetness on the tapestry; it was totally dry. Then Vivianne suddenly remembered how they'd had to clean the tapestry last April due to an unexplainable spill....

"You are about to meet your future husband and you're still busy weaving these childish pranks, taking up people's valuable time with crazy made-up tales when we must all be getting ready for the feast," Frieda bit out. "Might I remind you that rape is not a subject to be fooled with, Your Ladyship. *Herr* Baron will not take to this kindly when I tell him. *He* values my time! Take care, My Lady. You cannot be a prankster and a lady at the same time. You must stop this dreaming. Your place is to look after your lord's estate and keep his bed warm. Now, I suggest you ready yourself for the feast." With that last biting remark, Frieda spun on her heel and left the still bewildered girl alone in the gloomy hall.

Vivianne ran back to fetch her reliquary then returned and, after seizing a still unlit rush dip and lighting it on a nearby torch, she pulled aside the edge of the *Wild Woman* tapestry.

Behind it, as with its sister tapestries, lay a secret door etched into the stone wall that was the entrance to one of the narrow passages she'd found when she'd explored the castle as a child. She took in a hushed breath and opened the door.

✠

## ...6

VIVIANNE felt a shudder as though she'd walked through a ghost, and the rush of cool air rustled through her hair. She inhaled a sweet but cloying fragrance she could not describe; its stench had only recently invaded the dark passageway and Vivianne wondered if some small animal had died in there. She entered and hastily closed the wall door behind her then made her way carefully down the damp and steep stairway that wound its way to the great storeroom at the bottom northeast-end of the keep.

She thought it odd that only she knew of the secret doors and passages behind the *Wilde Leute* tapestries. After many skillful inquiries, she'd deduced that no one in the household, not even her father knew about the hidden passageways that riddled *Ordensburgen* von Grunwald. It was Vivianne's grandmother—the baron's mother—who had commissioned the tapestries from an atelier in France and had them put there. Was her grandmother responsible for more than just the tapestries? Vivianne hadn't shown anyone the false doors she'd discovered. Not even Wolfgang. She'd used them many times to escape the officious meddling of Berthold or Frieda's incessant ministrations or Uta's smothering scrutiny. It gave her a means to "disappear" at will. She'd often run away from all her well-meaning overseers and a world crowded by meaningless duty.

This particular passageway descended steeply into a

subterranean level below the level of the storerooms, then ascended again and terminated in a trap door to the great storeroom floor. Vivianne stopped at a small wooden ladder that led up to the trap door. On the well-worn stone floor, to the side, sat two bags, one was a large oiled duffel bag that held her purloined knight's gear—thanks to Wolfgang; the other container was her mother's knapsack of strange material that fit over the shoulders.

Vivianne put down the reliquary then squatted over the bag and touched it, imagining what lay inside: the strange and wonderful items her mother had bequeathed to her, the only things she had left of her mother: several bottles of her mother's alchemical potions: magnesium sulfate, penicillin, hydrazine and labetalol, and coumadin—the potion Doctor Grien had given her mother against her will—and vials of ampicillin, gentamicin and metronidazone too; a small leather folding purse with transparent windows that held two slim flat wafers of strong but flexible material with writing and heraldic designs; a strange smooth metallic-like box the size of her palm that opened on a hinge to reveal a square glass face and "buttons" marked with the alphabet, numbers and symbols she didn't understand; and, of course, her mother's magical books…

Vivianne opened the large pouch of the knapsack and rummaged through the books. She pulled out one of her favorites and let her hand slide across the smooth thin and malleable cover with its colorful image of people in a strange room. Perfectly shaped white letters on black background read: *Nineteen Eighty-Four* by George Orwell. It was a fictional satire about the far future. When Vivianne had first opened the soft cover and looked inside at the first page, she'd read: *Copyright 1949*; which was impossible. It meant that the book had also been published in the future! When she'd checked the other books her mother had left her, they too had been supposedly published in the future: Johannes Kepler's *The Harmony of the World*, in 1619; *The Manifesto of the Communist Party* by Karl Marx and Friedrich Engels in 1848; Albert Einstein's *Relativity* in 1916; Simone de Beauvoir's, *The Second Sex*, in 1948; Brian Greene's *The*

*Elegant Universe* in 1999; and *Roget's l'Histoire Compréhensif à 2010.* At first she'd concluded that *Roget's l'Histoire* was simply predicting the future using the language of certainty. But she eventually realized that the book itself came from the future!

Vivianne fished out another favorite, *Gargantua and Pentagruel* by François Rabelais, a French writer and priest. The book, published in 1534—yet to happen—was a satirical attack on scholasticism and superstition, written with lively and ribald humor.

But the fact that they were supposedly published in the future wasn't the magical part; the magic happened when she took any of the books from her secret passage to any other part of the castle. As soon as she crossed the threshold into or out of the passageway, the contents and cover of the book transformed! Some, like *The Communist Manifesto* and *Relativity* almost disappeared! They faded and went transparent, as if shrinking from the harsh outside world.

When she'd first experienced the transformation, with Orwell's book, Vivianne had stared in shocked alarm as the images on the cover blurred, writhed and rearranged themselves as if they were alive. She'd dropped the book with a startled shriek. Luckily, no one had been around to hear her and she'd eventually gained enough courage to approach the sprawled book on the ground and pick it up to stare at its totally new cover; a cover that changed with the light, flickering from one version to the other. One version was a satirical depiction of a dystopia; the other was a utopia. Vivianne had since read both versions of each book her mother had left for her, and they were very strange. One version was invariably less edgy than the other. Only Rabelais's book, *Gargantua and Pentagruel*, had remained exactly the same no matter where she took it.

This divergence she had observed in all but Rabelais's book was most pronounced in *Roget's l'Histoire* and it occurred to her that she was reading about two different futures. Two *possible* futures. In the version outside the secret hall, her father's Teutonic Knights resoundingly won the Battle of Grunwald; in the version inside the secret hall, the Poles and Lithuanians slaughtered them, every single knight except a paltry few. She'd giddily flipped pages in each version of *l'Histoire* and was devastated by either world depicted. In one version the Teutonic Order embarked on an atrocious genocidal purge and massacred all Jewish people; but in the other version the atomic bomb was developed by a Jewish scientist and dropped several times, killing millions of innocent people in one devastating stroke. War, disease and treachery plagued both worlds.

Vivianne put *Gargantua and Pentagruel* back and bound up the knapsack. She stood up, letting a frown crease her brow as she studied the only thing Dianne had left her.

She pushed the trap door above her open, catching the damp and musty scent of ripening fruit, grain, spices and fermenting wine. Once she made sure no one was there, Vivianne lifted the heavy wooden door, grabbed the large oiled duffel bag in the passage and scrambled up. She was certain she would find no one here at this hour; everyone was needed in the kitchen, the adjoining pantry, wine cellar and Great Hall, preparing for the guests and the feast. She closed the trap door and opened the bag where her gear was secretly stowed. Then she carefully laid out the squire's garb that Wolfgang had acquired by dubious means and hastily undressed. She stood naked for a moment, staring down at the knight's clothing and weaponry. Visions of the horrid rape from which she'd just fled shivered through her. Milda's anguished face, staring at her in a silent plea for help, promised to be the disturbing companion of her thoughts for years. The cruel beauty of the mercenary's face, out of which Devil's eyes of malice sliced into hers, would haunt her dreams forever. Did her father really know what went on in his castle? Did he care?

Vivianne bowed her head in shame at having abandoned the girl to that cruel animal and then doing too little too late. By the time she returned with Frieda, the ill deed had been long consummated. Vivianne knew that any of the other castle servants would have scoffed that the girl had probably asked for it and deserved it and would have ignored Vivianne's plea for aid. Despite being hurt, Milda would no doubt have preferred that it remain a private affair in any case; there was less shame in it and fewer bad repercussions. Vivianne knew this from Uta, who'd reproved her once when Vivianne, in an ill-temper, had spitefully blurted what she'd learned about the servants who whored with her father. Work was hard to come by and food even harder these days, Uta had scolded. Women had to get by however they could. Despite all this, Vivianne felt like she should have done *something* for the poor girl....

Vivianne heaved out a long sigh. A sigh for womankind. It wasn't easy being a woman these days. It probably wasn't easy for a man either, but it just seemed to her that men had more choices than women did. Then she set her mouth in a tight purse. There would come a time, she thought, when such actions could not happen because women could and would defend themselves! She found her hand on her *ritterkreuz*, fingers rubbing as if she were one of Scherarazade's characters and it was a magical lamp. *If only I was a knight....*

Her hand dropped and she balled her fists then she stomped her naked foot on the hard earthen ground.

After a long exhale, she slowly pulled on the warrior's garb. First she threw a long-sleeved white linen shirt over her head. Then came the linen breches, stockings and mail leggings. She then wriggled into the heavy long-sleeved and hooded chain mail leather *haubergeon* with padded head-piece. She paused to run her fingers over the mail, feeling its cool weight on her shoulders and body. Over the *haubergeon* she shrugged into the sleeveless black velvet surcoat embroidered with a red dragon, the coat of arms she'd chosen for herself. Last came the leather belt and scabbard that held her hand-and-a-half sword, that she'd heard was called a bastard sword. Vivianne had graduated from a *baton* years ago and reveled in wielding the bracing weight of solid metal.

Lethal metal, she thought, as she pulled the sword out of its wooden and leather scabbard. She enjoyed the clean sing of steel on the metal scabbard throat and gazed down to study her sword. It had a tapering double-edged blade of steel, good for thrusting and cutting, with a simple cross guard and a hilt bound with fine leather over cord and a plain brass fig-shaped pommel with an amber stone at its centre.

Vivianne replaced the sword into its sheath and picked up her *bascinet*. All her accoutrements were a hodgepodge assortment and in sorry condition, having been stolen or bartered for from the armory by Wolfgang or some local peasant who'd likely looted from a local battle. Most knights wore complete or partial armor; all she had was mail. The *bascinet*, too, was an ancient battered model that still contained the breath slit at the bottom no longer found in current *bascinets*. The *Klappuizier* was hinged at the top and was the common right-handed version, with more breath holes on the right, also weaker, side. It was meant for right-handed combat on a horse. Vivianne, being left-handed, should have worn a left-handed *bascinet*, but beggars couldn't be choosers, she decided with a wry smile, as she put the helm on her head and raised the visor. No matter, she thought. It all worked well enough. It wasn't as though she were a real knight....

Gripping the sword in both hands, left hand near the cross guard and right cupping the pommel, she set her legs apart and tried to still her mind from the lurid scene to make a few practice motions. Facing her imaginary opponent squarely, with legs slightly bent, she practiced her defenses, attacks, and counter-attacks in a flourish of steps and circles; slicing, chopping and thrusting, then half-swording with quick jabs of the blade point or hooks of the pommel. Within moments she became liquid fire, feet gliding in a warrior dance and shifting her hips and weight with each swing for momentum. When she finally paused, she was flushed, sweating and breathing hard but invigorated at having unleashed most of her angry energy.

She realized with mounting shame that during her practice she'd imagined those stabbing eyes of the mercenary and had killed him in her mind. And she'd exalted in it. It was a very unlady-like thing to feel, she thought, her face heating involuntarily.

"Good Lord, please forgive me," she sighed and removed her *bascinet*. "I fear I'm unruly."

She stared down at the sword, reminded of the last time she'd seen Wolfgang von Eisenreich, last month, and how her childhood friend had accused her of that very thing: unlady-like behavior.

She let her thoughts drift over the years they'd played hoodman blind, tag, hide-and-seek, and jump rope as children since he'd first come to the castle when he was seven; first as a page in the service of her father's employ, then as a squire at fourteen, learning the skills of a knight in preparation for knighthood at twenty-one—or earlier if he earned it in battle. When they were little, their favorite game had been "princess and the knight"; she'd dressed up in her best clothes and he in his warrior trappings and she would "knight" him with his sword for some act of valor. Then Vivianne had forced them to reverse roles to play "prince and the knight" but Wolfgang tired of "knighting" her and they eventually stopped playing it entirely.

Wolfgang was seventeen now, three years her senior. As they'd grown, Wolfgang had remained a true and loyal friend, her only real friend in the castle. None of the servant's children had played with her because she was a baroness. Baronesses didn't play with lowly servants, Uta had told her. But that didn't explain why the other pages and students who came to the castle to apprentice avoided her as well. It was only much later that Vivianne had understood that it was fear that had driven them away. Fear of witchery. Because they'd thought her mother was a witch.

Wolfgang, alone, didn't seem to care. He teased her like a sister and treated her almost as an equal when they were alone. She'd easily inveigled him into secretly teaching her the same skills he was learning as a knight-in-training; she'd convinced him that by teaching her he was learning it all better. She'd bound her breasts flat using scrap cloths—it wasn't hard to get them flat, she lamented. Then she covered herself in full gear, girlish hair tucked underneath the mail *aventail* and *bascinet*.

They'd brashly practiced in the courtyard, where he taught her how to use a long-bow, pike, halbert and mace. They sparred with a sword and shield or sword and dagger, then eventually graduated to fighting on horseback; he was the groom, after all, and could easily fetch her one of the horses from the stables. He always gave her Willy, the oldest palfrey, explaining to her that she should have the tamest of the horses because she was a girl. At first Wolfgang easily beat her in sword-fighting; he was faster and knew all the moves. It took Vivianne awhile to build up the muscles of her wrist, forearm, thighs and legs.

Once this happened and she'd caught on to the techniques, Vivianne usually bested Wolfgang in mounted combat—*Rossfechten*—being tall and rather strong and coordinated for a girl, particularly astride a horse. Vivianne took to the palfrey and to Wolfgang's dismayed surprise she managed to spark a virility in Willy that no one thought existed. During unarmored foot combat—*Bloßfechten*—she was not above thrusting herself into close combat and using Wolfgang's greater weight to lever him to the ground. She'd swiftly mastered the art of *Überlauffen*, outreaching his attacks by diving into or out of his action with *schiessen* strikes where he'd exposed himself by his own attack.

She excelled over him in close-in techniques or "wrestling at the sword" by means he considered unfair and unchivalrous: like striking with the pommel; or using *halb-schwert* techniques of grabbing the sword's blade with her hands and striking, thrusting, or deflecting; or trapping his forearms with her other arm and disarming him by tripping, kicking and grappling moves. He always called her on it; but Vivianne pointed out that these were legitimate fighting techniques that she'd found in *Fechtmeister* Johannes Leichtenauer's *Fechtsbuch*. They even had a name, she'd defended: *Ringen am Schwert*. Wolfgang only grew more cantankerous at learning that she was studying from books on top of the lessons he gave her. She wondered if it was more that he was jealous of her abilities, which she openly admitted were superior to his. She was faster, more aggressive with a quick mind for strategy; and a willingness to think outside the traditional. On the day

Wolfgang would ever have an original idea, he wouldn't know what to do with it, Vivianne thought with a sideways grin.

The two of them always ended up panting from their efforts; she with a victorious smile and he usually disarmed and glaring up at her from the ground.

Their sparring sessions often got the attention of the servants and guards. Warner, the gatekeeper eventually got curious: "Hey, von Eisenreich! Who's that whelp besting you? You let a skinny little rascal like that beat you! Look at his arms and hands…." Indeed, her limbs were slight for a boy her height. Warner didn't know when to stop: "Maybe *he* should be the baron's personal squire instead of you!"

Fearing exposure, Vivianne had glanced down at the coat of arms she'd embroidered over the von Grunwald crest of her "borrowed" tunic, and thought of her heroic knight in the chapel. She answered boldly in her lowest pitch possible under the helmet. "I'm Wolfram, scion of the Duke von Eschenbach!" she lied with another glance down at the image of a red dragon on her black tunic, the only piece of embroidery she'd embarked on with enthusiasm. Vivianne was certain that no one, apart from the chaplain, was sufficiently well-read to know the 12th Century knight-poet whose name she'd purloined.

"Ah!" Warner had laughed, upon hearing her voice. "And just a young sprout too, not yet with his man's voice!"

Undaunted, Vivianne finished her explanation, "I was sent here to help with the rye harvest."

"Were you, young Wolfram!" The gatekeeper chuckled. "Then I shall call you Wolfram, the Skinny!" He turned to Wolfgang. "What do you say to that, eh, von Eisenreich?"

Vivianne would have preferred a more flattering title, but she knew better than to argue. Wolfgang just scowled and Warner laughed again. It didn't seem to bother Warner that Wolfram stayed on long after the harvest. He was too entertained to question her presence within the castle walls well into the fall and winter months. From then on, the servants and guards eagerly watched their practice sessions, much to Wolfgang's discomfort. Vivianne had even learned of some heavy betting among the guards and had flushed with smug pleasure when she discovered that she was generally the favored of the two combatants to win in swordplay.

It became a sore point with Wolfgang. Every time he learned a new move, he sprang it on her only to have her instantly improve on his technique and fling him or his weapon to the ground, to the amusement of the gathered crowd. Vivianne had begun to consider Wolfgang a little oafish and a bit clumsy when it came to wielding a weapon. She considered that perhaps he'd be better off choosing another career to serve his Lordship. Since last month, Wolfgang hadn't come down for their ritual sparring. Vivianne thought she knew why.

Leaning on her sword with its tip against the packed earthen floor, she brought her other hand up and touched her lips lightly with her fingers. Last month, while in a dark mood from her father's molestation of the night before, she'd cruelly taunted Wolfgang in the hallway with his apparent ineptitude and had drawn out his anger. He'd retaliated with an insult that had cut close to home: how unlady-like she was—more like a boy—and it was about time she acted like a proper lady before she didn't know how to anymore. Affronted, she dared him to kiss her if he thought she needed taming.

"Make me a lady with a knight's kiss, then!" she'd said tartly. "Kiss me—if you dare!" At the time she'd had no idea why she'd said it, except to annoy him. Perhaps she'd been moved by some perversity of character. More likely it had been a peevish and blind retaliation for her father's unnatural intimacy the night before. But when Wolfgang unexpectedly accepted, she grew terrified. It was only her pride that kept her from backing away. To her surprise his kiss pleased her greatly. He'd leaned forward awkwardly, not daring to touch her with his hands, and his lips brushed hers with a sweet devotion that lingered like the taste of honey. The very connection of his soft flesh on hers was exquisitely thrilling and she realized with an exotic yearning how desperately she craved to be touched—

"Vianne!—"

Vivianne jerked and nearly fell forward as her grip

slipped on the sword she was leaning on. It clattered to the ground in front of her and sent her into a stumbling dance to regain her balance.

Wolfgang stood at the doorway of the great storeroom, dressed in his full squire mail and red tunic emblazoned with the *displayed* black Eisenreich falcon. He wore his sword on his back like her father, in a leather scabbard that hung diagonally off a soft leather *balderich*. The baron was the only knight she knew who used a *balderich* as a back-hanger. Apparently very well suited for one-and-a-half and two-handed swords such as the ones used by her father, the back scabbard style uniquely championed by her father—and now Wolfgang—had apparently made its way to von Grunwald during one of his campaigns against the Mongols early in his career. Her father had nearly been killed but he came away with an appreciation of their fighting methods, including use of the back-sling scabbard.

Wolfgang stared at Vivianne with obvious disapproval.

"—Er...My Lady," he swiftly corrected himself, though he kept his reproachful tone, "What are you doing here...like *that*?"

Vivianne recovered with a shuffle. Since that kiss, Wolfgang had avoided her. He'd failed to show up in the storeroom or the courtyard during their regular match times and she knew why. She bent to pick up the sword by the hilt then stammered, feeling some dismay at his baleful look, "I was just practicing."

"My lady, this is no time for our practices," he scolded, approaching her in a loping stride. "The baron, your father, is looking for you. You're expected in the Great Hall, bathed and attired like a...*lady*." Not like a *boy*, his eyes added with a roving critical glance from the unbound disordered hair that tumbled over her well-fitting tunic down the rest of her knight's trappings. "I must bring you to him at once." Emboldened by his declared duty, Wolfgang lurched forward to snatch her hand.

Vivianne twitched out of his grasp and recoiled, face heating with agitated excitement. He smelled of the stable and the fields and his face was flushed with awkward excitement.

"You're so unreasonable, Vianne!" Wolfgang rebuked, keeping his face stern and trying to look older than he was. But he'd forgotten his vow to stay formal with her and had addressed her by his childhood nickname for her. "Why do you disobey your father like that? He's your master. You should heed his wishes, Vi—My Lady. I've heard the castle servants talking."

"What? That my mother was a witch?" she said boldly, thinking to startle him. She stepped to one of the barrels overfull with apples, took one, wiped it on her tunic, then bit into the crunchy flesh and chewed languidly with her mouth purposefully open.

Wolfgang frowned. "You're not helping matters, Vianne, with this unlady-like behavior—"

"*My Lady*, if you please," she corrected him tartly, reminding him of his lower rank. Did he regret giving in to her dare? She knew the answer well enough. Perhaps he was regretting all their secret meetings and tutoring. "You're eager to remind me of my truant behavior when *you* share in it—"

"*Used* to share in it!"

She blinked as if he'd struck her and realized that her foolish outburst had cornered him.

"You're much too unruly, Vi—My Lady." He shook his head at her. "You appear to seek the baron's wrath."

"I just want to *live*!" she responded sharply. Wolfgang's expression made her feel as though she was a child being rebuked. "Like everyone else," she added.

He snorted. "You mean like a man!"

"Like a *person*!"

He shook his head at her with pursed lips of disapproval. "Vianne…" But she thought she noticed the stern gleam in his eyes dissolve at his mention of her nickname.

Vivianne dropped her gaze. She scuffed the earthen floor with her boot and absently tapped the point of her sword on the ground. "I don't want to go…just yet," she confessed in a subdued voice. She heard him sigh and, keeping her face bent low, she demurely peered up at him through her long lashes.

The urgent tension had drained from Wolfgang's shoulders and a sad liquid gaze drowned the fire in his eyes. Beautiful eyes, Vivianne thought suddenly. Why hadn't she noticed before? Dark and lustrous brown like deep pools of water in a forest glade, they glowed like dawn breaking in a new day of innocence. And such an honest naïve mouth set in a face now dusted in the light feathering of a virgin beard. He was not nearly as oafish as she'd once thought, and observed how the waves of his gold-brown hair tumbled nearly to his shoulders like a long caress. He, too, was growing up, she decided. Going to war had sobered him and given him something to think about. Did he now think of her as a foolish spoiled child? An irresponsible castle-brat? Maybe she was, Vivianne concluded gravely.

She considered Wolfgang's dire fate: tomorrow morning, he would join the left flank with other guests of the Order alongside her father to fight the unified pagan forces that would converge in the marshy fields between Grunwald, Tannenberg and Ludwigsdorf. She found to her shame that, while she fretted over Wolfgang's safe return, she felt nothing for her father.

Vivianne swallowed, suddenly overwhelmed with compassion for her childhood friend—now a young man. He was only three years her senior; just a squire, not yet a knight. But, in her imagination he was her *ritter*: respectful, devoted and chivalrously committed to protecting her. She momentarily lost her unruly defiance, and realized that she was afraid. She dreaded what her father intended for her. What possible bargain had the baron struck with that foreigner? It made him so giddy with desperate hope on the eve of a great battle that should otherwise be occupying his full attention. What was he trading her for?

Vivianne wanted so much to throw herself at him, seize him in a tight embrace and tell him how scared she was: for her and for him. But somehow she knew not to. She bravely stood her ground and, meeting his unguarded eyes with her own, let her eyes speak in soft silence. She felt that he too was holding onto this protracted moment, like a pause between the stanzas of an epic poem drawing to its inevitable conclusion. They stood each on a threshold. After this moment he would go from squire at table to arming squire in earnest and to his first real battle. And she would leave this place, her home, for a stranger's land to fulfill an unknown destiny long ago chosen for her by her father and mother.

"Can't we have one last practice, Wolf?" she blurted out in a pleading voice and put the apple down. "We're here, both dressed in our knight's mail, with our swords..."

He gave her a tremulous sideways smile, trying and failing to hide his own eagerness. "Very well, *pepin*," he conceded in a voice meant to show reluctant indulgence. But he'd used his old nickname for her and she'd caught the old glimmer in his eyes. "Here's what I learned this morning...on guard!"

He drew his sword and faced her in a *pflug* guard, with the hilt held in front of his body at waist height and point directed toward her. She responded by raising her sword behind her left shoulder in a *noble woman's* version of a *vom tag* guard. To Wolfgang's nod, Vivianne took her cue with her typical angled *oberhau* cut from the left to his open side. He raised his blade to parry then followed through by turning his blade into a sloped thrust to her face from above. Forced to displace it, she deflected his blade; but he snapped his blade flat and rapped her hard and painfully on the hand with the *flech*. She cried out in annoyed surprise as the sword tore out of her grip and fell with a clang on the packed earth.

With lightening speed Wolfgang flipped his sword, took the blade in his hand then hooked her leg with the cross guard and gave it a forceful yank.

Feet pulled out from under her, Vivianne was thrown backwards to the ground with a yelp. She landed hard, grunting in startled pain. Wolfgang barked out a loud laugh and knocked her lightly on her helmet with the tip of his blade. A dull tinny clank. "The technique is called *Das Verkehren* with a unique twist the baron taught me," he said, watching her regain her breath.

As she scrambled up to her feet and retrieved the sword that had flown from her hand, he sang out cheerfully, "*Was sehrt, das lehrt!*" *What hurts, teaches.*

Vivianne glared at him through her open vizor. She took in a long breath, closed the vizor and sprang forward in a swift series of *blitzen* hits. Startled by her wild single-handed *Überlauffen* thrusts, Wolfgang's levity dissolved to a fearful recoil. The fact that neither could see the other's expression was to her advantage. Vivianne noted with cruel satisfaction that he appeared genuinely apprehensive that she intended *Ernst Fechten*. It spurred her on her chase as her flying thrusts forced him stumbling backward, with retreating strikes, toward the short stairway to the brew house and ended in a *Gemechslich*, a thrust to his groin.

Wolfgang jerked back, teetered then lost his balance over the top step and sailed backwards into a hard fall. Vivianne flinched as she watched him bounce with a loud thud onto the hard ground of the brew house. The breath flew out of him in a dark shout of pain.

As he raised his head with a shake to regain his senses, she repeated tartly with a wry grin, "*Was sehrt, das lehrt.*"

Visibly irritated, Wolfgang scrambled up and flew over the steps to lunge forward. Refusing to panic like he did with her attack, Vivianne stood her ground. He let his anger misguide him and Vivianne coolly warded off his blows with downward cuts, eventually regaining the offensive and counterattacking in the middle of one of his strikes.

Following a clash of swords, she beat his blade aside with a front cut, turned her pommel forward in a bold thrust to his face. As he jerked back, she closed in with her left hip and trapped his forearms in an arm lock. Her move brought them up pressed against each other, panting, with blades clashing. She could have easily wrested his blade out of his hand with pressure from her pommel then tripped him to the ground; but she paused to stare at him instead. His shallow breath on her neck lingered with the fragrant scent of oranges and cloves. The heat of his body, pressed up against hers, surged up her face and fired her belly. She let go and recoiled with a gasp, heart racing like a rabbit in a snare.

"That's enough," she said, breathless, and pulled off her helmet and mail hood. Her hair spilled out over her shoulders like an unruly brook. She stepped back from him and forced her breaths normal as he removed his helmet and gave her an inquisitive look. She'd never until now been the first to call off a sparring session. "We better go," she added. Casually leaning her sword on the ground again, she then retrieved the apple she'd put down and added cavalierly, "I wouldn't want to get you into more trouble than I am." She offered him a bite of the apple.

Wolfgang relaxed at her remark and laughed wryly as if nothing had happened. His laughter reminded her of the boy she used to play with. He replaced his sword in its scabbard then took the apple from her and tore a large crunching bite out of it with his teeth. He handed it back to her, chewing with smacking lips, then grinned and said with a full mouth, "I don't think that's possible, Vianne. You'll always be in more trouble than anyone at Grunwald!" Then he frowned, as if reminded of some sobering thought.

"Are you afraid of going into battle tomorrow?" she blurted out.

"Of course not!" he scoffed but she thought she noted the thrill of terror beneath his blustering bravado. "I'm his squire, Vianne! The squire of the great Baron von Grunwald who fought alongside Conrad, the old *Hochmeister* in the battle of Gotland. They drove out the Victual Brothers for the King of Sweden. Your father's one of the best swordsmen in the Teutonic State. His unique *balderich* style of swordplay is renowned." Wolfgang proudly tugged at his own *balderich*. "This is what I've been training for, Vianne. It's exciting! I might come back a knight!"

You might come back *dead*, she thought. But she recognized a genuine spark of excitement surging through his fear and finally understood. He saw her father differently than she did. He still revered the baron, choosing to see the knight through the black and white lens of past heroism; when Vivianne had long ago stopped trying, and saw the real man before her in too garish color. "It's a little like stage fright, I guess," she offered.

Wolfgang brightened, accepting her remark as delivered inoffensively. "Yes, a little," he admitted and let his smile open to a brash grin, showing his old self, the Wolfgang who used to play dominos, joke, laugh and spar with her. "Are you envious, *pepin*?"

"A little," she admitted with a wry smile and thought of their differing fates. Which was the worse one? He going willingly to war at risk of an honorable death or she becoming the property of a strange man she knew nothing about. A man who's will she had to please; a man who might beat her for no reason in particular.

Wolfgang tapped her sword respectfully with his. "You *are* better than me with that, *pepin*," he said with a magnanimous nod to her. Then he grew sober and his large brown eyes looked sad. "I wish that you weren't—" He cut himself off. He regained his cool composure and took the apple from her hand then bit into it and returned it to her, quipping with a full mouth, "Well, you'd make a good knight. You'd stick quite a few of those pagan pigs for the Holy Roman Empire."

She laughed uneasily at his remark, and thought briefly of that mercenary she should have stuck instead. Fighting for noble causes was not what she yearned for, though she knew she longed for more than to just wait to become someone else's destiny; she knew in her heart of hearts that she was meant for more, that she was meant to *give* more, to *be* more. There was definitely something missing in her life right now. Perhaps she should look upon her fate with hope, not dread. It would get her out of here, at any rate, she reasoned: away from this confined existence and away from her truculent father and his dreadful mercenaries who raped and pillaged whomever and whatever they pleased...even if it meant marriage to a stranger from a foreign land.

She came out of her reverie to find Wolfgang staring at

her with an alarming intensity that surged through her belly in a throbbing ache. It was the same half-terrified wide-eyed look he'd given her the last time they'd been together, just before he'd kissed her. The heat of the sudden realization flushed up her face as Wolfgang threw himself forward in an awkward charge and stole yet another kiss from her.

It was more like two mouths colliding.

He withdrew as quickly as he'd advanced; yet when they parted, both were panting from the heated collision. Both swords had dropped, clashing, to the ground in the confused excitement of the moment. Her half-eaten apple spilled out of her hand and rolled off behind some barrels, victual for the rats and mice.

Vivianne sprang sideways to pick up her sword and replaced it shakily in the scabbard that hung on the belt at her waist.

Wolfgang shuffled his feet in nervous embarrassment then straightened and pushed up his face in a haughty show of cavalier coolness. "That was just for luck," he declared non-chalantly. "For both of us."

Vivianne abruptly said in a girlish voice, "Wolf, you must turn around while I change." Without waiting, she began to disrobe. He quickly turned. She caught his fierce blush and felt a vengeful smile tug her lips. In truth, she would miss him dearly. Despite his recent priggish attitude, he was innocently beautiful and he was her best and only friend.

The first boy to kiss her.

Vivianne dressed and stuffed the knight's garb back into its hiding place without Wolfgang seeing. They then left the storeroom the traditional way, up the main stairway, and she saw that Wolfgang had stiffened anew and returned to his formal demeanor.

✠

## ...7

UTA met them just outside Vivianne's chambers. She looked relieved and rushed toward them in a fluster. "*Gott sei Dank!* There you are, My Lady! Thank you, Wolfgang. Now look at you!" She seized Vivianne's hands and turned her palms upward, examining them with a frown. "Where did you get so dirty? One can tell so much about a person from their hands and feet, mark my words, child," she scolded. "And what I see isn't very complimentary!"

Definitely not lady-like, Vivianne thought to herself, hiding her hands behind her back. She threw a self-conscious glance at Wolfgang beside her. He looked impassively in another direction, as though not listening.

"We must get you quickly bathed and dressed for the Great Hall where your father and his guests already await!" Uta continued.

Reminded of what awaited her, Vivianne felt a hot wave of darkness sweep over her and an aching pain gnawed at her belly. Her color vision faded to black and white and starry lights sparkled in front of her. As if knocked by the swelling wave of a molten ocean, her knees gave out from under her. She would have fallen had Wolfgang not seized her by the waist.

"Vianne!" he cried out in alarm then stammered, "—eh, Your Ladyship...Are you alright?"

Vivianne righted herself and pushed off him self-consciously. She felt her face heat with a flush of confused excitement and straightened with a glance from Uta to Wolfgang. "I'm alright. Just...hungry, that's all."

Wolfgang shuffled awkwardly.

Uta turned to him in exasperation. "Well, go tell His Lordship that we have found her and we won't be long!" She waved an impatient hand at him. "Go on!"

Wolfgang welcomed his task with a curt nod to Vivianne. "My Lady." Then he rushed down the hall.

Uta ushered Vivianne into her outer bedchambers where a bath was already drawn, steam visibly rising from within her private bathroom. "Nice boy, that Wolfgang," Uta muttered absently and pulled at Vivianne's gown to help her undress.

"I'll do the rest myself, Uta," Vivianne said, twitching away. "Thank you."

Uta looked hurt. She stood her ground obstinately with a longing glance at the gown draped over the chair. "You will need help with the gown His Lordship has chosen for you."

Vivianne followed her glance and folded her arms across her breast in firm decision. "I'll manage, Uta. Thank you," she ended sternly.

Uta knew when to give in. She tightened her wrinkled lips and nodded in acquiescence. "As you wish, My Lady," she ended formally. Vivianne knew Uta missed the intimacy of dressing her, combing her hair and grooming her; Vivianne had to admit that she missed it too. But there was no way around it. Uta turned to leave and Vivianne sighed at having to disappoint her old nursemaid, who lived to serve her. Uta had taken care of her since she was a baby. But Vivianne refused to let Uta see how far her blemishes had advanced, knowing it would alarm the old woman. After today she would not have occasion to see Vivianne again, so there was no point in upsetting her. Uta was at the door when Vivianne called out after her.

"Uta, have you seen Milda lately?"

"Why, no, child," Uta responded with a frown of contemplation. "Why are you bothering about that slave now? She up and left us in April. So we figure, anyhow. Plum disappeared. Must have escaped and gone home. Or the wolves got her."

"Thank you, Uta," Vivianne said. "That's all."

Uta nodded then shuffled off in defeated silence.

Vivianne undressed and stepped into the now lukewarm bathwater. She reached and turned the left faucet on and watched the steam rise as hot water poured into the tub, practically scalding her feet. Thanks to her mother, Vivianne could enjoy a hot bath on command and in the privacy of her chamber. She stretched back, willing her muscles to relax, but knew she could not linger. They were all waiting for her. In truth, the baron was probably hopelessly drunk on a potel of wine and had no clear idea of how much time had passed; as for the stranger...he could wait for his prize, she thought. Nevertheless, she scrubbed herself clean and within a few moments she stepped out and dried herself and began to dress.

The baron had outdone himself, Vivianne thought, feeling the dress with her hands. It was beautiful, made of the finest cream silk brocade, a form-fitting bodice with rather low décolletage and a skirt that opened, flowing fully to the floor from a gilded belt at the hip. The sleeves, narrow up the lower arms flowed at the elbow with long draping tippets then flared slightly at the shoulders, all accentuating and flattering her female shape. As Vivianne admired herself in the mirror, she had the strong impression that her father had been thinking of her mother when he'd chosen this gown. She had barely finished brushing her long hair to braid and coil back when he, himself, barged in without announcement.

"Father!" she stood quickly, instinctively clutching her breasts. She might have been in a state of undress.

"Ahh!" He looked slightly embarrassed for a brief moment then collected himself with a burp, mouth puckering in its usual pout. His already bloodshot eyes flitted around the room for the nursemaid. Not finding Uta, he turned to Vivianne and waved brusquely. "Come, daughter," he growled. "It is time to meet our illustrious guest."

"But, my hair—"

"It's fine," he said, drawing near to her and fingering her tresses in dreamy pleasure. His breath was sour. "Your hair is beautiful this way. Leave it." Then he brusquely took her hand and led her out into the hallway. Her father smiled down at her with such warmth and pride—like she was his princess—that she almost forgot his earlier drunken cruelty and how he'd lately taken to touching her like no father should.

As they walked down the corridor, she basked in the warm blaze of his eyes and smiled back at him, thinking that he might still love her a little. Then he blinked as though he'd suddenly awoken to some grim reality. A shadow swept over him and the light in his eyes vanished, replaced by a cold glare. He looked away, pulling her with renewed haste as if they were being chased down the main corridor to the Great Hall. She felt the cold draught caress her skin into goose bumps and gazed up with uneasy feelings of portent at the long tapestry flying past her. The captivating scenes depicted the story of an English prince and the French princess he loved but who was about to be married to a Moorish prince. The English prince arrived at the wedding disguised as a fiddler, the King of France welcomed him, and the lovers eloped, followed by a sweet love scene and a final scene with a buzzard in a tree, bearing the ring of the princess.

Vivianne stared at the tapestry with new understanding. Why did she feel this inexplicable dread of careering toward some calamity? She'd felt it since she'd roused this morning, awoken from her recurring nightmare. It was more than the jitters of meeting her betrothed. *The fourteenth hour of the fourteenth day of her fourteenth year in the fourteenth hundred year*...was it a sign? The priest seemed to think it was. She shivered, feeling her hand grow clammy inside her father's hot clutch.

She wished now that she hadn't sent Uta away and the old nursemaid was here beside her. She wished her father was not squeezing her hand so tightly in a jerking pull, hell-bent on reaching the Great Hall as if what lay there were a life or death issue. Vivianne suddenly felt fearful of what they would find. Who awaited them? Who was this foreigner who incited trepidation in the von Grunwald *Ordensburgen* and even commanded her arrogant father's respect and fear. His name was Mortameur, according to *Père* Daniel. A French name, like her own. Like her mother's. Why did it strike fear inside her?

"You will have a chance to redeem all, daughter," the baron said with a giddy smile. It made her shiver.

✠

94

# ...8

THE heady scent of lavender, chamomile, rose and fennel competed with the sharp undercurrent of wood and torch smoke as Vivianne and the baron entered the high-vaulted Great Hall. They came in through the west front entrance so that they could be announced and could see the faces of all the guests already assembled, particularly those at the high table. This was the first time that Vivianne had seen the Great Hall today; it was splendidly decorated. Vivianne imagined the scented matted floor soon to be strewn with bone fragments, spittle, animal excrement, beer and grease from the impending revelry. The gilded hall glowed with the daylight that streamed in from the large stained glass windows facing the courtyard to the north and the candles and oil lamps that lined its length.

Vivianne glanced up past the high tapestries of elaborately stitched forests and frescos of knights chasing unicorns to the gothic-arched stained glass windows, interspersed with banners and von Grunwald coat of arms. Her gaze aimed further up to the intricately carved wooden beams of the Great Hall's ceiling, striving upward as if towards the very vault of Heaven. She remembered revering the empty Great Hall with heart-pounding trepidation when she was a child—before she was permitted to eat there beside her father at the high table. She'd thought it a hallowed magical place, a mausoleum with stilling echoes and massive tapestries. They depicted knights on horseback hunting mythical beasts.

She and her father stepped past the carpeted drapes of the front archway entrance to the desultory sounds of laughter and lively conversation mingled with a complex perfume of herbs, smoke and warm bodies. Vivianne felt her heart race anew with a different kind of awe and fear.

They walked past the lavabo without dipping their hands in the already filthy water. Tancred, one of her father's young footmen who stood by the archway acting as herald, nodded to them with averted eyes. He was a gangly pimple-faced youth with protruding teeth and a gaze that never made eye-contact; but he had a genuine smile. Tancred blushed fiercely as his eyes brushed Vivianne with a fleeting touch. Tancred seldom spoke to anyone and never spoke to her. He had a lisp and stuttered badly. It was one of her father's typical ironic decisions to assign Tancred the role of herald: a boy with a shaky voice who could barely string three words together before stumbling into a chaos of unintelligible sound. Tancred also helped the castle gardener and had often offered her a bouquet of violets, roses, carnations, or Madonna Lily that he'd no doubt purloined. He'd startle her by lunging forward out of the shadows with his gift of flowers, thrust out in front of him, and fix bright eyes on her for a brave instant. Then just as she accepted his posy and returned his gaze, he'd bolt and flee down the hall like one of her father's hunted deer.

Vivianne recognized two *minnesängers* from Gilgenburg standing beside him. One was a tall young man with a long but friendly face, dressed in a colorful checkered tunic, hat and leggings. The other was a short older bull-dog faced man with a lute. They nodded respectfully to the baron, who returned them a sporadic wave with his hand followed by a nervous scratch. The younger man bowed in a low sweeping gesture to Vivianne.

"Johannes the Brilliant at your service, Your Ladyship!" he said with a huge self-pleased grin. "You can call me Hannes."

Tancred cleared his throat and announced their arrival in a loud but shaky voice: "The Right Honourable Lord Ulrich Schoen, B-b-baron von Grunwald, and the…eh…Honourable L-l-lady V-V-Viv-v-vianne Schoen, *B*-b-baroness von G-g-grunwa-a-ald!"

Her father proudly took Vivianne's hand in a poised grip as all faces turned to watch them enter. The baron walked her toward the high table where his honored guests were seated on a small parapet in front of a huge rich tapestry of the *Roman de Sainte-Graal* that spanned the length of the table above a huge double fireplace.

As they passed the several dozen plain trestle tables and benches, crowded with people and waiting dogs, Vivianne couldn't help searching the less important guests amid the castle servants for that dreadful mercenary who'd raped the young pagan slave girl. Vivianne meant to report him to her father. But she didn't see him. Nor did she see the slave girl. Although the baron's slaves usually ate in the kitchen, on feasts such as this one they were permitted to sit in the Great Hall. Despite what Frieda had said and Uta had confirmed, Vivianne couldn't help searching for Milda among several other Lithuanians. Then they were too close to the high table and her attention shifted to the guests assembled there. One of them was her suitor, surely!

Feeling her heart throb with excitement and fear, Vivianne glanced over the guests—all men—in a brisk wave of eye-contact from right to left. This mystery man, her intended, had supposedly turned the castle upside down fourteen years ago with his demands and his temper—not to mention having incited her father with fear and giddy excitement regarding a mutual promise to be consummated today.

Realizing that she was the only female to sit at the table, Vivianne felt her steps falter. She recognized most of the men from her father's previous war-meetings. Several were Teutonic Knights, dressed in their long white tunics with the black, silver-edged cross pattée of the Order. Others were guests or allied to the Order, secular knights like her father. To the farthest right sat the tender-hearted chaplain, *Père* Daniel, in his elaborate silver chasuble, which was already stained from previous bouts of careless eating. He met her glance with kind eyes and nodded with a gentle reassuring smile.

He was followed by a guest knight of the Order, from Livonia. Holbracht Ekdahl had campaigned with Vivianne's father in Gotland and visited often from his convent in Livonia to drink with her father. Ekdahl was a huge barrel-chested man about her father's age. His thick beard failed to mask a face twisted with a long jagged scar from the bite of a sword; it dragged one of his eyes down into a permanent droop. He was the roughest looking man at the table, but his eyes were surprisingly gentle for a brutal warrior. Vivianne had overheard that he'd beheaded scores of pagans, earning him the nick-name of 'Holbracht the Beheader'. But he always treated her with kindness and respect whenever they chanced to meet in the hallways or at dinner in the Great Hall. Despite his overwhelming size and daunting looks he never intimidated her and Vivianne wished he came to the castle more often; he had a way of mollifying her father. Eckdahl nodded to her with a respectful smile of greeting.

Next came Nicholas von Renys, Komtur of Kulm, a middle-aged man with a clean-shaven pocked face and wild dark hair. He scanned her with canny eyes and an enigmatic half-smile. Vivianne decided that he had a cruel mouth. She remembered him from his many drinking sessions with the baron. He was a Pole of the clan Rogala and one of the founding members of the mysterious Lizard League.

Beside von Renys sat Casimir, Duke of Stettin, a Polish dukedom allied with the Order. He was a reddish-bearded man with a hooked nose, engaged in solemn conversation with the Grand Marshal Friedrich von Wallenrode, seated next to him. Both of them ignored her and her father approaching the table.

On the other side of the high-backed chairs sat the clean-shaven Mayor Schaumburg of Sambia, who returned her glance with a look of virile appreciation, which unsettled her; then Konrad the White, Duke of Oels, who raised a brow and studied her with ironic passing interest. Then came Markward von Salzbach, the Komtur of Brandenburg, a burly long-bearded man with a wide face. He sneered at her invitingly with thick snarling lips. She remembered his profane language from one of her father's war-meetings. Seated beside him was the *Großkomtur*, Kuno von Lichtenstein, a thickly bearded gruff-looking man in his forties with knife-sharp eyes and a steady shrewd gaze. He was reportedly the finest swordsman in the world; at least according to Wolfgang. He returned her a glancing look of general disinterest and focused a critical gaze on her father.

He was followed by the clean-shaven long haired Knight Templar, Seigfried von Heidelberg, who she'd met earlier in the chapel. The handsome knight looked splendid in his light mail and white tunic with its tell-tale red cross. She'd heard that he was to lead a charge of crossbow archers and some of his men were seated at one of the wooden tables to Vivianne's far left. The Knight Templar gave her an indifferent fleeting glance, as if to belie the warmth of their earlier exchange in the chapel. As her eyes fixed on his, he settled his gaze on the baron and she felt disappointment.

Von Heidelberg was followed by another Teutonic Knight, Heinrich von Schwelborn. He met her gaze with disrespectful eyes and sneering lips and she looked quickly past him.

It was like a role call for one of her father's war meetings, Vivianne considered, feeling a little overwhelmed. Save the Knight Templar, Vivianne knew every one of these men; all of them would fight at her father's side tomorrow. And none of them was Mortameur. Moreover, most were monks who had taken an oath to remain chaste and obedient to God and wanted nothing to do with women. Why had her father included her in the company of these great men of war? So, why was she here? Then she noticed that the seat right next to the baron's chair was empty and felt her heart plunge. *He has not yet arrived!*

Her father led her onto the platform of the high table, past the chaplain, then sat her to his right, at the center of the table, facing the rest of the Great Hall, below the salt. He then threw himself onto his own high-backed seat, madly scratching himself in jittery strokes. As Vivianne took her seat next to her father she felt her body tremble in anticipation. The baron was in no better shape, Vivianne considered, glancing at him. He slouched and pursed his lips like a dejected boy. Despite his careless posture, his hands were shaking on his lap and his entire body visibly shivered. He wasn't an especially patient man. Vivianne watched him nervously tap the nef with his spoon and tinker with the large silver, partly enameled, salt cellar. While the other men conversed about the impending battle tomorrow morning, the baron sulked in silence, preoccupied and tapping with his spoon. His fingers absently stroked the two naked figures adorning the salt cellar. They were of Poseiden and Amphitrite, half reclined and facing each other, her silky leg alluringly stroking his with the promise of more. As the baron's finger settled on rubbing the woman's smooth breasts, Vivianne glanced from the salt cellar to the baron's entranced face. He finally straightened in a jerk and turned to her in desperation.

"Where in God's name is he?" he stuttered out, glaring at her with wild eyes as if she had something to do with it. "I thought someone said he'd arrived in the castle already."

Vivianne could only shake her head at him and look out miserably toward the impatient crowd of servants, guests and mercenaries assembled in the Great Hall—

Then she saw him: the unnaturally handsome brute who'd ravished the slave, Milda! The man who haunted her dreams. He was cavalierly striding up the center of the Great Hall as though he owned it. He headed straight for the high table, shiny black boots clicking, and ignored the dogs that romped excitedly around him, snapping at his heels. His midnight black jacket, taut against his chest, emphasized his muscular build. *Fylfot*-shaped jewels glinted on his collar. His striking face split into a malicious grin and his eyes found hers. Vivianne seized in a stuttering breath and broke her gaze to turn to her father in alarm.

She was preparing to alert the baron to this man's transgression, when von Grunwald raised his hands in the air and shrilled out cheerfully to the man, "About time, Mortameur! You were spotted in the castle earlier but you kept us waiting!"

Vivianne caught her breath. This monster was her intended? The man she'd helplessly watched ravish a slave girl? A girl, not much older than herself! Surely both her parents—her mother—couldn't have known Mortameur's true nature?

Mortameur threw his head back and laughed, that same churlish laugh that had chased Vivianne down the hall. He hadn't looked surprised to see her sitting at the high table and she knew then that he'd known exactly who she was from the beginning. And he knew the battle that raged in Vivianne's mind.

"I was detained!" he boomed in a deep gravel voice. His eyes never left Vivianne's. They blazed into her like hot knives. He laughed again with great amusement. He stopped in mid-stride and pointed down his black cotehardie-like apparel where it glistened with something wet. The entire assembly of the Great Hall watched him, transfixed. He touched the place with his fingers and brought his hands up to show fresh blood. Vivianne heard an audible hush in the crowd. Even the warriors at the high table appeared mesmerized. "I had to stick one of your squealing pigs that got lost in the castle and I gave it to your cook to roast."

Vivianne tasted acrid bile in her throat. She shut her eyes to the horror of what her mind had deduced. If she'd eaten anything she would have lost it right then. This was proof of what she'd witnessed, Vivianne concluded. Had Milda struggled too hard? Mortameur's implied message was all too clear to Vivianne. Keep your silence and you might live. *Oh, Mary, mother of Christ! My father will give me to a filthy murderer! Someone who kills for pleasure!*

When Vivianne opened her eyes, she saw that Mortameur had pulled open his black coat, revealing a blood-stained gray-green shirt open at the chest—Vivianne flinched and lost her breath in horror. She recognized the same purple blemishes on his bared chest as those on her buttocks and back. What did it mean? *Lieber Gott, rette mich!*

Mortameur pulled out a device tucked in the leather pouch that hung off his belt. His hand wrapped around the handle and he pointed the long end of the thing toward Vivianne's father. Mortameur's finger pressed a trigger, discharging a sharp explosion. The baron's cup shattered, spraying red wine over him and Vivianne and the white elegantly cross-stitched tablecloth.

Everyone, including the baron, jumped in their seats.

Several women shrieked. Vivianne flinched and cried out then clamped her hand to her mouth, ears ringing. The Knight Templar jerked to his feet and unsheathed his sword. The *Großkomtur* pulled him down with some quiet words.

Mortameur laughed, enjoying the effect of his show. "I had to shoot the thing because it squealed so loudly," he explained casually, replacing his lethal weapon in its pouch. "And I made a mess. Apologies." He didn't look in the least apologetic, Vivianne thought soberly and wondered how that explosion had not been heard or reported by any of the castle workers.

The Great Hall fell into a hush of excited discussion as the men at the high table murmured among themselves. Was this the item her father coveted? Either way, it was clear to Vivianne that Mortameur had told his tale to permit him to demonstrate his mysterious weapon of instant destruction for whatever purpose he had in mind.

Vivianne must have blacked out for an instant because in the next moment the evil man was already passing behind her, long fingers languidly trailing her armrest. Then he sat down next to the baron with a cursory glance at her.

Once Mortameur had seated himself, children servants came forward with pitchers, basins and towels. Everyone who was seated washed then dried their hands. The baron then nodded to the chaplain, who stood up and bowed his head, followed by everyone else—even Mortameur—to give a blessing to the meal. He began with *Ave Maria*, in which everyone joined in, even Mortameur. Then *Père* Daniel proceeded with a special prayer for the Teutonic Order and the battle tomorrow.

"Pray to Our God for our spiritual father, the Pope, and for the Empire and for all our leaders and prelates of Christianity, lay and ecclesiastical, that God uses them in His service," the priest began. He prayed for the Order and its friends and for the Grand Master, that they all would act in such a way as not to depart from God.

Vivianne hardly listened as she stole glances at the French stranger, seated to the baron's other side with his head bowed. She should have guessed that it was he who'd come to claim her; he'd been most different in dress and looks, she thought, noting his form-fitting coat, silver buttons and stiff collar, adorned with swastika jewels, tailored shirt and loose crisp hussar-like trousers tucked inside sturdy boots to his knees. He was no knight: instead of a scabbard at his belt, he carried an upside-down L shaped leather pouch that held his cannon-like weapon of destruction.

"...Pray for those who have fallen into deadly sin, that God may help them back into his Grace and that they may escape eternal punishment..."

Vivianne found her eyes resting on Mortameur's stunning profile, bowed in apparent reverence like everyone else. He turned imperceptibly toward her, sensual mouth curling up in a smirk, then his eyes leapt up and slashed her lustily. She flinched as if struck and wondered how God could mar his own beautiful art work with such evil eyes of malice. Mortameur looked down again, laughing to himself.

Evil eyes; evil thoughts; evil deeds in an otherwise perfect face and body...*God, save me*, she prayed. *This monster will be my master*. Where was her knight?

✠

## ...9

"PRAY for all believers, that God may give them eternal peace. Amen," *Père* Daniel ended his prayer. He then invited those in the hall to recite *Pater Noster*.

Once they had finished, the *minnesängers* began their entertainment of song and dance as the young servants set wooden trenchers before each individual at the High Table and between pairs seated in the remaining hall. The servants then returned with Nuremberg-made *Edelzinn* pewter platters, laden with food, and flagons of wine. Vivianne, who hadn't eaten breakfast, found herself giddy with hunger but couldn't bring herself to eat. She found her body trembling with hunger and anxiety.

She watched with a kind of sick longing as servants, including Wolfgang, brought out roast venison cooked with *frumenty*, served with a jelly and a spicy rice pudding. There were also stuffed piglets, hare cooked in a thick spicy *Cameline* sauce, mutton stew with onions and peas, grilled trout with almonds and battered lamprey in green sauce, white bread and dumplings. All dishes were accompanied with pastry *soteltes* in the shape of lions, griffins, eagles and dragons, followed by pear and apple slices and "sweetmeats", sugared ginger, nuts and juniper berries.

Despite her feverish state and roiling stomach, Vivianne's mouth watered as she watched the dishes flow in. Theobald had even prepared her favorite dish: a swan, with its gilded beak, gold-coated feathers and feet floating on a green pastry pond accompanied by *chaudron*, a vinegary hot sauce. She helped herself to a little, knowing she couldn't stomach a bite, but not wishing to upset Theobald by not taking any.

As her gaze wandered the hall, Vivianne noticed that her father had magnanimously included the servants in this noble feast. Usually they were relegated to pastries filled with organ meat, *pease pottage*, turnips and baked beans or *macrows*. Today they ate like nobles. Though not in manners, Vivianne hastily added to herself, noting that most of the servants of the household ate with open mouths and heartily smacked their lips. She spotted Claus, the castle blacksmith, burnishing bones with his teeth; Brigitta, the laundress, buttered her bread with her thumb; and Hans, one of the watchmen, wiped his knife on the tablecloth. Several more carelessly tossed bones and other remains to the baron's begging dogs.

Of course, to help wash all the food down, there was plenty of wine.

As other squires served the two ends of the High Table,

Wolfgang—who still helped serve the baron and his guests during special feasts like this one—approached with hands full. One hand held a squat *Hanseatic* pewter flagon of red wine and the other an ornate silver-gilt pouring jug with coiled dragon spout for the baron and those seated immediately next to him. After genuflecting in front of Vivianne's father, Wolfgang set the jug down beside the baron. Vivianne could not help studying the translucent and opaque enamel with relief images made by a Parisian goldsmith. The images depicted Sir Gawain slaying the dragon, lovers embracing, and a wild woman with a unicorn. Wolfgang poured the contents of his pewter flagon into individual pewter cups; he started first with Mortameur, then he filled von Grunwald's personal tankard, made of Augsburg silver and horn, which the baron practically carried around with him everywhere he went. Its titillating *repoussé* relief of a Bacchanalia—naked men, women and beasts at the height of their revelry—did not escape Vivianne's gaze. *Why am I noticing all these things now*, she thought feverishly.

When Wolfgang came to Vivianne, she drew in her breath sharply. Their eyes met in an aching embrace that made her blush and she accidentally knocked over her cup as he poured. Wine spilled over her hand and onto the white linen tablecloth, mingling with the cross-stitched fruit and leaves in a blood red sea. They both quickly apologized in giddy laughter. As he hastily wiped the table with a cloth, their hands touched awkwardly. A furtive glance at Mortameur verified to her that he'd watched the exchange with interest. His cruel eyes fixed on hers and he leered. Heart beating madly, Vivianne turned back to Wolfgang with a haughty nod as he poured her cup. He avoided her gaze with a flushed face, then moved on to the next guest.

Vivianne, who seldom drank, took the freshly poured cup then raised it to her lips and swallowed a sizable gulp of the acrid wine. She felt it burn down her throat and nearly coughed, choking. It instantly warmed her and left a lingering aroma of pungent fruit in her mouth. *Surely, my father will not go through with this*, she thought and tried to distract herself by listening to a lively conversation that had erupted at the end of the table between the priest and Hannes. To the *minnesänger's* remark about how much he enjoyed his ale, the chaplain responded passionately, "I come by it naturally, my *minnesänger*! I'll have you know that my cock ale is considered the best in the county!"

"Is it, indeed!" The *minnesänger* laughed and wheeled around to face the crowd. Vivianne knew before he opened his mouth that some ribald remark would issue from his grinning lips: "Well, for an avowed priest, *Herr* chaplain, you must have one Hell of a cock to make such a fine ale!"

"Theobald always gives me his best cock," the priest said innocently. Most of the high table and those seated nearby below burst into a hearty laugh. Of course Père Daniel meant the boiled chicken essence Theobald gave him, but those seated in the Great Hall were enjoying the word-play at the priest's expense and the good-natured priest let them.

"Oh, it's Theobald's cock! That explains it!" Hannes screamed out amidst his own laughter. He had to bend over with his bouts of laughter, inciting the rest.

Père Daniel burst into a humorous prayer: "He who drinks beer sleeps well, he who sleeps well cannot sin. He who does not sin goes to Heaven. Amen!"

Most of the monks at the high table laughed cheerfully.

"Can I quote you on that, *Herr* chaplain?" Hannes asked.

"Certainly!" the priest said, raising his mug of ale to the *minnesänger*.

The baron cleared his throat loudly and the Great Hall quieted down. He twitched nervously. After taking a large gulp of wine, von Grunwald seized the jug and refilled his tankard. He reached recklessly past Vivianne, forcing her to sit back, to refill Schaumburg's cup then turned to fill Mortameur's cup, splashing some on the tablecloth. Her father then stood shakily and raised his tankard high to the rest of the Great Hall, as if to make a toast.

The baron released a belch then proceeded in a wavering though booming voice, "Welcome honored guests of Grunwald Castle, Brethren Knights and castle household. Most of you have companies of heavy and light cavalry, infantry and archers assembling even now in their tabors outside these castle walls not two kilometers away to battle the pagan Lithuanians and unruly Poles tomorrow. Which brings me to our special guest, *Herr* Leduc Mortameur, who has come today to fulfill a mutual promise we made some fourteen years ago. A promise that will ensure that, despite the greater numbers of the enemy, the Teutonic Order and those who have come to help us fight will prevail and extinguish those barbaric pagans in a final sweep. It will be a victory for the light of Christendom and the Holy Roman Empire over the dark and evil forces of heathenism. Here's to Mortameur and our successful battle tomorrow!" To which he drained his tankard. Some wine missed his mouth and spilled down his throat.

As the hall erupted to a din of cheering, drinking, and rapping feet and spoons, Vivianne felt her heart beat with the thrill of terror. This was no more than an arms deal and she was the payment. She found her eyes sliding of their own accord to his unnaturally attractive face and focused on his beautiful mouth, held in sullen disdain. Everyone was playing with fire, she thought...*including me*. Mortameur was obviously used to taking what he wanted. She'd seen him do it. What wasn't willingly given to him, he simply took by force. It was a deadly cat and mouse game her father was playing, using her as bait.

"What do you say, Mortameur?" her father pressed on.

Mortameur shook his head slightly at the baron with a look of contempt. "You are so myopic, Schoen," he said, purposefully neglecting her father's title. "All you see is this one battle."

Vivianne's father stared at Mortameur in confused silence.

"There's so much more," Mortameur went on, showing more emotion than he had since walking into the Great Hall. "We are poised here on one of several key events of Germany's *sonderweg*. An event that will jumpstart the entire *völkisch* movement. It is our destiny to achieve a *lebensraum* for our people."

"Whose people?" the baron asked, obviously confused. Mortameur was French, after all, not German; though he was speaking passable German now.

"You're an idiot!" Mortameur snapped back. "*Our* people, of course!" His arm swung out to the others at the High Table and he even deigned to include those seated below in the Great Hall. Seeing that everyone was as confused as the baron, Mortameur sneered in sudden understanding. "Let me put things into perspective. You think in terms of the Teutonic State. Right now, the state is just part of an empire, the Holy Roman Empire, though a decrepit, corrupt and disparate empire. But one must *create a system,* Schoen, *or be enslaved by another man's*....Thanks to what your state will accomplish, that empire will change and grow to such proportions that it will eventually have a French pope."

"What? Surely not another pope like that anti-pope in Avignon; we already have three popes!" The baron laughed uneasily, throwing searching glances for nods of agreement from the others seated at the high table.

Mortameur's otherwise beautiful lips curled into an obscene smile. "And she will be a woman, Schoen. Pope Jeanne."

"What? A woman!" The baron threw an amused but nervous gaze at his fellow guests, careful to avoid Vivianne. The others at the High Table remained silent, though it was obvious they were wondering where this man was taking his line of thinking.

"How do you know of this? What kind of magic are you consulting?" the baron pressed on. "Perhaps the magic that comes with copious wine, eh?" Then, as if suddenly reminded, the baron took another gulp and slammed the now empty tankard on the table with an expectant glower at Wolfgang. As Wolfgang sprang up and rushed over with more wine, Mortameur sneered at Vivianne's father.

"You're a barbarian and a fool, Schoen," Mortameur said and let his eyes graze Vivianne with cruel lust before resting contemptuously on the baron. "You have absolutely no idea of the import of your actions, do you? No concept of the series of events you are poised to affect. You lack vision, Schoen. You think this is all about crushing the Polish and Lithuanian pagan uprising and conquering Eastern Europe....You haven't the half of it. It is about so much more. It is about the swelling of a new *zeitgeist*, the ushering in of a romantic new era, the *völkisch* movement. Your victory and its ancillary events will incarnate into a *schutzstaffel* of immense proportions. Its momentum will galvanize the integration of the disparate German estates and create—a hundred years ahead of its time—the greatest world power ever known to humankind: the Nazi Empire." For the first time, Mortameur's gaze left Vivianne and blazed with a different fire, the fervent flame of insanity.

"We will enslave the inferior Russians and Slavic peoples and repopulate with our own. We'll exterminate the Jews, blacks and other riffraff polluting our gene pool. French, English, Italian, all will join this new empire. And your Teutonic Order will be our cherished and honored guard."

The baron blubbered some inept answer, much to Vivianne's dismay. Despite what she thought of her father, she felt fealty for him; he was bringing disgrace on their household with his pathetic drunken performance. She felt embarrassed for him and the rest of the Grunwald estate.

Seeing that the baron was more than tongue-tied, the *Großkomtur* helped him out with his own question. "So, what have you brought us, *Herr* Mortameur, that has the baron sick with happiness?" That was a polite way of saying 'skunk drunk', thought Vivianne. "Something that will usher in this new empire you mention? Something for our war with the Slavs and their infidel friends?" He was glancing down at the firearm that hung off Mortameur's hip.

"Something the baron's foolish wife should have provided," Mortameur said, giving Vivianne's father a snarling glance. "She didn't even have a chance to show you what you can do with a little chlorine and bleach, eh?..." He gazed out indifferently at the length of the Great Hall. "I came, *Großkomtur*, to finish what the good Lady Dianne didn't." His expression had once again returned to a languid sneer. He glanced over to

Vivianne without moving his head and murmured, "And to collect what is mine."

"What? More plumbing?" von Schwelborn jeered.

"Not all weapons are *things*, *Herr* Knight," Mortameur said sharply. Vivianne cringed and Mortameur continued, eyes flickering back to her "The best weapon is knowledge." He unleashed a wide conspiratorial grin and let his cold eyes slice into her. She shivered involuntarily. "And fore-knowledge is the best weapon of them all..." Mortameur then gazed directly at Vivianne and sneered. "Wouldn't you agree...*witchling?*"

Vivianne swallowed convulsively. What did he mean by that? Calling her a witch as if he expected her to understand. She stared at him. Despite who and what he was, she found that she *did* agree with the rest of what he'd said.

"For instance," Mortameur continued, "thanks to three fatal moves made by your *Hochmeister* and a treacherous act of betrayal by one of you seated here, in twenty-four hours your precious *Hochmeister* will be dead..." The entire hall fell into excited whispers. "Followed by most of you sitting right here." Mortameur swept his hand at the high table.

"This is nonsense!" Von Lichtenstein said in a deep voice of contempt. "What are you? A conjurer or a bombastic fool looking to stir some trouble?"

Mortameur laughed sharply. "And your arrogance will be your greatest failing. Even the apparent safety of your tabor will offer you no solace in the end, for the commoners you press-ganged into service will strike your desperate returning knights down. Of the two hundred and fifty or so Teutonic Order knights who will fight in this battle, only a handful will survive." He leaned forward and craned to study the face of each man sitting at the table. "Let's see..." Then he leaned back with a malicious smug smile and made his pronouncement: "With the exception of the good priest there, who will survive you all, four of you will die bravely in battle, two of you will be captured and later released, two more will be captured and executed for insolent behavior, one will be captured and beheaded for cowardice in fleeing the battle and the last one will escape, having done his treachery but will be found out and later beheaded for his treasonous act." Mortameur smirked, totally aware of the disturbance he'd just incited. "That's how it will be...or *not*," he ended with a leer and abruptly turned to stare at Vivianne, as if she had something to do with it.

"Is this your promised gift?" von Renys snapped, flashing angry eyes at Mortameur. His nasal voice was pitched high like a woman's. "It's worth nothing, because if you can't prove it, it's just a pile of dung!"

Several of the others agreed.

"Hear, hear, Mikolaj!" the Duke of Stettin piped in with a nod to his fellow Pole next to him. "If you mean to set us up against ourselves, I suggest you go elsewhere, Mortameur. We all fight the same cause."

"Do you?" Mortameur folded his arms across his muscular chest, totally nonplussed by the hostility he'd just ignited. He smiled in *schadenfreude*.

"Come, come, everyone," the Grand Marshal said, raising his hands to the others. "Let's hear him out, then. Find out what he has to offer us. This is surely just to tease us with intrigue."

"Yes," Ekdahl agreed. "Let's not let him terrorize us with useless fabrications. We're smarter than that. Come, what have you to offer us, *Herr* Mortameur?"

"Well, let's get this over with, then!" her father slurred out before Mortameur had a chance to answer. The baron raised his hand to the *minnesängers*. "This is your cue!"

Johannes the Brilliant nodded to the lute player then approached the high table and announced with a flourish of his arm, "Here's a ballad that was inspired and possibly written two hundred years ago whose subject, however, is eternal." Then he began to sing:

*Du bist mein, ich bin dein,*
*Dessen sollst du gewiss sein.*
*Du bist verschlossen*
*In meinem Herzen,*
*Verloren is das Schlüsseliein —*

*Du musst immer darin sein.*

Vivianne stared, aghast. It was the *minnelied* she'd written! Was this the special gift Uta had in mind when she'd mentioned it to Vivianne earlier? The baron must have given her poem to the *minnesänger*. Had she not been so shocked and mortified by it, her father's overture to true love might have moved her...or was he in fact mocking her?

After draining his third tankard of wine in a long draught and slamming it down resoundingly on the table, the baron pushed back his chair and lurched to his feet. Even though she kept her face forward, Vivianne noticed to her dismay that he staggered slightly and swayed before gripping the table to steady himself. Then he aimed an expectant gaze on her.

"Come then, daughter!" he snapped at her and pulled her to her feet with a clammy hand. She knew her face was already flushed with wine and felt herself redden more as she prepared for an announcement. It was her doomed birthday, after all. And she was Mortameur's present.

Still clutching her hand in his sweaty palm, her father turned away from her and aimed his glazed eyes on Mortameur, quietly seated and looking up with a sneer.

Her father cleared his throat. "As promised since my good wife was with child to be handed on the day of her fourteenth birthday, on the eve of her womanhood, to you...and in exchange for a promised boon from you, I give you my virgin daughter, the Honourable Lady Vivianne, the Baronesse von Grunwald."

✠

## ...10

VIVIANNE stared in sick horror and disbelief. Glancing from

the brute's cruel face, lips set in a lecherous smile, to her father's stern implacable stare she felt the intense alarm that came with realization of the bitter truth. *He's really going to give me to that beast! Does my father know what he is?* She turned a pleading look of anguish to the baron, willing that cold face to thaw. It was like walking into a blizzard. She forgot her composure in new desperation.

"Please, Father!" she heard her voice splinter as she pulled her hand from his wet grasp then laid both hands on his chest and saw him flinch. She abruptly let go and instead threw herself onto the floor to kneel before him. "I humbly beg you, for Jesus sake, and because you love me as a father, please don't do this thing." She seized his hand and clung to him as though he were a sanctuary. "You made this promise without consulting me!"

He glared down at her with disgust and pulled her gruffly to her feet. "You shame me, daughter," he scolded, drunken voice rising in pitch from embarrassment. "Get up! Get up!"

He threw a furtive glimpse at Mortameur, now slouched comfortably in his chair, inspecting his wine; it was clear to Vivianne that her father feared the man and was looking to Mortameur's reaction to gauge his next move.

Anger at his lack of strength of character swelled her bosom and gave her strength to speak further. "You're the powerful *Right Honorable* Ulrich Schoen, Baron von Grunwald..." she reminded him in a shrill voice that she fought to control. "Surely you can undo a promise you made fourteen years ago—perhaps made in haste—and strike a new agreement, mutual to *all* of us. You command ten knights as your vassals in your fief; you employ and provide the livelihood of a hundred working people, both in the castle and in the village. You are their keeper. And mine. And as I have a duty to you, you have a duty to me...my father!"

"You're not mine," he muttered, eyes glowing with something like madness. He shook her hand off. "You were never mine." His cold distant stare clutched her heart like a fist.

She felt suddenly cold with abandonment. Still facing her, he pointed behind him to the cruel barbarian who sneered at them. "*He* is your duty. Your duty is to please *him*."

*Lieber Gott!* She knew only too well how that was to happen.

"I've given my love to another already!" she blurted out, not thinking of the consequences of her untruth. Though she was very fond of Wolfgang, she could not admit that she truly loved the boy. The lie—the fabrication—had burst out in a desperate hope that her cold father would warm up to her declared feelings and heed her wish. Surely he knew something of true love! According to castle gossip her mother had bewitched him.

Her father's mouth dropped open then he closed it. "You've *what*?" His eyes flamed into her like torches. "What devil has taken your senses, girl!"

"I love another!" she persisted foolishly. "A squire in your service. He, there!" Finding Wolfgang staring dumbly at her from a table to her far right, she pointed feverishly and clung to unreasonable hope. But even as she pointed, her hope vanished when she saw Wolfgang visibly cringe. He vehemently shook his head and waved his hands up to indicate that he had no part in this. Then he jerked to his feet and backed into the crowd of standing servants behind, hoping to put more distance between them. Vivianne realized her foolish error: in her panic, she'd elevated him to something he wasn't; she'd conjured a dream, not even thinking of his feelings in the matter. Her chivalrous knight was just a boy who'd kissed her once on a dare and a second time simply because he could.

"What's this about a lover, Schoen?" Mortameur grunted, as if roused from a drunken sleep. He straightened from his slouch. "I expected a virgin, a girl not yet a woman. Not a whore!"

"And that is what you're getting!" the baron shrieked. Any composure he possessed was fast slipping away. Vivianne felt a cold chill claw up her back; she recognized terror in her father's voice. Her crime was his crime; her action his responsibility. "She is still a child!" von Grunwald insisted. He glared at Vivianne and his face twisted with rage. "You foolish girl! What are you blithering about? You belong to *him*!" He pointed to the brute. "You've belonged to him since your miserable little birth, you ungrateful wretched brat!"

The baron seized her gruffly by the shoulders and, spinning around, pushed her violently toward Mortameur, seated at his other side. Vivianne stumbled forward into the brute's waiting arms and seized in her breath. Laughing, Mortameur opened his legs and pulled her between them, crushing her into his purple-mottled chest in a brawny embrace of his arms. Face buried in the folds of his strange clothes, she suffocated in the stench of stale beer, sweat and horse manure.

"She has spirit!" Mortameur growled. "I like that in a wench, von Grunwald!" He stroked her hair with one of his massive hands and she shuddered and felt a renewed ache in her belly as a hot wave of nausea overcame her. Cheek crushed against his rough clothes, she saw the Great Hall splinter into a million pieces and fought from passing out. Her thoughts feverishly glanced over the lurid rape scene with the absent Milda as Mortameur teased, "I'll enjoy taming her and teaching her the arts and joys of becoming a woman."

To her humiliation and outrage, he swept her skirts up in an eager billowing motion and forced his legs between her. Spreading her legs over his lap he pulled her gruffly to sit, straddled, on him. Then, pinning her down with one hand, the other swiftly groped between her thighs, touching her where only she had touched herself before. Her eyes flew wide with shock and she struggled in sudden alarm, gasping out a cry of revulsion. But he was much stronger than she was and to her horrified dismay no one intervened. It was all transpiring out of view, below the table and obscured by the tablecloth, but surely everyone knew what he was doing!

The Knight Templar, face flushed with offended anger, surged to his feet and reached for his sword. Schwelborn restrained him by the arm and pulled him down with a whisper in his ear. The Knight sat down in a fluster and looked away in revulsion. They all did. No one else moved. Not the priest. Not even her father. She caught a glimpse of him with his eyes averted in disgust, and felt tears of shame heat her eyes. To these monks she was already Mortameur's, to do with as he pleased. No one saw, or cared to see what he was doing under the table.

"Ahh..." Mortameur groaned, vile fingers diving inside, intruding, and probing her as she shuddered with silent tears. "She's already wet and hot for me..." he crooned, fingers wriggling inside her. Then he brought his hand out from under her skirts as if to smell and his eyes grew wide at what he saw. There was blood on his fingers. "*What!*"

He pushed her violently off him and she fell prostrate with a grunt on the hard floor behind the table. "You're no longer a virgin! You've just been defiled!" Mortameur surged to his feet, eyes blazing with such fury that Vivianne trembled convulsively on the ground. Gazing back at him in mortified horror, she understood that she'd finally just then begun her woman's cycle and realized the impeccable irony of her body's timing. Mortameur's scorching gaze swept over the crowd like a wild fire. His voice boomed, "Who has stolen her from me just now! Who has just robbed her of her virginity! WHO!"

"Who has cuckolded my daughter!" the baron echoed in a high-pitched shrill, taking his cue from Mortameur.

Vivianne stood up giddily and saw where Mortameur's roaming gaze finally rested. Wolfgang! She'd betrayed him with her foolish and desperate remark: *I've given my love to another already!* How differently that might be construed!

Her father pointed a shaking finger, seeing where Mortameur was glaring. "*You!*" he shouted at Wolfgang like a madman possessed. "You've just soiled my daughter with your prick, haven't you! Seize him!"

"Oh, no," Vivianne moaned. She finally found her voice, even though it came out in a shrill cry: "He didn't touch me, father! We did nothing!" But she couldn't help flashing a guilty glance to Wolfgang at the thought of their kiss. She instantly felt Mortameur's eyes boring into her and glimpsed him leer. He'd seen their silent exchange. All was lost. Her betrayal of culpability for that small transgression, on the heels of her vehement denial, pointed to the greater crime and Wolfgang's guilt was sealed. *Oh, Mary, mother of Christ! What have I done!* She tried to explain, "It is only my woman's cycle, finally begun—"

"Silence, girl!" the baron screamed. His face, already puffy and red from drink, had gone scarlet with frenzied madness. She saw his eyes glaze with insane fear.

Uta stepped forward, shivering like a leaf in a winter storm. "I think she tells the truth, My Lord," she said in a voice shaking with fearful determination. Her eyes flickered from Mortameur to the baron. "She was feeling somewhat poorly earlier today and she is overdue for beginning the time of her flower—"

"Shut up, crone!" the baron yelled at her. "I'm not interested in your fiction to save the little brat you've nursed since she was born."

"I can prove it, My Lord, with an examination," Uta insisted. "Let me examine the girl. Or ask Herr Doctor—"

"Shut up!" the baron shrieked madly. The doctor was nowhere to be seen. Besides, Vivianne wasn't sure he would provide the right prognosis.

Her father waved impatiently at his guard. "Get that whelp over here now!"

Two of the baron's guard—Walther and young Nerdhart—grabbed poor Wolfgang, pale and shaking with fear. A moment ago they'd been friends of his; now they were his keepers. They brought him forward to face the baron. As he stumbled over the steps to the high table, Wolfgang's gaze brushed Vivianne's. She could not read his eyes past the fear that glazed them.

Her father turned a wrathful face from the shaking boy to Uta, still standing by the table on the floor below them. "Where were you when my daughter bathed and changed before the feast?"

Uta hesitated. Vivianne felt despair strangle her throat like cold fingers squeezing. "She sent me away, My Lord, as it is her custom to change in private—"

"Of course it is! I now see why. So her lover could join

her!" The baron shook with insane anger, pointing a shaking fist at Wolfgang. "*You* found her! You came to fetch me but only after you and she were alone together, in her bedchamber, where you did your pleasure with her!"

Wolfgang went white. It was obvious to Vivianne that he was tongue-tied with terror. She took one look at Mortameur, chillingly calm, then to her father's face, twisted with insane rage, and recognized the deadly game they were all in.

"No, father!" she cried, hearing the shrill in her voice. "When I was changing and bathing I was totally alone, like I always am." All her bad habits were conspiring against her today, Vivianne thought with mounting terror. Because of her insubordinate behavior she now had no witness to corroborate her claim. "I swear, Wolfgang didn't come in my room," she said, commanding her voice to a firm calm she was far from feeling.

"Look at the blood on you!" The baron pointed down her dress. Her eyes dropped down and she saw with renewed mortification that a bright red stain of fresh blood had seeped through the inner gown onto the outer silk brocade gown. As if that in itself made her guilty—as though a virgin couldn't menstruate.

Her father pushed her back onto her seat at the table then turned a steely gaze to Wolfgang, still held by the two guards. "I trusted you," he growled. "Took you into my household and taught you about chivalry. I entrusted you to train her and this is how you repay me, by deflowering my only daughter." Vivianne jerked her head to stare at Wolfgang then her father. He knew! Her father had known of—in fact had arranged—their secret lessons in knighthood? Only he hadn't counted on her making the suggestion herself first. Or had he? Perhaps he knew her after all. Her entire education, which she'd believed she'd stolen through inveigling, had been pre-arranged by her father and this beast. The baron's upper lip twitched into a humorless sneer. "I see your game, von Eisenreich. You saw fit to take my daughter before you lost the chance—before she left. A little prize before going into battle, eh?" That was not so far from the truth, Vivianne considered miserably, thinking of that last kiss he'd stolen from her. "Well, you like maidens so much...you can marry one; take him below to the Iron Maiden."

Wolfgang blanched in horrified disbelief. Vivianne gasped.

"NO!" she screamed. Her voice had projected more loudly than she thought possible. Her father flinched and stared at her. "If you must punish someone punish *me*! Please don't put him there!" she pleaded. She'd goaded Wolfgang into kissing her in the first place, after all.

The baron looked as if he would relent. "On second thought, whip the whelp until he bleeds then put him on the rack, Berthold. We'll do this right." He then fixed Wolfgang with a sinister look. "First you'll be partially hung in front of the villagers; not enough to kill you but to terrify your soul with visions of fiery Hell where you are surely headed. Then you will be very slowly disemboweled and castrated of your offensive part before we cut off your head and leave it on a pole for all to see. I will make sure that appropriate pieces of your dead body return to your lord and lady with a clear message of your criminal act of defilement."

Vivianne felt sick. She was about to scramble to her knees to beg but the baron saw it coming and clamped his hands down on her shoulders to keep her in her chair. Feeling helpless, she burst into silent tears. She watched longingly as Berthold and two guards pulled Wolfgang away.

*Forgive me!* But the words refused to come out and her throat closed with wracking sobs of guilt and overwhelming dread. His eyes never met hers. He looked ill and stumbled several times as they shuffled him out of the Great Hall. Vivianne dropped her head down over her arms and let the sobs flow out of her. The whole world had gone mad.

Her father leaned over her like a vulture and hissed down at her, "Don't worry, disobedient daughter, you will get your punishment too for bewitching the boy and whoring in my castle." His breath reeked of wine and fear. "There are many ways to deal with whores...and witches!" Her own father had called her a witch! Vivianne shuddered, imagining all the possibilities: exposure, the stocks, stoning, breast ripping, even the pear of anguish; they were all indescribably cruel, terrifying and sadly ended in an excruciating painful death. Surely her father would not subject his own daughter to those! Vivianne studied the baron's demented expression of cruel insanity and she shuddered with terror.

"But your punishment will be by *his* choosing," the baron went on with a glance at Mortameur. "*He's* your new master."

"There is still the matter of her defilement, Schoen," Mortameur said rather matter-of-factly, like this was some kind of business transaction and she was a piece of merchandize to be assessed. Which, she supposed was true. "The whore's worthless to me now. I think our bargain is terminated."

Vivianne squeezed her eyes shut in despair.

"Surely, you don't mean that, Mortameur!" Vivianne heard the shrill in her father's voice. He was desperate. "You don't understand!" von Grunwald gushed pleadingly, "I've held off my own banner in this battle because of your promised secret weapon. Von Jungingen is relying on me, Mortameur. We can't win without it. They outnumber us three to one at least and they have those barbaric Tartars. They raped and tortured our women and children and they pillaged our towns and desecrated our churches." She heard him straighten and sniff to gain composure. "I've kept my end of the bargain," he said more clearly. "They were childhood friends, for God's sake, Leduc! How was I to know? It's not my fault the boy got crazy at the last minute and pricked her for his own. I kept her safe and we managed her exactly as you instructed all these fourteen years."

Good God! *Everything* had been to Mortameur's bidding! Even Uta's service? In the long moment of silence Vivianne had to raise her head and look up. She found Mortameur eyeing her in contemplation with appraising eyes. It sent a new chill through her. She felt her thighs grow clammy with her spilled blood as Milda's probable fate raced through her mind.

"She resembles her mother," Mortameur said in a

subdued voice.

"Yes," the baron moaned miserably. He looked as though he was ready to weep.

"You lecherous bastard!" Mortameur sneered at the baron. "You've contemplated having relations with her, haven't you? First the mother, now the daughter, eh? Well, then..." He looked from the baron to the rest of the castle household, assembled like statues in the Great Hall, and let a malicious smile light his disturbingly beautiful face. Still facing those assembled, he said, "You won't mind, Baron von Grunwald, if I check the merchandise before I agree to our bargain... seeing the slut's already given herself away with joy..."

✠

# ...11

"YOU mean *right here*?" her father's voice went shrill. It was one thing to condemn a rabbit to slaughter; it was quite another matter to watch it being slaughtered. To think she'd once revered her father as a chivalrous knight and had longed for his approval. He was a simpering vulgar drunk who couldn't keep his honor any more than his liquor.

Studying her with restive eyes, Mortameur said absently, "You spoke of punishment, Schoen; I've decided on something less barbaric than torture: education. Let's see how she likes pleasuring from a *real* man. No harm, considering she's a whore." His eyes gleamed with lust. Mortameur turned to the baron and opened a cruel smile on him. Then he abruptly killed the smile and shifted his gaze to Vivianne with penetrating intensity. "She's so like Dianne..." he breathed out.

The baron blinked in miserable confusion, staring at Mortameur. Despite what had just happened and what her father had just done to her closest friend, Vivianne felt sorry for him. Torn between his lust for victory and his duty to a knight's honor—she had no delusions that it was out of any love for her—he was truly being tortured. And Mortameur knew it. It was his way of punishing von Grunwald, herself, and their entire household all at once. By forcing them to witness her appalling humiliation and the baron's as consequence.

"All right!" the baron shouted as if cursing. He threw up his hands in surrender, shaking and twitching, and glared briefly at Vivianne as though it was her fault he was in this mess. "Take her, then! She's yours, after all, to do with as you please. Just so long as you keep your end of the bargain." Then he looked away and wiped his hands as if there was dirt on them. "You must follow with your promised prize."

"Of course," Mortameur said with an ironic smile.

Heart slamming, Vivianne caught the eye of her chaplain and saw that his eyes glistened with tears. He looked ill. His mouth, twisted with revulsion, hung trembling open. But, like everyone else in the Great Hall, he sat stiff and immovable. This was madness, she thought. There were a dozen knights seated at this table and not one stirred to fight for her honor or come to her aid. Even the Knight Templar sat like a stone, his handsome still flushed face set in stern disapproval. She saw the condemnation on their faces; in their eyes she was a harlot who deserved this degrading punishment. They all sat mesmerized, along with the rest of the castle household, in stony fear and prepared to watch him rape her in public in thrilling anticipation of the prize he would give them for their obedience.

She bolted.

Mortameur was ready and caught her. He dashed in her path and she ploughed unwillingly into him. "No one will help you," he snarled down at her in a low voice meant only for her. "They are all sway to my power, now that they've gladly given you to me, my little *witch*."

He threw her face forward violently against the table, knocking over her glass of wine, and forced her down with a massive hand on her neck so her cheek jammed hard against the table. Hardly able to breath under his vice grip, she stared past the white linen cloth with its seeping river of deep red as Mortameur raised her skirts with his free hand and bared her naked backside toward the huge tapestry of knights in battle. She squeezed her legs tight but he kicked them apart and forced them to spread open with his knee. Exposed to the air, her thighs grew tacky with her own blood.

She saw the blurry image of her father's stony face, eyes averted, through a film of silent shuddering tears. Then he dissolved in a sea of sparkling prisms as her choking breaths grew shallow; Mortameur was slowly strangling her like a drake mating in the castle pond.

She couldn't believe that everyone would just stand by as this brute violated her right there in front of them, deserved or not. These were members of her household; people she'd grown up with, servants and mentors she'd respected, assisted and joked with; she couldn't believe that he had them all so enthralled in a stupor of fear that they stood as if transfixed in heinous complicity. Or was it something else? Had she been reduced to something so repulsive and immoral that they saw this as her due? Mortameur was her intended, after all; her future lord and master. Men typically beat their wayward wives. How was this any different? Taking her, even if by force, was his God-given right.

"Oh, ho!" Mortameur shouted in gleeful surprise and fumbled excitedly with his breeches. "She has the markings already. No doubt the boy's prick stirred them to appear! Welcome my Aeon, you are one of us, a true blood of the pleroma." Then he leaned close and she felt his foul breath on her neck. He snarled, "This will hurt a great deal, but only for a moment...you might even enjoy it."

He pressed against her with his stiff manhood, eagerly forcing entry. Vivianne squeezed her eyes shut, bracing for his intrusion. *Lieber Gott! If only I was a knight!* She envisioned the sharp points of the sword crest on the wall behind them. She saw them fall and skewer Mortameur in the back by macabre accident as she prepared to be skewered herself from his point—

No! She relented; the shield would just smash his head—

A loud crack split the air.

Mortameur grunted, startled, then abruptly released her neck. Vivianne gasped for breath as he slid off her in a fall to the ground. The entire castle household took in a sharp inhale. Several women screamed. Men surged to their feet and Vivianne heard the scrape of swords drawn from their sheaths.

What had happened?

She straightened, hastily brushing down the back of her dress to cover herself, and saw to her disbelief that the crest had indeed fallen as she'd envisioned and somehow struck Mortameur's head; one of the swords of the crest had glanced across his neck and back, drawing blood, and he lay utterly still on the floor. She flung her hands to her mouth, horrified and relieved at the same time. Dark blood flowed from the wound and already pooled beneath his body. Was he dead or just knocked out?

A deafening silence hung in the air for several heartbeats. Her father came out of his stupor first. "What have you done?" Then he pointed fearfully at her. "*Mein Gott*! Your eyes!"

Vivianne stared, mystified, at her father as the rest of the castle folk roused with murmurs and shouts. Why was he blaming her for an accident? Surely, it was an accident. Just because it had happened just as she'd envisioned it, meant nothing. Then why did he stare at her with such fear?

"Do you know what I sacrificed for this moment? We'll be crushed by the Slavs. I have nothing to offer my liege who waits for a boon. I promised von Jungingen. Mortameur would have given us his secret weapon. He said it was ten times more devastating than Greek Fire and with twenty-times more fire power than our cannons. You've cost us the war! You've killed us all, girl, with your selfishness!"

Then, with a final unintelligible gasp that wet her cheek with flying spittle, he convulsed violently and pitched to the floor, shaking and vomiting his dinner.

Vivianne stared at her father, rolling and twitching in a

seizure on the floor and crying out gibberish. She turned to the castle community, who were now pointing and shouting at her. Their faces had twisted from transfixed revulsion into fear and anger. Somehow they blamed her for both the stranger's accident and her father's sudden paroxysm. Perhaps for losing them a battle in the bargain too. Even *Père* Daniel's face looked stricken with confused accusation. Until now Vivianne hadn't realized how much his opinion of her meant to her. She felt his faltering faith drive like a blade into her heart and would have burst into tears had the crowd not suddenly grown very surly, which demanded her sudden attention.

Gertrude, the new dairymaid she'd assisted earlier, flung the first accusation: "She's a witch!"

"Witch!" another echoed. "You heard her father call her one!"

Another servant swiftly followed with, "Just like her mother! She's bewitched the baron! Put a spell on him with her wicked look!"

The crowd ignited to a raucous mob and a spate of accusations gushed out like a dam breaking: "My butter failed to churn because of her!"

"Look at the witchling's eyes! They blaze with the devil's own fire!"

"She appeared in Weikhard's dream and now he's ill!"

"She touched my cow and afterwards it couldn't stand!"

"I saw the nursemaid bringing her a daily potion of nettle, mustard and mint with wine to make her lustful!"

Oh, no! They were implicating Uta along with her!

"I smelled basil and cloves in her bed chamber!"

Vivianne had used both to mask the rank odor of Uta's anti-plague potions, completely innocent of their aphrodisiac properties. Vivianne stared in anguished despair as *Père* Daniel stood by, mutely sanctioning their actions. She'd thought him her champion once. But obviously this was too much for him to bear. He'd lost his trust in her. As their eyes met briefly, he suddenly gasped out strange words of gibberish. A violent shudder convulsed through him. It threw him forward, as if the devil itself were animating him, then felled him to the ground where he vomited alongside her retching father.

"She's taken the priest!" someone shouted. "He's doing the *Viper's dance!*" Another screamed in a panic, "Watch out for her eyes!"

Vivianne turned back to the crowd. Whomever her gaze alighted upon shrank back and averted their face in terrified alarm. They were convinced that she could strike them down with a glance. To her horror a few of the castle servants jerked out of their seats with startled cries of gibberish then fell writhing to the ground; some began to vomit. Vivianne recognized the true onslaught of an epidemic. The same illness that had inflicted her father and the chaplain was attacking the staff. And again, the timing was impeccable, thought Vivianne with wry cynicism. As though God was plotting against her.

Gertrude pointed to her. "Seize her! Burn the witch! Before she kills us all!"

"Someone find her demon cat too!" Vivianne heard the doctor shout.

Several of the baron's knights surged forward, swords drawn. As if suddenly awoken from a stupor, the Teutonic Knights at the high table leapt into action and drew their swords.

*NO!* Vivianne backed away in alarm. She envisioned their swords suddenly pointing back toward themselves. To her amazement, their swords flung back and the knights dropped them in shocked fright.

In that surreal moment, as the world staggered into slow motion, Vivianne saw the entire castle household draw in a long breath. Still on the floor, *Père* Daniel's shakes abated long enough for him to fix lucid eyes upon her and silently mouth, "*Cours, ma petite! Cours! Sauves toi!*"

After a last glance at her convulsing father, Vivianne took the *Père's* advice and ducked through one of the curtained archways behind the table to the kitchen stairwell, and pelted down the stairs.

"After her!" she heard the booming voice of Doctor

Grien. "The witch is getting away!"

✠

# ...12

SHE heard their pursuing steps behind her and ran down the hall past the kitchen, toward the wine cellar—and her secret doorway. If she could get through it in time, she would get away. If not, they had her, for she heard them coming down the west stairway of the Great Hall to head her off; that would force her outside, off the pantry. Chased into the open courtyard, she would be easily outrun and captured.

Then she was there! Panting with excited anticipation, Vivianne snatched the closest tapestry aside and slid behind through her secret door just as heavy steps made it down the stone stairs. She plunged past the murky wind into the pitch black safety of her secret tunnel and exhaled a sigh of relief as the sounds of confusion outside melted away; the two parties had no doubt met and found that she'd truly disappeared right in front of them. Unfortunately the passage now reeked of that same cloying smell that caught in her throat and made her gag. She hadn't had time to grab a torch or candle and found to her annoyed dismay that she could see nothing in front of her. She hadn't even been sure which tapestry she'd hurried behind, therefore which passageway she'd secured. There was nothing but to proceed by feel, she decided and stepped carefully forward.

As she made her way along the uneven surface, with left hand trailing along the wall and the right instinctively stretched ahead of her, the vile smell grew stronger. Overcome by the assault, she brought her right hand to her face and covered her nose and mouth. Thinking to escape from the smell faster,

Vivianne traded caution for speed and shuffled hastily along the uneven and slippery stones. She abruptly tripped over something large and nearly fell head over heels. Instead she landed on something bulky but soft. She flung out her hands to break her fall and they landed on what was unmistakably cold flesh. Vivianne started back with a scream.

It was a body! And she knew who's body it was.

With a moan of sickened dread, Vivianne scrambled backwards over the damp stones in the pitch dark, envisioning Milda's rotting corpse from when she'd been raped then killed several months ago. When Vivianne bumped up against the passage's secret door—where she'd started—she flinched at first then gave in to the wave of sickness that gorged up her throat. It spilled out in several retching coughs that left her weak and breathless. She leaned back against the cool stone.

*I can't go back that way*, she thought with a convulsive swallow. She decided to risk opening the doorway; surely her father's guards had left the corridor by now to search the rest of the castle.

Vivianne opened the door a creak, letting in a stream of light from the dimly lit corridor along with a breath of fresh air. She peaked out past the tapestry and noted that no one had lingered. Vivianne emerged, saw that it had indeed been the *Wild Woman* tapestry she'd ducked behind, which hid the passageway to the great storeroom. That was where Vivianne needed to go; but a dead rotting body barred the way. She would have to chance going the conventional route, past the kitchen and scullery, and pray they'd already searched the storeroom and brew house and left it to look elsewhere. Good Lord, didn't anyone else smell that foul odour emanating from her hidden passageway? Or maybe only she smelled it, Vivianne thought at length. It was magical after all, and existed in another time.

Vivianne stepped lightly, listening sharply for any sounds. She stopped a few times and shrank against the wall as she heard the distant echoes of gruff commands. Once she confirmed that they weren't heading her way or in the direction she was going, she continued on soft feet and finally made it without mishap or being seen by anyone past the kitchen and scullery into the great storeroom. There, she hurried to the trapdoor, opened it with shaky hands and climbed down to fetch her knapsack and her knight's apparel; she would require it for what she next needed to do.

Vivianne hastily stripped off her gown, soiled with her own blood, to change into her warrior trappings. Before she pulled on her breeches, she used her dagger to rip clean strips from her linen frock and stuffed them in her crotch to staunch her menstrual flow, which was streaming down her thighs. She felt brief alarm at the sight of so much blood issuing out of her and thought briefly of her mother, bleeding and dying as she gave birth to her. But it was only her natural bleeding, Vivianne reminded herself. She knew it would eventually end, though it didn't seem like it right now. She hurriedly replaced the first set of linens, already soaked, with another set. Then she proceeded with the remainder of her knight's trappings. She was just cinching in her belt when a shuffling in the scullery alerted her. She ducked behind a large barrel of apples and stilled her breath.

✠

# ...13

"VIVIANNE?..." came Uta's tentative whisper. "Are you here, child?"

Vivianne didn't reveal herself right away and listened to her nursemaid mutter fretfully to herself, "Oh, *Guter Gott*, where are you, *kleine Hase*....I hope they haven't found you...this madness will kill us all..."

Vivianne stood up and beheld Uta at the entrance to the great storeroom, the same place she'd first seen Wolfgang earlier today…when he'd kissed her. Vivianne didn't step forward but regarded Uta with cool suspicion. The scene in the Great Hall had rattled her and she felt she could trust no one, not even the nursemaid who had brought her up all these years. After what happened in the Great Hall she didn't think she had any friends left.

"Oh, dear child! I hardly recognize you in that!" Uta exclaimed, seeing Vivianne behind the barrel dressed in her knight's trappings. Uta rushed forward, ignoring Vivianne's reserve, and reached over the barrel to hug the girl. Giving in to an overwhelming yearning to be embraced, Vivianne relented and sank into the old woman's arms, biting back tears.

"*Gott sei Dank*! You're safe," Uta said breathlessly, leaning back to look Vivianne over with fearful eyes. "I thought they found you. Then I saw them come back up and search upstairs. They're shouting about a burning, to cleanse the castle."

Vivianne stiffened and gave Uta a hard searching stare. Uta betrayed fear in her eyes; not a good sign, Vivianne decided. "You're afraid of me, that I might be a witch."

"Oh no, poor child!" Uta sighed but shuffled back nevertheless, eyes faltering. Her eyes pooled with tears. "They want to burn you, child. For what you've supposedly done. They think I helped too, thanks to the doctor." That didn't surprise Vivianne. She knew Grien had targeted Uta long ago with his prejudice. "Crones like me are of no use to them; we're dangerous, especially when we help young witches with our potions and spells. The doctor called me out."

Vivianne sighed, realizing that she'd misread Uta. The old nursemaid wasn't frightened of her as much as she was frightened of what the guard might do to them both. Vivianne took Uta's hand. *Lieber Gott, I've brought her into this*! Fear of witchcraft had always focused on old crones, like Uta, with wrinkled faces, furred brows and missing teeth; women who conjured spells and murmured incantations. Everyone in the castle—Vivianne included—had suspected Uta of being a witch. But no one had cared…until now.

"I'm so sorry, Uta. I didn't mean to bring you into all this. I didn't mean to do it myself...whatever it was I did." She then considered soberly. "Maybe I *am* a witch," she ended in a shaky voice of growing despair. "I don't know how those things happened in the Great Hall...only that I thought them and then they..." she trailed, choking on her saliva, then continued in a nervous torrent, "And I never...with Wolfgang...we...he...I never..." She blushed fiercely despite the dire situation.

Uta patted her hand. "I know, *meine hase*. You're still a child, not deflowered."

Reminded of her mission, Vivianne straightened and made to brush past the old nursemaid. "I must go, Uta."

"Yes, you must escape and never come back, child. They're building a pyre as we speak. They've gone mad. So many have succumbed to this sickness your father and the priest have. You are at the forefront of their madness to be blamed for it all. Most of the Teutonic Knights have left in disgust but some have stayed for the burning. I fear it won't stop until they find you—someone—to punish."

*Lieber Gott!* Anyone who was her friend was liable to be blamed alongside her, Vivianne thought with growing fear. She could count on no one to help her; if they did, they'd be ensuring their own death. Uta was right; Vivianne had to leave. But she had to do something first. "I must save Wolfgang, Uta. It's not his fault. They've falsely accused him."

Uta restrained her by the arm. "Do you have to? They will find you, child! Wolfgang is already dead."

"You don't know that!" Vivianne cried, shaking off the old nursemaid's hold.

"No, I don't for certain," Uta relented. "But Berthold put him on the rack after whipping him. And what can *you* do?" she challenged, glancing with skepticism at the sword that hung off Vivianne's belt. It was obvious that Uta doubted the girl capable of disarming anyone. "The guards will stop you. They'll catch you surely and you'll burn!"

"I have to try."

This didn't sit well with Uta. Her body shook with

anxious fear and she mumbled to herself, making crossing motions over her chest several times. *"Guter Gott…rette uns!"* As Vivianne made again to leave, Uta seized her arm. "Wait, child. Before you go off, I have something to give you. It's from your mother. But before I do, I must tell you about the time you asked. When he first came for you. I was there, child." Uta drew in a long breath. "He came back when your mother was large with you. *Guter Gott*, when I saw him today, he didn't look an hour older than he was fourteen years ago—how's that possible if not by some evil spell? Back then they recognized one another, your mother and he. And there was fire between them, some history. He was in a full rage at her for leaving him. Mortameur said she'd run away from him; that she was his! He accused your mother of stealing something from him. Then he pointed to her huge belly: it was *you* he meant, child!"

Vivianne swallowed at the inference.

Uta continued with halting breaths, "Your mother screamed at him: 'she's not yours!' and he made a harsh laugh and called her some mad fool. He said you should have been, and that you didn't belong in this world, child. *Guter Gott*, I'd thought then that he meant you shouldn't be alive; now I think he just meant our land instead of his. Mortameur was ready to kill them both, but your mother clutched your—the baron—with such desperation, that the brute seemed to relent. He said he'd spare them if they promised you instead, child, because you summoned him!"

Vivianne felt her breaths grow shallow. The dream of Mortameur chilled through her. Had she unknowingly summoned him through her dream?

"He said that was how he could finally find you," Uta continued, unaware of Vivianne's increasing distress. "He burst into the castle and killed the old gatekeeper with that awful weapon; no one could stop him, though several tried. He came right into the Great Hall, where they were having their dinner. He stopped short of your father and in the end he had your father's own sword against his throat with his ultimatum and pointed his awful weapon at your mother's great belly. I can hear it as plain as day, what he said: '*I could kill you both right here and now. Or you can deliver that virgin girl-child to me on her fourteenth birthday and I will not only spare you both to a life of co-nuptial bliss but give you that which you ultimately seek.'*"

The secret weapon her father so feverishly coveted, Vivianne realized. Uta gazed at Vivianne with misty eyes of anguish. "Your mother was beside herself in tears but even she relented in the end and gave her promise. Oh, child, I fear *he* is your real father."

After all the tears she had already shed, Vivianne wouldn't have believed it possible that more could flow. But they did, swelling her throat, as she considered the ugly versions of truth set before her. What father would publicly rape his own child? Then again, what father would just stand by while another man did?

"I couldn't believe that your mother would give you away. And to such a brute," Uta went on. "But if he's your real father...Well, she did it to save the life of the man she loved, your...the baron...and her own life. Yours along with it, I suppose, for you were still in her belly then. *Guter Gott*, if that man is really your father...."

Vivianne could no longer bear it; she felt her body heave convulsively with wracking sobs and brought her hands to her face. Uta put her arms around Vivianne to comfort her; it triggered the release of a great torrent of pent-up tears.

"There, there, child...*meine kleine Hase...*" Uta mur-mured to her and patted her head. After letting Vivianne weep freely for a while, Uta pulled back the rumpled hair off Vivianne's face.

"Vivianne," she said in a different voice that made the girl swallow down her tears and look up. "Your mother wrote you a letter. She told me to give it and those other things to you just before you turned fourteen...if she wasn't around to give it to you herself." Uta pulled out a torn piece of parchment with shaking hands. "When the baron found out about the letter he told me to burn it. But I didn't have the heart to, after what happened to your mother. I tore it up in front of him. But then I retrieved it and pasted it back together again. I almost forgot to give it to you. Here." She handed the wrinkled and scored yellow parchment to Vivianne. "I can't read so I don't know what it says, dear, but you will."

Barely keeping her hands from shaking, Vivianne uncurled the parchment and read:

*June 14, 1395*

It was the year her mother had arrived at her father's estate. She was already carrying Vivianne she surmised.

*Dearest Vivianne and Mortague—*

Viviannes eyes darted sharply up to Uta. "Mortague? Who's Mortague?"

"Oh, my..." Uta's gaze flickered away and she fretted with her skirt to straighten it and murmured, "She even named him..."

"Who's Mortague?" Vivianne repeated more emphatically.

"Oh, my dear child..." Uta sighed and met Vivianne's gaze with sorrowful eyes. "He was your fraternal twin brother. He died with your mother."

Vivianne's throat closed and she brought a hand to her mouth. *Lieber Gott!* She had a twin brother? And no one had told her! No wonder she'd always felt there was something missing in her life. Only it was a *someone*!

"Only you were saved," Uta went on. "The baron gave strict instructions not to save the boy. But, it wasn't necessary; the boy was still-born because of your mother's womb fever."

Vivianne's mouth went dry and her knees gave way. She steeled herself by gripping the edge of the barrel for support with a free hand. "Did you know? Before, I mean, that my mother was carrying..." She gulped the rest of her words in a convulsive swallow.

"I guessed she was carrying twins," Uta said. "When I mentioned it to her she already knew. She seemed to know a lot of things..."

Like the fact that it was a boy and girl inside her, thought Vivianne. And she'd already named them. Still shaking from a mixture of excitement and dread, Vivianne returned to the parchment and read:

*...If you are reading this, I must have passed on and you are alone. Alas, the good doctor must have finally had his way with me; we never did get along. At least you have each other...* Vivianne quelled a convulsive sob. She felt her face twist with grief for a brother she never had as she read on through a film of tears: *I've left these things for you as they will be helpful in your journey, the one you must take on your fourteenth birthday. I hope you have read the books carefully, in all their versions—I'm sure you know what I mean by that and have grasped their significance to you and your worlds. You are* summoners, *after all; like me, and he who will come for you on your fourteenth birthday. We are* summoners, *beings of light and spirit who are able to summon and manipulate the world of matter. Have you done some of that already? Those who practice* gnosis *call us* Aeons; *others call us* Angels. *We are the* pleroma *and we come in pairs— twins—which the* Gnostics *call* syzygies.

*Here's the hard part: Every once in a while a choice is made that influences the two dichotomies in a significant way and on a scale that will affect many. This is called a* nexus *event. When linked to other cumulative phenomena, it can create a* Butterfly Effect *that will cause the dichotomous twin worlds to differ significantly from one another. Before such an event,* Aeon *twins are emanated—conceived by their parent* Aeons—*one for each of the twin worlds. These twin* Aeons *will summon the splitting worlds at the* nexus *event and then each will direct their twin world until the twin worlds join again as they always do eventually. A* nexus *event will happen on your fourteenth birthday, my twins, and will determine the fate of* the Battle of Grunwald. *I can't tell you what will happen but only that each of you is destined to summon, see in and live through each of the two opposite outcomes. The two worlds are always there for you—and only you can see them.* The secret passageway, Vivianne realized. It was the alternative world. *The two worlds will both be there until the shcizm event occurs, when one disappears for each of you as you each pass through into your world. Yes, this means separating from each other, no matter how frightening or lonely it may seem. If one of you does not take up his or her world and you choose instead out of cowardice or greedy appetite to stay together, this may promote a divergent pathway for humanity, and eventually result in two twin worlds so different from one another that they may never join again. Believe me, I know this to be true...I wish I didn't but I do, God help me—perhaps I can atone for what I've done through you, my beautiful children. You must be brave and separate so you can join; an Aeon emanation from an Aeon without a partner Aeon, results in a Demiurge, a reprehensible creature that should never come into existence—*

Vivianne seized in a halting breath. With her twin brother dead, was *she* now this thing, a *Demiurge*? And what did that mean? The parchment was visibly shaking in her hand but she pushed herself to read on:

*...Have you read all the books I left you? Use them as a Talisman. Keep them with you always, consult them to determine the success of your mission. Specifically pay attention to those that disappear or reappear and to Roget's l'Histoire. And yes, you have a mission, both of you: right now it is to stay alive and free, to escape the clutches of the one who wishes to kill one of you and take the other for himself—*

Mortameur! He wanted Mortague dead; well, the baron had done his bidding for him. And he'd just about given Vivianne to Mortameur too.

*...Before you fulfill your Aeon destiny, you must save yourselves first. I had hoped to brief you on your mission, but, alas, I am obviously not there for you now. You will have to trust in your instincts and these few notes I've left you (it's not safe to reveal more here). Use the tools I left you; they will help you to find friends and to avoid your enemies. You know where you must go before he finds you: to the tear between our two worlds that I created when I came here eight months ago. You will find it—you have the map in your mind's eye. And you alone will see it—because you are* summoners.

*I will just say this one thing: beware of the tear-sickness; it is a significant thing to pass through the tear. When you do, you will suffer a number of ill-effects and they vary with each individual, so I can not prepare you fully. Most certainly though, it will rob you of your wits and eyesight at first. You will both be blind and unable to speak rationally for a time. You will appear like stumbling incomprehensible fools to anyone who discovers you. And you will be vulnerable and sick for a time. Don't be alarmed; it will all eventually pass, but be aware and prepared. Don't fret; the tear will direct you to the one who will help you. The person who finds you will be very compassionate—that's how the tear works and you are* summoners, *like I am. It was the good baron who found me because he was meant to find me.*

*Help one another and when the time comes to return and see in your twin worlds when each of you must go your own way, I wish you courage to separate and the knowledge that you will be together again. Believe me, it is better to do your duty alone so you can gain your reward later than to be greedy at first and remain together and ruin everything, including yourselves. When it is time for the schism to occur and the nexus portal to open, you will know; you will feel it inside you with every breath of your being. The light inside you will guide you to where you both must pass—each to his or her opening. Be brave, bid each other farewell, and walk through; I was weak and selfish and cheated an entire world to stay with my love. I was wrong. You must do it right; for me. Go and may God and the* pleroma *be with you.*

*You must have figured out by now that the baron is not your real father. You were conceived in my world....*

*Love,*

*Dianne Mortameur—*

The parchment fell from Vivianne's hand. She covered her gasping breaths with trembling hands. Her mother had saved the worst for the end. It was true. Mortameur, that brute who tried to violate her, was her father! Vivianne staggered back and almost vomited.

Uta lurched forward to help steady her. "What did she say? You've gone so pale, child!"

Vivianne regained her composure and picked up the parchment she'd dropped then straightened. "I'm all right," she lied and tightened her face with determination. Aiming an intense gaze on Uta, she said, "Promise me that you will hide somewhere until it is safe. I fear an epidemic. Some sort of food poisoning or something. I must get Wolfgang and we'll leave the castle somehow. Don't worry about us."

"Here," Uta stuffed a small sack that smelled of herbs into Vivianne's backpack. "It's food and supplies. Some of my medicines: tinctures, oils and potions of comfrey, plantain, rosemary, and sage..." She listed a dozen or so additional herbs like self-heal, yarrow, vervain, ginger root, white willow bark, myrrh and wild lettuce. "They might come in handy."

Vivianne took the pack with gratitude and stuffed it inside her knapsack before slinging it over her shoulders again. "Thank you." She hastily hugged the woman who had come the closest to being a mother to her. Vivianne then pulled her mail hood up over her head, stuffing her hair inside, then put on her bascinet. With a wave goodbye she sprinted out of the great storeroom, down the corridor toward her secret passageways, and held back dour thoughts of never seeing Uta again.

Vivianne hurried through the secret passageway that ended in a trap door to the larger of the two dungeons. She carefully lifted the door and peeked out through the crack under the small rug. She faced several large kegs of wine; both dungeon rooms were seldom used and served as secondary wine cellars. Seeing no one inside, she opened the door further and scrambled out. It was only then that she saw Wolfgang on the rack, lying face-up and shirtless with his body tautly spread-eagled, wrists and ankles bound. He was deathly pale and beads of sweat glistened on his chest and face. His back stretched in an unnatural arch and his face grimaced in agony. Angry red streaks across his chest confirmed that he'd been flogged but was thankfully still only poised for the hanging and quartering.

"*Oh, Lieber Gott!*" she breathed out, rushing to Wolfgang's side. At her voice and approaching footsteps he stirred and opened his eyes. They widened as he briefly mistook her for a knight ready to take him to be hung. Then he recognized her trappings and choked out in a raspy voice, "Vianne!"

"Yes, it's me!" she said and pulled off her bascinet. As she loosened his bonds she continued, "I've come to rescue you! Don't move. I've got some medicine for you from Uta and my mother." He'd begun to shiver and she recognized that he was in shock and might already have a fever. "Here. Swallow this." She fished out one of her mother's vials marked 'ampicillin'. She shook out a few pills of hardened powder and shoved several into Wolfgang's mouth to swallow.

As he did, boisterous voices of approaching guards rang toward them.

Wolfgang's eyes widened and he went pasty white.

"Quick! Try to move, Wolfgang!" she urged, shoving the vial into his hand. He struggled to move but his limbs wouldn't respond. Vivianne ignored his cries of pain and dragged him to the trapdoor. She pushed him into the hole and cringed as he dropped down with an awful thud.

"I'm so, so sorry..." she called down to him. It was all that came out of her mouth, all she was capable of saying. Then she had to slam the door shut on him as the guards clanked at the door.

Vivianne scooped up her bascinet then ducked behind a large keg of wine and plastered herself against it as the guards burst into the dungeon. She stilled her breath, hoping no one would creep around to see her. Instead, one of the men discovered the trap door. In her haste to take shelter, Vivianne had left the mat off the door and a man with keen eyes had spotted it. He approached it then bent down to open it—

Vivianne seized in a sharp inhale as he did. The guard bent to look down and saw nothing. There was no one there. Wolfgang had disappeared! How was it possible? But she had no time to ponder this because another guard had heard her sharp intake of air and was moving toward her.

Thinking she was better off in the open than being caught trapped in a corner, Vivianne drew her sword and burst out from behind the keg to meet him. Despite the fact that he suspected someone of being there, he flinched and shrieked in surprise. She recognized young Eugen, one of the baron's footmen. Of course, he didn't recognize her beneath her shroud of knight's armor and trappings.

Vivianne took the offensive and attacked, lunging

forward with a women's guard. Not experienced in real fighting, Eugen fled in fear but two other squires met her, swords flashing.

She beat them down quickly, using her close combat techniques and easily knocked each one out with the pummel of her sword. Then she sprinted up to the ground level passageway.

At the top of the stairs, she came to a sudden halt. Someone stood there! They both started. It was *Père* Daniel! Vivianne swiftly pulled off her bascinet to reveal her face.

"*Père!*" she cried out softly. "You're alright!"

"Yes, *mon ange,*" he whispered hoarsely with a fearful glance to either side of them. "My fit has ended. I came to warn you. They are pursuing you from both sides and will cut you off unless you leave the building through the courtyard. You must leave the castle. They are mad. They wish to—"

"Yes, I know," Vivianne cut in. She clasped his hand and added imploringly, "Oh, *Père!* I'm not a witch! I didn't do all those things they accused me of. Please don't judge me as—"

He squeezed her hand. "*Enfant,* I refuse to judge you. Only God can do that." Then he turned his head sharply at hearing a sound. Fear rushed into his eyes and he urged, "Now go, *petite*, before they find you! *Sauves toi!*"

Vivianne seized his hand between hers and kissed it.

"*Cours, ma petite! Vites! Et Dieu soi avec toi!*"

Vivianne threw her bascinet back on then wheeled and ran. She thought she caught a glimpse of him abruptly twitch and bat at nothing but she kept on running.

✠

# ...14

SHE spilled out of the service door into the wet heat of the courtyard and a din of angry shouts. It was drizzling outside and a summer's storm wind whipped across her *bascinet*. The wind whistled through the eye slits, making her eyes water. Vivianne blinked several times and flinched at what she saw and heard in the far north corner of the courtyard.

A dozen or so of the castle household were eagerly gathering and building up a log pyre. Dark smoke billowed out of the sputtering fire like angry storm clouds. Vivianne recognized Frieda and Gertrude among those tending the fire. She spotted the doctor, standing apart, overseeing them. Two of the footmen had already constructed a 'ladder' onto which they would lash Vivianne, once they caught her, for easy vaulting into the fire.

Vivianne shrank back and shivered. She reminded herself of her disguise; no one would for a moment suspect she was the baron's wayward witchling daughter. She was just another of the squires of the castle. She needed to act swiftly, though, before the dungeon guards gave the alarm in the courtyard. They had, after all, contended with her dressed as she now was in knight's trappings. Vivianne turned and sprinted to the stables where she found Willy, the horse Wolfgang usually gave her for their sparring matches. The horse snorted, apparently happy to see her. He was always glad to get out for some exercise.

"Come on, Willy," she said, outfitting him with riding gear. "Today, if I'm lucky, you're going to get a lot more exercise than you usually do."

Vivianne pulled out a parchment from her backpack, readjusted the pack over her shoulders then hastily led Willy out of the stable and mounted. She lowered the visor of her *bascinet* and rode to the castle gate, making a point of not glancing back at the growing mob by the raging fire; they were pretty certain of finding their prey, Vivianne thought and prayed that Uta had found a good hiding place. She threw a furtive glance up to the battlements of the castle and curtain wall, where she spotted a few guards stationed. They were on the lookout for a young girl in a cream brocade gown and obviously hadn't yet been alerted to an interloper in knight's trappings. But they soon would be, once the guards she'd tangled with in the dungeon woke and spilled out of the hallway into the courtyard. Feeling her heart thunder, Vivianne reached the gate and held up a rolled parchment in front of Warner.

"I have an urgent message for *Herr Hochmeister* von Jungingen!"

"Ah, it's you, *Herr* Skinny!" Warner laughed, recognizing her coat of arms. "But where's von Eisenreich, the baron's squire-at-arms and personal messenger?"

"He's too busy attending to certain castle matters—"

"Ah, you mean the little witchling!"

Vivianne flinched and shifted in her saddle to hide it.

"Ah, the poor sod!" Warner said, clearly referring to Wolfgang. "I heard what she did to him. I always knew that girl was trouble. I recognized her for a spoiled trollop and a witch," he continued proudly. "That hair and those eyes of hers, so soft and dangerous, wicked in their sweetness. I saw how she could bewitch anyone to get her way…"

Vivianne felt hurt by his words. She was doubly glad of the concealing quality of the *bascinet*; it kept her face in shadow and made it harder to make out her eyes.

"Women, eh?" Warner went on blithely. "Imperfect animals they are. Just like the bible says, there's nothing as wicked as a female…" Then he snorted and made an obscene gesture. "I'd sure like to taste some of her wickedness though, eh?—"

Vivianne gruffly cut in, "At any rate, I'm free and the baron knows my father intimately so he could trust me with this letter. It's urgent."

"Indeed!" Warner laughed again, quite unaware of Vivianne's morbid play on words. "Then go, *Herr* Skinny!" he said cheerfully, cranking up the portcullis. "And God speed!

They've been arriving for the past hour!"

As soon as she cleared the portcullis, Vivianne spurred on her horse and, without a glance back at the red brick *Backsteingotik* castle, she coaxed Willie into a gallop past the castle outer wall into the open road and fields of Grunwald.

✠

Open was a misnomer. Vivianne reigned in her horse and stared out at the sea of moving men. As Warner had informed her, the German infantry, light and heavy cavalry with their artillery and caravans, were converging in the fields. Camps were being set up to the north as men, horses and caravans trudged at least four to ten abreast, cutting a muddy sea made by hundreds before them along the road from Frogenau in the northwest.

The queue appeared endless as they snaked down the hill in a force march from Löbau, some twenty kilometers away to the West. Mud was smeared up to their knees and their heads bowed and nodded in exhaustion. It was easy to spot the stalwart Teutonic Brothers on horseback, wearing white surcoats with black crosses. The secular mercenary and vassal knights in various armor and coats of arms, along with the burgers, were also mostly riding on horses. The remainder of the men, who made up the majority of the troops, were on foot; they formed a chaotic mixture of city-folk, hired soldiers and peasants, reflected in their mixed attire. They looked solemn and dour to Vivianne; all of them appeared weary. They certainly didn't look ready or willing to do battle.

She was suddenly reminded of what Mortameur said of the commoners and knew this to be true. They were here because of obligations to their lords rather than any personal conviction to fight an opponent they didn't necessarily consider an enemy.

Vivianne recognized several banners of the various squadrons among many she did not know in a sea of amassing soldiers. She'd studied them with Père Daniel and knew most of the standards of the Teutonic State. She spotted the banner of the Order to the north of her already; it was carried by Grand Marshal von Wallenrode's Brethren Knights of the Order and was a simple black cross on a white field.

She scanned the slope and counted others she knew: the black and white countercharged paired cross-pattée of the town of Braunsberg; the red deer in a white field of the Komturia of Strasburg; the angel of the town of Engelsburg; the horizontal yellow, white and red bands of Ekdahl's Livonian contingent. To the far left she spotted the white cross on a red field, the banner of St. George, led by a fierce knight, Georg Kerzdorff. Further down in the long queues still arriving, Vivianne glimpsed the white and red horizontal bands of the town of Tuchel, the standard of that arrogant von Schwelborn knight and farther down she observed Duke Casimir V of Stettin's banner, a red griffin *salient* on a white field. Not far from it she saw Brandenburg's red and gold eagle *displayed* of Markward von Salzbach and the red and white wave of Kulm Town, the banner of that Lizard League knight. There seemed no end to the marching soldiers.

Within a few heartbeats Vivianne realized that she could not avoid them to get to her destination, the swampy bog that lay to the northeast toward Tannenberg. She would have to cross their path somehow. She decided to attempt to ride through the thinnest part of the queue, cut straight north, then skirt behind the amassing encampments through the back of the boggy forest to where she thought the tear her mother had written of lay. It was far from a direct route and meant negotiating far more of the treacherous marsh than she'd have liked but she decided her options were severely limited. The less of a presence she made among these warring parties, the safer she'd be. It was bad enough that she'd have to cross their path once.

Despite her unrecognizable coat of arms, Vivianne's armor and other accoutrements were decidedly Germanic and the horse displayed the von Grunwald coat of arms on its caparison. Theoretically, she should not have any trouble getting through. However, she still fully expected to be challenged by someone. Security was important and there were spies and enemy scouts everywhere. Straightening herself on her horse, Vivianne urged Willy forward toward the thick line of marching men, choosing a section devoid of cavalry. When she reached them she wormed her way through the exhausted warriors, uttering her thanks in German. She noticed to her amazement that most of them paid her no mind. Their exhausted faces gave her the barest glance of disinterest, as they gave way for her in an unconcerned shuffle. She began to think that they would all ignore her and she'd slip through them without incident—

"You! Boy!" someone shouted. "Stop!"

She made the mistake of turning and beheld a large craggy-faced blond-bearded knight. He was dressed in armor overlain by the white Teutonic Knight tunic with cross *pattée*, now considerably muddied. Vivianne realized he was shouting at *her*. The stocky old knight had stepped out of the moving troops and waved wildly at her from some twenty meters behind. Mud darkened his legs up past his knees. Vivianne thought it strange that he was on foot among the infantry.

Here it comes, she thought, the challenge: *Who are you, wandering about by yourself? Who's banner are you with?* She toyed for a brief moment with the thrilling idea of kicking her horse into a gallop in a mad dash to the swamp, still a good hundred meters away. But common sense prevailed over panic and, despite her urgency to slip away, Vivianne reigned in her horse and felt her heart pound as she maneuvered Willy past the thick of marching men toward the burly knight.

The knight urged on, "Here, boy! Are you from the castle? You're one of von Grunwald's boys, aren't you?" He'd obviously recognized the von Grunwald coat of arms on her steed. "I need your help!" he urged.

She was never one to refuse help to another when she could give it. Her disguise was still intact, after all, she reasoned; he'd called her 'boy'. When she'd ridden closer and dismounted, the old knight lumbered toward her with a stiff limping gait and wheezing breaths; the long trip had not sat well with him, Vivianne concluded. The part of his leathery face not veiled beneath his long wiry beard was a well worn map of scars and lines, suggesting a man who had journeyed long and hard; yet, his canny eyes sparkled with a kind of heat that belied the weary demeanor of his body.

"I have an urgent message for you to deliver to the *Hochmeister*, there." He pointed to the largest canopy being erected a few kilometers to the northeast of them and generally in the same direction that she wished to go. The tent was so large that it was quite visible from where Vivianne stood. She realized that this Teutonic knight mistook her for one of their own squire-at-arms. "Before he goes too far in setting up, he must consider the cavalry," said the knight. "This mud is not good for the horses. He must seek higher ground for them. That's all swamp in there." He shoved the parchment into her hand then clapped the other rough hand over hers and squeezed. "Now go!— Wait!" He looked down at her with a stricken expression. "You're bleeding, boy! You've been injured between the two thighs! "

Vivianne pulled back but the knight held her fast. She followed his concerned gaze down to where blood seeped through her mail along her thighs. Her initial alarm sank quickly to mortification and she felt her face redden. The linen 'bandages' she'd recklessly stuffed in her crotch to staunch her menstrual flow had shifted, letting the blood flow freely through her breeches and mail. It left a shiny soaked blotch of dark red on her thigh. Her stomach clenched and she was glad her visor was only partially up so her deep blush wasn't obvious.

In that startled moment she recognized the wizened face of the knight: this was Werner von Tettingen, the Grand Hospital *Großmeister*! It was only then that she spotted the banner of his Komturia and town, Elbing; a pair of counated crosses, a red cross on a white field beside a white cross on a red field. The banner danced up and down past her as the standard bearer passed them by with a brief curious glance and nod to the *Großmeister*.

"Here," von Tettingen said gently in a softer voice, but still holding her hand in a steely grip. "Let me have a look at you..." He bent down to have a better look at the 'wound'. His eyes brushed across her hand clasped in his. "*Guter Gott.*" He stroked her skin. "You have such fine soft hands, like a girl's..."

Vivianne twitched her hand out of his loosened grip and stumbled back with a stutter, "There's no need, *Herr Groß-meister!*" She winced at hearing her shrill girl's voice and tried to sound more gruff. "It's just a superficial flesh wound. I will deliver your message!" Clutching the note in her hand, Vivianne hastily clambered up her horse and was about to spur him on when von Tettingen waved his hand at her.

"Wait! What is your name, brave squire?"

Her heart beat like a drum. "Er—Wolfram...the Skinny!" Then she kicked her horse into a frenzied gallop away from the troop line to prevent Tettingen from asking more. It was only when she neared the huge canopy that Vivianne realized that her lie to Warner had turned into a truth of sorts; she was indeed taking a message to the *Hochmeister*, only it wasn't from her father, it was from the Hospital *Großmeister*!

✠

# ...15

AS Vivianne approached the seven pinnacled canopy, the pungent bog aroma of the swamp cut sharply through the fresh scent of rain and loam and she noted that the softer ground was dotted with puddles of liquid mud. Sweat from the growing heat of the day beaded on her forehead as she cast her eyes toward the drowned marsh forest behind the encampment...where she was ultimately headed.

She recognized the *Hochmeister*'s huge flag hanging in front of the camp that marked the main entrance of the huge tent: a gold cross, fimbricated black and a cross *potent* with a shield at the point where the arms of the cross met. The shield bore the Imperial Arms, a black crowned eagle *displayed* on a gold field. As she wound her way through the warren of wooden covered wagons strewn about the camp, Vivianne glimpsed piles of handcuffs and shackles in several: obviously meant for the enemy prisoners they expected to capture. Other wagons brimmed with torches soaked with tallow and tar and arrows prepared the same way. Other wagons contained barrels of wine and ale.

As she rode up to the main entrance of the canopy, her heart raced with thoughts of abandoning her task for the *Großmeister* and continuing on her own mission. But somehow she felt honor-bound to see the message delivered. Tettingen had entrusted her with an important message on behalf of the horses. She couldn't let him or the horses down, not even when it meant taking a chance that she might be found out and shipped back to von Grunwald Castle…to be burned alive as a witch.

As she approached the main canopy, a thin young man in his early twenties rushed out to meet her. He leapt toward her and seized her reins. Cold eyes sliced into hers and he demanded, "Who are you?" Then, recognizing the von Grunwald coat of arms on the horse's caparison, he answered himself with a sneer, "Oh, you're from the castle." He'd uttered the word like it was a profanity and Vivianne flushed with both anger and shame. She knew what they all thought of her father; he was a bit of a laughing stock, a drunken has-been. There was nothing worse, it seemed, than a great warrior who'd lost it and gone to the dregs. "What do you want?" the boy snarled.

"I bring a message from the Hospital *Großmeister*," she responded. She held out the parchment and deftly slid off the horse, landing on the ground with bouncing light feet. The boy was about to snatch it from her but she quickly retracted her hand. "It's for *Herr Hochmeister*."

"Don't you know who I am?" The boy was definitely annoyed that she obviously didn't. "I'm Jurge Marschalk, von Jungingen's companion, imbecile." He looked her over like she

148

was livestock. "Give it to me." He went to snatch the parchment from her hand. "I'll get it to the *Hochmeister*—"

Vivianne twitched her hand out of his grasp and stepped back. "That's all right," she said evenly, craning to see inside the entrance of the main tent . "I'll do it myself. Where is he?" Even as she insisted, Vivianne reproved herself; it would have been more prudent to let the boy take the note to von Jungingen and she could have been safely on her way. But Marschalk's contemptuous arrogance had piqued her and assaulted her sense of integrity. It suddenly and inexplicably became important for her to see the *Großmeister*'s note safely into the *Hochmeister's* own hands.

Marschalk's sallow face twisted with anger and he stiffened as though poised to wrestle her to the ground and force the note out of her clutching grip. Vivianne tensed and found her left hand hovering over the pommel of her sword. The little *klugscheißer* could use a lesson in manners, she thought, bracing for his attack—

It never came. Instead the *Hochmeister* barged out of the tent, half-dressed, and buttoning his undershirt in an angry bluster. "Jurge! Where is my new tunic? I told you to find it NOW you *lümmel!*"

When he saw Vivianne, he halted and blinked, looking her over. She met his gaze head on.

He was quite tall, with excellent posture, but otherwise looked his fifty years. A long reddish wiry beard covered most of his seamed face. Wide-set intelligent eyes flashed with cruelty. He had an impatient hubristic nature to his long gait and a casual but brisk demeanor. Emerging from the tent half-dressed, for instance, suggested to her a certain lack of propriety, that he considered himself above certain rules; rules which he flouted unless they were to his benefit. "Ah, what do we have here, Jurge? One of your little playmates?"

Despite the vows of the Teutonic Order, there was something about the *Hochmeister's* informal manner and the boy's reaction that suggested impropriety.

The boy began, "He's—"

"I have a message for you from your Hospital *Großmeister*," Vivianne cut Marschalk off and kept her gaze directed at von Jungingen. "He begs you to please reconsider placing the horses on higher ground out of the bog." She held out the note with a deep bow and dropped her gaze to the ground. The heat of the day, trapped in her knight's garb was starting to get oppressive.

"Oh, does he..." von Jungingen said in a rather surly tone.

Vivianne didn't dare look up but after a moment, during which the note was not removed from her hand, her gaze slid up from her still bowed head and she beheld von Jungingen regarding her with an amused but cold smile.

"Well, well..." he said, finally snatching the note and eyes skimming its contents. "Since when does Werner use castle riffraff to deliver his commandments?" He'd obviously recognized her castle knight's trappings, if not her specific herald. Von Jungingen flung it to the ground, breaking out into a snarling laugh. Marschalk followed with a churlish cackle. Vivianne felt her face burn. This was not at all what she'd expected from the Grand Master of the Teutonic Order. She gaped at him, shocked by his petty and childish response and his disrespect for his own Hospital *Großmeister*. "Perhaps," the Hochmeister went on, "Werner should have sent the drunken baron to find him some higher ground, though I can't imagine him finding anything outside of a pot of beer—"

"My father isn't that—" She cut herself off too late. She'd blurted it out. She knew it was personal between von Jungingen and her father but nothing merited showing such disrespect in public.

Von Jungingen stared at her then suddenly frowned. He abruptly reached forward and gruffly pulled off her *bascinet*, forcing her head forward with a hard snap. Eyes now flashing, he pushed off her mail hood. Dark curls of long hair cascaded over her shoulders.

Von Jungingen's eyes sparkled with amusement and he let out a sharp laugh. "Well, if it isn't von Grunwald's little brat!"

Marschalk muttered some churlish remark; Vivianne only heard part of it and was glad she hadn't heard the rest. Her face flushed nevertheless and she glared at the *Hochmeister* with growing anger. How dare he! She couldn't help defending her father, despite his sorry state, despite what he'd done to her and allowed to transpire...and despite his not even being her father. But, he'd brought her up, looked after her, kept her safe in his castle and she felt a kind of fealty to him and his household. They may have all turned against her just now, thinking her a witch, but they were the only family she had.

"So, you're the little darling everyone's talking about," von Jungingen added with a whimsical smile to Vivianne's puzzlement. Who was calling her a *darling*? Certainly not her 'father'. And why were they all talking about her? Then von Jungingen's face tightened into a stern mask. "The baron promised me a new weapon," he snarled. "Where is it? Or did he imagine that also from the bottom of a wine pot?"

"No. He spoke truly," Vivianne defended.

"Ah..." von Jungingen glanced over at his companion with a snarling grin. "And what would a little girl know of that? You dress like a knight from the 1300s and carry a bastard sword." He leaned over to study it more carefully and Vivianne slid her hand from the pommel to the grip. "A rather decent one though." Then he straightened. "So, you think you're some kind of knight now?" He shook his head with a sneering smile. "The coward must be desperate indeed to use girls in his banner to do his dirty work."

"I'm not in his banner!" Vivianne retorted. "And he isn't a coward! He doesn't know I'm here!" She immediately regretted her outburst and knew that she'd committed a great error in her admission.

"Oh, a runaway?" He glanced again at Marschalk with an amused smile then returned a critical glance at her. This time he noticed the blood on her leggings and stared down. Vivianne followed his gaze to where the bandages had balled all the way down her breeches, bulging uncomfortably at the knee. As she looked down with renewed mortification, he seized her by the arm. She snapped her head up to meet his malicious gaze. "I have a mind to ransom you for that prize he promised me!" he said with malicious glee.

Realizing that she was in deep trouble, mainly because the baron did not possess any kind of prize for the *Hochmeister*—especially if Mortameur was dead—Vivianne kicked out. Her knee connected with his groin. She'd caught the *Hochmeister* off guard. He might have expected her to struggle but not to make such an offensive move. He bent over with a whining grunt and let go of her arm.

She bolted.

As his companion went to his aid, Vivianne snapped up her *bascinet* and threw it on. She leapt onto her horse from a dead run and kicked Willy into a gallop.

"Not me, you *lümmel*!" von Jungingen puffed. "Her! Get *her*!" the Hochmeister shrieked desperately. But Willy was eager and Vivianne plunged into the coolness of the marsh forest. Within moments she'd entered the muted silence of the swamp, losing any sign of pursuit.

She knew why; the swamp was treacherous and no one dared or could be bothered. Uta had fed Vivianne yarns of people drowning here in the flooded forest. Vivianne had discounted the gruesome stories as folktales to keep her from going there, but now, as she negotiated around oily black pools in slimy marsh grass and rotten-egg smelling mud she was inclined to believe them. She'd heard about the huge smelly sinkholes that lay beneath mats of fluorescent green algae, disguised as green swards. Once a man and his horse plunged into one of these, there was often no way of getting out. Like Lucifer's groping hands, the soft bottomless mud gripped you and sucked you down like desert quicksand. The more you struggled, the faster you went down to a gruesome death.

Vivianne guided her nervous steed through the skunky swamp, keeping to the hummocks as best she could. She had no idea where she must go, except to follow a vague vision of a place and a general direction. Her focus kept being disturbed by unruly and morbid thoughts. Thoughts of a twin brother she never knew she'd had…never did have. Oh, *Lieber Gott, I'm the one who should have died! And he should be here now*, she thought, lamenting his early demise. The baron would have been happier with a son. Mortague might have done well for himself if he'd survived instead of her. In the end, apparently, it had been sheer luck that she'd survived their mother's womb fever unscathed and not he. Would he have done what she had done? *And what have I done…*she pondered miserably. *I might have killed a man and ensured the death of the Teutonic Knights and their armies.* Père Daniel was right about her and a calamity. But he hadn't anticipated that she'd be its actual cause.

All at once she felt certain that the tear was somewhere near, very close-by, then grew dismayed when she could not recognize any landmarks. *And, why should I,* Vivianne scolded herself, *I've never been here before!* It was all in her over-active imagination, she lamented.

*What am I doing?* she thought in growing despair. *This is foolish and will achieve nothing!* She thought of going back to the castle to attempt another rescue of Wolfgang, but realized the futility of it; she'd only get caught and burned on the pyre in front of her insane father. She needed to escape into this land of her mother's and get some help before returning, she convinced herself. So, she pressed on, shivering, not from the cold—for it was quite warm—but from fear of failure. She instinctively slapped her chest, looking to feel her *ritterkreuz*, but couldn't find it through the buckskin mail and tunic. It was an omen.

Her ordered life had truly fallen apart. Vivianne thought of her imaginary knight; a cross between the praying knight in the *Glaßmalerei* and the fierce one she'd drawn in her illumination. There was no shining knight for her…perhaps no God either. Only magic and its evil followers. The thought brought her to *Père Daniel's* portent: on *the fourteenth hour of the fourteenth day of her fourteenth year in the fourteenth hundred year* a calamity would befall them all, which she would somehow carry. Then *Père's* prediction came to her in a blinding moment of realization: *a devenir ce que vous cherchez…to become that which*

153

*you seek...*She was truly alone: *she* was the knight she'd been searching for.

*Gott rette mich....*

Vivianne had settled into a kind of morbid despair in her plodding when bellows from where she'd come rang through the wet forest. She flinched and nearly slipped off the horse. It was a clarion call; they were pursuing her after all!

Her heart beat in her throat and she dug her feet into Willy, urging him to hurry.

She saw the mistake of her foolish haste too late and shrieked as the ground suddenly gave way in a sudden stench of rotten eggs. They plunged into a dark sinkhole. Willy whinnied out a desperate wail and they sank fast, submerging into a turbulent boil of pitch-black water.

Terrified, Vivianne's mind screamed as she gulped in murky water, *Oh, dear Mary, mother of Jesus! I don't want to drown!*

She thrashed toward where she thought the surface was. Then she spotted a bright light cutting through the darkness. A sudden stillness fell upon her...*your body is the temple of the Holy Spirit*...and she struggled toward the light, knowing it for the tear she'd visualized but could not recognize because it was underwater. She fell into it—

✠

There was a moment of excruciating pain, accompanied by a vision of unimaginable beauty and splendid wonder...Of a knight on a quest, wading through a swamp littered with the remnants of war...jeweled swords, discarded pollaxes and flails, all glinting in the eerie light, but no bodies. There was just a single knight, her knight...and yet she felt it was she doing the wading. Above her yawned the vaulted ceiling of an immense cathedral and through its ethereal 'walls' streamed a million golden threads of liquid light that kissed her face with heavenly song. Immediately before her shone a light so pure and deep it hurt her eyes to look upon it, though she could not stop herself. She lay suspended between life and death, between Jesus and

God as if carried by the Holy Spirit. *For one brief moment thou shalt see thy Lord...that sight of the Most Fair will gladden thee, but it will pierce thee too....*

Then she knew she was through, for she abruptly sailed easily, rushing through air rank with the stench of grease, sewage and smoke. She tumbled down. She heard her own wail: *"Lieber Gott, rette mich!"*

She was flying—no falling—through the air. She grazed a boy about her age, running down a dark street. She knocked him down. Then she landed hard on her back and head on unforgiving pavement. A sharp cracking pain stunned her and forced the breath out of her. She saw stars. She briefly glimpsed the boy through her vizor in a thick darkening film. His face looked vaguely familiar to her, framed by a wild mop of dark hair. Beneath those unruly wavy locks he flashed an animal's fierce gaze at her through intense brown eyes. His sensual mouth—made for laughing—wasn't laughing now. Then it came to her: he reminded her of the illumination she'd painted of her charming *ritter*. But this rude boy was anything but charming. He'd scrambled up and was shouting belligerently at her in French as she lay on her back, paralyzed with pain.

He waved his arms like a madman as he hurled his invective: *"Connard! Tu pourais m'a tué, petit con! Tas de merde! Cochon! Salot!"*

He wasn't in the least concerned for her welfare, she thought as she drifted slowly out of consciousness. Her mother had assured her that the tear would lead her to a kind savior. *Mary, mother of Christ! I've made a mistake.* It was her last thought as she slid into darkness.

✠

She drifted awake, or thought she did...to urgent whispers. She thought her eyes were open but she couldn't see. Was it the tear blindness her mother had warned her about in her letter? Or was she dead and this was Hell? Surely, she'd gone to Hell for what she'd done—killed or almost killed a man.

And what she hadn't done, she added, thinking of how she'd failed Wolfgang. Her helmet was being removed and the sharp pain returned. Did she cry out?...Then gentle hands lifted her head and slid the mail hood back. Her hair spilled freely out from its former confined state, awakening a deep throb that drew out a moan.

"*Tabernac!*" An older man's voice bellowed. "*C'est une fille!*"

"*Qu'est-ce qu'ons va faire?*" a young voice; the boy's?

"*l'amenes à ta place! Vites! Depeches toi, François! Et soi prudent! Elle est blesse! Regardes, elle saigne là.*"

They were speaking French very fast and it took her awhile to understand it. Then she felt herself being pulled and with a twinge of pain slid back into the blackness. When she awoke—still in darkness to a throbbing pain—she was lying on something not as hard as pavement but not much softer. She inhaled garbage and mold. Her arms and legs were being pulled this way and that; then she realized that she was being un-dressed. She was weak, disoriented and blind; struggling was futile, so she gave in.

"*Ah!*" the older voice exclaimed. "*Mon Dieu!*"

The boy stuttered out a giddy laugh and he said with forced casualness, "*Quoi? N'as tu jamais vu une fille nue, mon oncle?*"

"*Ha! Mettes tes yeux dans ta tête, François!*" the uncle reproved. No doubt the boy was staring despite his cavalier show. Then the uncle burst out, "*Mais, regardes...elle porte la marque. Elle est un Aeon!*"

"*Un quoi?*"

She had the sudden urge to vomit then blacked out.

✠

# Book Two: Illumination

"He who binds himself to a joy
Does the wingèd life destroy;
He who kisses the joy as it flies
Lives in eternity's sunrise."

—William Blake

## ...16
*Paris, France, 2010*

FRANÇOIS thrust his way through the thick crowd in Place de la Bastille. He craned to see the parade of greycoats and several blackcoats goose-stepping down the Boulevard de la Bastille and Rue Saint Antoine to converge at la Place. They were followed by heavy artillery that had begun its trek all the way from the Arc de Triumph and Avenue des Champs-Élysées. It was a great show of military power for the Nazis. Today was July the fourteenth, 2010: Bastille Day. In earlier times, the Porte St. Antoine was defended by a drawbridge and the Bastille. All that remained was a gilded statue of *liberté* in the center of the square to commemorate the culmination of France's long struggle to establish democracy with its final 'liberation' by the Nazis in the mid 1800s.

A clammy wind stirred up tiny dust tornadoes in the square and people flung up their hands to protect their faces from the flying grit. François watched them, like the pocket thief he was. There would be a few easily taken today.

He caught the eye of Philip, one of his neighbours on Rue des Rosiers and the best pick-pocket François knew. The lanky boy nodded to him with a look of surprised delight; he hadn't expected François to come. There were several dozen kids like he and Philip, scattered throughout *la Place*, poised to wreak havoc on the crowd at just the right moment. They were only a diversion for the real crime. François glanced briefly at the

*Banque de France* on the corner of Rue St. Antoine, then checked his watch. It was ten minutes to the hour. At 1800 the artillery would give its booming show; and at precisely that moment, masked under the cacophony of the blasting artillery, his anarchist friends inside the bank would blow the safe. They would make their getaway once chaos set in as people realized that they'd been robbed. *T'is a godlike thing to lend; to owe is a heroic virtue,* he thought with a smirk.

François's role in all this was very profitable though actually quite dangerous; he and Philip and the other pick pockets were placing themselves in the direct line of attention—and fire of the *flics*. Their safety lay in their scattered numbers, in their nimble feet, and their ability to negotiate the crowd and blend in when they wanted to. They were all kids, like him; mostly ten to sixteen year olds. They'd all lost their parents and other adult relatives to the Nazis.

Many of the middle class workers had lost their jobs and the will to live when the Nazis introduced efficient city bots and turfed people out of their rich homes. Left behind by dead, imprisoned, or conscripted mothers and fathers or simply abandoned by overworked uncaring parents, most children lived on their own in the streets of Paris with whole district slums devoted to the 'street brats'. François's parents had been killed in the Latin Quarter uprising of 2007. There were at least half a million "homeless" children, fending for themselves in the city, according to his uncle; all finding shelter in derelict huts and bivouacs. They were the discarded refuse of a series of purges by the fascist government.

Purges were not new to the empire. They'd begun hundreds of years ago with the Jews, who were pretty well extinct now, François considered. During the early development of the empire, Jews were massacred by the Teutonic Knights, who later became the strong arm of the new Reich as the feared Black Knights. But the purges weren't enough. Like an old building, the empire was crumbling from within through its own debauchery, and from the outside pressure of war and rebellion. The empire was at war with the Chinese and rebelling

Muslims to the east and dealing with the unruly British and upstart North Americans to the north and west. The two English-speaking countries had allied in rebellion against the Reich and were causing Fuhrer Hitler III no end of grief. It was eroding his empire, sucking it of funds, men, arms and resources. And bleeding it of morale as well as the pitifully little humor the Germans might have had in the first place. François saw its effect in the uncalled for cruelty meted out by the Black Knights and greycoats to his fellow Parisians.

Grand Marshal von Eisenreich seemed to call a purge almost weekly. First it was the restless students of the Sorbonne, then it was complaining workers in Nanterre. Then the school teachers of Lyon. Or transit workers in the Mont Parnasse area. No group or person was immune to their indiscriminate wrath. One day you were scorned for dressing in black; the next day for dressing in white. Something drastic would have to happen for it to right itself, his uncle kept saying. Luckily for some, von Eisenreich talked in his sleep and his light-sleeping wife, Lizette, listened. She, in turn, gossiped to François during their pillow talk and François then warned those intended victims through his uncle of the coming purge.

But all that was largely Antoine's concern and those in the *Résistance*, like Philip and André and most of the other children assembled here and poised to do mischief. They had a right to be skeptical of François's presence here. He did what he could, but only if it suited him. His motives weren't with the liberation of France. His motive was with the liberation of François.

Each for himself, he figured. *I come first*. That was the rule by which the government operated, he reasoned. *Why should I be any different?* Now take Sylvie, for instance, he thought, mind recollecting the thirteen-year old girl from the 12ème Arrondissement he'd left only moments ago; she gladly spread her legs for him anytime, anywhere for a cigarette or an apple.

There were no kids these days, François reflected as he caught sight of Collette, Alain and René, working the crowd. They were all shrewd midgets, who'd learned early in life to do what was necessary to survive according to the rules of the street. François was twelve when his parents were killed and members of his family pursued for their apparent allegiances to *le Societé Secrêt pour la Liberation de France*, the insurgent movement dedicated to destroying the oppressive Nazi Reich. Forced to take shelter in the anonymity of the streets, François did it so successfully that it took his uncle two years to find him. By then François had become very self-sufficient. He'd discovered, like his friend Sylvie, that sex was a commodity that he could sell, barter and buy and there were plenty of women and men—though he didn't like the men as much—who were eager to taste him.

Some, like Lizette, Colonel von Eisenreich's bored third wife, became regular patrons and kept him well fed, well powered and tech'd. Lizette, in turn, had taught him to be a consummate lover, introducing him to oral sex, among other things; he recalled how she'd first seized him by his wild mop and shoved his face into the furry place between her legs. She'd perfumed it with lavender and musk and it made him dizzy with desire. She'd talked him through the art of tasting her between her own sighs and moans of ecstasy. Then she'd arched and screamed her climax, startling him with a sense of incredible power.

He was a regular Valentino, François figured, and felt something stirring below. He grabbed his crotch and scratched his unruly penis with a leering smile. "Down, boy," he whispered with a grin. Lizette cooed over François like he was a doll and called him her sweet *putain*. *Baisses moi, mon putain...Tu as un beau cul....*He was her little darling peasant to dress...and undress. He didn't care; he could eat, and live half-comfortably on Rue des Rosiers because of her and other patrons like her. He had a running Pal with naughty vids of all his clients that he rented out to his street friends. And the girls on the street, like Sylvie, thought he was hot.

He jammed his hand in his jeans pocket and smirked at the silver Pal in his palm before re-pocketing it and pulling out a small innocuous-looking black package of *rapture*. They also called it the *black rabbit* because of the package and where it took you: through a fantastic black "rabbit" hole.

When his Oncle Antoine finally found him, he tried to get François away from all that. But Antoine was no better off, having been recently chased out of his own house by Black Knights who accused him of helping the anarchists. Antoine wasn't helping them...he *was* one, François thought with scathing humor. Antoine was always trying to recruit François to join the Résistance by berating him: "Why do you keep whoring? You're worth more than that. You're selling yourself, François. And for what? Half the time you don't even get money; just that stinking *rapture*..."

François rubbed the small black package of *rapture* between his fingers and felt his nose flare with desire. Stinking *rapture*, indeed. *You wouldn't think it was stinking if you tried it, l'Oncle!* He ripped the package open and threw his head back to pour the slightly acrid white powder in his mouth, then flung the wrapper onto the street. Within an instant, the street burst into sharper contrast and he knew his eyes dilated. A grin split his face open and he laughed, feeling invincible. Everything was all right now. Even those stinking Nazis with their swastikas, high-stepping black boots and batons...and whoring wives....

"You're the Nazi's *putain*. They've turned you into an addict and they've got you on a leash, François," his uncle had gone on. "Honestly, you should stop all that whoring."

"Why? And for what?" François had retorted, thinking he made a pretty good living by it; better than his destitute uncle. "Besides, I like it!" he'd ended maliciously. Antoine had lost all that he owned and now had less cash than François. "If I stop, what do I gain?"

"Something you've lost, François. Your dignity."

"My parents lost it for me when they joined *la Societé Secrêt* and got themselves killed for some lost cause," François said bitterly. To which his uncle had nothing to say. François knew it was cruel to say that; Antoine loved his brother, Marcel, and his wife, Angeline. Heck, Antoine had even dated François's mother before François's dad stole her heart. It had been

Angeline, in fact, who'd brought the two brothers into the Résistance in the first place. *She* was the original anarchist. She'd apparently been one of the founding members of the SSLF. Until joining the SSLF, Antoine had just been an unruly student, one of millions in France. Antoine never married and judging from the pictures he'd seen François thought that he'd shriveled up like a prune when Marcel married the only girl that Antoine had courted.

It was François who helped Antoine find a niche in the street community as a techno-salvager. His uncle was very good with computers, virtual tools and AI; he'd worked for years as a technician for *European Robotics Inc.* He could build anything from scrap. He and François finally made a deal: l'Oncle would build AI parts out of scrap that he found in the dumpsters and general refuse of the profligate city and give them to François in exchange for services rendered by the boy for the Résistance movement. Things like delivering and helping to distribute subversive pamphlets, helping with Pal broadcasts and other acts of sabotage. François didn't mind most of the time; he was usually able to get something for himself on the side. Like this little act of sabotage he was currently embroiled in, for example.

Except the Black Knights always seemed to know what they were up to. Every time the SSLF came up with a brilliant plan, something happened to thwart their efforts—

Gunshots exploded inside the bank. François caught Collete's stricken expression and Alain's confusion in the crowd. That wasn't supposed to happen. They were early—it wasn't time yet! Then the doors of *Banque de France* burst open and two of their colleagues spilled out, followed by flic who opened fire on them. They fell and the crowd scattered like flies. More flics emerged, aiming their weapons into the crowd.

François bolted. The two-tone sing-song siren of the *flics* rounded the corner. François ducked into a side street and ran. He wound his way down several lanes without stopping then eventually the lane that spilled out on the dilapidated, garbage-filled Rue des Rosiers and audibly sighed with relief. The rancid smell of stale oil, garbage and sewage cloyed in his nose with thoughts of home. Rue des Rosiers was a haven for rag-tag street people, beggars, thieves, misfits and artists. They crouched inside or squatted in front of their modest shanties of corrugated metal and old plaster; others lay in a drugged sleep on the sidewalk, huddled under musty blankets. The tiny shacks—and their decrepit occupants—all looked the same to an outside observer; François's was no different.

Still panting from his run, he forced himself to slow and nodded to a boy squinting at a canvas he was painting in the waning light. Patrice was an obsessive Renoir-wanna-be, who stole his paints so he could work on the same painting for two months.

"Salut," François called, trying not to look like he was in a hurry to dive into the safety and obscurity of his shack. As if sensing François's chase, the lanky thirteen year old nodded briskly and went inside.

After another fearful glance behind to ensure that no one was following him, François let a grin split his face open as he sprinted to his shack. What better way to hide a thief than among a crowd of thieves—

A sudden gust of wind swept in and something large abruptly appeared in mid-air in a dazzling blaze of light and raining water. An armor-clad figure, glittering silver, burst into being above him. A river of water flew out behind him like a waterspout.

The figure cried out in a girlish voice, *"Lieber Gott, rette mich!"*

Before Francois had a chance to veer, the figure collided into him, knocking him to the pavement. The man sailed on and landed in a hard bouncing thud and a grunt of pain.

Francois scrambled up and unleashed his terrified surprise—and relief that it wasn't a Black Knight's weapon that had caught him—by shouting a string of curses at the stranger: "Asshole! You could have killed me, you little prick! Pile of shit! Pig! Bastard!..."

The figure didn't move. Apart from his initial cry and startled grunt upon landing, the stranger made no sound. He just lay there on the pavement, limp. François crept forward to inspect the still figure. Apparently the man behind the armor was unconscious from the fall. It gave François a better chance to inspect him closely. He was dressed in awesome warrior garb: head entirely hidden by a full-vizored helmet, a splendid sword in a scabbard on a leather belt, glistening mail and a black tunic with an elaborate red dragon stitched on front. In spite of his cynical regard for most material things, François was impressed. His experience in antiquities was limited but something told him that what this person wore could fetch a great deal in the right market. His friend, Jacques, would drool.

After a swift appraisal of the darkening lane, François began to loot, starting with the sword and belt. Then he heard a telltale loping gait and wheezing breaths and glanced up to recognize the black rumpled leather jacket and red scarf of l'Oncle Antoine. His uncle had been waiting for François at his shelter and may have seen the whole thing. François swore under his breath. His opportunity for rare fortune had vanished; Antoine would not condone robbing an injured and likely innocent stranger, even one who had practically killed him. Besides, the stranger appeared to be waking up. As Antoine reached them, François heard him moan.

"What have you found, François?" Antoine whispered urgently. "Tell me what you saw."

"A blinding white light up there like lightening." François pointed above them. "And then this...*jerk* came hurtling toward me out of it."

"I saw the light shine the whole street briefly with a crackling sound," his uncle said in a low voice. Then he glanced furtively around him. François followed his glance; they were alone, well practically—a few huddled forms remained on the street, hibernating in a drugged stupor. His uncle bent down on one knee and checked the stranger's left arm. "He's just a boy," Antoine whispered, turning over the small hand of the stranger to expose the wrist; there was no ID tattoo. They exchanged a glance and Antoine raised a brow.

François turned his own hand over and checked the

seven-digit number indelibly marked on his wrist. Embedded just beneath it, hidden from view, lay his *Riech* DNA-GPS chip. Every citizen of the Reich had one; it was placed there when they were born and registered with the *Reich*. Why didn't this person have one?

Antoine struggled with the stranger's helmet. "Help me take this off."

"Are you sure we should do this, l'Oncle?" François said, standing up.

Antoine jerked his head around to glare at François. "Good God, boy! He's hurt. We must help him."

"But what if he's with..." François trailed off at Antoine's expression of disgust. There was nothing for it. The old man was a Samaritan and he was going to get them both into trouble. The stranger wore no *Reich* ID. That meant only a few things, and every one of them spelled trouble. But once his uncle got an idea into his head there was no stopping him, so François bent down and helped his uncle remove the stranger's helmet.

The stranger cried out again as they moved him—a girlish sound. And François knew why; as the helmet came off, he saw she was a girl. A pretty one. Her eyes weren't focused and he concluded that she was on the edge of consciousness. Could she see and understand them?

Antoine carefully lifted the girl's head and slid the mail hood back. Thick dark hair spilled out in waves of silk, except where it was matted with sticky blood. She moaned and her eyes sparkled with pain.

"*Tabernac!*" Antoine exclaimed. "It's a girl!"

"What should we do?" Francois asked, suddenly interested in the stranger.

"Take her to your place! Quick! Hurry up, François! And be careful! She's injured! See, she's bleeding there." He pointed to the dark blood stain where her upper right thigh met her other leg then he proceeded to pull her away from the middle of the alley. Francois saw the girl's eyes roll back as she passed out.

They managed to get her to his place without seeing anyone. Dusk was not a popular time to be out, unless you were a Black Knight or one of their spies, François reflected as he straightened from laying the girl down on his lumpy mattress.

"We need to undress her," Antoine said.

"What?" François said, recoiling with unreasonable fear.

"She's injured in the groin. It's one of the common injuries of a medieval knight—"

François started back in surprise and frowned. "A *what*?"

"She's dressed as a knight," Antoine said simply, as if that clarified it. "We need to check the rest of her body for injuries and see what needs to be done." Uncle Antoine had some knowledge in medicine. It had come in handy a few times already after a few skirmishes he and François had encountered in their clandestine anarchist dealings.

François nodded to his uncle. He straddled the mattress behind the girl's head and hooked his arms under her armpits then hoisted her into a sitting position so she was leaning with her back against his legs.

"It looks authentic!" Antoine said in a hushed but excited voice; there was little privacy on Rue des Rosiers and their voices carried in the night. But his excitement was getting the better of him. Stranded with his arms around the limp girl, François glanced askance at Antoine with an impatient glower as the old man's fingers lingered over the material. "Look at the splendid hand-embroidery on the tunic," Antoine went as François struggled on his own to get the girl's tunic off. "No one does that anymore. And this mail leather shirt..." He fondled the chain and leather outfit between his finger and thumb.

"Help me get it off her!" Francois bit out as the girl's head lolled forward onto her chest.

"Ah, sorry."

Antoine helped François remove the girl's sword and belt then the tunic and leather mail jerkin. As they struggled with the clothes, Francois whispered, more to himself than to his uncle. "Where'd she come from?"

Antoine replied, "The sky, Francois. The sky..."

"But why is she dressed as a medieval knight—"

The girl moaned awake in the midst of their removing her tunic and Francois winced, feeling guilty. Her head lifted and her eyes opened suddenly but they remained glazed and unfocused as she murmured strange confused sounds. Babbling. François glanced at his uncle with raised eyebrows. Antoine shrugged.

At Antoine's urging, Francois maneuvered around her so he faced the girl and straddled her thighs with his knees. Her glazed eyes were unfocused and her mouth slack, like she'd been drugged. Grabbing her by the shoulders, François gently pulled her head forward to lean on his chest. He was careful not to touch the place where blood had matted her hair. His uncle then pulled off her linen shirt. Francois blinked and stared down at her naked breasts.

"*Ah!*" Antoine gasped, looking at her from behind. "*Mon Dieu!*"

Francois released a nervous laugh and said with forced casualness, "What? Haven't you seen a naked girl before, Uncle?"

"You're one to talk. Put your eyes back in your head, François!" Antoine reproved then pointed. "But, look…she's got the mark. She's an Aeon!"

"A what?" François craned to see her bare back. He saw a dark rash that ran the length of her back.

The girl sighed and lost consciousness again.

Antoine instructed François to lower her down on the mattress again. Then the old man swiftly tugged off her leather mail leggings.

"Oh, dear…" Antoine muttered, gazing down at her.

François stared at her body. She was a thing of beauty—

"There, boy!" Antoine shook him from his reverie and François saw what his uncle saw: dark crusts of dried blood and smears of new crimson blood coated the inside of her legs.

François gasped. "*Merde*! She's been cut—"

"No, you idiot!" Antoine reproved, smacking the boy's head with his open hand. "She's menstruating…I think. It's pudendal blood. I don't see a wound."

They glanced at one another. "Then why isn't she wearing...eh...protection?"

"How should I know?" Antoine retorted back uneasily. Then he bent down to inspect the leggings. "She *was*. At least, a makeshift version." Using a finger and thumb as pincers he pulled out the blood soaked linens that had migrated down her leg. Then he smiled like a boy who'd found a stash of candy. "Very curious. *Very* curious!" He tapped his lips in nervous excitement with his wrinkled hand. "She was running away...."

"How do you know that?"

Antoine didn't answer as he carefully inspected the girl's crotch to make sure his prognosis was right and she wasn't truly injured there.

Francois pressed on, "Running away from what Halloween party?"

"A medieval one," Antoine replied, looking up with a smirk and covering the girl's lower body with François's only blanket. "Women in that time would have remained in bed during their period. It was considered unclean." He frowned at the blanket. "Like this blanket." He leaned down and sniffed then made a sound of disgust. "Don't you *ever* wash things around here?" He shook his head as if to clear it then continued, "Anyway, she was not only out and about but wearing a knight's—or squire's—trappings, more befitting a boy. With a few odd exceptions, there were no women knights."

"You're not making any sense." Francois frowned. Antoine was talking as though this girl had actually travelled a millennium from medieval time to collide into him. Sure. He smirked at his uncle, then grew uneasy as he thought of that eerie flashing light.

"Here." Antoine passed François the girl's linen shirt and removed the dirty blanket with a sound of disgust. "Stuff that up her crotch. It's cleaner than that maggot-filled smelly thing of yours. We can wash it later." François accepted the shirt with a bewildered look. The old man was enjoying all this. "It'll staunch the flow for now until I bring back some protection." Antoine bounced around the room in excitement. "Listen, she probably has a mild concussion. But the bleeding has stopped. It's all matted in her hair, which helped it clot. Let her lie still and she'll probably wake up in a few hours. Don't let her go anywhere." He turned with sudden inspiration to the knight's trappings piled on the floor. "Hide those, so she can't leave. I'll fetch some proper clothes for her. We must keep this a secret!"

François blinked at his uncle, standing at the makeshift door, then settled his gaze on the naked girl.

Catching the boy's mesmerized stare, Antoine laughed in a loud bark then used François's own line: "What? Haven't you seen a naked girl before?"

"She's...different," François blurted out, jerking from his stare to face his uncle.

Antoine laughed again. "Glad to see that despite your line of work, the female form hasn't lost its particular appeal...or mystique." With that remark his uncle took the opportunity to let his gaze linger appreciatively down the girl's naked figure. Then he sighed and left to fetch the girl some street clothes and other sundries.

François frowned to himself. He didn't really know why he thought her different, except that she was. Of course, there was the bleeding obvious...ha, good pun, he thought to himself with wry amusement. The strange markings on her back, her abnormal dress, lack of protection, and lack of *Reich* ID certainly marked her as a foreigner, not to mention her atypical entrance in a crackling flash of light. Though, to look at her—especially this way—she was a normal looking girl. She was a little more filled out than the anorexic girls in his neighborhood, but still slender. He'd seen plenty of naked girls and women, most with better looking bodies too—the girl's breasts were too small, he abruptly decided—but none as interesting. Except for the purple marks on her back, her creamy soft skin was unblemished, supple and the color of an angel's. Dark waves of unkempt brown hair cascaded over her shoulders like a river of soft silk. When he'd carried her to his shelter, François had caught the faint but heavenly scent of lavender and pears in her thick hair.

His gaze settled on a small gold necklace around the

girl's neck. The arms of the silver cross that hung off the necklace were slightly flared at their ends, like an iron cross, and each arm was studded with jewels. He bent closer: sapphires and diamonds, by the look of them. Then his eyes narrowed as he recognized the cross: it was the cross of the Black Knight! What was this girl doing with a Knight's Cross? His nervous hands drifted over the cross pendant. It would fetch several good meals and maybe even an upgrade to his Pal—

The girl emitted a low moan and stirred.

François jerked back, then lurched forward to shove the girl's linen shirt between her legs as he'd been instructed and stepped back again, staring. She remained silent. François crossed his arms over his chest and watched her in brooding silence. Who...what was she? Where did she *really* come from? He settled into a cross-legged sit on the dirty blanket on the floor by the mattress and studied the girl. He rocked gently, watching her as if hypnotized.

His uncle soon returned with supplies, including sanitary napkins, a pair of girl's jeans, briefs, a black beret, sandals, an olive green tank top and a black cotton cardigan. François had long ago stopped asking where his uncle got all the stuff he usually came up with; he didn't want to know. But he was curious how the old man had found these savory clothes so quickly. He eyed his debonair uncle; was Antoine a cross dresser?

Antoine glanced at the girl, resting quietly on the mattress. "She looks better," he noted. "Some color has returned to her face."

François nodded but hadn't actually noticed that detail.

"Help me get this on," Antoine said, fingers awkwardly fumbling with the sanitary napkin package.

François recoiled and threw up his arms with a shake of his head. "That's your department. *You're* the medicine man."

Antoine laughed uneasily. "*You're* the lover!"

François pressed his lips together in stubborn determination.

"Okay, okay," Antoine grumbled. "Make yourself use-

171

ful, then, and get me some water and a cloth…A *clean* cloth!"

François leapt at the chance to get away. There was a public fountain with plenty of clean water that most of the street people here availed themselves of. He found a cloth hanging off the pail by the door of Thibaut's hut. When he returned with his pitcher of water and a not so clean cloth, Antoine snatched it with a frown. François watched in morbid fascination as his uncle set to wiping the girl's bloody thighs then slid on the briefs and protection.

When it came to dressing her, François gladly helped and within moments she was transformed into a normal Parisian girl. A rather good-looking one, François decided with an appreciative smile. Antoine had ingeniously found a top that was sufficiently low cut in the front to be alluringly revealing yet with a high enough backline to conceal her strange markings.

"I must go," Antoine said finally, drawing François's gaze from the girl. "I have two comsets to deliver to Etienne Farigoule and I haven't even started assembling them yet." He glanced at the girl. "When she wakes up, she'll be woozy and may even get sick. If she can't stop vomiting then it's bad; if she doesn't wake up soon it's bad too. Either way we should take her to the hospital. But I think she'll be fine. She seems on the verge of waking. I checked her vitals and her eyes. Her heartbeat is regular and she doesn't have a skull fracture or contusion. When she's able, call me and bring her to *Café Toujours* in Place Sainte Michel," he commanded. "Tell her to put on that beret; it'll hide the bloody mess on her head." Then he pointed emphatically at François and added sternly, "Take the métro and stop no where else in-between, understand?"

François nodded to his uncle then watched him leave. He'd never found out where his uncle had finally found accommodation after he'd lost his house. They always met in some café, park or square. Antoine still had a lot of secrets. François shrugged, then let his gaze stray to the girl's backpack and smiled like a fox in a hen coup.

✠

# ...17

FRANÇOIS squatted over the girl's backpack and rummaged. He found the oddest assortment of things. He pulled out mostly books, which he laid aside without reading their titles. There were several vials of common antibiotics—did she have some girly infection or was she just overly prepared? He could make some good money selling these; antibiotics were hard to come by and highly valued in the slum community. But François decided to be magnanimous and save them for his uncle. He stashed the vials in his little hiding place beneath his fake upraised floor then returned eagerly to the pack. He pulled out a few burlap sacs filled with smelly herbs that he dropped to the floor then fished for more valuables. He found a leather cardholder, which contained an ID with le *Banque de France* and a virtual map and year-pass for the métro. Bingo! Smiling like a wolf, he jammed the holder with the cards into his pocket then greedily thrust his hand back into the pack. He felt something silky smooth, cold and hard—

He drew in a sharp breath. She had a Pal! François yanked the slim data-communicator out of the pack and turned it over in his hand. A grin split his face. The Pal was in mint condition. His was battered, scratched and old. François stabbed a button for the menu and the screen lit up with the picture of a handsome gentle-faced man with square features, probably in his thirties. Some relative or friend, no doubt, he surmised. Then he noticed—Good Christ!—This was the latest version of Pal— the one that ran on localized EMP with the latest upgrade and apps! He fingered his way deftly through her latest communications and whereabouts registered on the Pal's GPS and found that she'd last been where he'd collided with her. Her last ten communications, several days ago over the space of a few hours, had all been with a Julien Boulanger, numero 23345. François tapped the GPS and let his eyebrows rise at what he saw: Boulanger lived at 22 Rue Cortot.

Christ! That was Renoir's old studio on the hill of Montmartre. This once cheap bohemian section of town was now a wealthy residential center and an almost exclusive area for Nazi officers. Why would this girl know someone who lived there? Was this rich guy the person she'd run away from? And a Nazi officer? Was he the same guy as the man pictured on her Pal? Was she his slave? Or his concubine?...He didn't look like the type. And neither did she, François thought with a glance at the unconscious girl. Then again, they never did look the part, François decided. With a deft flick of his finger, he opened the last few messages that had passed between them:

It was Boulanger first: *Come to your senses, cherie! Why run away? It won't solve anything. And in your state! You're not well. Come back. I beg of you. I'll take care of you. I've kept you safe from the awful world all this time, haven't I?*

The girl's answer came next: *You can't forever. Don't try to stop me. I have to go, for both our sakes. Before he finds out. Don't look for me. You won't find me.*

Then Boulanger's ominous response: *But he will.*

The communications ended there. *In her state...*what did Boulanger mean by that? Was the girl crazy? Was he her keeper after all? Were they involved in some illicit liaison? Was she pregnant?

After a swift glance at the unconscious girl, he slid the Pal into his jeans pocket then replaced the books and smelly sacs in the backpack and returned to her side. François studied the girl's passive face, so innocent...out of place...and kind of sweet. She was no concubine, he decided. More like his prisoner...his ward, maybe his niece or something. François brushed a wayward lock of hair from her face and stared on. She was an odd case: dressed in authentic medieval knight's trappings, complete with functional sword; not protected, though obviously in the middle of her menstrual cycle. It betrayed a naïveté and lack of sophistication contrary to her possession of both wealth—a bank card from *le Banque de France* was hard to come by—and the most current technology. Or was it because of a sudden haste in fleeing. Who was chasing her besides this Boulanger guy? Without a *Reich* ID tattoo, she wouldn't have gotten very far in Paris. So, what was she doing here? And where *did* she come from?...*the sky*, Uncle Antoine had said.

He found his hand hovering over her necklace again. In a rush of fear, he had it in his hand and unleashed a predatory grin—then met her dark piercing gaze—and flinched. She'd just awoken and had raised her head to aim a look of suspicious accusation at him.

François gave her a shaky laugh. "You should hide that," he quipped and tried to tuck the pendant underneath her low cut tank top. It was cut too low and his hand brushed against the swells of her breasts. He blushed. "Someone's liable to snatch it right off your neck," he added giddily. He straightened and stepped back from her.

The girl gave him a look of obvious distrust but he thought she at least understood what he said. Her earlier half-German half-gibberish, hadn't given him any confidence that she would, although her perfect French text messages with Boulanger belied that. She raised herself on her elbows and after briefly casting her eyes around his meager place, she glanced down at the clothes she wore then blinked up at him in inquiry.

"Wo *sind meine Sachen*—eh..." She looked confused for a moment and shook her head as if to clear it then looked as though she wished she hadn't. She closed her eyes for a moment and placed her hand on her head, fingers gently probing the matted mess of dried and sticky blood that, in truth, neither he nor his uncle had done anything with. François was sure she was suffering from one pounding headache. Then she looked up and said in slow and deliberate French, "Where are my things?" She sat up in a jerk, ignoring her pain and dizziness, and looked around with sudden urgency. "*Meine*—eh—my pack?"

"It's okay," he assured her, relieved that she spoke French. It carried a slight accent but was otherwise very good. "Look, it's all there. See." He pointed behind him, worried now about what he'd already taken, which was burning a hole in his pocket. He quickly thought up a ruse; someone else must have stolen those things before he'd found her lying in the middle of the lane. "There's your pack." He didn't offer to bring it to her. "And your clothes are in a safe place. My uncle gave you those so you'd blend in. You looked a little out of place dressed as a medieval knight." He offered her a lame smile.

She seemed to understand most of what he said and calmed down to his relief, although her gaze remained guarded. François didn't fancy dealing with a hysterical female. Sylvie's ringing shrieks of condemnation had already given him a headache today. He watched the girl give his place a good look. He'd built his shack from sheets of corrugated metal, rebar, paving stones and old plaster; cemented with the refuse and decay of an oppressive government. It had no windows, unless the large tear left from a street fight that had invaded his place counted. It leaked like a sieve when it rained. But it was home. He'd wall-papered the ugly utilitarian walls with old posters from the May 68 riots that he'd found during a raid. François knew she was reading them and followed her gaze.

One had a stereotypical silhouette of General de Gaulle with his hand over a youth's mouth. The slogan read: *Sois jeune et tais toi*. Another read: *Lisez moins, vivez plus*. She perused each one: *Be realistic, ask for the impossible*; *Poetry is in the street*; *Power to the Imagination*. Her gaze lingered thoughtfully on the slogan that read: *Forgive, but never forget*. She narrowed her eyes and frowned at the last one: *Neither God nor master*!

Just as François started to relax he noticed the girl's sudden look of panic as her eyes darted down at herself. He knew exactly what she was thinking and glanced at the bag of sanitary napkins on the makeshift table beside her.

"It's okay," he assured her, pointing to the bag and annoyed at himself that he was blushing. Damn! Why wasn't his uncle here when he really needed him? "You're wearing one of…those."

She obviously didn't understand.

"It's a pad…for your…eh…period…" God! How could

she not know about these things? Didn't she have a mother? "To catch the blood. You've got your...eh...period, don't you?"

"Period?" she echoed, still totally clueless.

God! He felt like he was being pulled down a fucking black hole. "Eh...when you bleed every month—"

"Ah!" she exclaimed and blushed. She finally got it.

"Girls here wear those pads or something like it so they can get around. And they keep replacing them as they need to...." he trailed, feeling his face heat to the color of hers.

For a very long awkward moment they stared at one another, both fiercely blushing. Then she offered in a soft voice, "*Danke*...eh...thank you." She studied the package to avoid looking directly at him and seemed compelled to explain herself: "Where I come from we usually stay in bed. This is ingenious—"

"So where *are* you from," he cut her off and jammed his hands nervously in his pockets, stroking her Pal in one of them. The question had been genuinely on his mind since she'd literally dropped in on him like an alien from some other dimension.

She seemed to pull inside herself at his question. "I'm...from...." She hesitated, reluctant to tell him, and turned the question around. "Where is this place?"

He nodded in acquiescence. "Fair enough. I'm François and this is my place. It's not much." He thought of Boulanger's place on Nazi hill and blushed with shame. "But it's mine," he ended in triumph.

"And where is your place, François?" she asked demurely. She'd cleverly maneuvered the subject of their conversation back to him, François reflected.

He gave her a casual grin. "You're on Rue des Rosiers, in the 4ème Arrondissement."

"You mean...." she hesitated, hand straying to the cross below her neck. "... in Paris?...*France*?"

He stared at her. Didn't she know where she was? Maybe she really *had* dropped from the sky. Or that bump on her head had removed some of her brain cells, François decided. Maybe that Boulanger guy had locked her up for a good reason.

Or was Boulanger a slave-trader? He wrinkled his brow and gave her a skeptical smile, remembering the flash of light. "You're really not from here, are you?"

She shook her head with a guarded smile then straightened and introduced herself, "I'm Lady Vivianne Schoen, Baronesse von Grunwald."

He wanted to laugh but realized she was dead serious and obviously unaware of the strange image she'd just presented him with. Although what she'd said sounded pretentious, she didn't seem that way; or he would have given her an earful. Instead he said, "Now that's a mouthful. How about I call you Vivianne." It was a French name, at least. But he was sure he'd heard her speak German at first. Her last name sounded German. Her French, albeit very good, was flavored with the slightest foreign accent and some of the words she chose were rather antiquated.

"All right." She gave him her first friendly smile. He felt it glow on his own face.

They faced one another in awkward silence for a few moments until François, trying to be friendly, broke it with a question, "Are you hungry? I've got some fresh apples." He'd offered them to her as much to simply get away from her earnest gaze as to share his stolen booty. "Here." He brought out two juicy apples and handed her one. She accepted it and took a hungry bite. François smiled with amusement and wondered when she'd last eaten. He decided to be blunt: "Why don't you have a *Reich* ID? Are you a runaway or something?" With a name like 'Lady Vivianne' and the title of 'Baronesse'—not that he for a moment believed her—he was sure that she must be in some kind of trouble. He felt entitled to know, François reasoned to himself, since she was taking shelter in his shack.

But the girl clammed up; she averted his eyes and ate quietly, chewing slowly, and stared at the floor with a slight frown of deep contemplation. He wasn't getting anywhere with her, François thought, growing frustrated. And here he'd shared his precious food with her!

As if to make up for her earlier reserve, the girl looked

up with another affable smile and said, "My teacher, Father Daniel, lived in the Rive Gauche of the Seine River, when he studied at the Sorbonne."

"He probably lived in the Latin Quarter, then," François added then suddenly wondered with dread: was she a Catholic? The Nazi *Reich* had reduced that once powerful religious order to a small cult, often persecuted and at best tolerated. That might explain the girl being a fugitive—if she was Catholic, that is. He hadn't yet established her status thanks to her unreasonable reticence. Maybe if he offered her something, he'd get something back. He said, "We're in the Marais, on the Rive Droit; it's one of the oldest intact pre-revolutionary parts of Paris…"

"We are?" She instinctively cast a skeptical glance at her surroundings, as though wondering if she'd strayed rather into some noble's dungeon. "Isn't the Marais where the nobility live?"

So, she did know something of Paris. Only she was two hundred years out of date. François laughed, following her critical gaze at his slummy hovel. "Yeah, funny isn't it? Now it's the biggest slum in Paris. You might be thinking of Montmarte, up on the hill, there." He pointed to the north. "That's where all the rich and powerful live." *Like your old sugar daddy,* he thought to himself. It gave François smug pleasure to know that his *quartier* was located in the shadow of one of the exclusive Nazi officer residential parts of town. "The Marais is our working class quarter too," François went on, feeling like a tourist guide, "mostly cheap shops, artisan studios, and scummy housing like this." He shrugged, not wanting to apologize, but feeling like he should.

"Le Marais," she repeated quietly, looking away in contemplation. When she met his gaze again, her eyes sparkled with excitement. "Is it near the Notre Dame Cathedral or Saint-Chapelle?"

"No, they're on Ile de la Cité." Deciding to change the subject, François added, "Do you feel well enough to get up and see a little of Paris?"

She wrinkled her brow in contemplation then nodded

with an eager smile. "Yes, I'd like that."

"Good," he replied. He thought of what his uncle had said to him. "Because my Uncle Antoine would like to meet you. He knows a lot so you might like to talk to him. I think we all want some answers, you included, right?"

She swallowed what she was eating and nodded. "Yes, I'd very much like to meet your uncle."

"Good," he said, curbing a frown; she appeared more eager to see his uncle than he'd expected for someone who'd barely shared two words about herself with him. "Try to get up. My uncle told me you might still feel a bit dizzy from your head injury. So take it slow."

She understood. Firming her lips with effort, the girl slowly raised herself to her bare feet and stood up as François got beside her, ready to catch her if she fell. She was tall, almost his height, François conceded. How was it, François thought rather peevishly, that l'Oncle Antoine had guessed her size so well? And found such savory clothes for her in such a short time?

François pulled out his Pal and made a call to his uncle, turning his back to the girl while she stared at him in curiosity. He cupped a hand over his mouth and used a hushed voice so she wouldn't hear him. Then he texted Jacques with particulars of his new stash. After a furtive glance at the girl, he sent three pictures that he'd taken earlier of her knight's gear.

She looked confused. "Were you…talking to someone?" she asked, once he'd shoved his Pal back into his jeans pocket. "There's no one in the room…"

He barked out a sharp laugh. Surely she knew about Pals—She *had* one! And had obviously used it. François let his brows come together and studied her for a sullen moment without replying. What kind of game was she playing?

"Let's go," he said tersely. François showed her the sandals Antoine had provided her and she slipped her feet into them then gingerly put on the black beret to cover her messy head injury. As François went to douse the oil lamp, she put on the sweater, even though it was too hot to wear one, then pulled on her pack. At the last minute, she dashed back to retrieve the package of protection and stuffed it in her pack. Smart move, François thought.

They emerged into the gusty darkness of Rue des Rosiers, and François caught the girl wrinkling her nose at the complex street smell that assaulted them in the warm breeze. It was just the comforting stench of old cooking: over-used grease, fried scrap meat and cabbage. It made him hungry. *No clock is more regular than the belly*, he thought with a wry smile. It seemed to have the opposite effect on the girl.

✠

# ...18

THE wind had picked up and François looked up at the dark night clouds. A storm was coming, he thought and glanced at the girl. The wind played with her hair, whipping it across her face in teasing gusts. With an elegance he wasn't used to seeing in a local girl, she seized her thick long mane and coiled it to tuck under her beret. Before he realized it, their eyes met and he nodded to her in appreciation.

As he led her down the filthy cobble-stone lane, François observed a new edge to the girl. Her head kept turning slightly from side to side, tossing sharp glances around, as if looking for someone and listening attentively to the sounds of the city. He watched her listen with narrowing eyes as she tried to decipher the repetitive sing-song klaxon of distant sirens that came and went with the wind.

"*Les flics*," François offered. "Black or gray coats roaming the city, looking for prey." She stared at him with a blank look. Obviously his words of explanation were equally obtuse to her.

For the first few times, when a plane rumbled overhead, she cringed slightly and looked up as if expecting some shrieking monster to swoop down on them. She was clearly nervous. It made him nervous. Then he remembered her cross pendant and felt the back of his neck prickle. What if she was somehow connected with the Black Knights? Was this Boulanger guy a Black Knight and was she spying for him? Was taking her to l'Oncle Antoine a mistake? No, that was stupid, he decided. If the girl *was* spying for the Black Knights she wouldn't be wearing that cross. That would be dumb; and she certainly wasn't dumb.

They picked their way along the cobble alleyway littered with garbage and rubble. Shanties and huts like his lined either side of the narrow lane like rip-rap. They were mostly one-person hovels, erected with corrugated pieces of dead buildings and daubed with garbage and sundries. The chaotic blend of slum aromas gusted at them in a cloying mixture of kerosene, old cooked meat, stale wine or vomit and urine. François noticed that the girl stuck pretty close to him. She betrayed nervousness by touching her cross pendant as she glanced from side to side, looking for occupants in the shadows. Where a few lamps flickered they could make out the odd huddled form and could hear the complicated murmur and sighs of the slum.

Trying to help her relax, François pointed to the various shanties and described the more colourful occupants. That neighbour for instance, he pointed to a well-thatched hut, was a mean old man in his seventies who spoke to no one and seldom left his hut. His name was Vincent Rouard and he used to be a drug lord with the notorious gang *les Foux de Paris*. "He dealt particularly in *rapture* and *crystal D*—nasty stuff," François went on. "According to slum myth, Rouard is actually filthy rich. During a huge drug deal a colleague ratted on him to the Black Knights. But they never found the stash and had to let him go. Apparently he's kept under surveillance and even though he still has those millions of Euros he doesn't show He lives here in the slum, where no one can touch him. Rumour is he has the best high tech stuff inside like a Reuental VC entertainment system.

But no one's ever been inside…and come out, that is. According to Patrice, the old man snatches and eats children." The girl had cringed initially at this part then quickly gave François a glaring smile for his tease.

"What about that place?" She pointed to a small mud hut with a tiny raised garden plot crowded with aromatic lavender flowers.

"Oh, that's Crazy Annette," he said. "She's one of the old folk on our street, like Rouard."

"Old folk?" the girl echoed.

"Older than eighteen. Annette used to be a fashion designer with Jean Paul Gaultier on Rue Saint-Martin. Then they came to her house and shot her husband and twelve-year old son right in front of her for apparently plotting against the Reich." He made a whistling sound with puckered lips and twirled his finger around his head. "She lost it and ended up here."

The girl looked suddenly miserable. "That's so sad."

"Yeah," François said gloomily. "Life's sad."

She jerked her head to flash him an intense look of reprove. François avoided her eyes.

After some silence, the girl turned to him with a wistful smile. "This place is rich with wonderful herbs."

François followed her gaze to the plants growing along the roadside and in the pavement cracks. "You mean the weeds?" he smirked.

"They are natural medicines." She met his eyes with stern honesty. "That one helps to disinfect wounds and staunch bloodflow." She pointed to a small yellow-flowered plant that sprang between the pavement. "That one there is soothing against burns." She pointed to the common plantain weed.

At one of the street corners a hunched form dressed in jeans and a black t-shirt abruptly approached them. François felt the girl briefly tense but she otherwise kept her cool. It was only Luc, one of his neighbours.

"Got a cigarette?" the boy said in a gravelly voice. He threw glances at the girl. "New chicklet, eh?"

François gave him a wry smile and avoided looking at the girl. She wasn't his chicklet, but he wasn't about to tell Luc that. "Here," François said, producing a pack of *Gaulois* from his back jeans pocket, and pulled two cigarettes out. He lit both then handed Luc one, noticing the girl staring with curiosity as Luc drew in a deep appreciative breath then sighed out a column of smoke. It coiled over his shoulder and dissipated into the darkness. The girl caught a breathful and coughed.

Luc kept looking at the girl, sizing her up. It made François nervous.

"*Beau cul,*" Luc finally said, taking another long draw on the cigarette and casting wolfish eyes on the girl. She felt it and shuffled her feet nervously. She had a right to be nervous; Luc was a bastard when it came to women...come to think of it, he was a bastard when it came to anything, François amended.

"Catch you later," François said, grabbing the girl's hand to pull her away, and turned to go.

Luc closed the space between them. "*Je te donnerais dix Francs a me faire foutre la connaise...*" He leaned out to touch her. She might not have understood his vulgar French but she certainly understood his vulgar intentions and shrank back from him with a look of revulsion.

"Maybe later," François said. He pulled her away to his opposite side, placing himself between Luc and the girl.

Sensing possessiveness, Luc shrugged. "That new, huh? Okay, my friend. Later...*ciao!*"

François lifted his hand to wave goodbye without looking back.

They walked quietly and the girl stayed close beside him.

"What's a chicklet?" she finally asked, not looking his way, and keeping her eyes straight forward, like she knew it wasn't a complimentary thing to be called a chicklet and was sparing him her *look*: that dangerous penetrating gaze that cut through his bullshit and stirred his heart with gallant thoughts.

"Just a name for a girlfriend," François lied. He wasn't going to tell her that it meant she was his little whore to rent out.

A whore for a whore. He felt sudden shame. This girl was a lady. Even in jeans and tank top, she looked like one; the way she held herself, her dignified stature and gait, her confident gaze. It was obvious to even Luc, an ignorant street bum, that she wasn't your everyday street girl and he was willing to pay for it. She wasn't like Sylvie. Not even like Lizette, who would have been a street girl if she wasn't the field marshal's wife.

When they reached the entrance to Rue Vieille du Temple, the girl recoiled with a repressed gasp and clutched her cross. It took François a moment to figure out what had spooked her. Then he realized it was the traffic; cars and mopeds on the streets and rushing city bots on the sidewalks. Moving machines, especially the ones with people inside them, had her cringing back with a stare. François wanted to laugh. He did, in fact, and noticed her look of mortification. But it worked; she swallowed down her fear and quickly rallied her composure with a long breath.

"They're just cars," he said. "We use them to get around. Don't you travel?"

"Yes," she answered. "By horse."

"By horse," he repeated. Right....

She followed close behind him as he skirted around the city robots and crossed the street. How could she be so ignorant of everyday life? Perhaps that Boulanger guy had really kept her shut up all this time in his house; she wasn't wearing an ID tattoo. She had lived a very sheltered—and illegal—life.

Once on the other side, François headed south but had to stop when he noticed that the girl wasn't beside him; she'd remained at the corner, staring wide-eyed at the street sign. When he went back, she turned to him with breathless excitement. "This is where Louis de Valois, the Duke d'Orleans, was ambushed then brutally assassinated while he was mounting his horse."

François glanced from her to a pair of lovers walking down the street. "This street?" he said, forcing down a scowl.

"His murderers cut off his left hand for fear he would raise the devil with it and his brains were knocked out onto the road. Jean de Bourgogne, the regent of the royal children of Charles the Mad, later confessed to ordering it."

It bothered François that she knew this obscure historical fact about his own arrondissement. He took pride in knowing the history of Paris and the Marais, in particular. And how could she know this yet not know anything about cars and city bots? To his awkward silence, she added, "It was basically a feud between Louis and Jean over who should be the regent of France and guardian of the children of Charles VI."

François quickly did the math. That was six hundred years ago, he thought. "You know a lot about this place..." he said, managing to keep the petulance out of his voice.

"Father Daniel told me all about it."

"...that was around the time of the Hundred Years War, wasn't it?" François said off-handedly, hoping to impress her.

She looked at him with a blank face. "Hundred Years War?" Like she'd never heard of it.

François wrinkled his nose at the girl. How could she know this incredible detail and not know it took place during the Hundred Years War?

"Well, your Father Daniel sure knows his history," he said and saw her wrinkle her brow at what he'd said.

"History? But it was only three—"

François shrugged and brusquely directed them south to Rue Saint Croix de la Bretonnerie. He thought he heard the girl say 'three years ago' but decided he'd heard wrong. In any case, the girl didn't pursue her thought because François led her into the bustling pedestrian street full of shops, crowded cafés and boisterous bars. Spotting a few grey-coats, François wove a zig-zag path across the cobble street past several boulangeries, poissoneries, an aromatic fromagerie, charcuterie, tabac and other shops with brightly colored awnings and displays. Sidling close to the pastry display at a pâtisserie, he boldly stole two meat croissants then hurried the girl on, past two grey-coats. The grey-coats, hands resting on their side-arms, never noticed them; they were too busy watching and laughing as two girls successfully solicited their colleague in one of the cafés.

Once safe in the milling crowd, François pulled the warm croissants out from under his t-shirt and handed the girl one of them.

She studied the croissant he held out to her with puzzled suspicion. "Did you bring that from your place?"

François grinned and bolted the still warm pastry in silence. The girl was pretty naïve, he thought, watching her finally accept the pastry and gratefully eat in rather less dainty mouthfuls than he'd expected for a 'lady'. She probably hadn't eaten in a while, he realized, remembering how she'd devoured the apple he gave her. And judging from her slim figure, she wasn't that much of an eater to begin with.

As they continued down the seedier part of the lane, François recognized more people loitering in front of 'apartment' doorways. Girls and boys, mostly his age. Street brats, the grey-coats called them. Rue Saint Croix de la Bretonnerie was, like Pigalle, known for its sex market, particularly of youth. Kids, like himself and younger. François had picked up a few of his clients here.

François was rather known in these parts and had to fend off several suggestive gestures for his attention. He noticed that most of it was beyond the girl, who was quite unaware of the attention she was attracting from both the boys and girls. The grey-coats he'd seen were actually here on duty, to watch for illicit goings on. They were supposed to arrest any illegal youths partaking in sexual favors or selling *rapture* on the street; instead the grey-coats partook of both themselves. Now, if they were black-coats—Black Knights—that would have been another matter François thought, ignoring the air-kisses a young man was making to him.

"Is he a friend of yours?" the girl naively remarked. François didn't bother to answer her. "This place is very friendly," she continued, watching the girls, dressed in short skirts, halters and too much make up as they leaned seductively against the walls of the buildings. She caught one of them in a direct gaze. It was Dominique, one of his neighbours on Rue des Rosiers. The girl smiled.

Dominique sidled up next to them and rubbed up against the girl suggestively. "How do you want it?" she asked the girl, who looked confused.

François guffawed. "Get lost, Dominique! She's not a les like you."

Dominique huffed and frowned at the girl, looking her up and down. She made a loud phfft sound of disgust with her lips. "Bitch, then. *Con* tease." Then she made an obscene gesture with her finger.

As François dragged the girl off, she glanced back in agitated confusion. "Why did she say that to me?"

"You're not supposed to smile; it means you're interested. Don't you know anything?" he hissed out, letting out his simmering frustration in a long breath. "God! You're so stupid!"

That remark silenced her and for a moment he regretted his sharp outburst and the words that he'd used. But not enough to apologize. They continued in silence until well out of the busy commercial part of the lane and more into the quiet residential part.

"I never had the chance to walk in a city like this before." The girl looked up at him from peering inside a 1998 Peugot parked on the sidewalk where a post had been detached. "In fact, I never walked in *any* city before!" she gushed then blinked and clammed up with embarrassment as if suddenly deciding that she'd divulged too much. He didn't know what to make of her. It was as though she'd been suspended in another time or place and had just awakened, like H.G. Well's character in *When the Sleeper Wakes*.

As they walked in silence, François glanced at the girl with a wry smile. He wasn't sure if he was amused or annoyed with her. She kept flip-flopping from secretive adult to naïve child. First she was like a child; every small detail seized her awestruck attention. Then she'd try to hide it under a veil of reserve. What secrets was she hiding?

They reached Rue Beabourg, another wide busy street and François felt her tense beside him. Across the street the avante-garde exoskeletal structure of Centre Pampidou loomed neon yellow, red and blue like a Miro painting. The girl did better this time crossing the street to Place Stravinsky and into the treed park of Place George Pampidou. Lit with golden light from city lamps, the place, usually bustling with mothers and playing children or strolling lovers, was empty save an old man sleeping on a bench. They skirted the idle Stravinsky fountains, past a church, and onto Rue de la Verrerie, where to his frustration the girl lingered to stare at the old structure.

She'd relaxed a bit as they strolled the quiet cobbled street, lit with old-fashioned wrought-iron lamps. The street was mostly residential and the apartment buildings that lined it were typical Hausmann style elegant neo-baroque with wide facades, mansard roofs, wrought iron balconies and tall windows. The kind that graced most of Paris, thanks to the *Haussmannization* of Paris in the 1850s after the Nazis took over. François frowned. Most of his neighbourhood had thankfully remained untouched by Haussmann renovations. But they were getting into some now, he thought, noticing the girl slowing and gazing with the rapt interest of a dazed tourist at the buildings. She studied everything with the avid interest of a serious student; from the parked cars to the small sidewalk posts and the cobble brick streets and sidewalks. Her open eagerness annoyed François as he studied the architecture along with her.

The Nazis had embarked on the scheme to modernize medieval Paris shortly after the revolution. They'd cited the lousy traffic conditions and poor hygiene of the narrow streets and cramped buildings. "Let air and men circulate!" their Paris prefect had said. But François knew better; their true motivation was to facilitate troop movement, permit artillery to fire on rioting crowds and prevent rioters from forming barricades in previously narrow alleyways. So, the Nazis hired the exacting Baron Georges Haussmann as prefect of the Seine. He cut great swathes of straight wide streets and boulevards through the labyrinth of quaint narrow lanes and alleys, opening up and beautifying Paris. Like their destination ahead, François thought wryly: the Boulevard de Sébastopol, which ran through the heart of Paris. Haussmann didn't stop with roads; he tore down hundreds of buildings and erected entire blocks belonging to a "unified urban landscape". He also rebuilt several bridges. Most of them, like the Pont Saint-Michel where they were headed, bore the brand of an engraved "N", reminding all Parisians who had rebuilt their city for them.

As they neared the larger boulevard, Rue Verriere became littered with cafes and restaurants, then spilled out onto the bustling tree-lined Haussmann-style Boulevard de Sébastapol. François led them to the cross walk and pushed the signal. The lights changed, the sing-song signal chimed and François went to cross. At first the girl hesitated, glaring at the stopping cars with suspicion. Then, with his cajoling, she bolted across only to halt like a stunned deer.

François let loose a string of curses then grabbed her hand and pulled her to the other side. Once there, he quickly let go, jammed his sweaty hands in his pockets, and strode south to the laced ironwork gateway of the Châtelet Métro stop beneath a grove of plantane trees. He didn't bother to look back to see if she was following.

When he finally turned at the gate to le Métro, the girl was toddling behind.

"This way," he said to her then strode beneath the 'Méropolitain' sign and down the steps to the station. He glanced over his shoulder. She was following but with obvious reluctance. Harp music from a station busker swam up from the depths of the station like perfume: the plaintive notes of Pachabel's Canon, beautifully rendered into a kind of fluid dirge. François smiled; he recognized the music of Marie-Louise. Upon descending the stairs they reached the pedestrian walk to the station and François saw her, a grandmother in her seventies, dressed in a long multi-layered dark blue cotton skirt and top. She perched like a young woman on a stool with her great harp between her legs, coaxing seductive notes with agile fingers. Marie-Louise had been accused of sedition and kicked out of her house in Montmartre by the Black Knights. They threw her harp down the stairs when they expropriated her mansion. She'd been a wealthy woman; now she was destitute. When François confronted her with that, wondering if she would try to regain what she'd lost, Marie-Louise had answered: "Why? I have my harp and my music. And people to play for." She was amazing.

"*Salut*, Marie-Louise!" François said and threw a coin in the small bowl beside her. It would pay for a croissant, the kind he'd stolen. "*Ça va?*"

"Always," she sang out.

"*Au revoir!*" he said, continuing on past her.

"*Ciao, framboise!*" she sang out, using the nickname she'd given him. Marie-Louise had quieted her strumming but not ceased altogether as she eyed the girl beside François with interest. The girl, in turn, watched the old woman and the harp with quiet fascination, turning her head to look back as they passed.

"Hey, *framboise!*" Marie-Louise called. François turned and glanced over his shoulder at the old hobo. "You should keep that one."

"*Ya*," the girl added, making François blink at her rather sharp tone. "*Nicht wie einer seiner* chicklets…"

Despite her failing ears and the girl's German, Marie-Louise heard and understood the girl; she burst into a cackling laugh. Still laughing, she launched into a lively piece. François threw a furtive glance at the girl without turning his head. All that he caught was her pensive profile. Like Marie-Louise, he'd figured out what she meant; it didn't take much, particularly judging from her disparaging tone. As naïve as she seemed to be, the girl was no slouch. She caught on fast. If she didn't exactly know what a 'chicklet' was, she sure as hell knew what it wasn't.

✠

## ...19

BY the time they'd reached the station platform, the girl had visibly tensed and cast distraught glances around her. Her hand slid up to clutch her cross again as if it would save her. What was she afraid of now? He followed her gaze and saw nothing; only some innocuous waiting passengers, the platform on either side of the depressed train track and the yawning blackness of the tunnel. That was where she was gaping in visible fear.

The faint buffeting rush of stale air accompanied the high-pitched squeal of the oncoming train. François was totally unprepared for the girl's panicked reaction as the train burst into the station. She violently recoiled, bumping into him; her eyes flew wide and she unleashed a muffled shriek beneath her two hands. It made him flinch. *Merde*!

He forcefully grabbed her arm to steady her. "It's just a métro train," he said, losing his patience.

To her credit, she quickly regained her composure and let him lead her toward the doors. Her steps faltered as the doors slid open and several people got out, glancing at them. Still holding her arm tightly, François pulled her inside then immediately let go and slouched into one of the empty seats. She followed his lead and tentatively took a seat beside him, sitting stiffly with her back straight. She jumped in her seat when the doors shut. The train lurched into motion and she began to shake. François noticed that the girl was attracting undue attention from the other patrons in the car. She'd gone deathly pale with unspoken terror.

François felt an embarrassed laugh bubble up. What was wrong with the girl? When they dove into the tunnel, she let out an involuntary squeak. She broke out into a sweat and seized his shirt, releasing a quiet moan of terror. She clutched his arm in a painful grip and he heard her breaths come out in shallow spasms. *Merde*! She was having a major panic attack. Her fingers dug into his arm like the claws of a cougar. He didn't push her away but his patience gave out.

"*Merde*! Okay, okay!" François gave in. "Let's get out of here." At the next station, he surged to his feet and seized the shivering girl's arm. As the door slid open, he gruffly pulled her to her feet and they rushed out of the train and away from the staring patrons. François swiftly navigated the shaking girl up the stairs to the exit for Cité. Might as well let her see some of Paris, he decided, and was relieved to see her stop shaking once they'd emerged into the open air. Anything was better than suffering her disastrous claustrophobic fit.

Totally recovered, the girl turned to him with a solicitous smile. The color had returned to her face. Her hair had escaped from her beret and tumbled down over her shoulders. The gusting wind teased it into a playful dance around her face. "I'm sorry," she offered. "It was just like a nightmare I used to have." She waved a hand casually around her. "This is all so foreign to me. And those moving machines..." She shook off a last shudder, eyes flickering to the moving cars on Rue de la Cité beside them.

François shuffled his feet. "They were just trains." And cars and people and....God knows what else freaked her out, he thought with growing frustration. Why had he agreed to take her to his uncle? It would have been easier to just dump her; he'd gotten his boon from her already—Jacques had probably already dropped by out of intense curiosity and grabbed the stuff. He'd have it all sold on E-Pal by tomorrow morning and François would have his cash that afternoon.

"But no one drives them," the girl went on about the trains.

"They run on AI—"

"AI?" she echoed. She looked uncomfortable again.

"Artificial Intelligence...it's...." he trailed seeing the baffled expression on her face. How could she have a Pal and not know what a subway was? Or AI, for that matter. "I'll explain later." Jesus! She was so ignorant! "Look," he said with an involuntary sigh, "since we're on Ile de la Cité, I thought you might like to look at *that*."

He pointed to his left, where the looming towers of the

cathedral, lit in an orange glow against the night sky, were already visible over the acacea trees. Completely forgetting her ordeal in the subway, her eyes lit up like glowing lanterns. She usually veiled her earnest gaze with a reserve that was tricky to interpret. But now she betrayed surprised delight and wonder. Despite his annoyance with her, it brought a smile to François. He found her suddenly very attractive.

His uncle had told him not to stop anywhere, but they were just going past it, François reasoned. Seeing the girl's broad grin, his smirk widened and he took her hand in a flush of pleasure. "Come on, then!"

When they rounded the corner of l'Hospitel Hôtel Dieu and emerged into the open space of Place Parvis, the girl gasped. The full splendor of the massive cathedral revealed itself. François had to admit that it was an awesome structure. It was built so long ago, before the Nazis came and turned the city of light into the city of darkness. Of course, it took close to two hundred years to build, he'd heard. They stood for a while, staring in silence.

"Can we go inside?" the girl asked.

"No," he said brusquely and lied, "It's closed." He saw her disappointment and felt a pang of guilt. In truth, the cathedral was open. Despite the anti-Catholic stance of the Nazi government, their politicians appreciated the splendid grandeur of the place and permitted travelers who came from all over the world to worship there at all hours. The last time he'd been here the place *was* closed because someone had leapt off the sacred building; apparently twenty suicides a year took place off those magnificent balconies.

"We can come back another time, when it's open," he offered the crestfallen girl. She accepted his offer with a defeated smile. He didn't think she believed him. Of course she didn't. His heart clenched as the girl's penetrating eyes pierced through his bluster and she expressed a kind of sad disappointment; she seemed to know every time he lied.

François pushed them on, past the statue of Charlemagne. She slowed to stare with a frown at the tall black

Nazi banners that draped off the first set of balconies and obscured several of the twenty-eight kings of Judah.

"The banners are hiding the frescos; you can't see the Last Judgment!" she said. It was the second time she'd shown him her temper and although both times it was controlled, François recognized the potential for a boiling passion beneath her usual reserve. Her gaze drifted to where several armored guards, dressed in grey, were stationed and François saw her eyes narrow. Then her steps were straying toward them like a moth to fire.

"This way," François urged, grabbing her arm and pulling her away toward the bridge to the Left Bank. She resisted only momentarily then let him guide her away. That was when he saw them: Black Knights! Dressed in jet black with capped hats and shiny sable boots, three of them loitered by the entrance to the Pont au Double; their way across to the Left Bank. *Merde!*

"I hear there's a great view of the cathedral's flying buttresses...*this* way," François abruptly said. With a furtive glance back at the Black Knights, he steered her down the riverbank walk toward the back of the cathedral.

He urged her at a pace far speedier than she would have taken down the walkway beside the huge church and they crossed over le Pont l'Archevêche, the small bridge behind the church that crossed the murky Seine to the Quai de la Tournelle. François took them down the stone stairway to the cobbled riverbank walkway that still bustled with the green metal stalls of *bouquinists*—used book stalls—and artists with their paintings and sketches lined against the walls. He walked beside the girl beneath the warm amber glow thrown off by old-fashioned lamps beneath the plantain trees. Across the Seine, they had a panoramic view of the lit cathedral with its flying buttresses and the wisteria covered embankment of the Île de la Cité.

The river was behaving itself tonight; François could barely smell the sewage and garbage. Fishing boats, barges and other working boats were moored along the steep stone embankment. Murmuring lovers, nestled in each others arms, glided past them without looking up. François had walked here hand-in-hand with a girl before. But, somehow, walking with this girl—not even holding hands—sent a thrilling surge through him that he'd never felt and couldn't explain. She was just a strange girl with very strange habits, he decided and caught furtive glances at her attractive but thoughtful profile. A mystery he needed to unfold...or avoid.

The girl's steps faltered at one of the *bouquinists*. François noticed that she'd leaned in to stare at the magazines displayed in the stand. Her hands strayed, fingers gliding, over the laid out glossy covers: *Regards, Paris Match, Photo, La Researche*. The young vendor sidled next to her, trying to persuade her to buy *le Vogue*, a fashion magazine. But she was perusing le *Monde*, a popular newspaper. As François came beside her, she turned to him with a sober frown and held up the newspaper in front of them.

"What year are we in?"

Surely she knew, he thought, with an embarrassed glance at the vendor, who shrugged. François said, "You're kidding me, right?"

"It's 2010?"

"Yeah, July 14th."

She returned the newspaper to the stand and thanked the vendor. "July 14th, 2010..." she murmured then grew silent with solemn thoughts. It suddenly occurred to François that perhaps she was mentally challenged and was Boulanger's psychiatric patient. He dismissed the wild thought as soon as he entertained it; she was far too lucid and clever. She was simply ignorant. His theory of her being held prisoner by that Nazi guy made more sense.

When they came to the Pont au Double, the two passed beneath it and François peered furtively up; no Black Knights lingered on the bridge. Once through, he led the girl up another set of stone stairs to the street level and urged her across the fairly busy road eventually to where his uncle's favourite ancient bookstore nestled off the Petit Pont. They made it across without mishap but the girl hesitated when she saw the sign: Place

Viviane. François had to smile. It was somehow fitting, he thought.

Once in front of the bookstore, the girl's attention was diverted by the green water fountain of nymphs holding up a sphere. Metal mugs for drinking the water hung off the hooks below the caryatids. She helped herself to some water. She was awfully trusting, François thought, watching her drink. Either that or she was very thirsty. Perhaps both, he concluded as he hesitantly accepted the mug when she offered it to him. He sipped a little, thinking that her warm lips had just been there.

He found her studying the trees overhead. When she saw that he'd replaced the mug and she had his attention, the girl said, "These trees—all the trees I've seen in Paris—look, dried out and …."

"Sick?" François offered. "Yeah, we've had a few really dry, hot summers lately. Global warming." He shrugged. Then he pointed across the river to the lit spire of a gothic church with its weathervane angel. "That's your Sainte-Chapelle cathedral," he said and watched her face light up with a smile as she gazed longingly at the spire that poked out behind the trees. He enjoyed her open smiles. Not that easily given, they were so genuine. They opened her reserved face with an inviting vulnerability that thrilled him to the core of his loins.

He wanted to sleep with her. But he recognized that she wasn't like the promiscuous Parisian girls who chased after him; it made her all that more alluring.

Thinking to prolong the walk, François steered them south, away from the river along another busy street, then west along the quiet Rue Saint Severin, past yet another church. He watched the girl stare at the gothic church with prickly spires that were meant to resemble flickering flames. She turned to him with a girlish grin. "You have so many beautiful churches," she remarked "Your people must have a strong faith."

He started to laugh but covered it with a cough. She'd mistaken these relic monuments for practicing houses of God. Although a few remained—like Notre Dame and Sainte-Chapelle—the Nazis had converted most of these old magnificent structures into offices, administrative buildings or museums. They were a sad reminder of an age when people believed in something. No one believed in anything now, thought François, as he steered them back toward the river along another quiet narrow lane.

They emerged into the bright amber light and lively din of Boulevard Saint Michel. It bustled with rushing cars, mopeds, and people carrying on lively discussions in well-lit outdoor cafés and bistros. The boulevard opened to the Place Saint-Michel, where several streets converged with the Pont St. Michel that crossed the Seine to l'Ile de la Cité. His uncle would be around the corner.

François led her past the mètro entrance—where he'd initially intended for them to emerge—and several crowded outdoor cafés. The girl had gotten used to traffic by now. But he still had to consider her annoying inclination to freeze or bolt at the wrong time. As François's eyes darted to the milling traffic before attempting to cross, he felt the unexpected delight of the girl's hand slipping into his. A quick glance at her profile—she was deliberately not looking at him—revealed her tense fear as she steeled herself to cross the square.

With her hand secure in his grasp, François led them across the busy intersection toward the central structure, a large fountain, presided over by the magnificent statue of the archangel Michael slaying the devil. Two fierce-looking dragon-like creatures spouted water out of their gaping jaws into the churning pool in front. To the west of the fountain, at the entrance to Rue St. Andre-des-Arts beneath a thick canopy of plantain and horse-chestnut trees, François spotted the tricolor umbrellas of Café Toujours. There he would find his uncle, enjoying some escargot and a pastis or an espresso. How Antoine managed to afford suppers and lunches at cafés and bistros all the time was beyond François, who made more money than his uncle...and didn't spend his cash on food—something he could too easily steal. Antoine was a true Frenchman though, François decided; someone who could never give up the experience of dining out no matter how poor he was. He'd often told François that food and drink fed the sanctuary of the soul and in some important ways represented the very fiber of the French soul. It was the Frenchman's God given mandate to enjoy the sensual pleasures in life. Probably the reason the Nazis despised them.

Once they reached the general safety of the fountain, the girl relaxed; enough to stare at the statue and then remark, "He's using a flamberge."

"A what?"

"The sword." She pointed and made a squiggly motion with her finger. "That wave-like blade makes a nasty vibration in the opponent's blade on contact. Some people think the flamberge inflicts a more deadly wound, but it doesn't."

What an odd thing for a girl to know, François thought to himself. Then he reminded himself that she was an odd case and had been carrying a real sword when he ran into her. A sword he was hoping to make a great deal of money on.

As his gaze wandered, François caught sight of Antoine at the outdoor café dotted with bright red umbrellas. Antoine sat cross-legged with a cigarette between his fingers, reading *le Monde* as he sipped an espresso. François squeezed the girl's hand and noticed that she hadn't been in a hurry to let go this time. "There." He pointed to his uncle, who hadn't seen them yet. "That's my Uncle Antoine. The grey-haired man in the leather jacket and red scarf, sitting behind that flower box." He squeezed her hand again. "Come on."

✠

## ...20

THE hypnotic notes of Charles Tatou's "La Mer" floated on the warm breeze as they approached the café. "*...Et d'une chanson* *d'amour…la mer…a bercé mon coeur pour la vie…."*

Café Toujours was crowded with its regular patrons, who discussed politics, art and literature with quiet intensity. And no greycoats. Greycoats seldom frequented the cafés of the Rive Gauche; they preferred the ritzy cafés of the Rive Droit and the Champs-Élysées. A large blackboard sat on the sidewalk in front of the café, proclaiming the *Plat du Jour* for 9.75 Euros and *Salades* for 7.50 Euros. François read several down the list and felt his mouth water as his eyes rested on the *Cote de veau sauce porto au truffes haricots verts*. Maybe his uncle would treat him again.

Antoine looked up and the corners of his eyes seamed with a beaming smile. When they reached his round table, François took his uncle by the shoulders and leaned down to kiss his cheeks in the typical greeting of the French. When he straightened to introduce the girl, she beat him to it, "I'm the Honourable Lady Vivianne Schoen, Baronesse von Grunwald," she said then held out her hand in greeting. Her name was getting longer each time she introduced herself, François thought to himself. She'd added 'Honourable' this time. What next?

Antoine surged to his feet and took her hand lightly in his with a bow. "*Enchanté*, My Lady," he said to her, annoying François with his obsequious response. Antoine motioned for them to sit across from him and as he sat back down himself he waved at a waiter. "Two more coffees. Oh, and the cheese plate I selected with a basket of baguettes and a bottle of Languedoc," he added. Antoine turned back to the girl. "You're looking much better now. How's your head?"

To François's annoyance, she returned Antoine a warm smile. She'd never given *him* a smile like that. Then again, he hadn't treated her injuries, just tried to steal her necklace right off her neck.

"A little sore," she admitted, adjusting the beret.

"To be expected," Antoine said with a kind smile. "That was quite a crack you got."

Noticing the girl's warm response, François decided that

he should practice that smile for himself.

"Welcome to Paris, Lady Vivianne," Antoine said respectfully and raised his cup to her with a slight bow of his head. François had to hand it to his uncle; François could never have pulled that off without a smirk. Antoine continued, "You speak French very well for someone not from here…"

It was a leading question, but the girl didn't take it; instead she responded with, "Father Daniel—my teacher—taught me French along with Latin and English."

"Ah, an accomplished lady." Antoine nodded, genuinely impressed. "The French are really descendants of all the tribes and races that ever invaded France and all the immigrants that flocked from other countries. You could say the French are the Aborigines of France." He chuckled and François settled back, preparing for an obligatory history lesson. "First it was the Romans," Antoine continued to the girl, who listened with interest, "then the Visigoths—your ancestors—took the south and the Franks won Paris and northern Gaul. Charlemagne came in 800 AD to unite a hodgepodge of Celtic, Roman and Frankish people under the Holy Roman Empire." At his mention of the Holy Roman Empire the girl brightened with recognition; this was something she knew. "But France had a long way to go to get to where it is today," Antoine added. Then he leaned forward with an open grin. "Charles de Gaulle said: '*La France est la lumière du monde, son génie est d'illuminer l'Univers.*'"

"That's beautiful," the girl said, reflecting Antoine's smile.

"I don't know what my nephew has already told you but you're sitting in the traditional core of the Rive Gauche's liberal bohemian district." Antoine casually waved his hand around them. "This *quartier* is an artistic center and melting pot of poets and philosophers…and winos like me," he ended with a chuckle. The girl, much to François's annoyed surprise, laughed heartily, obviously charmed by the old man. When she laughed her mouth opened unabashedly, stretching alluring lips widely across her face; her eyes sparkled with the hint of mischief and her nose pinched with an urchin's pleasure. It was a sweet laugh and he wished he'd caused it, not his uncle. "La Place Saint-Michel has always been a gathering place for the city's malcontents and misfits," Antoine continued to the interested girl. "Back in the seventeen and eighteen hundreds the citizens of Paris took the streets from the government troups, set up barricades and fought against royalist oppression—"

"And brought in the Nazis instead," François muttered. "If we hadn't weakened our own country's rule they could never have taken over so easily—"

"*Voyons*, nephew! *Tais toi!*" Antoine railed at him. "Let *me* tell it." Then he turned back to the girl excitedly, like he wanted her all for himself. "You see, Paris has always been a center for the free expression of art and literature. We are a nation of diverse people. We like to argue and discuss things. There are three million French people in the Paris city center and three million different opinions—"

"Which the Nazis want to stomp down into one opinion."

"*Voyons*, François! *Tais toi!*" Antoine turned on him with renewed frustration. Then he turned to the girl, calm again. "In the 1890s painters came here from all over the world to paint; in the 1920s writers came; then in the 1960s film buffs came and created *La Nouvelle Vague*. Paris became the cinemaphilia capital of the world. We were always at the forefront of artistic expression and intellectual freedom. Something, yes," he continued with a nod to François, "the Nazis have tried to suppress—"

"I take that back," François cut in again. "The Nazis don't care about all that blabber because that's all it ever is—blabber. Empty rhetoric."

"*Eh, voyons*, François…" Antoine raised his hands to the boy, trying to calm him.

François waved a hand back at his uncle, keenly aware of the girl staring at him and bolstered by it. "Two hundred years ago we didn't just talk—we acted. France was all about innovation. When the Nazis took over they cut off our…eh…" he glanced at the girl and amended, "they emasculated us; they left us our voices, but we argue like impotent old men..."

Antoine cut in, leaning forward and pointing with his cigarette at the boy. "I beg to differ François—"

"We're all talk and no show—"

The girl grabbed his arm with a stern look to quiet him.

At François's confused hesitation, Antoine barged in: "In spring of 1968, students battled riot batons and tear gas right in this place. We were fed up with artistic oppression. We set up barricades and attacked them with everything from homemade explosives to rocks. We took over the Place and declared it an independent state. I was just a boy and a little idealistic."

"What happened?" the girl asked, entranced.

"They brought in the Black Knights." Antoine let his face grow long with dark memories. "Hundreds of students were killed and hundreds more imprisoned. I was lucky. I got away." He was clearly remembering his friend getting caught and beaten to death, thought François. It had apparently affected his uncle greatly, and had no doubt helped to cement his active participation in the Résistance.

Antoine finally drew in a long breath. Then his eyes lit up with a flame of excitement and he smiled like an old wizard. "The energy in this place is positively electrifying, don't you think?" His eyes darted between François and the girl. "Do you feel it?" He paused expectantly.

François was about to retort when the girl responded to his surprise.

"Yes, I do," she said. "Something incredible will happen here."

"Something that will change the world," Antoine added brightly then nodded to François as if he should know what they were talking about.

*Merde*! François fought from making a sour face and slouched in his chair. He hated conversations like this. He wasn't a philosopher or a dreamer like Antoine. It had surprised him that the girl had engaged in it too. He decided that she was more annoying than attractive. And was glad that he'd already contacted Jacques with details on where to find the girl's gear.

She was a lost cause. François knew women. The girl's naïve and conservative nature and diffident attitude toward him—not to mention her secretive and contradictory mannerisms—were a barrier that he decided he had no patience to surmount. He'd find a way to ditch her tonight and would collect his money from Jacques tomorrow. She obviously didn't know the city, so chances of her finding her way back to his hovel on Rue des Rosiers were slim. He'd deal with his uncle's disappointment later.

"Who are the Black Knights?" the girl asked Antoine. She turned suddenly to François with an intense gaze. "Are they the men we saw at the cathedral, the ones in grey uniform?"

François opened his mouth to answer but his uncle cut in, "No. The Knights are dressed in black from head to foot. And they're black inside too, like coal, with no heart," he added, his mood obviously darkened by memories of 1968. François noticed the girl's face grow pale at Antoine's description. She seemed to recognize Black Knights without knowing who they were. His uncle volunteered darkly, "They're the Führer's henchmen and the ones who make sure we all behave like good little Germans."

He was pushing all her buttons, François observed. At his mention of 'Germans', the girl put her fidgeting hands on her lap and dropped her gaze to the table. As quickly as he'd charmed the girl, Antoine alienated her.

Just then the coffee, bread, cheese and red wine arrived. The girl eyed the food with hungry appreciation then glanced with puzzled curiosity at the steaming coffee set before her. François took a sip of his and nodded to the girl. "It's coffee," he said, barely hiding a grin. "Don't you have coffee where you come from?"

She shook her head, rousing herself from her estranged quiet. "Only ale, wine or cider. Sometimes we make a mulled wine or hot cider, but nothing like this..." She bent her face down and brought the espresso cup to her nose to breathe in the scent of freshly brewed coffee. François smiled inside at her open enjoyment.

"Well, you'll like it," he said, waving his hand for her to try it.

She glanced at Antoine for reassurance and he nodded with a smile. She took a careful sip. Her eyes immediately widened and she grinned back at them. "You're right," she said to François. "It's very good." Then she took a large appreciative gulp.

Antoine cleared his throat and the girl looked up. "You must sip it," he instructed. "The French sip their drinks. Otherwise we would have nothing left to lubricate our lively discussions of the *grand philosophie.*"

"Besides, it's a stimulant," François added, trying to gain points on pragmaticism. "And you're not used to it, so you should take it slow."

"All right," she agreed and let her gaze stray to the pungent cheese and fresh bread with large eyes of yearning hunger. François's mouth watered. Except for that apple and pastry he'd stolen, he hadn't eaten since early yesterday.

Antoine smiled, watching the girl with amusement. Then he caught François's eye and winked. "Please pour the wine, François," he suggested then moved the platter of cheese and the basket of bread closer to the girl, who looked down at it and hesitated, waiting for a signal from either of them before digging in. If she had been any of the girls François knew, she'd have charged right in there without need of invitation.

Just as he was about to help himself to a piece of bread, Antoine leaned forward, barring the way with his elbow.

"You must begin with the lighter soft cheeses, like camembert, coeur de Neufchâtal or Saint-félicien." Antoine pointed to each cheese as he named them. "And then finally end with the goat's cheese." He pointed finally to the pyramid-shaped Valençay. "This cheese," he pointed with his knife to a plump round ball of pale cheese, "is called Boursin and it's made in Normandy." He took his knife and cut into soft cream cheese then spread it on a piece of bread. "You know what they say: *du pain, du vin—*"

"*Un peu du Boursin!*" François finished for him with a

laugh and followed his uncle by grabbing a piece of bread and spreading it with cheese for himself. Needing no encouragement, the girl helped herself as well. She briefly closed her eyes and breathed in the cheese and bread as she ate. Antoine approved with a grin. Between exultant savoring, they sipped the flavourful but not overpowering red wine.

Once Antoine had guided her from the mild camembert to the sharper heart-shaped Neufchâtel, he had the girl taste the Époisses de Bourgogne, with its distinctive soft red-orange colour, then they moved on to the Bleu d'Auvergne, a pungent creamy buttery cheese that melted in François's mouth then finally to two goat's cheeses, a Rocamadour and the Valençay.

"The French love their cheeses," Antoine told the girl. "We have hundreds of different cheeses in this country and a *fromagerie* on every street corner," he added with a smile of satisfaction. "We need to eat cheese every day." He brought a piece of Rocamadour to his nose and inhaled. "We need to smell it too. Ah...it smells like the feet of an angel..." Then he popped the pungent cheese straight into his mouth with half-closed eyes and pursing lips. "Ooh la la..."

The girl grinned, appreciating his passionate lecture, then helped herself to more cheese, bread and wine. They fell into a silence of savoring for some moments. Despite Antoine's lecture on patient appreciation, the girl was done in several bites and leaned forward to face Antoine with an intense look. "You called me an Aeon," she stammered, blushing a little, and hastily explained, "I heard you just before I passed out...You recognized my...er...markings...."

"Ah, yes." Antoine stroked his grey bristle with a gnarly hand. "The Gnostics call you Aeons. Others have different names for you. It doesn't matter what you're called, though. We've known about you for millennia. We're the *Guardiens*—a secret society from a long line of prophets and healers dedicated to protecting you and helping you through your threshold—"

"Threshold?" François cut in. This business about *Guardiens* was news to him. He blinked in confusion at Antoine then glanced at the girl. Oddly enough, she looked more interested than confused. As if she'd been handed a puzzle piece.

Antoine ignored François and went on, "Aeons have always had threshold guardians to help them in their journeys through our inter-dimensional network of realizable realities…"

"Realizable realities?" François laughed uncomfortably.

"So, tell us where you're from," Antoine asked the girl, again ignoring François. "Where were you before you burst onto Rue des Rosiers through that rift and fell on top of my nephew?"

She swallowed down her distress and gazed hesitantly from one to the other then rested large eyes on Antoine. "I came from my home in von Grunwald Castle…in Prussia."

Antoine leaned back and brushed his stubbled face with his hand, staring through her then at her. "And what year was that?"

"What year!" François burst out scornfully. How condescending could his uncle be? Did he think the girl had Alzeimer's or something? Then he remembered the girl's question at the *bouquiniste*.

She didn't blink an eye as she replied, "The fourteenth hundred and tenth year of our Lord—"

Antoine smacked the table, making François flinch. The girl jumped too.

"Ah, ha!" Antoine said cheerfully as if to himself. He looked past them both with a manic smile on his lips. Then he focused back on the girl. "You've just traveled six hundred years into the future, My Lady! We're presently in 2010." He let that sink in to the girl's brain before going on, "When you introduced yourself, you were telling me where you're from; it's in your name, of course. As for the year…wasn't a major battle fought there around that time?"

The girl went pale again and she stared at Antoine. "The Battle of Grunwald… the day after I left."

"Of course—"

"Wait!" François interjected. He stared from the girl to Antoine. "Are you suggesting that she traveled in time as well as space from 1410 to now?"

"Yes," Antoine replied without looking at him. "Now, as I was saying—"

François cut in, "Through this rift in an inter-dimensional network—"

"My mother called it a tear. Like a rip," the girl said.

François turned on the girl. "You mean you *did* come from medieval time?"

"Medieval?" she echoed.

"She wouldn't know that word, François." His uncle touched his arm. "That term only developed later."

"But—"

"She's a traveler, François," Antoine said brusquely. "That's what an Aeon is, someone who travels beyond our limited visible world of four dimensions like we negotiate the city streets; only she negotiates probable realities through 'tears', tears in time and space that they summon," Antoine ended with a smug smile at the girl. *She* didn't look smug, thought François. It was hard to read her, in fact. François felt his brows come together. None of it made any sense. What about the girl's dozen calls of a few days before on her Pal to and from that Boulanger guy? How could she be back in 1410 and yet be here to make those calls? Unless she was lying, leading his uncle on with this stupid quantum physics crap.

…Antoine was nattering on about how two parallel time-space realities, once created by a major fateful decision, had the tendency to rejoin on their own accord as if God had created it that way…with one usually dominated by the other, itself becoming a shadow or "dream" reality…the vivid dreams, déjà vu's, intuition, and moments of unexpected clairvoyance, prescience or genius that stir every human being….

"Wait a minute!" François burst out. As both the girl and Antoine turned to him expectantly, he swallowed down his challenge. How could he share his question without revealing to the girl that he'd taken her Pal? He glanced from his uncle to the girl and shrugged. "I…well, I…never mind. It wasn't important."

Antoine waved his hands at him. "That blinding light

you saw, François; that was *her*." François caught the girl's astonished expression before she quickly hid it. Clearly, she was learning all this along with him. And finding it equally unbelievable, François thought. She looked like an ordinary girl; the only magic was in her sparkling eyes, he decided. Antoine continued, "There are hundreds, perhaps thousands of you Aeons, each shepherding a thread of reality within a fabric of probable time and space. You weave the tapestry of history. You summon reality."

François stared. So did the girl.

Obviously in his element, Antoine went on, "Aeons— who always come as twins—split off at a nexus in time, a major decision point, each twin intuitively choosing one of the two realities based on their individual comportment, a kind of yin/yang thing, I guess. And it seems that *you*," he nodded to the girl, "gravitated to *this* reality, whereas your twin must have chosen the other."

The girl's lips tightened and her eyes glazed with discomfort at the mention of a twin.

Antoine merrily went on, "Each twin Aeon sees-in one of the paired realizable realities until they rejoin years, sometimes hundreds of years, after." He turned eagerly to François. "You always need a pair of Aeons to bring those two split worlds back together. You see, without an Aeon's energy to guide that reality, it goes off kilter, essentially spiraling into destruction, and collapses; like a remnant or diseased branch of a growing tree that loses its nourishment. It dries up and gives way to the stronger branch guided by the living sap of the single Aeon. Therefore, if only one of the two Aeons survives, he has to make a choice which branch will be realized."

The girl blanched at that. François thought she was going to be sick but she reigned it all in under a mask of calm. It was amazing how she could do that, he thought. What Antoine had divulged had obviously troubled her greatly.

"There is a legend among *les Guardiens*," Antoine continued, "that the last of the summoners to emanate will cause the most significant nexus of them all, which will lead ultimately to the *Suntelia Aeon*, the catastrophic end of all ages. No doubt an Aeon that has no twin, because only they would be able to see a world through to such an event."

The wind suddenly gusted hard, whipping the trees above them and the umbrellas flapped as if trying to escape the ripping wind. The girl jerked her head to look up and knocked over her wine glass. It spilled over the table and she let out a desperate sound of apology.

As François helped the blushing girl mop up the mess, Antoine laughed to himself and tapped the table with his finger; he was on a roll and would not be diverted. "Perhaps I use the wrong metaphor for an Aeon's realized world. It's more like a symphony vs. an aria," he said to no one in particular, therefore inviting comment from anyone wishing to partake. When no one did, he continued with his train of thought, "It has its basis in science and metaphysics, alike. With the *Music of the Spheres—*"

"Expressing the energy tones of numbers, shapes and sounds connected in a pattern of proportion," the girl added eagerly, fully recovered from her embar-rassment and discom-fort thought François. She went on, rather animated, "Pythagoras showed that the pitch of a musical note is in proportion to the length of the string that produces it, and that intervals between harmonious sound frequencies form simple numerical ratios."

"Yes! Yes!" Antoine said, reflecting her animation with his own. "The *Harmony of the Spheres* ... He proposed that—"

"Planets all emit their own unique hum based on their orbital revolution," the girl finished for him. They were on a role again, leaving him behind, François thought petulantly. She continued, "Then Kepler—as part of his celestial physics—connected sacred geometry with harmonics and music through his *musica universalis*."

François stared at her. "How did you know that," he challenged in a voice sharpened by intellectual shame. This one thing he knew: "Keplar lived way after your time period...if you're telling the truth."

She shrugged and Antoine filled her glass with more

wine. "It was in a book that I read...a book given to me...from my future, I guess," she mused.

"Ah! My little Aeon!" Antoine raised his hands in a gesture of fatalism. "You have no future or past...only decisions."

The girl could no longer meet his gaze and let it falter. They fell into an uneasy silence and sipped their wine. *La Mer* had concluded and was replaced by some accordion music. François listened to the quiet murmur of his fellow café patrons over the low howling moan of the wind through the trees. He welcomed the silence; the conversation had been a little too strange for him. And this *Guardien* business that his uncle claimed to be part of was too bizarre. Why had he never confided in François about it?

Antoine, who'd been watching the girl, cleared his throat, a signal to François that he would broach an important topic in a reckless guise. "I'm curious, my lady, about what brought you here..."

*Now* he was finally asking the right questions, thought François.

"I was told that the Tear would direct me to the one who would help me," she volunteered and threw a cursory but dismissive glance at François then rested intense eyes on his uncle. "I think that person is you."

François felt slighted that the girl hadn't envisioned him as her saviour; not that he wanted to be, he added petulantly to himself.

"You were nearby and are a Threshold *Guardien*," she added to Antoine without glancing at François. "As for my purpose in this time and place, that is something I must still discover. I've only just arrived...and met you."

"Yes, yes," Antoine conceded heartily, rather eager to claim her as his responsibility. "Aeons, I'm told, when they travel through a tear, will either consciously or unconsciously direct themselves to a figure or place of inter-dimensional stability. Someone or someplace, or sometimes both, that tends to remain the same no matter which reality they are in." He smiled amiably and rather self-pleased. "It takes a person of great character to remain the same no matter what their reality is, and I thank you for the unintentional compliment. But that's not what I meant." The girl leaned forward attentively, inviting him to continue. "You're about fourteen, right?...That's the age most Aeons travel their first nexus split. I'm guessing that your nexus split was the Grunwald battle. So, why did you leave before it and come straight here? Aren't you and your twin meant to live through your separate dimensional worlds once you've created the split realities only to join years after? You seem to have skipped that..."

Her face darkened. When she finally looked at him directly with a pained expression, she said in a shaky but determined voice, "I'm alone...there was an accident, a mistake—"

"Which will be corrected now," interjected a man's deep voice behind François and the girl. She jumped, obviously recognizing it, and winced with a grimace as if someone had struck her.

François turned to see whose rich baritone voice it was and flinched: a Black Knight. *Merde*!

✠

## ...21

SHE knew a Black Knight!

François should have been alerted by the sudden hush of the café's patrons, but the girl had distracted him. The Knight was tall, François guessed in his early twenties with handsome features and thick shortly cropped dark hair. He had the kind of mouth women liked to kiss but his eyes blazed with something cruel and François felt danger prickle the back of his neck.

"Hello, Vivianne," the Knight drawled with a malicious smile.

She bolted to her feet but the man grabbed her shoulders and pushed her gruffly down. François surged up to protect her. With lightening speed the Knight hooked his arm and sent him tumbling to the cobbled ground. Totally embarrassed, François scrambled up to his knees then found the muzzle of a phantom gun pointed at his face. Nearby patrons of the café turned discreetly away, as if all this was normal; it *was* normal with a Knight. They were the law and no one wanted trouble.

"I suggest you sit down nicely or I'll have to do something more drastic," the Knight addressed François like he was a dog requiring a lesson in manners. "I'm only after the girl. Don't interfere and all will be well." He turned to the girl and said in a condescending voice, "Come, Vivianne."

"I'm not going with you, Mortameur," she said more firmly than she'd ever sounded.

*Merde*! She even knew the guy's fucking name! What kind of trouble had she gotten herself—and them—into? François threw a glance at his uncle, who gave him a barely imperceptible wink. *Merde*! What was Antoine going to do? It wasn't as though the girl was *his* Aeon. He didn't have any allegiances to her. *Don't do anything dumb, uncle!* François had to think fast or they were all going to get killed on account of this stupid girl. He was still figuring out what to do when Antoine made his move. A dumb move:

In a sudden dramatic gesture, he averted his eyes toward the bridge, to the Knight's left, and pointed. "My God! What's that!"

Mortameur automatically turned to look. Antoine jumped to his feet and grabbed the wine bottle, ready to swing at Mortameur's head. The Knight caught his swing and the bottle sailed to the cobble ground with a loud clap of breaking glass. Red wine spilled over everyone's feet. Mortameur followed his parry with his own swing, gun butt connecting in a sickening crack with the side of Antoine's face. The old man dropped like lead to the ground.

"L'Oncle!" François cried and surged to his feet.

Mortameur hooked his leg hard and pulled him down, sprawling on the paving stones with a grunt. Still winded, François saw the girl leap to her feet. With lightening speed, she seized the umbrella stand off the table and swung the pole toward the Knight with a strength that amazed him. The gun flew from Mortameur's hand and he yelped where she'd rapped him hard. She continued in a follow-through arc, rod striking him full in the chin with a loud crack. Then she thrust out full force, stabbing him in the chest. Mortameur jerked backward with a grunt and stumbled in a daze into a backward fall toward the traffic of Place Saint-Michel.

François saw his chance: a scooter, parked with its key left in the ignition, stood a meter from their table. He scrambled up, grabbed the girl and went to straddle the bike. The girl started back with a moan of terror. "*Nein!*" she said. "*Ich kann nicht!*"

"Come on!" he shouted. "It's our only chance!" She knew it and let him hoist her behind him. "Grab my waist and hang on!"

The engine sputtered on and he skidded into the street as Mortameur scrambled up and lunged toward them like a drunk. He caught the girl's arm in a violent tug. She shrieked. François gunned the throttle and the scooter squealed. The girl desperately clung to him and fought from being ripped off by the Knight's grasp. It was a loosing battle. Already one arm recoiled off his waist and the Knight was pulling her off—

The girl's eyes lit as if on fire. The umbrella pole flew up from the ground—as if by a ghost's hand! It knocked Mortameur on the head with a loud crack and he let go in a dazed stumble. Suddenly released from the brute's clawing grip, the scooter sprang into the street and the girl seized François around the waist to keep from flying off.

A string of curses—no doubt from the scooter's owner—followed them as they squealed out of the Place and down the Quai de Conti, along the river, toward Orsay. François didn't look back. He felt the exhilaration of giddy relief as a warm wind beat against his face and the gold sparkles of Parisian lights reflecting on the Seine merged into dancing streaks of a fluid watercolour. The girl clung to his waist and buried the side of her face against him. She was being quite brave, he thought, deciding to be impressed. Of course, she had no choice, he reflected and let a manic smile curl his lips with cruel humor.

François headed west, staying on the riverbank of the Rive Gauche. The Eiffel Tower, splendidly lit against the night sky, loomed ahead of them, lighting a bright beacon in the darkness. The city of light. It was a beautiful city, he decided. *My city—*

The girl's arms abruptly tightened around his waist as she turned to look back and shrieked, "He's following us!"

"What?" François threw a glance backward and the scooter swerved with his movement. The girl shrieked again and hooked her arms around him in a vice grip. Sure enough, a two-seater VW bug was aggressively weaving around the traffic behind them and leaving a confused wake of screeching brakes and honking horns from angry drivers.

"*Merde!*"

François could already make out Mortameur's angry face at the wheel of the little red and black car. He forced the screaming bike around le Place de la Résistance and onto Avenue Rapp, the VW squealing right behind them. Traffic came to a sudden halt. *Merde!* François threaded his way between the maze of slow traffic, imagining his pursuer cursing as he was left behind, and thought of trying to lose Mortameur in the crowds of Champ du Mars; maybe ditch the scooter and go on foot—

A loud boom, followed by the machine-gun stutter and flashing lights brought the scooter to a swerving halt. He didn't hear her but François was certain the girl had screamed. The whole night sky exploded and burst into flaming lights of the rainbow. François laughed and watched the fireworks display then glanced at the girl, her upturned face reflecting the sparkling lights of red, blue, yellow and green. She stared in awe, mouth gaping open at the beautiful fanning out stars and fountains of sparkling light in the night sky.

"Fireworks," François told her as they got off the scooter. "It's Bastille Day," he explained with a glance at his watch: it was 22:30 and the fireworks were right on time.

Even though she couldn't help flinching at some of the bigger booms, the girl was obviously fascinated. "It's beautiful," he barely heard her over the noise.

François then made out Mortameur's VW, parked in the gravel parking lot behind the girl — he must have driven along the sidewalk to get here so fast. François flicked his eyes quickly from side to side in search of the Black Knight. He couldn't be too far away. Then François grinned in sudden inspiration.

"Come on!" he urged the girl, still looking up, mesmerized.

"Where—"

"There!" He pointed to Mortameur's car and the girl paled. She'd lost her beret, probably during the scooter chase, and she looked frazzled, hair flying in the gusting wind as she shook her head in denial.

"But—" she stuttered out as he pulled her to the car. It was empty but Mortameur had to be nearby, looking for them.

When they reached the car, François swiftly picked the lock then turned with a wry smile to the girl. She recoiled and violently shook her head, hair thrashing around her pale face. "*Nein!*" she barked it out then added in a moan, "*Ich kann nicht!*" François bit back a grin; it was the only way, and she knew it too.

She reluctantly let him push her into the passenger seat, uttering something under her breath: "*Leiber Gott, rette uns…*" Then he took the wheel and gunned the engine. The little car leapt out of the parking lot with a scream, spitting gravel. The girl shrieked and François couldn't help another ruthless grin. He was enjoying this. His whole body thrilled in the giddy exultation of a good chase; of course, it was because he intended to win. He thought he caught a glimpse of Mortameur running and shouting behind them. Then he disappeared in a chaos of cars, trees and buildings as they careered out of the lit park into a dark street.

Hand shaking from adrenalin, he flicked on the radio. The girl flinched as heavy metal blared out. François barked out a laugh. The girl glanced wide-eyed from the radio to him with a painful look of confused agitation. "It's *MegaDeth*," he said simply. "I guess you don't have thrash metal in the Middle Ages, eh?" he cavalierly shouted over the howling music.

Her gaze jerked from his face to ahead of them then back again. He glimpsed her gripping the dashboard and grinned.

"Don't worry," he reassured her with a conspiratorial grin. "I can drive, even though I don't have a license yet. And we've lost him, I think."

"Not for long," she said with ominous prescience. It drew a sharp glance from François and he grew silent with foreboding.

When he reached one of the entrances to the *Bois de Boulogne*, François silenced the radio and slowed the car beside a hunched boy in rags. He trudged in little steps against the buffeting wind, litter and garbage whirling around him in tiny tornadoes of grit. Not much more than eighteen, he raised a haggard face up to them and stretched out a filthy shaking hand for alms. François recognized the telltale streaks and pock marks of *sparkle* overuse on his drawn face. He was a ghost under the gibbous street lights. *Sparkle* was a far more potent and addictive drug than *rapture*, François considered, and this boy must be doing big-time crime to support that habit. François got out of the car into the howling wind and motioned for the girl to follow. She did, though she eyed him with a puzzled look, blinking hard. Her hair whipped across her face in thrashing waves.

Clearly fearing some kind of violence, the boy backed away from them. "Please…don't hurt me…" he stuttered out.

François seized him gruffly and shoved him at the car. "Don't worry, old git. What's your name?"

"Jean."

"Well, Jean, today's your day. Do you drive? The car's yours, provided you drive it back into the Latin Quarter. After that you can do whatever you want with it. Do you understand?"

Jean nodded vigorously then let his gaze stray to the girl.

François grabbed Jean by the arm. François shook him to draw his gaze from the girl. Then he threw Jean gruffly at the car. "Go now! The key's in the ignition."

Jean scrambled inside with a last fearful glance at François and the girl, then drove off with a jolt and squeal of the engine brakes. François wasn't so sure Jean could drive. No matter; so long as Jean managed to get the car out of here, he thought.

They stood briefly in the wailing wind and watched the car wind its way down the street. It headed toward the *Jardins du Trocadero*. Satisfied that he'd managed a good diversion, François grabbed the girl's hand and they ducked into the forest. The wind picked up and sent the trees pitching with loud groans and creaks. The forest hissed like an angry exhale. The moonlight winked on and off behind moving clouds. François led the girl hastily down a dark and spongy leaf-littered path.

They continued in silence for some time, following soft winding paths through the park, then finally veering into the wild unkempt forest after they glimpsed a couple on the path ahead of them. A girl and a boy, leaning into each other. Lovers, no doubt. But François wasn't taking any chances. To his surprise, the girl didn't hesitate when he urged her off the path. They had to feel their way at times through the pitch dark forest as the gibbous moon hid behind storm clouds. She was more agile than François expected. She kept up with him, uncomplaining, as they thrashed through thickets of shrubs, brambles and ferns until he found a small open knoll by a small brook. When the moon revealed itself briefly, he glimpsed an arched stone bridge farther down where a path obviously intersected with the creek. It was down a bend in the waterway and he reasoned they were safely out of sight here, blending in with the dark forest. Both he and the girl were aptly dressed for camouflage, wearing jeans and dark tops.

The girl removed her backpack and sat herself on the

soft moss beneath an oak tree. She pulled her sweater closed, drawing her knees up and wrapping her arms around them. The wind hissed through the forest. The girl squinted at the forest around her, hair flying in every direction. François sat down not far from her.

She ran her hands over her head to reign in the hair whipping across her face and pulled it back then held it with one hand as she turned to him to finally break their long silence. "What is this place?"

"It's called *le Bois de Boulogne*," François muttered. He was trying to decide what to do with her: dump her or...help her, *then* dump her....

"It reminds me of home," the girl said quietly. François tried to detect any sentimentality in her voice but she'd carefully hidden it beneath her cool reserve again. Then she added softly, "We had a large forest just outside Grunwald. My fa-father used to hunt there." She'd stumbled over the word 'father' and François guessed that there were issues between them. The girl was more talkative now, making an effort at communication, François reflected; just when he didn't care to be talkative himself. "I think we've lost Mortameur..." she whispered into the silence that had fallen between them. François sensed her shivering beside him despite the warmth of the night. He still felt the odd after-shock tremble himself. But he fought his initial inclination to get close and put his arm around her, like he would have with any other girl. She was the reason he was here in the forest, being chased by a madman with a gun; why his uncle was lying on the cobblestones of Place Saint-Michel with his head cracked open.

"We might have lost him...for now, maybe," François said cynically.

"You did a smart thing there with the car," she said, giving him a brief shy glance.

So, she'd recognized his ploy. Good. She wasn't a total imbecile, he decided and fixed a long gaze at her. "So, where'd you learn those cool moves you used back there? Tai Chi class?"

"I trained as a knight," she said, not quite looking him in

the face.

François barked out a sharp laugh. "Sure!" Then he realized from her earnest expression that she wasn't kidding. "Really? But I thought that only guys trained as knights...that girls didn't..." he trailed.

"They didn't," she agreed soberly, raking her hair back with her fingers against the unruly wind. "I did it in secret."

François was suddenly intrigued, despite still being skeptical of her supposed origins. "So, you took secret lessons in knighthood in this place in Prussia six hundred years ago..."

"Yes."

They fell into another awkward silence. The wind moaned through the trees. Watching the wind throw up some leaves into the air, François remembered the freaky umbrella stand, rising of its own accord like from the hand of a ghost to knock Mortameur senseless. It gave them the chance to escape. Had he dreamed it? It couldn't have been the wind. He'd thought he'd seen the girl's eyes light up like a stoked fire. "So, what happened back there at Place Saint-Michel?" he said. "That umbrella post...how did it do that...it was like magic..."

The girl's eyes flew wide at his words but she offered only silence. François was getting fed up with her silence.

He thought of just leaving her here and running away. She could never catch up to him and he'd be done with her. She was nothing but trouble. But as his eyes grazed her briefly, shivering beside him with the aftermath of an adrenalin thrill, he felt he couldn't abandon her. Even though she made him angry. She'd be lost without him, he decided, and turned to her angrily. If he was going to help her he needed some answers...NOW!

"So who is this guy?" he abruptly demanded and saw her flinch. "Why are the Black Knights after you?"

"Just one," she corrected him.

"Yeah, and he knows you quite well. What have you done?" he pressed her. "Did you rob a bank or something?"

"No."

She was clamming up again. He could tell from her taciturn response and lack of eye contact. "Well, what then? You must have done *something*."

Her hand unconsciously fingered the cross pendant on her neck. "I ran away."

"Why? What did you do?" he persisted. She just pressed her lips together in stubborn silence and avoided his gaze. "Okay, so why's this Black Knight, this Mortameur guy, chasing us with a gun, then? What'd you do to *him*? Who exactly is he?"

"He's my—"

François watched her choke on her words. She visibly shuddered and shook her head at him, unable to continue. He'd definitely hit a nerve with her. Any other time or situation she might have moved him to take pity and leave off; but he was too obsessed and pressed on: "*What*? Some guy you cheated on? A partner. An employer. Or your older brother, maybe. Your *father*, then. Hell, maybe a lover. Your husband—"

"He's my betrothed!" she practically sobbed.

François blinked at the girl. She was coming apart but he ignored it. She'd given him an answer he hadn't expected. He'd thrown out his suggestions rhetorically; her reply now intrigued him. "So, what's the problem? Just fuck him—"

"That's exactly what he wants me to do!" she said breathlessly.

"I mean—" He bit down an exasperated laugh. She took everything so literally. "Just tell him to go to hell." Even as he said it, he realized how ridiculous it would be to tell a Black Knight to go to hell. "Tell him that you don't give a flying fuck for him...eh..." he quickly amended, "that you don't want him—"

"It doesn't work that way. Where I come from we're promised to one another from birth and it's a binding promise..."

"What a stupid rule! So fuck it!"

"Why do you keep using that awful word!" she shrieked at him, suddenly very upset. He saw tears glistening in her eyes. In a minute she would burst out crying. Up to then she'd pretty much held it together. But she was on the edge of losing her composure. And that made him very uncomfortable.

"Okay, okay," he said in a soft voice of truce. "I wouldn't want to offend a *lady*." It wasn't much of an apology but it was all he could muster for now. François rubbed his face with the palms of his hands and exhaled a long breath. He aimed his glower at the deep forest and let his mind toil. She was one dangerous commodity. Why was he staying?

The girl opened her backpack and jammed her hand inside to rifle for something. François turned a sidelong glance at the girl and felt his heartbeat increase at her discovering his burglary. Her movements grew more agitated as she didn't find what she was looking for right away. *Merde!* Was she looking for her Pal? He was still searching for an answer to her obvious question when she finally pulled out a tiny book with a sigh. He sighed inwardly. Within a few moments, he heard her whispering to herself. Clutching the little book to her breast, she bowed her head and murmured some mantra in German:

"*...Unser Vater im himmel, dein Name werde geheiligt, dein Reich komme, dein Wille geschehe wie im Himmel, so auf der Erde....*"

When she finished, the girl released a long exhale as though what she'd said made everything all right. They remained silent for several awkward moments and François finally thought that he should break the quiet with something.

But it was she who spoke first. "You really don't like me very much, do you?"

He hadn't expected such a blunt remark from her and laughed sharply. "Well, what's to like?" the cruel words had spilled out but he didn't care; she'd opened up a sluice door and let him rush in. "First you suddenly appear in a sparkly show of light and nearly kill me. Then you let me take you in, all lady-like, damsel-in-distress—knowing full well that that madman was out there, chasing after you. But, of course you didn't tell us about him either. You put my uncle and me in danger, you deceived us into helping you—"

She winced with surprised dismay at the last words then her face darkened with rising anger and she straightened to retort. But he silenced her with a violent gesture that made her jerk back with alarm. "My uncle got a nasty crack on the head from that boyfriend of yours and I should get him to the hospital. But instead I'm here hiding in the forest with you. I think you fucking used us both with your malicious lies. You cheated and lied—"

"Lied!" she shrieked, face heating with fury. She sprang up, making him flinch, and advanced to face him. He winced back from her as she hurled out a string of German invective he could only imagine the expletives they contained: *"Du bist so klein! Du bist arrogant, selbstsüchtig und unverschämt und du bist der rücksichtsloseste und gemeine Junge, den ich mich je getroffen habe! Du kummern dich um nichts oder irgendjemand!—"*

She shook her head all of a sudden, realizing she'd lapsed into German, gathered her composure and continued: "Listen, I'm sorry about your uncle and you have to believe me that I didn't expect to find Mortameur here." Then her eyes flashed. "But you're one to talk about lying," she bit out sharply. "You're nothing more than a common thief with no consideration for anything or anyone except your own fat belly to fill. You take what isn't yours...and without asking. I saw you trying to take my necklace when you thought I was unconscious. And you stole something else of mine..." she trailed with ominous expectation.

He swallowed. She'd been awake for *that* too? How much had she seen?

"That's right." she nodded with disgust. "It's in the left front pocket of your breeches. I've been watching you fondle it."

He pulled out her Pal and looked down at it with shame. Suddenly inspired, he jerked his head up and his eyes flamed with challenge. *"Yours?"* He waved the shiny Pal at her. "Then why didn't you know what it was? I saw your reaction to what I was doing with mine. It's called a *Pal*, by the way," he said condescendingly with a smug sneer. "Pal is actually an acronym that stands for *Personal Artificial Living* and it costs—"

"It was *left* for me, idiot," she muttered sharply. "Like everything else in this backpack, along with that travel pass I saw you use and my other cards." Great, she hadn't missed anything, he realized with dismay and mounting shame. He might still be safe with the knight's gear; she didn't mention them. The girl went on, "They were given to me by someone from here so that I might better navigate your world. Unfortunately she died before she could explain it all to me."

François felt his face redden as yet another piece of her puzzle slipped into place. Of course. That explained her paradox of possessing the latest technological tools and conveniences of the city, yet having no idea what they were. It probably wasn't the girl who'd made those calls on the Pal either, he realized. If she could travel from the past into the future why couldn't someone from the future travel into the past, he reasoned. Each was as ludicrous and improbable as the other. Like Antoine being a *Guardien*.

The girl turned from him and lay down, settling into a mossy corner. She curled herself around her backpack with her back to him then turned her head and glanced over her shoulder at him. He couldn't make out her expression in the dark. "You don't have to stay," she said coolly. "I'll manage. I won't trouble you any further with my affairs. You don't have to worry. They're not after you." She then turned back around to face away from him. She'd just dismissed him. Like a noblewoman would her servant.

He blinked and fidgeted, not sure why he didn't bolt. She'd released him, after all, and he had all he needed from her. She hadn't even asked for her Pal back. "But what about that Mortameur guy? Won't he keep looking for you? What are you going to do? Where will you go?"

"I said I'd manage," she repeated tersely. "Like I said, you don't have to worry; it's me he's after. He doesn't care about you. I'm not your concern any longer." Then she mumbled quietly to herself, but he overheard, "Not that I ever was...*Père* was right..."

"But what are you going to do?" he persisted. He really wanted to ask her: *what's your next move?* She was an Aeon, after all! Whatever that meant.

"I told you. It's for me to figure out. I don't need you for that."

François felt suspended by conflicting feelings. Logic and self-preservation told him to leave the girl to her strange fate, that it wasn't his affair and she'd released him from any obligation; another part of him yearned to stay and protect her, embark in this intriguing adventure he'd stumbled upon and ride it to its end. He wasn't sure why but he convinced himself that he couldn't leave the girl on her own, despite her calm reassurances. She needed someone to protect her. She was just a girl, lost in the forest. A lady.

The girl was wrong, he reasoned: she *was* his concern. He might be a thief and a scoundrel, but he wouldn't abandon a young girl in need. For better or worse, she had brought him into her perilous journey by colliding into him; she, the Tear, Fate had chosen *him*. And Antoine, apparently; perhaps her *Guardien*. Besides, he decided, feeling uncharacteristically gallant, he'd stolen all her stuff. He felt obliged to give her something, considering what she'd unknow-ingly given him.

Whenever the gusting wind died down, François heard the low hush of the Paris nightlife traffic. For some Parisians the night had just begun.

"There are wild animals in this forest," he said, desperate for an excuse to stay. "If I stay we can share the watch. Then I can show you where you need to go in the morning— once you decide, that is," he offered in a kind voice, probably his first of the evening. And too late, he realized.

She didn't turn around to face him and he barely heard her muffled response, "Suit yourself."

That was a 'yes' he decided and settled down beside her. "I'll take the first watch," he announced to her huddled figure. She didn't respond and within moments he heard her long even sighs of sleep. He marveled that she could fall asleep under the circumstances; she must have been exhausted. She'd had quite a day, he decided as he sat cross-legged onto the soft turf next to her. He inched his way closer to her, getting as close as he thought was decent without actually touching her and peered up into the turbulent night sky. The trees swayed and creaked and the leaves hissed in the gusting wind. Rain wasn't far away.

The Bastille heist seemed so long ago. It seemed so long ago since the girl swept in like a stormy wind and changed his day into a thrilling nightmare.

As if drawing in a halting breath, the wind quieted. Then, like a sluice box suddenly opening up, it poured. Sheets of rain pelted down in a drowning hush. François was instantly drenched and the girl jerked up, aroused from her sleep in stricken confusion. She stared, blinking at him, hair streaming down her face.

"Come on!" he urged her, grabbing her pack then her hand and hastening toward the stone arched bridge. They scrambled down a gully to the dried portion of the creek bed and crept under the bridge out of the pelting rain. François squatted into a sitting position under the low bridge and hauled her on top of him, using his lap as a seat, then put his arms around her shivering body.

She didn't seem to mind being held by him as they huddled under the bridge in silence and listened to the rain hissing on the trees and shrubs. To François's amazement, the girl let herself drift off into a restless sleep.

He swept the wet hair plastered to her forehead away and she murmured in her sleep. Her eyelashes were still wet with raindrops that glistened in the blue light thrown off a lamp on the bridge. François couldn't fall asleep. Too much had happened and this strange girl nestled in his arms was stirring something inside him, foreign feelings he didn't feel comfortable having. Dangerous feelings. He glanced from her small form, sighing in deep sleep, to the veiled forest revealed from under the bridge through the thick sheet of rain.

The girl kept twitching and shuddering. She murmured and uttered sounds of agitation. François watched her passive face tighten into frowns or grimaces of distress. Nightmares, he thought, stroking her wet hair until she calmed down. But it was fleeting; within moments she was whimpering like a hurt child. He swallowed down his emotions and kept stroking her hair.

During her waking hours, the girl had remained pretty cool, he thought; she'd kept everyone and everything in this foreign world at a distance; she'd betrayed little vulnerability, and had mastered herself under great duress—if, indeed, she had really traveled in time from the Middle Ages, then she was coping extremely well, he considered. But in slumber the demons of her existence and circumstance openly tormented her and she succumbed to all her girlish vulnerabilities. There was more to her story, he decided. Much more than she'd told him.

Before he realized it he was nodding off and sleep claimed him shortly after.

✠

## ...22

FRANÇOIS bolted awake to the screech of a wild animal and the dawn light of a new day. It took him a moment to realize where he was. Then, the smell of her and her soft form pressed against him brought the recollection of the strange events of the day before. He glanced down at her as she lay asleep, nestled against him like a warm but damp blanket. Morning light filtered through the trees of le Bois de Boulogne in strings of gossamer through the early morning mist. The girl smelled of peaches and lavender. He gently swept back the hair that had tumbled over her face and noticed that the spate had washed away the blood crusted in her hair. François watched her body rise and fall in soft sighing breaths. Her sweater hung open and her still wet top clung on her like a second skin. He smiled wistfully. She felt good there, snug and trusting in his arms, as he waited patiently for her to awaken.

The girl abruptly stiffened then awoke with a scream that made him flinch. She squirmed out of his arms and surged to her feet, avoiding his eyes in awkward embarrassment. When they finally made eye contact, she gave him a small smile of greeting, as if nothing happened. *"Guten Morgen...*eh, good morning, François," she said.

"Good morning," he said. Then he smiled mischievously. "Come on, we can clean up in the creek." He promptly removed his grey t-shirt and stripped off his jeans to his bright blue boxers. The girl stared at him at first, then averted her eyes as he wandered into the creek and splashed himself briskly with the cold water. She followed hesitantly and took off her sweater but stopped there. François stood in the ankle deep water, watching her bend awkwardly over the steep bank and splash her face with water then wipe her arms and hands. He found himself wishing she'd fall in. He'd never met a girl as modest as she was. She had no reason to be, he thought, eying her slim athletic figure and remembering what it looked like without anything on. But he found her humility rather sweet and refreshing. He watched her scramble up the bank and glance back at him with an expectant look.

"Are you hungry?" he asked. She didn't have to answer; he saw it in her face and grinned. "I know where we can get something to eat." He got out of the creek and dressed.

"What about your uncle?" she asked him once he was fully dressed and she clearly felt it decent to look at him.

"He's okay," François answered enigmatically, thinking of all the times she'd given him an obtuse answer. He'd already checked on Uncle Antoine with his Pal while the girl had been sleeping. Antoine had texted him that he was okay: he'd awoken, still at the café, and its patrons had helped him recover by solicitously plying him with wine and fresh bread. Mortameur had disappeared and Antoine had been worried sick about François and the girl. Antoine had suggested to François that they meet later that day to discuss what to do with her. François was looking forward to talking to his uncle about what being a *Guardien* meant and why he'd never mentioned it before. "Have you figured out what you need to do?"

"Not yet," she said honestly. "I might want to meet with your uncle again."

François nodded."Let's get some food first," He smiled

at her. *"A bellyful is a bellyful."* He'd decided to take her back to his place but the long way, first to the morning market at Rue Mouffetard for breakfast then past Sainte-Chapelle. He'd promised to take her to a church, after all, he reasoned. Although Sainte-Chapelle wasn't Notre Dame, it would do nicely. Notre Dame was too open and full of greycoats. Besides, someone had told him that Sainte-Chapelle had the most spectacular stained glass windows and today was proving to be a sunny hot day.

By the time they got to the métro, the sun was blazing and they were mostly dry. They took the subway to Censier Daubenton in the Latin Quarter of the 5th Arrondissement. The girl was a lot better prepared and willing to take the subway, although he recognized her fear just under the surface in her furtive looks, poised stance and quiet disposition.

He decided to help by distracting her with his observations on human behavior—a skill he'd perfected over many a crowd-watching moment and his numerous interactions with clients.

"You see that man over there," he said, flicking his eyes toward an old man, absorbed in reading a newspaper. "What do you think he's thinking about or going to?"

To his satisfaction, the girl fully engaged him and with an eager expression. She raised her eyebrows in inquiry.

"He's listening to the two girls chatting behind him and getting turned on—"

She practically rolled her eyes in disbelief. "What makes you think that?" she said skeptically.

"His eyes aren't tracking across the page and he hasn't moved it in too long. Plus his face is a little flushed."

She nodded to him, impressed. Then she pointed discreetly to a tall well-dressed middle-aged woman further back. "What about her?"

"Ah," François said with a low chuckle of confidence. "She misses her little boy who's just started school."

Vivianne hiked up her brows again.

François grinned. "She looked very maudlin when she gazed at that little boy with his mother."

Vivianne nodded again.

At the Censier Daubenton Station, François led her to the escalator, where they ascended from the dark and deep throaty rush of trains into a heavenly cacophony of dazzling colour, scent and sound. They emerged into Rue Mouffetard's bustling open-air market next to a treed park and old gothic church.

The market spilled out in all directions before them in a giddy chaos of competing perfumes. It oozed with the ripe scents of fleshy fruit, exotic flowers, fresh coffee, crepes, almonds, sausage and bread. François led the girl through the crowded maze of stalls and shoppers. Shouting vendors enticed them with a seductive collage of colourful fruit and vegetables, cheeses, meats and fish. François glanced alongside the girl at the long-stem glasses brimming with dark olives and whole fish on ice, where a metre-long shark with an apple in its mouth was displayed. The girl turned to him with a beaming smile.

The market ached with scent. It made François drool with hunger. He noticed how the girl kept eying the *boulangerie* at the entrance of the Moule.

"Come on!" François abruptly grabbed her hand and they wormed through the crowd past the display of fat breads, croissants and long baguettes. Pushing the girl in front to distract the *boulanger*, François snatched a baguette. He stuffed it up the back of his shirt and tucked it under his jeans. Niether vendor nor girl had seen; she was smiling at the old man behind the counter as he proudly showed her his products.

"*Non, merci,*" François said briskly to the vendor and seized the girl's hand. She glanced back with disappointment as he dragged her across the narrow cobbled lane to a *charcuterie* where he again set her before the vendor and snatched two sausages.

After a hasty stop at a *Fromagerie*, François grabbed the girl's hand again and led her out of the Mouffe toward the old gothic church grounds. There, he pulled out their breakfast. He ripped off a piece of bread and handed it to the girl along with one of the cooked sausages and a round of Boursin.

"I didn't see you buy those," she said, looking puzzled as she accepted the items. She then tilted her head slightly and eyed him suspiciously. "You didn't..." she trailed, not wanting to hear his answer. She was starving. François watched her smear the bread across the soft cheese then tear into it and the sausage with hunger. Her eyes closed in brief euphoria as she breathed in the savory tastes and aromas and chewed slowly. François smiled wryly. She wasn't too proud to eat what he'd stolen.

When they'd finished their breakfast, they walked to Sainte-Chapelle on l'Ile de la Cité. Without the wind of yesterday, the heat of the day was already rising. They would want to retire indoors by lunch to escape the hottest part of the day, François thought.

✠

The girl stared up in fascinated wonder at the tall vaulted structure. Finials crowned its wall buttresses and huge jeweled windows sparkled in the late morning light. François had never seen anyone so entranced by a church before. But after giving the impressive structure a good view, he decided there might be something in it.

"It's just as *Père* Daniel said: a giant reliquary!" she said excitedly, throwing him a gleeful glance then turning back to stare at the church with clasped hands.

"A...what?"

"Reliquary. A shrine where sacred relics are stored," she explained. "Your King Louis IV walked barefoot in the streets of Paris with the relics and eventually placed Jesus's Crown of Thorns, part of the True Cross, and the nail of the Passion in his royal chapel, there." She pointed to the church. "*Père* said that the inside also resembles a reliquary. It has twelve imitation *repoussé* Apostles along the sides, just like *Père*'s own reliquary."

François quelled a frown at the girl's rapt grin. This was yet another fact she knew about his own city.

"Shall we go in," he said, deciding they'd stood admiring the chapel long enough. The girl nodded enthusiastically.

✠

They entered through the dark entranceway of the thirteenth century cathedral into the lower chapel and the girl seemed to instinctively know where to go. She led them up a spiral staircase where the smell of candles, smoke and incense pervaded. When they entered the sanctuary, the girl drew in a breath. The tall and elegant hall was bathed in a rich colorful light; it resembled a giant lantern. The girl made the sign of the cross over her breast and bent briefly on one knee with her head bowed. François stilled his breath and stared at the enormous panels. They seemed to float in the dark of empty space, like holograms animated by the light that streamed through them.

"Light shines through it like God's grace, creating lanterns of divine light," the girl whispered. Her voice echoed in a hollow reverberation, as if it too floated in the air. "God is light."

He glanced briefly at her and found her smiling tenderly at him. It drew a smile from him and he returned his gaze to the rose windows, feeling a warm glow surge through him. François almost believed her. He'd never been inside this place and now that he was, François exalted in its unearthly splendor and felt deeply humbled by it. This place was built by those who believed in something. François recognized the girl's description of the interior as he gazed from the arcades of floral ornamented arches, spandrels filled with angels and colonettes from which projected the twelve Apostles to the vaulted ceilings and tall jeweled windows of light. Everything in this place pointed upward, toward the heavens. Toward God, the girl would have said. Feeling her eyes still on him, he glanced back to her.

"*Danke*," she said softly. "Thank you for bringing me here."

For a brief moment, he felt like her hero and exulted. The place reminded him of a vivid yet disturbing dream he'd had two nights ago. Of a medieval knight, wading through a swamp with the spoils of war scattered about on the rocks, but no bodies. The knight was himself. The vaulted ceiling of an immense cathedral towered above him. An eerie light streamed down through its translucent walls and straight ahead a great ball of light lured. He'd woken in a sweat. François wondered that he'd only now remembered the dream that he seemed to have forgotten until now. And odd that he'd dreamt of a medieval knight the night before the girl, dressed as one, had swept into his world.

She leaned close to him and whispered, "This place reminds me of a vision I had. Of a knight wandering on a quest through a swamp. He encounters a cathedral of heaven and stands, with sword in one hand and shield in the other, mesmerized by its utter beauty."

François stared at her. That was *his* dream! He met her gaze with a confused stare and their eyes locked—

An old woman, seated in a side bench near the front, coughed and broke the silence—and the spell. François tore his gaze from the girl to glance at the old woman and noticed that they were the only ones there; it was a weekday morning after all.

The girl headed toward the alter, where the shrine of sacred relics lay, and kneeled on the stone floor to pray. Feeling suddenly uncomfortable in this hallowed place, François lingered in the back. He saw a priest, dressed in a long black robe approach the girl from the side. She looked up at him like a child.

"Can I help you?" François heard the priest ask the girl.

"I wish to make my confession, Father," she said very quietly, but the impeccable acoustics of the sanctuary carried her clear voice to François. She glanced inquiringly back at him, as if to ask permission, and François found himself nodding. Maybe it would do her some good, he thought. Loosen her up; she was wound tight, bouncing from terrified to euphoric with nothing in between.

"Certainly, my child," the priest said, glancing briefly at François. "You are a Catholic?"

The girl nodded with an assenting whisper, something François couldn't make out. She and the priest disappeared to the side into one of the confessionals and François waited, wandering the sanctuary and inspecting the various stain-glass windows. He grew impatient and was beginning to think it was a bad idea, when the priest and the girl emerged. While the girl looked relieved and momentarily at peace, François noticed that the priest looked truly bemused. What had the girl told him? Some mad tale, no doubt, of medieval treachery, time travel and Aeon magic, François decided and hid a smile.

As François approached them, the priest turned to him and raised a brow. "Your sister may benefit from a visit to Salpêtrière."

François nodded and motioned for the girl to leave with him when the priest looked expectantly at him. "What about you?"

François backed away. "That's okay. You don't want to hear my confession. Besides, I'm an atheist." Then he pulled the girl by her arm and led them to the back of the sanctuary.

Before they got to the stairs, the girl stopped at one of the candle stands. "I wish to light some candles for my...loved ones," she said.

"Sure."

She found a long match and was about to light it when she turned back to François with a sad expression. "Why did you say that? That you're not a believer?"

He shrugged. "It's complicated. It was easier to say it than explain." If she could evade issues, so could he, François decided. "I'll wait outside," he added, feeling suddenly very uncomfortable under her gaze. He left her there, lighting candles, to wait for her outside. He was uncomfortable with the whole praying thing. He never prayed. Who would he pray to, after all?

François sat on the grass in front of the church. He soon grew impatient and cast nervous glances around, unconsciously looking for Mortameur. François kept thinking of the girl. He thought of her naked on his mattress then asleep in his arms, vulnerable and smelling like a flower…and him doing nothing both times. It triggered a sudden desire for *rapture* and he shivered with urgent need. François jammed a trembling hand into his jeans pocket for a rabbit, noting that there was only one left. He ripped it open with furious urgency then poured the magical powder into his mouth, flinging the black wrapper aside and reclining with closed eyes on the grass. He uttered a growl of instant orgasmic pleasure—

"What is that?" he heard the girl's voice above him.

François snapped his eyes open and squinted at her harsh silhouette against the sun. He couldn't make out her expression, obscured in shadow, but he saw that she held his black rabbit wrapper in her hand. He gave her a goofy grin. "A piece of heaven," he admitted and watched the prism of light play about her wild hair like a sun's eclipse.

"Some kind of potion, more like," she said in a reproving tone.

"That's right," he drawled, sitting up. "A *love* potion…" His mouth twisted into a lascivious grin as he made a grab for her.

"*Your body is the temple of the Holy Spirit,*" she said sternly, stepping aside from his grasp. "To abuse it like you do is…" she trailed.

"What? An abomination?" he barked at her, suddenly sober, and getting up to face her.

She dropped her gaze and pressed her lips together. He had the impression that it was not in her nature to lecture and he'd caught her about to do it. "I'm sorry," she apologized with a tight face of quelled concern. "I was just…" she trailed off with a light shake of her head. "It's not my life or my body. It's yours to do with what ever you wish."

"Damn right!" Francois agreed in a strident voice of strained cheerfulness. "Mine to destroy if I want to."

"Or not," she said softly.

Their eyes locked and he thought he recognized real concern in hers. Something he'd never received from anyone, including his uncle. They were always looking out for their angle, what *he* could do for *them*. Even his uncle...what François could do for the Résistance. No one had ever just looked at him—into him—as a person before and offered him their selfless concern. He blinked at her and eventually had to look away. "It helps keep the demons away."

"You think you're the only one who has demons?"

He turned back to gaze at her through his stray locks of hair and remembered her nightmares as she slept in his arms under the bridge. Her mouth was set in stern challenge but her eyes were compassionate and invited honesty. He blurted out, "You don't come from a world oppressed by power-hungry fascists who don't value your way of life, who're so busy changing your home into something else that you fear someday you won't recognize it anymore..." Her eyes sparkled with a knowing plaintive look, suggesting that he was wrong, that she shared that very fear; but he pressed on, "You don't live in a world that has no hope, no freedom, no soul...You didn't lose your mother and father to fascists either."

Her gaze hardened briefly. "What if I *did*?"

"But you *didn't*, did you?"

She backed off with a cryptic smile and put her guard back on. "Perhaps not," she conceded strangely and released her gaze to look away.

It was an odd answer and disturbed him. He knew she hadn't been teasing him; she was far too earnest for that. Not that she lacked guile, he thought. She was plenty clever and manipulative in her own way. But, unlike him, she wasn't a dissembler. What had happened to her loved ones? Maybe she didn't have any, he suddenly thought. Perhaps she'd just made them up in the church. Or worse yet, they did exist but they were dead like his and she'd lit candles for their departed souls. She hadn't told him anything about her parents or other relations. There'd only been her betrothed. And *he* sure wasn't worth a candle.

"What does your old boyfriend want with you?" François asked.

"Stop calling him that!" she huffed. Then, as if reminded

of the danger, she glanced fearfully around them at the people wandering the grounds. "We should go. This is too open."

He suggested that they return to his place to figure out their next move. She nodded vigorously, glad to leave their discussion behind, and they headed for the métro.

She was definitely getting the hang of it, François observed, watching her slide her ticket through the slot at the gate like a regular Parisian commuter. The rushing trains still made her nervous but she hardly showed that now. Within a few moments of entering the station they'd boarded a north-bound train and settled into two adjacent seats facing forward. The car was mostly empty except for a mother and her three-year old boy, face glued to the window, and an old man who looked like he'd slept on the street. François could smell him from where they sat; a strong unwashed odour, undercut with stale beer and urine. He was sure the girl was disgusted although her purposefully calm expression revealed nothing.

Once the train plunged into the dark tunnel, she turned to François with a guarded smile but plaintive eyes. "Why are you helping me? You don't know me, yet you're giving me aid at great risk to yourself." She sort of grimaced. "And your uncle, like you said last night..."

So, she'd taken his accusation to heart, he thought. Probably the reason he'd aroused such defensive anger in her earlier. He couldn't tell her that he felt compelled to help her because of the price her trappings had fetched for him; Jacques had texted him earlier with a promise of 2,000F for this afternoon. "Because you looked so lost," he said instead. It wasn't a lie; it just wasn't the whole truth.

At his words she lowered her guard and let herself look really unhappy. "I don't understand the people here." She glanced briefly at the other people in the car. "You're right; I do feel lost. When *Père* told me about Paris, he called it the city of light, and described a great city that celebrated innovation, art, and intellectual freedom. He said it was the most splendid city he'd ever been in. A city of reverence, beautiful art and culture, and with people of taste, an incredible *joie de vivre* and intellectual honesty."

That was before the Nazis came, thought François.

"I expected…" She trailed, throwing another brief glance at the filthy old man slouched in the seat across from them. His stench permeated the car. "I don't know…and no one smiles at you…"

François stared at her with a puzzled smirk. He hadn't realized that she'd made an effort to interact with other people. "That's because they don't know you," he quipped, the logic obvious to him. Then he added with cruel humor, "If they did, then they'd at least have a reason not to smile."

She pouted, clearly not appreciating his malicious tease. It was the first time he saw her pout. He wanted to laugh. But he bit it back.

"It's a joke," he said wearily. "I was just kidding. You should expect men to look at you. But you don't smile at a stranger unless you're being suggestive. If a girl smiles at a strange man he'll think she's an idiot, a simpleton, or—in your case—that you're coming on to him."

"Coming on?"

"Wanting to make out." She still didn't understand. He decided to be blunt: "That you want to have sex with him."

"Oh." She looked down quickly, blushing. Perhaps she was remembering the scene with Dominique. Then she looked up with a quizzical frown. "Why in *my* case?"

"Because…well…" Now it was his turn to blush. "Well, because you're pretty and they'd rather think you're coming on to them than think you're just a simpleton." François gave her a lame smile. Then he decided that since they'd broached an uncomfortable topic he might as well continue with another: "You never answered my uncle. Why *did* you come?"

She drew in a breath, bracing herself to share. Their eyes locked and for a moment he glimpsed a deep sadness and pain. Then the moment passed, her eyes faltered and she withdrew. She dropped her gaze and shook her head slowly with a sad complicated smile.

"Or was it just that you were running away from that

creep?" He thought of the messages she and Boulanger had exchanged. Was Mortameur the man they both had feared would find her?

Her head jerked up and she stared at him. "Yes," she responded quickly. "That's what I was doing. Running away from him."

François sensed there was a great deal more that she wasn't telling him. She'd seized his gift of half-truth to avoid revealing the whole. He wasn't used to this kind of reticence from a girl and found it infuriating yet deliciously intriguing. She was complex. Not like the simple girls who chased after him, usually for sex or cigarettes or food. Not like Sylvie who had nothing to share between her ears, but who was willing to share everything between her legs....

François had the sudden thought of shopping for some supplies on their way back, so they got off at the Rambuteau Station and he led the girl into her first underground mall. The mall linked underground with the Pampidou Centre and part of it was above ground. The girl stuck close to François and gaped around at the glittering shops and strobing signs like a kid in a candy store. It was an impressive mall, he admitted, following her gaze to the vaulting sky-ceilings and floating holo ads.

"It looks like a cathedral," she breathed out in awe. François laughed out loud and grabbed her hand as they wove through the already crowded mall of mid-morning shoppers and droids.

François took the girl to *le Grand Marché* to buy some fruit. As she marveled at the colourful display of fruit and vegetables, François paid for some peaches and cherries, happily using her bank card and aware that it might be traced. As they left, he caught the girl staring through a shop window at a pretty summer dress on a mannequin in the adjacent clothing store. "Come on." He dragged her to a pharmacy, where he let her unknowingly distract the clerk so he could steal a bar of soap.

Once out in the open square of the mall, François stopped to decide if there was anything else they needed. The girl tugged his arm lightly and he turned to find her gazing at him with a look of mild distress. *Now* what had he done? Had she seen him steal the soap?

"I must...I need to...*Ich*..." she trailed off into a kind of grimace. She looked very uncomfortable. "*Ich muß die Garderobe benutzen.*"

François squirmed. "I don't understand," he said brusquely, throwing nervous glances around them at the crowd. He was impatient to leave. They'd lingered long enough and it wasn't safe here. Most of Paris was under computer surveillance, linked to their GPS tatoos. He spotted at least five surveillance cameras high up, overlooking the sea of shoppers below. There were too many people to account for all their individual movements. And François was acutely aware of having just used the girl's bank card to buy the fruit. He hadn't discounted that her card could easily be traced by Black Knight surveillance. But the girl refused to move.

She gave him a sad straining look. Then, clutching her hands on her belly, she bent her knees slightly in a rocking motion.

He suddenly understood her urgency. "The toilet! You need the toilet!"

Recognizing the word, she straightened and nodded vigorously with a relieved grin. "*Ya! Die Toilette!*"

"Okay, don't pee your pants! I'll find you a washroom," he muttered and craned to find a sign for the Lady's washroom. "We can get cleaned up there too," he added. He spotted one in the far north corner of the mall and hastily directed them there. Once in front of the washrooms, François entered the men's washroom to clean up. The girl followed him inside.

"No!" He pushed her gruffly out and pointed toward the Ladies washroom door. "Ladies go in *that* one. See? This is only for men. Understand?"

She nodded with a slightly embarrassed smile and made for the right door. As she disappeared through it, François sighed and shook his head with a frown. It turned into a wry smile; she was probably going to freak out at the self-flushing toilet. He prepared himself for a shriek as he did his business.

But he heard nothing from the women's washroom. When he was done, François left the men's washroom and stood outside the door she'd gone through, waiting for her to emerge. Patiently at first. He soon grew impatient as the minutes dragged on and the girl still didn't come out. He began to get nervous again and surveyed the crowd suspiciously.

Okay, François told himself, she's probably having a hard time of it; she'd had to go really bad. She'd looked really uncomfortable. Then he began to worry that maybe she was sick. Maybe she was puking or passed out on the floor.

"Hey!" he called softly. "Come on!"

She didn't respond.

"Hey, you okay?"

Still nothing. "*Merde!*" He'd been inside a Ladies washroom once before but that was with Jacqueline who'd dragged him inside to make out in one of the cubicles. This was different. This girl was a lady. She wouldn't understand. Then he reminded himself that she'd initially followed him into the men's washroom. "*Merde!*" After a swift glance at the mall crowd, he slid inside.

He found her standing at the row of sinks, mesmerized by the running water. She glanced at him when he entered and gave him a big grin then returned a rapt gaze to the running water. When it automatically stopped, she put her hands underneath and triggered it to start again to her utter glee. Obviously puzzled by the mechanism, she bent and peered at the faucet, awestruck. François stared, incredulous. She really *was* ignorant!

With relief came the surrender to annoyance at his former concern for the girl.

"What are you doing!" he bellowed, unleashing his tension of the morning at her. The girl looked at him like a wide-eyed child caught with her hand in the cookie jar. He immediately regretted his angry outburst but refused to apologize or quell his crankiness for her sake. Instead, he grabbed her gruffly. "Come on! We need to get out of here!"

"It's incredible," she uttered, glancing back in rapt

wonder at the sinks as he pulled her out of the washroom and they wove their way through the crowded mall. "Your world is incredible."

"*Merde*, it's just a God-damned tap," he grumbled and instantly felt her wounded glare of disapproval. He wheeled on her with a retort, "What *now*?"

She stood her ground. "Do you always use such bad language?" she reproved. "It's offensive. You're profaning our Lord."

He rolled his eyes and laughed with cynical sarcasm. So, she *was* a Catholic! God help them both.

✠

## ...23

BACK at his little hovel, François tossed the cherries and peaches into a bowl then pulled out the stolen soap and threw it into the pail by the door. After confirming that Jacques had indeed removed his stash, François pulled out his Pal and read through his messages. There was one from Lizette, which he ignored, and one from Jacques, which he opened. It was just to confirm a meeting place and time this afternoon. Jacques had offered him two replica medieval swords as a gift for getting him those savory items, which he'd already confirmed were genuine. No doubt he'd get or already got over 10,000F for the stuff. With a beatific grin, François checked his watch and turned to the girl. It was just past noon.

"You get comfortable, have a peach and some cherries, maybe have a nap or something," he said, feeling awkward with her suddenly. "I have to meet a friend about something. I'll be back in a few hours and we can go out for supper after, okay?"

She smiled at him and nodded. "I will read my books;

that's what my Moth-eh-my guide suggested I do." She looked like a little girl just then and he felt a pang of guilt; he was abandoning her to get money for selling her stuff.

"Eh, good," he said. "Maybe you'll know what you need to do by the time I get back." Then he left in a hurry.

✠

François met Jacques at Place Stravinsky, where the old vendor paid him and gave him the two replica swords. They shared an expensive lunch together then François giddily went back to the same mall he and the girl had been to earlier that day. *Frugality is for the vulgar*, he thought as he bought the dress that had caught the girl's eye in one of the store windows. He included some sleepwear and a few pairs of briefs. He couldn't believe how embarrassed he felt, blushing at the store clerk when she asked him what size his girlfriend was.

"Eh, she's actually my sister."

"And you don't know her size?"

He'd guessed by pointing to another customer, "She's about *her* size, a little taller and bigger...eh..." He'd trailed, hands straying up to his chest. The clerk had understood. As the clerk folded the dress with the boxers, light t-shirt and briefs and put them into a bag, François suddenly realized that, despite all the girls he'd made out with, he'd never bought anything for a girl before. He wondered how l'Oncle Antoine had so easily managed to purchase those female things like briefs and feminine hygiene pads.

✠

When he returned around 1600 with his purchases, including bread and cheese from the local market and the two swords wrapped in a bag under his arm, François halted at the door.

The girl was kneeling beside one of his walls with a cleaning rag in her hand. The place was hardly recognizable.

She'd straightened everything. She'd found a place for each item, whether valuable or not, and thoroughly cleaned every surface and corner. She'd even fixed his rickety table and chair and filled in the leaks in the roof and patched the hole in the side wall. And it smelled nice. Actually smelled nice! She'd found some flowers and a vase and had hung lavender posies, now in season, in several places. He spotted his old guitar, polished and leaning invitingly against a corner wall.

François stared around, glanced at the girl, then stared at his place again in shocked delight. She was a baroness who lived in a castle with servants to do her bidding and yet she'd bent down on her hands and knees, perhaps for the first time in her life, to scrub his filthy floor clean. He was touched by her enthusiastic domestic attempt. Then he got mad. Feeling suddenly threatened, even trapped—he had no idea why—he exploded with anger: "Why'd you go and do that? Now I won't be able to find anything!" He swung around dramatically and aimed a raging gaze at his newly cleaned walls. She'd even straightened and re-glued his posters. "You don't touch my stuff! Never touch my stuff!"

She'd flinched at his initial outburst; she certainly hadn't expected it. Then she surged to her feet as if bracing for an argument. François stiffened, preparing for a diatribe. Instead she swallowed hard and apologized as if she'd done something wrong, which of course she hadn't, "You're right. I'm sorry. I won't touch any of your stuff again. In fact, I should leave—"

"Here, it's for you," François said, lunging forward with what he'd bought her. She accepted the large bag then sat down on his chair to look inside with a curious glance at him. She drew out the boxers and t-shirt and looked up inquisitively.

"They're for sleeping in. It's what Parisian girls wear at night when they go to bed." Unless they're naked, of course, he added to himself.

She then pulled out the cotton wrap-around blue-green patterned dress with spaghetti straps. Her face suddenly brightened and she grinned at him with unalloyed joy. It made him blush with pleasure.

There was more: a soft clean blanket and sheets, a toothbrush and toothpaste and hand cream. When she looked up at him again, François said quietly, "You can stay here as long as you need...no questions asked. As for time travel from six hundred years ago, Aeons and twin worlds, it doesn't matter. I know you're in trouble and I know you're a good person. That's all I need to know."

She blinked at him, speechless; probably the first time she'd been without a comeback since he'd met her, anyway. It made him smirk. He hid it behind his hand as he turned to inspect his place again, appreciating the work she'd put into refurbishing his shack. It looked a little more like a home.

When his gaze returned to her, she said, "*Vielen Dank,*" looking overwhelmed still. "Thank you."

"Yeah, sure," he waved his hand casually, in an attempt to diminish what he'd done. Then hoping to repair the damage of his earlier wrathful comments, he added, "Eh, *Vielen Dank* too, for this. The flowers...they're from?..."

She grinned. They both said in unison: "Crazy Annette!" Then both laughed. It broke the ice between them and he saw her relax.

"And you found a place for everything and straightened out my posters..."

"With help from Patrice."

"And you even fixed the wobbly table and the chair..."

"Philip and André helped. And I washed everything and aired out the mattress. Actually Dominique helped with that."

"Dominique?" The whore who'd hit up on the girl then insulted her when the girl rejected her. *That* Dominique? She was the most selfish brat he knew. "*She* helped you?"

"She's a very nice girl, François," the girl said matter-of-factly.

"Maybe when she wants something..." he trailed. *Like your ass, girl,* he thought. Burning with curiosity, he wanted to ask the girl how she'd handled the pushy whore. But he didn't; they'd obviously fared without mishap.

"How did you do that?" He pointed to the daubed hole. "It looks great."

"Actually, that wasn't me," she gave him a lame smile. "It was Vincent."

"You mean Rouard?" He couldn't believe she was using the old man's first name.

"I asked him what materials he used on his place and he showed me by doing yours."

"You talked to Rouard?" François exploded, feeling his warmth toward the girl boil over again. Why did she keep doing that? Like she had an 'annoy François' gene inside her that he kept tripping. "Rouard is a mean cold-blooded killer! He got twenty *flics* killed before they finally threw him in jail. I warned you about him, I told you before that no one talks to him. *No one!* People leave him alone. He kills people! And for no other reason than that no good bastard simply doesn't like the way you look…"

"Well, that *no good bastard* obviously didn't mind how *I* looked," she quipped.

He stared at her in quiet rage, not sure if she was teasing him. It didn't seem in her nature, but he wasn't sure. She couldn't be that stupid…so, she must be teasing him, he decided, studying her face. She'd carefully kept it closed from expression. Then he noticed a softening in her lower jaw and lip.

"He said he would teach me how to use a phantom gun," she said with an air of smugness and now barely hiding an amused smile. "So I can defend myself on the streets of Paris."

"Oh my God!" François wailed out dramatically and smacked his hand against his head.

She knew he wasn't a practicing Christian or that he believed in God; she knew he'd just profaned God's name by using it as an expletive. This time she didn't even have to glance reprovingly at him. "Sorry," he muttered an apology. *Merde!* *She's got me apologizing for every little thing now! Merde! Merde!* François let out a long breath of frustration. Why was this girl such a confusing source of pain, such delicious pain….

François felt a wry smile cross his lips. For a reserved

girl, she hadn't done too badly; in one day she'd befriended his entire neighborhood. And like a competent and commanding noblewoman, she'd enlisted every one of them to cheerfully help her. Even the old man....

"Oh, by the way," she added in a half tart, half amused voice, "he *does* have a Reuental VC entertainment system." Then she smirked...actually smirked at him. Damn her! *Merde! Merde! Merde!*

As if suddenly reminded, the girl returned to her backpack and pulled out her little prayer book. She only consulted it briefly as if to make sure it was still there, certainly not to read; then she closed her eyes tightly and clutched the book to her breast as if it were her savior and murmured from obvious memory. All this praying was starting to really annoy him. Her head was slightly bowed with downcast eyes of sincere reverence.

"...*Unser Vater im himmel, dein Name werde geheiligt, dein Reich komme, dein Wille geschehe wie im Himmel, so auf der Erde...*"

François frowned and interrupted in a more clipped voice than he'd intended, "Do you honestly rely on your faith in God? You really believe in that—" He cut himself off just before uttering the word "crap" which he knew would offend the girl.

She looked up at him with big earnest eyes. Their quiet complicated gaze spoke everything, just waiting for his interpretation. He found he couldn't—there was too much there—and let his gaze falter.

"I didn't used to," she said simply then returned her attention to her prayer book and continued, "*Gib uns heute das Brot, das wir brauchen. Und erlaß uns unsere Schulden, wie auch wir sie unseren Schuldnern erlassen haben.*" At this she glanced up pointedly at François, as though what she'd just said had particular significance to him. He knew it had something to do with their earlier quarrel or what he'd done today and felt his face heat. "...*Und führe uns nicht in Versuchung, sondern rette uns vor dem Bösen.*"

François shrugged, giving in to the girl's rhetoric, and glanced at his watch. It was approaching the time for him to meet his uncle at the *Café La Chope* in the Mouffe.

"Listen, I have a meeting with a colleague. You have to stay here, okay?"

The girl looked up at him and nodded. She didn't like the idea but it was okay with her.

"I'll be back and we'll have supper together," he said. "No more cleaning. Thanks, but no more, okay?"

"Okay." She nodded to him with a small complicated smile.

✠

François found his uncle seated, cross-legged and smoking a cigarette at the *Café la Chope*. He was dressed in his usual worn leather jacket and red scarf and managed to look impeccable despite his situation. The old man didn't look too worse for his beating last night either. A small dark bruise grazed his temple where Mortameur had hit him. As if sensing his presence, Antoine looked up and smiled with obvious pleasure. He looked past François for the girl. "Where is she?" he asked right away as they exchanged *les bisous*.

"I don't know," François lied in false despondency as he slouched in the chair across from his uncle. He had no idea why he'd lied about the girl except that he foolishly wanted her for himself. He felt eclipsed by his uncle. The girl hardly seemed to notice him when his uncle was there; she appeared to belong to his uncle. Antoine was master of everything. He knew everything. Antoine impressed her; François was lucky to amuse her. It was Antoine who she thought she was meant to seek out after passing through the tear. It was he, after all, François reminded himself, who was the *Guardien*, the guardian of Aeons, perhaps of *this* Aeon. François had no role to play; he was nothing. "*Je m'en fiche.* She was a pest," he grumbled, toying with the flower vase of lavender and thinking of the wonderful gesture she'd made to beautify his place. "She nearly killed us."

"You ditched her in the middle of the city?" Antoine looked amazed and disgusted at the same time.

François smirked. His uncle didn't think much of him, he thought. "Some park in the 5ème Arrondissement."

"The *Jardin du Luxembourg*?" Antoine looked aghast. Then he frowned at François with a stern gaze. "You sold her things too, didn't you?"

He'd guessed right. François felt his heart rumble with the truth. His uncle was sharp; he'd guessed most of the truth, but not all of it. François nodded and hung his head like a little boy caught stealing cookies.

"You bastard!"

François jerked his head up to blink at his uncle. He'd been more emotional about it than François expected. "So, what," he said peevishly.

"You idiot! She's important. Important to me! And to you, François." He pointed emphatically with his cigarette, ashes falling on the table.

"Why to me?"

Antoine jammed the cigarette between his lips to sweep the ashes from the table into the ashtray. "Because you're her protector," he muttered around the cigarette hanging out of his mouth. "You need to keep her from getting killed by that madman, Mortameur."

François drew in his breath to steel himself. He liked the girl. A lot, he had to admit. As for being her bodyguard, that was entirely something else, especially considering who was after her. The flower he'd been stroking snapped in his hand and he leaned forward. "Are you crazy, l'Oncle? That's a Black Knight who's chasing after her! *Merde*, he nearly killed you last night!"

Antoine leaned forward to meet the boy's frightened gaze. "Listen to me, François. You must find her. Find her and take her to your place. She'll be safe there."

François laughed sharply and stole the half-smoked cigarette out of Antoine's lips to take a long inhale. "As if my place is safe..." he drawled, blowing smoke out of his mouth and nose.

"It's a tear sanctuary."

François blinked. "A...what?"

Antoine leaned back and poured water from a carafe into the two glasses of *pastis*. They immediately clouded and he handed François one, even though he knew the boy hated the stuff. After taking a sip with puckered lips, he said, "A tear sanctuary is a natural force field that is produced around a tear for a radius of about half a kilometer. It forms every time a summoner calls forth a tear and uses it to get across time-space." He took another sip of *pastis* and studied François to make sure he was still with him, then continued, "What's important is that once a summoner calls up and uses a tear, it's matched with their signature alone and no other summoner—no other Aeon—can go near it, or they get zapped into a gazillion little pieces. It's a kind of failsafe mechanism built into the process to prevent paradox, I guess. To keep competing Aeons, who may have other motives, from messing with the singularity."

François sat back and frowned at his uncle. He took a sip of the liquorice liquor and water despite his distaste for it. "Are you saying that this Mortameur guy is an Aeon too?"

"That's what I'm saying." Antoine shrugged. "I'm guessing."

"What if you're wrong?"

Antoine smiled condescendingly. "I'm seldom wrong."

"I guess it makes sense," François said, grudgingly accepting his uncle's logic. "The guy knew her from her time period and he's obviously here—as a Black Knight—so he must be a traveler like her..." François abruptly brightened at his own logic and burst into a self-pleased grin.

Antoine nodded with a patronizing smile. "I concur, François. As for what he wants..." He shook his head solemnly. "Did the girl tell you anything?"

"Nothing," François said honestly. But, just as the words left his lips he remembered her revelation in the Bois de Boulogne about Mortameur being her betrothed. François decided not to tell his uncle. Was it really just a case of her fleeing from a poor match and Mortameur wishing to claim his betrothed? Somehow, François thought it had to be more. Not that she wasn't worth claiming, he thought. She was a sweet girl with a beautiful face. But François just couldn't imagine an ordinary girl inspiring such a passionate action from a Black Knight. Then he reminded himself that she wasn't exactly an ordinary girl. And this Mortameur guy wasn't your regular Black Knight either. Antoine picked up on his expression and, not wanting to share, François instead fed a real frustration he felt with the girl: "The bi-eh-girl never talks. She's a fu-eh-Marcel Marceau." It somehow felt better not to swear, even though the girl was no where near him.

Antoine threw his head back and barked out a laugh. He then nervously tapped his cigarette on the ashtray and took in a long inhale, blowing smoke out his nose and mouth. He eyed François shrewdly. "I suspected that under all that whoring you were a misogynist. You're not used to a girl like that, eh? So secretive..."

Deliciously mysterious, thought François.

"...Manipulative and deceiving..." Antoine continued.

Intelligent and cunning, thought François.

"...An evil witch..."

An incredible woman. And it was Antoine who was the misogynist, François decided.

"Well, the trick is to find her, François," his uncle reminded him. "I can't believe you dumped her in the middle of Paris like that..."

✠

## ...24

FRANÇOIS returned to find the girl dozing in the chair with one of her books on her lap. She stirred and tensed then relaxed, relieved it was him. She gave him one of those smiles she'd up to now reserved for his uncle.

"Are you hungry?" he asked.

She nodded enthusiastically and put her books away.

Feeling pleased with himself, François took her to *le Coude Fou* down the street. It was a *bar à vin* that he and his uncle used to frequent when Antoine had first found François a year ago and tried to lure him from his bad habits of sex and drugs. Many a lively discussion had erupted within those premises under the discreet care of Sabine and her husband, Etienne.

François and the girl entered the old place, with its checkered floor and simple pub-style wooden tables. He led them past several patrons to a table at the back and sat himself facing the door. Sabine, the proprietor's stylishly dressed and attractive wife, immediately came forward. Like with many of the small family-run cafés and bistros, she also happened to be the waitress.

"*Bonjour*, Sabine!" he said, betraying giddy joviality.

"*Bonjour*, François," she responded with a friendly smile and a brief glance at the girl. "It's been awhile since we've seen you...not since you and your uncle were here seven months ago."

"Yes...well...we'll start with a dozen *escargots* in garlic butter and a Gewürz," he said to her.

"*Ah, bon*," she said, glancing at the girl with curiosity. "Good choice, *monsieur*. But for now perhaps a *pastis* or a *kir* for you and the lady as you wait?"

"Good idea, Sabine. Yes a *kir* would be nice."

When Sabine left the table, the girl leaned over the table toward François with a shy smile. "The name of this place...Crazy elbow?" she glanced back at Sabine, who'd gone behind the counter and was speaking through the window to her husband in the back.

François grinned. "It refers to the crazy turns our elbows make when we chug back a few." The girl didn't look like she believed him. "Did you know that this whole place used to be a swamp?" François continued. "That's what Marais means: 'swamp'."

"That's like where I come from, in Prussia. My father's

castle was built in the Grunwald valley, next to a huge flooded forest."

She was opening up, François thought gleefully; his small-talk was paying off. He said with a grin, "And did you know that there are three times as many chefs in France as there are lawyers?"

The girl laughed this time, a wide-open laugh that showed her teeth.

Sabine returned with a tray and placed two stemmed glasses of aromatic deep crimson liquor mixed with white wine in front of the girl and François. Then with a smile she left them again.

François raised his glass. "*Santé*," he said to the girl.

"*Santé*," she responded, raising her glass to his. Following his lead, she took a sip. The strong sweet black current liquor topped with crisp white wine was both invigorating and refreshing. François smacked his lips in appreciation. He saw the girl stare into the drink with a look of genuine appreciation then take another less lady-like sip.

Within a short time Sabine brought the steaming *escargots*, a basket of bread and the wine to their table.

The girl stared down at the rectangle of aluminum foil, marked with a dozen shallow indentations, a snail in each. François felt the heat rise from their shells. Sabine set a napkin and a wooden toothpick in front of each of them then said, "*Bon appetit.*" She left them again. François hid a smile as he watched the girl inspect the exotic dish; it was obvious that she'd never had snails in her native medieval Prussia.

The girl intrepidly picked up one of the shells, then jerked her hand back with a stifled cry and blew her singed fingers.

"Watch out, it's very hot," François said, biting back a grin.

He caught her watching him closely as he hollowed out a slice of bread and used the crust like pincers, wrapping it around a shell to insulate his fingertips from the burning hot surface. Using his other hand, he stabbed the toothpick into the snail and with a half-twist of his wrist, extracted the sizzling flesh of the snail from its house and popped it into his eager mouth. The garlic was buttery, not overpowering, and his teeth sank into the snail's flesh like a tender filet mignon. The girl was still staring at him when François raised the shell to his mouth and sipped the juice with closed eyes of appreciation.

Then it was her turn. He nodded to her with an eager smile of encouragement. The girl did as he did but hesitated when she brought the snail up to her mouth to stare at the rather unappetizing dark and wrinkled mass.

François remembered what his Uncle Antoine had told him long ago, and repeated the words with a smug smile of amusement, "*Escargots* should be eaten through the nose, not through the eyes."

The girl glanced up at him past the toothpick-skewered snail poised before her and nodded. François could see her steeling herself to put that questionable mass into her mouth. Then, after a deep intake of air, she bravely slid it between her teeth and blinked several times as she chewed and tasted the delicacy with obvious pleasure.

François grinned in vindication.

The dozen were soon gone and François ordered another dozen, this time *à la bourguignonne*. They were in no hurry to return to his hovel, François decided. He ordered one of their *plat de jour*, the *Roti d'agneau du lait P. Sautées* and another wine while they finished the *escargots*. He lit a cigarette and smiled across at the girl who'd just given him a warm smile. The girl's guileless enjoyment of food and her eager and substantial conversation about philosophy and religion filled him with a sense of home. He tried not to think of where he'd gotten the money to pay for the meal.

As they feasted and shared stories for several hours, François relaxed and forgot about the Nazis for a while. Instead, he concentrated on the girl and what he could learn about her and her strange medieval world. And what she was doing here.

She was, however, consummate at negotiating a one-way conversation without giving the impression that she was interrogating him, François considered. The upshot was that by the time they were about to leave *le Coude Fou* late that evening she knew a great deal more about him than he did of her. She'd effortlessly drawn it out of him without revealing much of herself, he thought as they lingered over a strong freshly brewed coffee and crème caramel.

She'd learned of his anarchist parents; about his cynicism and nihilist view of the world; of his inclinations toward anarchy against the Nazi regime but refusal to commit himself to the movement; she'd learned all about his passionate and dedicated uncle; of Paris history and culture; that he would have liked to live in the Latin Quarter and learn music at the Sorbonne; that he hadn't traveled outside of France, although he knew a little bit about North America, the rest of Europe and Africa; and that he dreamed of some day traveling the world as a free man.

By contrast, he'd only learned that she lived with her father and a small household of servants and knights in Grunwald Castle, that she had a cat named Fritz and learned to speak fluent French, English, and Latin from her teacher, *Père* Daniel Auger, for whom she cared a great deal and respected highly. For a girl of her time, she appeared extremely well read. She knew a great deal about science, astronomy, geography, art, literature and history—up to her time period, and beyond, thanks to her time-traveling books. More, in fact, than he did, which didn't sooth his wounded ego. It felt strange and somewhat demoralizing to be outsmarted by a girl from six centuries ago. No matter, he thought at length, he'd never held much store in formal education. Particularly the kind of schooling the Nazi government promoted. That was less education and more propaganda, he'd decided. He'd preferred the schooling of the street. So, although he regularly attended the lycée during the school season at the insistence of his uncle, François put little effort into it.

He decided on the direct approach: "Did your books help you decide what you're supposed to do here? What does an Aeon do when she travels through a tear?"

The girl shrugged and frowned sadly. "I don't know, François," she said. "I don't know why the Tear brought me *here*; I just know I had to use it to leave my world."

He sensed that she had finally revealed the truth and felt compassion for her. If what she and Antoine discussed was true, she carried a responsibility to history itself. It was like discovering that you are a king without knowing anything about your kingdom. Or finding out that you were a superhero without knowing your true powers and your agenda. It was like being blind.

✠

He was just about to ask for the bill when two greycoats sauntered into the bar. *Merde*! François felt his heart thunder but kept his cool as he railed himself for bringing the girl here. He'd smugly strutted within the radius of the tear sanctuary, totally forgetting that although Mortameur couldn't enter, he could send his henchmen in. The officers were both young and wore surly faces of self-importance.

The obvious leader of the two was tall and lean with a harshly chiseled sallow face, short cropped sandy hair, and cruel eyes. His colleague was dark and hairy, shorter and heavy-set with the belly of a man who enjoyed several beers every day. François didn't recognize them and thought they were new; not a good sign. They'd be aiming to make a mark, shake up the place. Plus the tall man looked inebriated; another bad sign. François noticed the *Schutzstaffel* insignias on their shoulders and arms: the leader was a *Sturmhauptführer* and the shorter man a *Truppführer*; a captain and his sergeant. The *Schutzstaffel* were an elite guard of the Paris *Orpo* directly run by the Black Knights. *Merde*!

He and the girl were trapped. If they tried to leave now, these greycoats would certainly take note of her. She was too pretty to ignore. If the Black Knights had issued an all points bulletin on her, these *Schutzstaffel* officers were bound to recognize her. They worked directly for the Black Knights.

*Merde*! Luckily, the girl's back was to them; from behind she looked like any other ordinary Parisian girl. But if one of them decided to walk to the back of the bar in arrogant curiosity....

As if sensing the importance of the girl, Sabine caught the officers' attention right away by sashaying up to them and barring their way to the back. She said in neutral welcome, "What would you like, gentlemen?"

"Well, *fraulein*," the captain drawled, looking Sabine up and down appreciatively. "Are *you* asking?" He let out a sinister laugh as the two of them settled in an arrogant sprawl at a table near the front. He was already drunk. "What would I *really* like? *Ich will Sie ficken!*"

The girl flinched and her eyes flew wide. She would have turned sharply around but François seized both her hands tightly and murmured, "Not now..." He could only guess what the captain had said to Sabine. It was written on the girl's fuming face. Then François said a little louder, "What do you think of this wonderful desert, Phèdre?"

She didn't respond; she was listening with a stony face to the conversation behind her.

"But I don't see '*ficken*' on the menu," the captain went on. "Perhaps it's your special, eh, *mein Schatz*?"

He made a grab for Sabine's waist but she deftly slid out from his encircling hand. The sergeant laughed with embarrassment, as if he was used to the captain's drunken behavior.

"Let her be, Carl," he made his plea in a forced casual voice. Then he turned sternly to Sabine. "Give us some red wine. You know why we've come. Never mind *meine Sturmhauptführer*, here. He's impetuous. *Und er begehrt nach alles*. He would love to bring a traitor to the Reich back to question. Perhaps an anarchist with the *Résistance* who runs a bad restaurant to front his illegal activities, eh?"

The girl squirmed in her chair and gazed directly at François with alarm and anger. She understood what was going on and definitely didn't like it. François held her hands tightly. For someone so reserved, she seemed to have quite a temper on her. If she turned, the game would be up. Besides he and the girl, two other couples sat in the bar and they ignored the commotion at the front of the restaurant. They knew how to behave in front of greycoats, thought François.

Knowing just how to handle the German officers, Sabine managed to be neither obsequious nor haughty. She served them their wine quickly. "May I suggest the Pinot Noir. It's on the house, of course, for officers of the Reich," she said evenly then handed the older grey coat a fat envelope. She'd emptied her entire cash register to fill it.

The captain snatched the envelope before the sergeant had a chance to retrieve it and stashed it in his jacket pocket. Then he pulled out a holo-device and activated it. "We're looking for this girl." Sure enough, a three-dimensional almost life-size portrait of the girl appeared above the device. She looked exactly as she did right now, facing him: long hair tumbled wildly around her face, eyes blazed with fearful determination, her full lips parted slightly as if frozen in concentrated thought. François felt his heart hammer in his chest. They were sure to recognize her, even from her back, he decided in sudden paranoia.

"Pretty little thing, eh?" the captain drawled. "Maybe she's one of your patrons here, eh?" He cast a cursory glance around and briefly met François's surly gaze. "Or maybe you've got her hiding in the kitchen...maybe she's fucking your husband."

He cut the holo and lurched to his feet, ready to search the place. François felt his chest squeeze tight. The way to the kitchen was past them. The captain would recognize the girl—

Sabine threw herself at him and kissed him. Forgetting everything else, he embraced her and mauled her backside, pulling up her skirt. She gruffly pushed him off, panting and flushed. "Come back later. Let me serve my customers first." She looked self-consciously at the other patrons of the bar, eyes glancing over François's.

The girl's hands squirmed inside his like a rabbit in a snare. She would have jumped to her feet and given herself away if he hadn't held her down in a vice grip.

Both officers laughed. The girl glared at François.

"Ah, she's a real French coquette, Hermann!" the captain shouted and slapped Sabine's rump. "I told you we'd like it here. French beauties everywhere you look."

This confirmed to François that they were fresh German imports. It explained the captain's swagger. "We'll be back," he slurred. "For my pleasure!" He seized his colleague by the arm then lurched out, laughing maliciously. The door banged open then closed, as they spilled out into the evening light.

Once the door shut, Sabine visibly sighed and leaned against the counter. She looked straight at François. He swallowed, feeling guilty for bringing the girl. The other two couples, spooked and fearing the return of the Reich officers, quickly paid up and left.

Once the door shut behind the last patrons, François surged up with a scrape of his chair. He didn't need to rush the girl on; she was right behind him. François pulled out his wallet to pay Sabine, who'd been talking quietly with her husband through the kitchen window behind the counter and throwing glances at them.

The girl opened her mouth to speak but François cut her off. "Here, *Madame* Sabine, for your troubles," he said, handing her 200F of the girl's money. "Keep the change." Then he was hastily pulling the girl to leave.

"Hey!" Etienne called through the kitchen window, rubbing a hand across his rakish mustache. "Don't you go stealing it back from them, François. You have that look in your eye."

It would have been easy to do it too, François thought.

"Don't worry. We'll manage," Etienne assured them.

The girl burst out, "I'm so sorry! It's *me* they're after!"

"Yes, we know," Sabine said calmly. "I recognized you right away on the holo."

"I should have given myself up. Now I've gotten *you* into trouble!" The girl glanced at François then Sabine's husband in anguish. Then she seized Sabine's hand. "He'll come back and try to…to…" She couldn't finish, though she certainly knew the words; she'd heard them often enough, from François himself, in fact.

"Have me?" Sabine helped her out. "Don't worry, my husband won't let that happen," she ended with a wicked smile. "Etienne knows how to handle *connards* like them."

"But won't you get into trouble?" the girl insisted.

"This happens almost daily, Phèdre," Etienne explained, leaning muscular arms under rolled up sleeves over the windowsill to face the girl. "My wife is too pretty," he said with a brash smile at the girl then a long appreciative glance at Sabine. "Don't worry. We'll handle it. You and François better go." Then he aimed an intense gaze at François. "And I meant what I said, François. Leave them be."

They were easy marks, François contemplated. He'd have had their money back in no time.

"But…Are you sure?" the girl blustered. "Why did you?…" she trailed, staring bemused from Etienne to Sabine. "You know nothing of me—"

"Anyone who makes trouble for them is a friend of ours," Sabine said simply. "That's enough for us. I know your name isn't Phèdre. You're a German, aren't you?"

The girl looked surprised.

"It's the way you speak, the way you pronounce certain words in French," Sabine explained. "And you understood everything they said. I saw you react. Good thing they weren't paying attention. Now, go! Out the back, through the kitchen!" She pointed behind them to the back door.

François and the girl slipped out the back of the bar into the small alley behind and made their way without incident to his shack on Rue des Rosiers. When they'd safely returned, François lit his small gas lamp and motioned for the girl to take the only chair in his one-room hovel. His shack could be made into two 'rooms' by sliding his makeshift curtain across the small space occupied by his old mattress. He fully intended on giving the girl the mattress to sleep on. He would sleep on the floor. He'd done it lots of times before; he didn't always have a mattress.

It was too early to bed down but too late to go for a walk, François thought, suddenly feeling awkward and tongue-tied. Not that either of them was in the mood for a walk after the incident at *le Coud Fou*. He glanced furtively at the girl, who'd tried to make herself comfortable on his musty foam chair. Within a short time her brows furrowed in contemplation and she cast her eyes down. Was she thinking guilty thoughts of Sabine and those German officers? François traced the lines of her creamy smooth face, deliciously shaped mouth and slightly upturned nose.

He'd never met a girl who was quiet before. Usually they were silly and giddy or loud with him. Usually they talked all the time and he couldn't shut them up. They always seemed to talk about nothing. Nothing that mattered anyway. This girl was the opposite. It bugged him and intrigued him at the same time. Earlier, he'd found himself asking her questions, soliciting her comments and opinions, attempting to draw her out. He'd never done that, never needed to with a girl before. But everything she said was interesting. He found that it drew him out of his isolated world into hers. Even her name was different: Vivianne. It was an old French name. No one used it anymore. A beautiful name...like her. *Merde*! He realized he'd started to like her a lot—

She was staring at him.

He couldn't help a glance down to the swells of her breasts, only teasingly revealed by the low-cut tank top his uncle had gotten her. She looked suddenly self-conscious and brought the sweater around her to hide her exposed bosom. François blinked and met her gaze with a lame smile. "My uncle told me to tell you that you'd be safe at my place."

"And you believed him?"

François blinked again, puzzled at her skeptical response. He'd thought that she considered his uncle an authority on these things. "Why not?"

She pressed her lips together and shrugged.

"He said that no other Aeons can enter another Aeon's

tear sanctuary," François went on.

"Tear sanctuary?"

François was glad to see that she was as confused by the words as he was. "That's what he said. He was sure that Mortameur was another Aeon—"

"He is," she brusquely confirmed.

François nodded. "Well, apparently once a tear is made by an Aeon, it's hers and no other Aeon can come near it or they get zapped. It's like some kind of force-field specific for Aeons. Anyway, so you're safe here."

She seemed to accept his statement on the surface. But he could tell that she remained skeptical and suspicious. Perhaps she was thinking of the German officers. There was something she wasn't revealing to him still, he thought and felt sad that she hadn't included him in her confidence. He pressed on, "Why don't you trust my uncle? He only wants to help you."

She sighed, reluctant to share her suspicions. But he stared insistently. She finally met his eyes with challenge. "Then why does he deceive you?"

"What do you mean?"

"He told you that he was forced out of his house onto the street, right?"

"Yeah. So?"

"Look at his shoes."

"His *what*?"

"And his hands."

François blinked in confusion.

"You can tell a great deal from someone's hands and feet," she said, glancing at François's hands then his feet with a faint half-smile. He followed her glance down to his old worn sneakers then turned his hands, palms outward to study them. They were smeared with old dirt. She elaborated, "Your uncle may wear an old rumpled jacket but his shirt and slacks are always laundered and his shoes polished. They're very good quality shoes and fairly new; I'd guess about two months old. As for his hands, they're clean, soft and manicured; not the hands of a man who lives on the street…"

François studied his own hands. Filth was ground into his pores from living in the slum and too little washing. What she said made sense and he realized that there were still some mysteries surrounding his uncle. Of his generosity and convictions, however, François had no doubts. The girl simply didn't know Antoine.

François shrugged. "Well, speaking of hands, I'm just going to get some washing water," he announced and bent down to take the pail, now neatly and logically placed by his shack door. "You can draw the curtain and change behind it," he added. "You've got the bed. I'll sleep out here." He pointed to the outer part of his hut, where he stood.

"No!" she surged to her feet. "I can't take your bed—"

"I insist. I got you those sheets for that reason. Besides, I'm used to the floor; you aren't." He saw that she didn't like that idea but he ignored her plaintive expression and quickly left, giving her no chance to argue, then took his time fetching the water at the public fountain. When he returned, the curtain was drawn and he could hear the girl rustling behind it. "I'm back," he announced and started brushing his teeth. The girl came out from behind the curtain, wearing the boxers and t-shirt, and looking slightly self-conscious. François grinned at her through a foam of toothpaste. She lost her self-consciousness staring at what he was doing. "Don't you brush your teeth?" he asked.

"We use salt and chewing twigs...we rub the salt into our gums and against our teeth with our fingers like this..." She poked her index finger into her mouth briefly and stared at his brush. "That is so ingenious..."

"Yes," he grinned. "Another milestone for modern technology. Grab the toothbrush and toothpaste I bought you. You can join me."

She eagerly did and soon they were brushing and spitting and laughing together. Somewhere, in the midst of their mirth François realized that a strong desire to make her laugh burned inside him. And she was his when she laughed. He mugged and blew bubbles. Then he guffawed and as they laughed together, it felt almost as good as making love, François concluded.

François taught her how to spit like a man into the garbage pail. She wasn't very good at it. She didn't know how to coax up the bile in her throat.

"Is that the best you can do?" he'd asked when she'd first spit some toothpaste into the pail.

She glanced at him with a frowning smile. "I thought it was pretty good," she said.

He laughed. "Well, it's obvious that you're...well..." he trailed, then finally said, "not like the girls I know."

She seemed affronted by his remark and straightened. "What do you mean?"

"Well..." he began, searching for the right words and finally settled on, "you're more like...a proper *lady*..."

Her response was not what he expected. She broke out into wild laughter. "Where I'm from," she volunteered. "I was accused of being rather *unlady-like*," she said through a foam of toothpaste. He couldn't help laughing as he watched the green foam on her lips part into a chaos of bubbles. She hardly looked like a lady now. Recognizing that his mirth was at her expense, the girl flicked her toothbrush at him and he felt the spray of toothpaste on his face. She guffawed in surprised delight at the effect. It was war. And she knew it. She shrieked again and bolted at his attempted retaliation from the bucket of water. He missed her with the water and got himself instead. Seeing him dripping, the girl let loose a wild girlish laugh from the other side of the room, then shrieked again as he chased her around his little place. He'd just grasped her by the waist to pull her down onto the mattress when a loud shout from a neighbor made him jerk to a halt—

"Hey! Shut up in there! *Tu me fou!*"

Suddenly self-conscious, François hastily let go of the girl and gave her a giddy grin. The insult was obviously aimed at *him*. "It's your friend, Vincent," François said with a gleam in his eyes. "He can't stand it when someone else is having a good time."

She tilted her head at him with a wry smile. "He really is a nice man, underneath all that bluster, you know…"

"Maybe to pretty girls he is…"

Still smiling, she shook her head and dropped her gaze. "Well, thanks for helping me. Goodnight, François," she said, drew the curtain and slid behind it.

"Good night," he replied and doused the light. He pulled off his jeans and damp t-shirt then lay down in his boxers on the blanket on the hard plywood-covered floor; the filthy blanket he'd initially placed the girl's unconscious body on yesterday. Emitting an audible sigh, he pulled a flimsy old sheet with large holes over himself. The blanket he lay on still had a small dark stain from where the girl had lost some menstrual blood. Somehow that seemed so long ago. It was hard to think that it had only occurred yesterday. So much had happened; so much had changed.

He lay on his back and linked his hands then slid them behind his head, listening to the murmurs of the city. The occasional sing-song of a distant siren warbled close then drifted away. He could hear the odd neighborhood sounds: the bark of a dog; the occasional car horn or motorbike howling; or the sound of sudden laughter or a shouted greeting. He found himself straining to hear the girl's even breathing. There it was finally. She had a talent for falling fast asleep. He supposed that it made up for her generally restless slumber during the night. Would she get those nightmares she'd had the previous night? Or would his mattress afford her a good night's sleep? Only time would tell, he thought as he checked his Pal for messages. Six lit up the screen; four were from Lizette. Impatient, no doubt, for his company. Tonight was their usual night for a tryst. The Grand Marshall was in all-night meetings in Montparnasse. Lizette would have to wait, François thought. Absence made the heart grow fonder, didn't it? This girl was too interesting and too important to him, he'd decided. He refused to abandon her to have wild irresponsible sex with that selfish woman.

He found himself comparing the girl to all the other girls and the women he knew in Paris. For a girl of fourteen, she seemed quite mature, he reflected. More mature, in fact, than any of the girls his age he'd known, even the older girls he'd dated; hell, even most of the woman. But then again, she probably had good reason. Hers was not a normal life. The girl appeared so serious most of the time, sullen even; and yet, there was a naivety, a simple sureness and lack of sophistication that made her appear very young...and vital. It annoyed him that he liked that about her. François recognized too that this latter trait was responsible for her beautiful guileless smile that seemed to light the room. She was refreshing and invigorating. He decided that she was an oxymoron: so earnest and naïve yet so clever and wise. And she had spunk; she wasn't afraid to put him in his place or stand up to authority or wield a weapon for some honorable cause but shrank back in inexplicable fear at the silliest things like moving vehicles, elevators, and large machinery. It made her seem brave and deliciously vulnerable at the same time. Respectful, honorable to a fault, and dangerously faithful. Charismatic in her utter conviction.

"*Merde!*" François muttered to himself under his breath. *You'd think I was falling for her! She's just a spoiled rich kid who ran away from home and her duties.* Then he added, *I'm one to talk.* He didn't want to count all the things he was running away from. Besides, she was pretty, he reflected with an absent smile, especially once she'd gotten out of those strange clothes and put on those form-fitting jeans and snug tank top that l'Oncle Antoine had given her. They really suited her tall and fit body. And when she unleashed one of her wonderful smiles, she was downright dangerous. Sometimes he thought that she knew it and used it against him to get him to do whatever she wanted. "Girls..." he muttered to himself. They were all the same no matter what time period they came from, he decided.

François felt himself stir with the thought of the girl in her boxers and flimsy t-shirt, sighing in sleep just meters away from him, in his own bed. His body suddenly ached with a surging heat that sang through him like a sword across metal. *Merde!* He was getting a hard-on just thinking about her. François threw the sheet off his damp body and sat up with a long sigh. He listened to the girl's even breathing across the room. He knew she was out-of-bounds.

He reached over to his pile of clothes on the floor and searched his jeans pocket for his last black rabbit. He had one pack of *rapture* left...time to visit Lizette for more, he thought soberly and he ripped open the shiny black package with a guilty glance at the drawn curtain. Then he cast the magical powder down his throat. He shuddered with empty exaltation, feeling it slice through him like a razor. It split him open like the cracking rind of overripe fruit. He arched his back and gazed up at his filigreed ceiling with dilated eyes, appreciating the myriad of texture, nuance and shade. *Rapture* sang through him in a plaintive love song, resonating like the strings of a violin. He was a guitar, vibrating to the gentle rhythm of soft breaths beyond the curtain as his thoughts strummed over the girl. She had the face of an angel when she was sleeping. He recalled his vision of her when she'd snuggled against him in the park. He imagined himself slowly undressing her...straddling her naked body and caressing her velvet skin...then making slow delicious love with her—

Hell! He stood up, shaking in a sweat. His erect member poked his shorts like a tent pole. He crept to the curtain and peered inside through the fold, hand straying down under his shorts to clutch himself in erotic euphoria. The girl lay on her side and his eyes traced her girlish figure under the blanket. She'd partially thrown off the cover in her fitful sleep and a naked arm and leg were flung out, exposed to his gaze. He strained to make out her face, surrounded by a thick curtain of hair. Her mouth was parted in the unconscious bliss of sleep. He leaned forward and felt the surging tide of passion swell up. His head sang with the poetry of her. What was it about her that made him ache with such tender yearning?

Okay...it was the *rapture*, he told himself. He wasn't enraptured with *her*; it was the drug screwing with him. But...she looked so innocent...so vulnerable in sleep...so warm and inviting....He stumbled back with a gasp, heart thundering, and jerked his hand out from under his shorts. He retreated quickly with a rush of breath. *I have to get out of here!*

He pulled on his pants with jittery hands, then threw on his dirty t-shirt. The girl was asleep. She was safe from harm here, according to his uncle. Even if she didn't trust Antoine, François did. He'd be back here long before she woke up, François thought, slipping out of his hut into the dark of night with a shiver.

✠

# …25

LIZETTE was glad to see him, although she pretended she was mad at him for keeping her waiting. But she knew better than to ask him for an explanation. "I should punish you," she said petulantly, pulling him with gruff eagerness through the door into the foyé of her expensive flat in the 17ème Arrondissement. Her fair hair was rumpled and she wore only a nightdress and night coat; he'd clearly woken her from sleep.

"Go ahead," François sneered, not really caring and beginning to wonder why he'd really come here. He wasn't interested in Lizette or her money or even the first grade *rapture* she usually paid him. His restlessness had brought him here. He studied her face, young and attractive yet ravaged by the cynicism of living with the Furher's Grand Marshal. He'd never asked her age; he'd guessed her to be in her late twenties. She was von Eisenreich's third wife. The forty-year old Grand Marshal had arranged for the arrest and execution of his previous two wives; she was living a dangerous life and knew it. So long as she pleased the old bastard, she lived. So, she filled her bouts of terrified boredom with loose whoring. She was going to Hell anyway. She might as well earn it and enjoy the journey.

Lizette picked up on his surly mood and raised a brow. "Maybe I *will* punish you," she said coquettishly. "Come here, *mon petit con...*" He let her pull him by the collar of his shirt down the hall into her bedroom.

She gruffly undressed him—it was her ritual—then pushed him, naked, on the rumpled bed covers. She immediately lashed him, spread-eagled to the bedposts. He'd given no resistance and when she finished, she was panting with excitement. Baring her teeth in a malicious grin, Lizette turned to an antique dresser and pulled out a leather whip. François inhaled sharply, more for her benefit than out of fear. In truth, he didn't mind; a part of him invited the punishment as he thought of the sweet girl he'd left behind in his hovel, sleeping in quiet innocence while he freely submitted to the sadistic whims of a Nazi's wife.

Lizette sneered at him. "It's Dietmar's," she quipped cavalierly. "He likes to use it on me." Her eyes sparkled with malice. "Now my little *putain...*"

She barely hurt him, swinging the whip fecklessly as though afraid to draw blood. It aroused her to see him flinch in pain, muscles tightening as he grew rigid and made his toes curl. François clamped his eyes shut and thought of the girl, lying naked on his bed. His penis swelled and rose. Lizette shrieked and flung the whip to the floor. When he opened his eyes, he saw that she'd flung off her nightclothes and presently threw herself on him. "Kiss me! Kiss me! OH!"

François obliged as her hands groped his groin and directed him into her with a gasp of pleasure. She rocked him and he shuddered with an ardent moan, thinking of the girl. She panted and wailed then keened wildly as François thrust into her and thought only of the girl.

When they were lying quietly in the dazed aftermath of making love, Lizette drew her fingers slowly along his mouth. He was still tied up and her naked body, damp with sweat, lay draped over him like a wet cloth. She'd brought out her stash of high-grade *rapture* and a pile of black rabbits lay on the nightstand, waiting to be abused. She sat up and tore one open then poured the *rapture* into his willing mouth and took some herself. He saw her eyes instantly dilate. She arched her back, pushing out her breasts at him, and closed her eyes with a gasp of pleasure. When she opened them to look down at him, she rubbed herself suggestively over him and cooed, "What were you thinking, *petit con*, eh?" She stroked his lips with her finger. "You were tender tonight. Maybe I should tie you up more often, eh?"

He didn't answer.

"What would you do to me if you were free? Unleash your wrath on me?"

"Untie me and find out," he challenged, knowing how she'd react. She liked receiving abuse as much as giving it.

Breathing heavily with *rapture* euphoria, she hastily untied him.

As soon as he was free, François channeled all his frustrations and unspent passion for the girl at the woman he was with. He seized Lizette's arms in a vice-grip, knowingly hurting her, and drew out a cry of pain from her. Then he spun her around so she lay face down on the bed, face smothered in the blankets. After pressing her down uncomfortably for some time, he gruffly turned her to face him and lashed her as she had done to him, spread-eagled on the bed. She gasped in her breaths.

Just as she recovered, he slapped her, stunning her. François grabbed several black rabbits and tore them open. After throwing some into his own mouth, he poured *rapture* down her throat and she gladly swallowed it down with a moan of intense pleasure. Feeling *rapture* course through him like the flood of a desert rain, he bent down to lick the blood off her lips as she panted in a mixture of fear and desire. He murmured, "Tell me about the Zarathustra Plan. I know your precious Dietmar shares all his little secrets with you in his sleep." He gnawed her earlobe with his teeth, tongue flicking into her ear. She gasped and shuddered. He shouted, "Tell me!"

She did; she told him everything. How von Eisenreich planned to execute his Plan Zarathustra to remove all opposition. It was no less than a ruthless genocidal plan to exterminate all "lower forms" of humanity once and for all and achieve world domination for the Reich.

"He keeps the documents for the plan in a safe right here," she blurted out. "I saw it once and he got mad at me and beat me for being too curious! He keeps it here because he thinks this is the safest place and he doesn't trust his own colleagues at the City Hall."

If François wanted to reveal the Grand Marshal's plan to the SSLF, this was a perfect opportunity, he thought. All he had to do was get Lizette into a "state", which would give him the chance to find the safe, pick it open and steal the plan. If he was inclined, that is.

As she continued to reveal all that she knew, François used his tongue, lips and fingers to tease her whole body into a frantic quivering mass of unfulfilled desire. "Oh, François!" she finally wailed."Come to me now! NOW! Please!" she wailed. "Oh, please!"

"Tell me about Dietmar's domestic plan," he said. He slid his hand between her spread out legs and teased her with his fingers. She moaned then whimpered like a dog. Her body arched and bucked in desperate yearning. "Tell me how he always manages to figure out what the SSLF is doing!" he insisted over her pathetic wails.

"He has a spy!" she cried out in gasps. "In the SSLF!" After a pause to whimper, she gasped out, "One of your big shots—Oh, François—I don't know who. I swear—Oh, please, François!—I don't think even Dietmar knows. He has a code name, it's—Oh, God!—It's Wasserman!"

Darkly elated with thoughts of hollow victory, François snatched the remaining black rabbits. He took some and forced the rest down Lizette's choking throat. *Rapture* spilled out of her mouth and she desperately tried to retrieve it with her tongue. Her eyes sparkled dark with *rapture*, yet her wet and glowing body heaved with painful unspent desire. He'd primed her up like a bomb and she was ready to explode. He glanced down at his penis, already swollen and erect. The fuse. With a cruel grim smile, he released her agony and thrust into her with the force of a machine gun. She came instantly with a loud reverberating scream as he continued pounding into her until he was spent. He then collapsed from an exhausted climax on top of her wet body.

He could have left her there. He could have gotten up and dressed as she struggled. He could have simply left, never to return. But he didn't. Instead, François undid her bindings.

He knew he was drowning in *rapture*. This would be his very last time with Lizette, François decided and gave in to the perversity of the night.

✠

The dawn was just breaking when François trudged gingerly with aching limbs to the Rue des Rosiers. Lizette had had her will with him last night, he reflected, walking painfully bow-legged. His head pounded like a drum and he still felt the dizziness of *rapture* after-burn. What a comedown, he thought. His back ached with the wheels Lizette had left from the second dose of torture she'd applied with perverse excitement. Thanks to the *rapture*, he'd been more accommodating and she'd been more insistent.

He mulled over what he should do with his discovery of the SSLF traitor. Who was Wasserman? Someone he knew? And what about Eisenreich's safe? Was it worth the risk and one more tryst? He thought of the girl and her integrity. Part of him wanted badly to make her proud.

François breathed in the quiet amid the faint scent of baking bread, cooking sausages mixed with the cloying odor of rancid oil and rotting garbage. The quiet daze of the city was broken sporadically by the occasional bark of a dog.

When François opened the crooked door of his shack, it creaked open and he started. The curtain was open and the girl was awake. She'd already gotten up and dressed. She was sitting in his crooked chair, reading one of her books. She wore the cotton print dress he'd bought her and it looked ravishing on her. She'd even done her hair up partly with braids and some ribbon she'd found to hold it back; it exposed the feminine features of her face in elegant simplicity.

He marveled at how girls were always doing these awesome things with their hair. He preferred her with her hair down, tumbling in an unruly thick river of silk over her creamy shoulders. But he liked her this way too: elegant and sophisticated…a true lady. He found himself blushing to his annoyance.

"Good morning," he said in a subdued voice.

"Good morning," she replied softly and closed the book. She looked somewhat self-conscious in the dress. Perhaps it was like an undergarment for her; he'd seen some images of medieval dresses. This summer dress resembled the undershirt women wore beneath their gowns. No matter, it looked great on her. He liked how it revealed her slender legs and arms and how the light material clung to reveal the lines of her feminine figure.

She stared at him with an expression he couldn't read. He expected her to ask him where he'd been. But she didn't. Did she know? He felt like she could smell the other woman on him. Smell the spicy perfume of Lizette's cum smeared on him. See the smudges of Lizette's makeup over his face, lips and body. Recognize the after-burn of *rapture*-induced eroticism. Why did he feel like he'd betrayed the girl? It wasn't as though she was his girlfriend or anything. She was just a strange girl who'd barged into his life, intrigued him, and whose safety he'd been tasked by his uncle to ensure. Why did he feel guilty then? She looked so innocent, he thought, unable to look at her directly. François started to shiver and his eyes couldn't hold hers any longer. They entered an awkward silence. Maybe she thought him loose and callous with women. Maybe he was. Unleashing an anger at her for making him feel guilty, he cavalierly pulled off his clothes in front of her to change as he swung toward the wash basin. Damn it, if she'd made herself available to him he wouldn't have gone, he thought selfishly as he stood in his dark blue jockey shorts and washed his face and brushed his teeth with last night's wash water.

When François turned, he found himself unnerved by

her stare. He'd expected her to have averted her gaze in her typical modesty.

"I wish you'd stop that!" he lashed out. "You're always judging me!"

She looked stunned for a moment but recovered quickly and continued to gaze at him with an intense but sullen expression. "I refuse to judge you. Only God can do that," she responded quietly. It infuriated him. He wished she'd said something in anger back at him. Then he could understand and react. François glared at her. He made an exasperated sound and grabbed his clothes to stalk out of his shack when she added plaintively, "I wasn't judging you, François...really."

He turned to her. "Then what *were* you doing?" he challenged with pursed lips.

"I was just...just staring at you. I'm sorry." She blushed. It set him blushing again and they stared at one another in the heat of an awkward silence. He suddenly wanted to kiss her.

He might even have boldly lunged forward had she not added, "Your back...it's been injured!"

He quickly pulled on a new t-shirt and grinned at her. "I'm okay. Someone surprised me, that's all." Then, thinking to change the subject, he added as he stepped into his jeans, "You said you trained secretly as a knight. Do you mind showing me some of your moves?" He instantly felt his heart race with thoughts of her sword, no longer on the premises. Would she want to use it to demonstrate her moves?

"I'd be happy to," she said then saved him: "Do you have some sticks we can use?"

"Ah!" François said with an exhale of relief. "I have something even better!" He crouched by his false floorboards and opened a trapdoor then pulled out the two fake swords that Jacques had given him yesterday as a gift for providing him with such a good deal. Forged of cheap metal on some assembly line, they weren't worth much, but they were swords, none the less.

The girl beamed and clapped her hands with joy at seeing them. "Training swords!"

François handed her one of them and she accepted with

a smiling nod and a few critical swings.

"It's heavier than mine," she said, studying the blade. "With a blunt edge and a one-and-a-half grip. Nice." Then she looked back up at him with a bright smile. He thought her strangely alluring in her cotton print modern dress, wielding an old sword like a warrior princess. It seemed to suit her.

François suggested they go outside where there was more room to maneuver. They stepped out and thankfully no one was nearby to watch. François watched as she bent to put her sword on the ground then stood up to face him empty-handed.

"Sword fighting, like any form of combat, relies on the proper carriage of the body, a good sense of timing and an understanding of distance," she explained to François. "You fight with the entire body. So, here is the basic stance." She stood upright and extended her right leg forward, toe pointed straight at François; she kept her left leg back with her foot angled to the left slightly. François mimicked her moves. "Good," she said. "Okay, this is the part I hated the most during training but is the most important. The three basic types of footwork are passing steps, gathering steps and compass steps." She went through each type and explained their purpose as François copied her moves with an indulgent smile; he was getting impatient to use the swords. "Timing and gauging distance are critical," she went on to François's frustration. "The sword fighter is constantly moving from *zufechten*...the approach." She stepped toward him. "To the *krieg*...or close-quarters combat." She came aggressively up to within a breath of him.

François smiled suddenly and felt his heart race. He thought they would finally pick up the swords as the girl stepped back.

"We'll start with the guards," she said to him and picked up her sword then faced him again. François retrieved his sword from the ground and smiled like a predator. This was going to be fun. "There are *vier leger*—four main guards," she went on, "two low guards and two high guards. Think of them not as static positions of defense but rather as moments of transition between various offensive moves like cuts or thrusts. You're always moving from one guard to the next, initiating attacks." She made a few swings and moves that more resembled a jazz dance step than earnest combat. *I'm going to take this little lady down*, he thought smugly.

François nodded, feeling excitement course through him. She was taking this seriously but it was also clear to him that she was enjoying herself fully.

The girl stood with legs straddled in her print dress and held the sword with both hands just below her waist. She pointed the blade slightly up toward him. "This is a low guard," she explained, watching him mimic her move with a nod. "It's called the *pflug*...the plow. It's the most versatile guard and considered the best defensive posture because it protects the torso and can parry almost anything that comes at you." Then she lowered the sword and pointed it toward the ground still ahead of her. "This is another low guard. It's called the *alber* or fool's guard—"

"I can see why." François laughed. "It leaves you wide open to attack, especially from above—"

"Okay, try it," she challenged quickly. "Attack me."

He swung and she swiftly parried him with an upward swing and a clash of steel. But she didn't stop there; she continued with her momentum by flipping her sword around their bind to knock him in the chin with the pommel. He stumbled back in annoyed surprise as the girl barked out a brief laugh.

"Is that allowed?" he asked a little peevishly.

Biting back a smirk, though not very well, the girl said, "Of course. It's all part of hand-to-hand combat." Then she continued, "Anyway, the *alber* is called the fool's or trickster's guard because someone who uses it can fool their opponent into giving them an opening like you just did. It's a daring person who takes the fool's guard. They're either very foolish or very good."

She went back into the plow then curled her arms up so the hilt was over the side of her head and the blade pointed directly at his face. "This is one of the two high guards. It's called *ochs*...or the ox guard. The *ochs*, like the *pflug*, is a position that you should be in when you cross swords with your opponent," she explained.

"This one," she said, holding her sword up over her left shoulder with the blade slightly angled backwards, "is the *vom tag*...from the roof." As he mimicked her, she shook her head. "No, other side. Over your right shoulder. I'm left handed; you're right-handed and that's a weak hold for you." Then she moved the sword back behind her shoulder. "And this variant of *vom tag* is called the noblewoman's guard—"

"Because it's a sissy move—"

"Because," she cut in, "it's an over the shoulder guard which is a good defensive and versatile guard as the posture can be assumed both before or after a horizontal cut." The girl then lowered her sword and straightened to look at him with challenge in her eyes. "Shall we try a few moves?"

"Sure!"

The girl immediately took her guard. He should have guessed it would be the woman's guard. He took the *pflug*, deciding to play safe, and after a moment realized that she was waiting for him to make the first move.

He boldly lunged forward, thinking he would frighten her into recoiling. Instead, she met him with fierce eyes, side-stepped and sheared her blade up to his cross guard, pushing forward, then kicked him in the groin. He cried out and staggered back, panting in pain and prickly anger.

"This isn't some gentleman's sport," the girl calmly announced as he regained his breath. "It's combat with a sword, and it doesn't just rely on the sword. Remember, the intent is to gain the advantage. This doesn't mean you have to strike a fatal blow; a move that unbalances your opponent so that you can go in for an easier kill after is just as good."

She then resumed her guard and invited him to come forward again. With more serious intent to do harm, he swung up, aiming to graze her upper body. She parried him easily, then stunned him by flipping her sword with the momentum to knock his cheek with her pommel. Again, he staggered back and brought up his hand to touch his burning cheek. Although no blood was drawn, he was certain it would bruise later.

She was grinning at him. "Remember, the blade isn't the only part of a sword."

He was forced to give her his grudging respect beneath a growing frustration. She was good, that was the simple of it. Her movements were actually quite spare. There was no Samurai flourish he'd seen in the movies. Yet, with every move he made she was there, not only parrying it, but turning it into her own.

The girl resumed her guard, tacitly inviting him to come forward again. In sudden desperation, François feinted a merciless lunge, fully intending to grapple her to the ground. He wanted the satisfaction of pulling her disheveled form off the cobbled dusty street and helping her smooth out her ruined little dress; he'd buy her another.

But she'd anticipated his feint and sidestepped him again with a clash of swords. She then beat his blade aside with a front cut, turned her pommel forward in a bold thrust to his face. As he jerked back, she closed in with her left hip and trapped his forearms in an arm lock. Her move brought them up pressed against each other, panting, with blades clashing. She abruptly wrested his blade out of his hand with pressure from her pommel then tripped him to the ground.

The sword clanked as he fell hard, with a grunt, on the dusty pavement.

She burst into wild girlish laughter and had to bend over, because she was laughing so hard. Despite his embarrassment, François found her laughter deliciously infectious and joined her. Feeding off each other, their laughter sprouted bouts of uninhibited roaring cackles and guffaws that had both of them convulsing and gripping themselves.

"That was actually quite good," the girl finally said, reaching her hand out to help him to his feet. As he took her hand and rose, she added, "You have an aptitude for this. You've got some original ideas and you aren't afraid to use them. You did instinctively in your first lesson what Wolfgang had to learn after two years...." Her laughter petered out. Her face paled with a dark thought and she blinked at him. Then she forced on a calm composure and murmured, "Thank you, François. I enjoyed that." She handed him the sword then turned back to his hut. What had just happened?

After giving her a moment to recollect her cool, he followed her inside with the two swords. She'd dropped into his only chair with glazed eyes. She'd cupped both hands over her mouth and gazed in absent misery at the floor. It was clear to him that her mind had traveled far away from him, to her old home. Who was Wolfgang, besides her secret sparring partner, that is? Was he a knight? *Her* knight? To his surprise, François felt jealousy coil inside his belly as he put the swords away.

When he rose and turned to face her, he found her staring at him with those big eyes that pierced his heart. They stared at one another for a long moment.

"Oh, François," she murmured quietly and he wondered if he was in trouble again. "I left them all behind...Wolfgang, Uta, Father Daniel...my father...all those brave men who are going to die in that battle because of me. I convinced myself that I was getting help or answers back to them. I've done neither. I really just ran away. From everything and everyone." She averted her face and brought a hand up to partially hide it but he still saw her grimace with silent tears and felt something clutch his heart. This was the first time she'd let him see her cry, though he guessed it wasn't the first time she had wept since she came here; she'd simply done it in private. She'd had a hard time of it and he'd been a regular bastard.

"I know why the tear brought me here," she said quietly.

He laughed uneasily. "You make it sound like it's an entity that has intelligence and a consciousness."

"It does...mine."

He stared at her.

"I'm the tear, François," she went on. "I summon it, whether consciously, willingly or not. I control it. For beings like me there is no time or space...only light and how to use it."

She'd repeated what his uncle had said. *Merde!* She'd bit

it, hook, line and sinker. Trouble was, he was starting to bite it too. She seemed so sure. "What's it all mean?"

She leaned forward, head resting in both hands now. He could barely make out the expression on her downturned face. "You said you knew why you came," he prompted.

"Yes," she looked up. "It's simple, actually; I need to discover my path: which world to herald and nurture." After a long sigh she explained, "I need to determine which of the two worlds created by the split at the War of Grunwald should survive and flourish; because there's only one of me, François— my twin was murdered, abandoned to die. Only one world will have an Aeon. The other will go off kilter, destroy itself like a rogue planet. But the decision isn't an easy one. If an Aeon lacks perspective, they could be swayed by a moment in time instead of the overall reality. Compelled to ensure a small personal good, they might ignore the greater bad. Without the perspective of history, an Aeon is nothing but a self-serving bully." She looked up at him again with shiny eyes and ended in a broken voice, "All I've ever wanted to do was *make my world a better world. Gutter Gott*, I don't know what to do…"

"You need help," he offered with sudden inspiration. "Help from someone who knows you…or of you."

She cocked her head to one side with curious confusion.

"I know where we can go," François said, reaching inside his pocket.

"Not your uncle," she said forcefully.

"Not Antoine," he said. What was it with her and Antoine? Why didn't she trust him? Wasn't he a *Guardien*? Her *Guardien*? François pulled out Vivianne's Pal and punched a button. "Your friend's place," he said smugly. He turned the Pal toward Vivianne with Boulanger's face on it and watched her face, wondering what she'd betray.

She glanced from it to François with a puzzled expression. "*My* friend?"

"Well, you spoke to him a dozen times a few days before you and I collided—"

"I wasn't here until we collided—" She cut herself off

and her face grew quiet with enlightenment. "But my mother was." She looked back at Boulanger's face on her Pal. "He's my mother's friend."

"Okay. Your mother, then." François sighed; so, the girl wasn't Boulanger's lover. "He could help us, don't you think?"

She nodded, though her face betrayed some reluctance. François had never asked the girl about her parents. He'd told her about his; how he'd lost them when he was twelve. She'd shown great compassion and had suggested a comparable loss on her part. But she'd remained very silent about her life and he'd had to guess at things. He recalled her mentioning, almost in passing, of the person who'd left her the Pal and other stuff in her pack. He remembered her telling him that the woman was dead. It was her mother. As for her father…there was some issue between them…if he was still alive, that is.

✠

## …26

VIVIANNE looked more agitated than usual in the mètro station. She'd gone a long way from that first terrified encounter; but François still caught an echo of terror's shadow in her dark eyes as they entered the train. She caught him looking at her with curiosity when they sat down and gave him a lame smile. "It's my nightmare," she explained. She told him the terrifying details of her recurring twisted dream, of how she and her friend, a boy who resembled François, were being pursued through a métro station by a monstrous man—Mortameur—and how he chased them down the platform as various inanimate objects came to life and attacked them like something out of a horror movie. It didn't end well for either of them. When she finished describing her grisly dream, François felt a shudder go through him at the thought of her suffering that dream nightly. He slipped his hand around hers and gently squeezed.

The next stop was theirs and the two disembarked. François led Vivianne through the winding cobble streets of Montmartre and they eventually stood in front of 22 Rue Cortot. As François stepped toward the door, Vivianne recoiled. He turned to her and saw fear in her eyes. He took her hand gently and they stepped forward. François rang the bell.

Antoine answered the door.

"Uncle!" François said. The girl looked a bit dismayed.

"When you phoned me, I came right away," Antoine explained.

François felt the girl's eyes boring into him and shrugged. He'd wanted to keep Antoine informed, so François had covertly phoned his uncle with the news while the girl was using the bathroom. She obviously didn't like the idea of Antoine being here. What did she hold against him all of a sudden? Hadn't he been her protector and mentor? Her *Guardien*? François remembered being jealous of how she'd given Antoine all her trust and attention at François's expense. That seemed so long ago; it was only three days ago.

"Come in, children!" Antoine greeted them both. "How are you, My Lady?"

The girl recovered fast and smiled graciously. "I'm well, and you? I trust you've fully recovered from that unfortunate injury of the night before."

"Yes, yes," he said, leading them up a narrow staircase. As he did, François turned and leaned down to whisper his excuse to the girl, "I needed to know if Boulanger was okay, being a German officer and all…I knew Antoine would know."

She nodded.

When they reached the top of the staircase, Antoine waved them ahead into the living room. François immediately recognized Julien Boulanger, seated in a wheel chair. He was smartly dressed in good trousers, an expensive shirt and cardigan. Boulanger perked up at the sight of them.

"Dianne?" he asked incredulously. It was only when she

came closer that he realized his error. "Oh, no...not Dianne...Is it possible? Are you?..."

"Her daughter," she finished for him. "Vivianne."

"Vivianne," he echoed in a whisper. "It's a beautiful name. It's also my sister's name, did your mother tell you?" he said. "We decided on it together."

The girl looked suddenly agitated.

Julien picked it up right away. "Your mother didn't tell you? I'm your father, Vivianne."

The girl recoiled in shock. Then she stared in wonder with a tremulous smile.

"Only, she was pregnant with twins," Boulanger went on. "Where is your fraternal twin?"

François watched the girl steel herself to explain. It was imperceptible but he could catch her subtle actions of mind-control; a slight tightening of her jaw as she set it, the little lines that formed around her mouth and the slight flare of her slightly upturned nose. She'd pressed her lips together and worked her lower lip, worrying it slightly, to betray a far greater agitation inside. She was otherwise outwardly calm, an expert in the art of deception. Deception in comportment only; what she said was always the truth: "My twin brother died in childbirth...as did my mother."

Boulanger slumped back against his chair as if struck. "Oh, my Dianne!" It was obvious he hadn't known. He looked heartbroken. François saw tears well up in his eyes as he shook his head sadly. He hadn't known; but he didn't look surprised. Once he'd gathered his composure, he said, "I'm so sorry, little one. You look so like her, did you know?"

She dropped her gaze to the floor and nodded. "Yes, my servant, Uta, told me." Then she looked up. "But...my mother's last name..." she stammered to get the words out, "it's... Mortameui."

"Yes." Boulanger sighed. "She and Leduc are brother and sister...Fraternal twins, actually. They were lovers until I came along."

This time it was the girl who needed to sit down.

Antoine, always attentive, caught her wavering form by the arm and ushered her to a plush chair. She gratefully took it. She'd gone pale.

"Does it shock you?" Boulanger said. "Brother and sister being lovers? You forget they are Aeons. No doubt, you and your fraternal twin, if he'd survived, would have had the same inclination. It is so with Aeons, I'm told. You apparently feel an incredible bond, in every way, including a strong sexual one. Not quite as abhorrent as incest is for humans. It has been so for …well…aeons," he ended with a smile at his pun. "Its purpose, I believe, is to ensure that you share a strong motive to rejoin your worlds once you've separated. Of course, the danger is that you may decide not to separate in the first place like Leduc and Dianne and end up totally abandoning one of the worlds—"

"But what about…"

Boulanger smiled, as if guessing what the girl wanted, but could not, say. "They were cheating. They never wanted to be apart and never wanted to die. That meant never getting pregnant, so they were always careful not to conceive. But in the end your mother wanted a child. She wanted to live a normal life, with a family, and grow old with someone. When she left Leduc to be with me, we let it happen; we conceived. You see, when she had you, she basically signed her death warrant. Aeons are like salmon returning home to create a new generation. Once she becomes pregnant, an Aeon and the mate with whom she conceived, who is bonded to her chemically through the act of conception, change physiologically. They lose their immortality, see in their babies and then finally die. I'm a human mortal already so it didn't affect me. But, because she conceived with me, Leduc remained unaffected, alone and condemned to live forever without his twin who had become mortal. When he finally discovered what we'd done, he was enraged, as you can imagine—"

The door crashed open.

Mortameur burst in on them. "Enough!" It was clear he'd been there the whole time, eavesdropping and waiting for the right moment to enter. "You stole her from me!" he shouted at Boulanger.

"You lost her for yourself!" Boulanger shot back.

Mortameur pointed to the girl like she was a meal gone bad. "*That* should have been mine!"

Anger swelled inside François. How dare he call her '*that*'! He surged forward. "She has a *name*, you bastard! It's *Vivianne!*" He didn't realize, but it was the first time he'd thought of her with that name or used it himself. It sounded achingly real and wonderfully connected to him.

Mortameur seemed to notice him for the first time and sneered. "She's *your* girl now?"

François felt his face heat, embarrassed by the disclosure. He realized that Mortameur had only verbalized what François subconsciously thought. *Yes, she's my girl!*

Vivianne threw a pleading glance at François, warning him not to do anything stupid.

"You're just a puppy," Mortameur goaded him on. "You have no idea what to do with a woman. And make no mistake...*woman* she is already." He turned sharply on her with a malicious grin. "Aren't you, Vivianne?" He flashed his gleaming eyes back to François with a challenging glare. "She ran to the first boy who'd have her! And it wasn't *you!*" He barked out a sharp laugh.

"Don't, François!" Vivianne pleaded in a hoarse voice, pulling him back by his arm. "Don't you see what he's doing? You know it's not true. He'll just hurt you. Don't let him—"

François shrugged her off with a violence he hadn't intended. He didn't care if it was or wasn't true. It was a matter of honor. Mortameur couldn't dishonor her like that without reciprocity. He was vilifying an innocent girl. One François had sworn to protect, body and soul. He flew in a rage at the large man.

He didn't get very far.

Mortameur swerved and caught him in some kind of stronghold. François was suddenly spun around in a dizzying circle. A violent tug on his arm tore a cry from him and he blacked out. When he came to his senses on the floor, eyes focusing through a haze of pain, he saw Vivianne staring at him, stricken. He puzzled briefly that she hadn't rushed to his side or made any move toward him. Then he realized why: Mortameur clutched her by the arms and held her in a locking embrace. Antoine, obviously less courageous than last time, stood still, beside Boulanger.

"When are you going to start picking on people your own size, Mortameur," Boulanger said wearily. "First you pick on a boy half your size...I think you broke his arm. Now this helpless girl..."

"Not so helpless," Mortameur snarled. He squeezed Vivianne.

"You're disgusting—"

"*Me* disgusting!" Mortameur spun to face Boulanger. He released one of Vivianne's arms and threw her off balance by firming his grip on her other arm. "*You* stole Dianne right from under me—my twin. She's an Aeon. You soiled her with your hands and your lips. You impregnated her with your common seed!" Mortameur spat out the last part in total repugnance. "She was never meant to fornicate with a commoner, a mere human...You tainted a goddess, robbed her of her immortality, and to bring forth *this*!" He pointed gruffly at Vivianne like she was a leper. "You created *that*!"

From his crippled position on the floor, François helplessly watched Vivianne's reaction of sick horror. She'd put something together, a piece of her ever-evolving puzzle, and it sent her over the edge. Her face went deathly pale. François didn't understand exactly what Mortameur meant but he knew it wasn't nice. And it couldn't therefore be true.

"Dianne and I were meant to usher in a new world— when we were good and ready...*only* when we were good and ready," Mortameur growled.

"Which is never," Boulanger challenged. "You never intended to have children. You wanted to live forever. You avoided the nexus three times and stayed together in this world. You cheated the fates, cheated your duty for hundreds of years and got away with it, figuring that you were the last summoners;

286

all the others joined with their other worlds. But not you...you let the other world go to pot, along with this one—"

"Shut up!" Mortameur spat out. He turned and barked at Vivianne, "Then *you* came along and ruined it all!" He let go of her and she crumpled to the ground in a half-faint as he turned on Boulanger with seething anger.

Boulanger puffed himself up in his wheelchair. "You don't frighten me, Mortameur. You're just a bully. Dianne left you. I just came along at the right time. She was fed up with your controlling nature. You were suffocating her. She wanted to be free. Free of you—"

"Liar! She only loved *me*!"

"She stopped loving you a long time ago—"

"Shut up! Shut up!"

Mortameur pulled out his gun and shot him. A brilliant red beam screamed out of the muzzle. Boulanger slumped in his chair and Mortameur panted out his satisfied pleasure.

Antoine finally moved and Mortameur caught him in mid-stride with a hard punch. Antoine collapsed, unconscious. Vivianne made a choking sound, between a terrified gasp and a moan of anguish. She was staring at Boulanger.

Reminded that she was there by her muffled sound, Mortameur turned on her in a violent tirade. "As for you, bastard child...*Demiurge*!" He pulled her up by her hair and she cried out. "*This* is where you belong. Here, with *me*!" He'd pulled her close to him until their faces were a breath's distance from each other. "You'd be dead in either world, don't you know?" he hissed at her. "They burned you as a witch. Might as well stay here with me, mut." He locked his great arms around her waist and drew her snug. She appeared to have lost all of her will and with a desperate sob, let him crush her in a smothering embrace. "I had my way with your mother...I'll have it with you too—"

"NO!" François realized only after that it was he who had cried out. He suddenly found himself able to move as Vivianne came to life and struggled against Mortameur. François seized a nearby desk lamp with his good arm and propelled

287

himself at Mortameur with it. Vivianne's struggles were just enough to slow the Black Knight down and the lamp connected with his head. Mortameur dropped to the floor, pulling Vivianne down with him.

François pulled her up with his good arm and was about to get the gun, when Vivianne urged him away.

"We must go. NOW, François! Before he wakes!" They gaped down at Mortameur and a jagged gash where the lamp had struck him. "Your uncle's alright; it's ME he's after!" she shrilled urgently, following François's uneasy glance to his unconscious uncle. Antoine stirred with a groan and was already rousing himself. Did she think François was going to kill Mortameur with the gun? The thought had actually crossed his mind.

Then she was pulling him fiercely away and he let her lead him, stumbling, out of the house. Surging adrenalin was the only force keeping him from throwing up and collapsing in pain.

✠

## ...27

CRADLING his bad arm against his body with his good arm, François guided them in a panting run to the Larmarck Caulaincourt Métro Station a several blocks away. With every pounding step he took, the pain shot through his smashed arm. He led Vivianne down one of the double stairways flanking the station entrance and they plunged inside. They were in luck; a train was just coming in as they entered the station. Vivianne stiffened and recoiled, trembling visibly with unreasonable fear.

"What?" François turned to her, unable to hold back a grimace. The pain in his arm pounded like a hammer. They'd just witnessed a cold blooded murder; for all he knew the murderer was still chasing after them. And she was having a panic attack about the métro?

"I don't know..." she whispered, as if to herself. "I've got a bad feeling about this place...It reminds me of..." She blinked several times as if to shake it off and focused on him, noticing his damaged arm for the first time. "He hurt your arm."

He followed her gaze of concern. "I think it's broken," he said, hearing his fragile voice as if from far away.

"Oh, *Lieber Gott*," she breathed out.

"I'll be okay," he reassured her, forcing a faint smile and made ready to enter the train, which had just stopped. He felt suddenly very hot and dizzy and wanted badly to sit down. But he needed to be strong. He was sweating and felt nauseous; probably shock, he reasoned.

Again Vivianne's steps faltered and she glanced at him with nervous concern. "Don't you feel it? The heat..." She threw an apprehensive glance around the station then shrugged to herself. "Perhaps the fans aren't working..." she breathed out like a ghost. She was freaking out, François decided. But he didn't have the energy to be frustrated with her. He needed all of it to stay conscious. Once they got in the train, he could collapse on a seat, he told himself. They'd be safe from Mortameur at François's place, inside Vivianne's tear sanctuary—

A sudden explosion behind them made him flinch. Confused shouts and a woman's shriek drew their attention to the back of the station. François stared: Mortameur, bloody face twisted in a mask of outrage, was stomping down the platform toward them. A raging fire towered behind him. He pulled back his thick lips in an open snarl and pointed his gun at them.

François pushed Vivianne down ahead of him and ducked. The weapon discharged and a brilliant red beam sang past them in a high-pitched squeal. People scattered and made for the exits. Mortameur stormed toward them, leaving a wake of groveling and relieved bystanders.

"Run!" François seized Vivianne's hand in his good one. They ran for the escalator. Mortameur pelted after them. The station grew suddenly hot as a devil's wind blew over them like a flame.

"Stop, Vivianne!" Mortameur shouted. "You'll burn in this world too, then!" The hot wind licked them like a flame and François felt his legs burn.

He suddenly realized with terrified alarm that this was Vivianne's nightmare! They were living it! And the way she'd described it to him, it wasn't going to end well.

He glanced back—a mistake—and saw Mortameur closing in, looking like the devil himself. The station's fire blazed behind him. François tripped on his own foot and fell headlong with a grunt of pain. Their grip tore but Vivianne lurched back.

"NO!" he shouted at her. "Go, Vianne! Save yourself—"

Mortameur was right there and kicked him hard in the ribs. François felt incredible pain—and a burning heat—where Mortameur's boot had connected. The Black Knight glared at François with insane rage. "You little pest!" He pointed his gun at François. "This is what I do with little pests—"

Vivianne threw herself on Mortameur and knocked him off balance. The gun flew from his hand and discharged. It singed the floor, leaving a dark, smoking hole. Vivianne hissed at him, "Leave him alone!"

Mortameur cuffed her hard with the back of his hand. She yelped and jerked back into a dazed sprawl on the floor. François fumbled with his good arm to grab Mortameur's leg and pull him off balance but Mortameur sidestepped him easily with a snarling laugh and kicked him again. The blow sucked the air out of him. François curled up into a ball of agony. But he'd slid to within reach of Mortameur's gun. Mortameur watched François grab for the gun and pulled out a knife from his belt. François's head pounded with alarm as he pointed the gun at Mortameur and fumbled with the trigger.

Mortameur grinned maliciously. In a blur he plunged the knife into François's side.

Time collapsed.

The gun dropped and clattered to the floor. As if in slow motion, François heard himself suck in his breath with the lancing pain. Then Mortameur gruffly pulled the knife out. François knew he must have fallen but didn't remember falling. He lay on the floor, unable to move, and found himself helplessly blacking out. *I'm done for...just when things were getting interesting —*

... As if in a dream, Vivianne surged up from behind in a swirling haze and wrapped her arms around Mortameur like a lover. The Knight looked startled and was about to fling her off when she seized the bloody knife he was brandishing. To François's amazement, Mortameur's hand shook under the force of Vivianne's grip as they struggled briefly.

"This will hurt a great deal," Vivianne snarled into Mortameur's ear. "But only for a moment." Her eyes blazed with feral hatred. François watched the knife jerk then plunge into Mortameur's heart. Mortameur gasped. She added, "You might even enjoy it," and pushed the knife in deep.

Mortameur's eyes flew wide with pained shock then the life died out of them and he sagged to the floor in a heap. François gasped out a laugh and felt himself pass out. As darkness claimed him, Vivianne's face appeared, looking down at him with pained concern. It was the last thing he saw.

✠

# ...28

HE came to, leaning against a warm wonderfully-scented body and staggering like a drunk down the steep cobbles of Monmartre. Vivianne was the warm body. She'd hooked her arm around him and grasped his arm around her. Acting as his crutch, she struggled with him down the stairs of one of Monmartre's steep hills. She'd drawn her face taut. Sweat covered her upper lip, as she exposed her teeth in a grimace of labor. The neat braids of her hair had come mostly apart and rogue skeins fell turbulently around her. Like a drowning sailor going 'home', he drank in her alluring scent of lavender. Sensing his conscious state, she glanced briefly at him.

"That's it, François…stay with me," she gasped out in panting breaths. Even as she said it, her face swam into a kaleidoscope that merged with the golden streetlights and her hair lit with an amber glow as if on fire …then darkness flooded in as he heard her vaguely ringing cry, "No, François! Don't—"

He vaguely heard her shriek then grunt as he felt himself fall with her down the stairs. Then he heard no more. Until he heard a singing kettle and soft voices, the low murmur of a grown man and a girl. Vivianne, he thought, and forced his eyelids open.

The first thing he saw was her face, smiling tenderly at him, hazel eyes looking deep into him. He couldn't think of anything nicer to wake up to. "Hello," she said quietly then took his hand in hers and squeezed slightly.

François smiled back and squeezed back. She was sitting beside him on a bed. He responded in a shaky voice, "Hello, Vivianne." Now that he was calling her by her name, he couldn't get enough of it. *Vivianne, Vivianne, Vivianne….*

She answered his obvious question, "You've been unconscious for three days. But you're okay." She glanced behind her and for the first time, François looked past her to his surroundings. It was a small tastefully decorated room, lit from a skylight above with impressionist paintings on painted plaster walls. Then he recognized who was puttering by the kettle. The man turned to face him and François was looking straight at the ruggedly handsome face of Vincent Rouard.

He jerked up and tried to squirm into a sitting position. "Why did you bring me here!" He glared from the rugged forty year old to Vivianne.

She gently restrained him and urged him to lie back down. "I'm sorry. I couldn't think of who else to take you to. François, you were bleeding to death and half-conscious. You needed medical attention and I don't know Paris. So I used your—my Pal—to call Vincent and he picked us up." She continued in a whisper as Rouard made to leave, "He's a doctor too, did you know? He bandaged you up and fetched a specialist he knows to tend to your knife wound and broken arm—"

"But you have Vivianne to thank for stopping the bleeding and tending your wound with her herbal medicines as well as her antibiotics," Rouard cut in from the doorway. "She had several of us picking plantain, yarrow and willow leaves in the alley way for the concoctions she put on your wound!" He laughed, showing perfect teeth in a maverick smile. Rouard made an imposing figure at the door. Long unkempt hair tangled over his eyes and fell to his shoulders. His chiseled jaw held a mouth that might be cruel or gentle, depending on a whim, thought François.

Then Rouard went out the door, leaving them alone. François looked back at Vivianne, mind racing: he'd stashed her antibiotics in his hiding place beneath his flooring—

She must have read his mind. "I found them, François. When I was cleaning your place." She tipped her head to one side and gave him that wide, close-mouthed almost smug smile that was her hallmark. "It's not really a very good hiding place..."

"That's okay." François returned her a loose grin. "I never thought you'd use them on me, though..."

"I never expected to use them on anyone. I'm just glad Uta gave them to me. She might have saved your life...along with Vincent." She glanced outside, past the open doorway to where Rouard was obviously pacing.

François put his other hand on hers and squeezed a little harder. "*You* did the saving. Dragging me down those thousand and one stairs of Montmartre, then getting help. Thanks."

She squeezed back. "I just let you fall flat on your face and we rolled down the steps together," she said with amusement. To his bewildered expression, she burst into laughter and he had to grin.

"You got a few bruises from that, I guess," he said.

"I did," she said and innocently slid her dress up to

show him a large dark one on her thigh. "See?"

"Oh, my!" François gave her slender leg an appreciative look then looked up with a quizzical frown. "How did you...I mean...Mortameur is, well, a lot stronger than you but you still managed..."

She glanced away for a moment, gathering her thoughts. Then she met his gaze with a self-conscious look. "I can bend metal—give it a will." She laughed with embarrassment and he realized that his mouth gaped open. "It seems that every Aeon, once we get our markings, can manipulate matter in some way. Mine is through metal. Apparently it's not his." She gave him a self-conscious smile and let her gaze drop.

"Of course! The pole," François said in sudden revelation. "The flying umbrella pole at the Café Toujours—that was *you*!" He laughed then grimaced in sudden breathless pain.

Vivianne touched his lips gently with her fingers. "Shh..." she said tenderly. "No more laughing for you...not for a little while, anyway."

He let his gaze drift around the room, searching.

Again, she second-guessed him. "The gun is safe in your place, François." Then she added awkwardly, "Your clothes were bloody and torn..."

François let go of her hand and peeked under the blanket; he was buck naked under there! Vivianne smiled with some amusement and got up from the bed. "You had a fever and we had to keep it down..." She moved toward the doorway. "Now that your fever's broken and you're awake, I'll get you some new clothes from your place." Before he had a chance to respond, she'd disappeared through the doorway. Why that little scamp! Just as he'd undressed her while she'd been incapacitated, she'd done the same to him.

He wanted to laugh but Rouard appeared, with a glance behind him at Vivianne as she disappeared down the street. Rouard ambled over to François.

"That's quite a girl you've got there, Rabelais," he said in a gravelly voice. François flushed with embarrassed delight at Rouard's misplaced observation. She wasn't exactly his girl; at least, they hadn't discussed it...yet. "Don't know if you deserve her," Rouard went on. "She bathed you twice a day to keep your fever down. She dressed your wound and gave you medicine. And she never left your side. I just fed her and gave her lots of my tea...She's devoted to you."

François felt his throat swell with emotion. Then Rouard chuckled. "Youth! She makes me wish I was young again. I think I'm in love with her too!"

François squirmed, uncomfortable under Rouard's expectant gaze. To his surprise Rouard turned wistful. "She's remarkable," he shared. "She has a unique energy that just sings through her. Don't you feel it?" François had just thought it was lust at first. "From the moment I set eyes on her, Rabelais," Rouard went on, "I knew our destinies were enmeshed. It was as though I knew her from a dream..." Then, catching François's bewildered stare, Rouard shook himself and glared at him.

Vivianne returned and set down François's clothes beside him. Rouard announced that he was going shopping for some food and left them alone again. Vivianne sat down on the bed next to François.

"Did I tell you that Vincent is related to the physician in von Grunwald castle?" she said with odd excitement. "Doctor Grien was the first doctor to discover and use antibiotics. He discovered penicillin and studied its properties then shared his work with the world and brought us new medicine. Somewhere between his moving to France and several descendants later, a Marline Grien married a René Rouard and then Vincent came along."

François shook his head in bemusement. "That is bizarre. Surely, it's a coincidence."

She smiled strangely at what he said and he knew she didn't believe in coincidence.

✠

# ...29

VINCENT put on a pot of tea as Vivianne and François hunched over her backpack, rummaging. She peered up at François. "How is Antoine? Not too worse for wear I trust?"

François cocked his head to one side and studied her. Why did that sound sarcastic? He knew she was still very sad about her real father's death. She'd only discovered that he was her real father moments before Mortameur took him away from her. And Antoine came away with just a scratch—again. No matter. There would be no more run-ins with Mortameur, he thought. That was a few days ago. Of late, Vivianne had become very preoccupied and edgy.

"My mother told me to consult these books for my answers, especially Roget's," Vivianne explained, pulling out her books. "She called them talismans. But this one," she tapped Roget's, "has most of the answers." She gazed at the titles one by one as she pulled out the other books.

"I see you have my book there." François smirked, picking up *Gargantua and Pantagruel* by François Rabelais. "That's me...my name, that is..."

She stared at him from leafing through Roget's. "You mean *you're* François Rabelais, the writer?"

"Of course not, silly!" He laughed then clutched his side that twinged. "But my father claimed we were his descendants." Vivianne was the most astute and thoughtful girl he'd ever met. But every so often she still said something really dumb. He found it endearingly sweet and knew it was one of the things about her that he loved.

She drew in a sharp breath then murmured sadly, "Oh, Uta, not you too...even Fritz..." she breathed out... Then she gasped, "Oh..." followed by a whisper, "Wolfgang..." and fell into a low moan.

François edged over to see what had upset her and glimpsed two lithographs on the pages of the book she had laid open on her lap. The title at the top of the page read: *The Battle of Grunwald*. He read how the battle marked a pivotal victory for the Teutonic Knights. The Knights became an extremely potent arm of the growing German Empire, especially to the East, conquering Russia and eventually parts of the orient. Fearing the growing autonomy of the Teutonic Order, Kaiser Wilhelm II, the German Kaiser in the late eighteen hundreds, tried to destroy the order; instead he was destroyed and the Nazi Reich was born. The order formed the strong guard of the Nazi Reich and they renamed themselves the Black Knights. It was interesting, François reflected, how they'd gone from using a black cross on a white field to a white cross on a black field.

Then he spotted two lithographs on the sidebar that made him jolt. The first was a poor likeness of Vivianne! He knew it was her only because her name appeared in the caption: Lady Vivianne Schoen, Baronesse von Grunwald. He stared at the drawing; she hadn't lied about herself after all! She was a noble...a true lady. The second lithograph was a gruesome drawing of a witch burning. The etched plate depicted a castle courtyard with a huge fire at its center that was surrounded by a wild crowd. A young girl, lashed to a ladder-like structure, was being lowered over the fire by several men. François knew that the girl portrayed was Vivianne and feverishly read the main text first:

*...Ulrich Schoen, the Baron von Grunwald, who led five lances in Jungingen's left flank and later became the Grand Master's Chief Commander, was instrumental in turning the tide of the battle. Schoen introduced his personally designed field-cannon in the latter part of the battle when Jungingen's reserve had split and was surrounded. It was during this battle that mustard gas was reportedly first used, also invented by Baron von Grunwald, and used in concert with his new weapon. Together, these turned the tide of the battle and gave victory to the flagging Teutonic Knights over the Lithuanian-Polish army. The Knights slaughtered over ten thousand Polish and Lithuanian soldiers as well as Mongols and Tartars before the battle*

ended in their unconditional surrender. Of those that surrendered, the Polish and most Lithuanians were spared; no Tartars, Saracens or Mongols, who'd helped the Polish, were taken prisoners. All were summarily executed, mainly through beheading.

François swallowed hard. In a sidebar, where the book placed matters of interest and where the two disturbing lithographs sat, Francois read under the title: 'Ergot's Tragic Birthday Party':

Before Baron von Grunwald saved the Teutonic Order, he had to recover from a madness due to Ergot poisoning from eating the tainted local rye bread. Unfortunately for his only daughter, it was not soon enough. Consumed by Ergot hysteria, the baron executed his only daughter on her birthday for committing adultery. They burned her at the stake as a witch, along with her loyal servant, Uta Wolkenstein — also accused of witchcraft — and the baroness's demon cat. The cat was disemboweled and hung on a pole next to the pyre. Though unproven, the Lady Vivianne, who had been caught with a bloody dress had apparently committed the sin of taking courtly love to her own bed and lost her virginity to a local servant the very day of her handing off to her betrothed. The Servant was hung and quartered....

François threw a glance at Vivianne; he desperately wanted to ask her if it was true, especially the last part. He noticed that she didn't seem as upset about her death as she was the death of the servants or even the cat. She murmured again, "oh, no...not Wolfgang but Tancred...why...why would he say that? To save me...to realize a fantasy...oh, lieber Gott..."

François read where her finger rested: Although the baron had initially accused his own squire-at-arms, Wolfgang von Eisenreich, of having his pleasure with the baroness and had tortured him, it was another servant who confessed his crime. But too late: one of the baron's footmen, Tancred Frosch, burst upon the burning scene and shouted over the crowd that the Lady Vivianne was innocent of seduction. He'd ravished the baroness. He announced that he'd burst into her room while she was dressing and forced himself upon her. He claimed that she didn't tell on him because she was too modest. The crowd refused to listen and burned her anyway. The baron, who'd heard the boy's confession, punished him by hanging and quartering *him.*

Just then she choked on her breath and let out a little peep that he recognized was the repressed gasp of a sob. Her index finger lingered over a line and François read around her finger:

*...Once recovered from his Ergot hysteria, the baron was so overcome with grief at his daughter's death that he abandoned the castle, never returning. He left it to his loyal squire-at-arms, now a proven knight in battle, Wolfgang von Eisenreich.* As Vivianne looked away with misty eyes of contemplation, François read on with a frown: *von Eisenreich later went on to become one of the Reich's most prominent officials, eventually becoming second in command to the Kaiser. Eisenreich's descendants maintain an important place in the First Reich and the Fuhrer's ruling government.*

Damn! François had known the name was familiar and he'd had a hard time placing it—until now: it was the name of Lizette's husband; Grand Marshal von Eisenreich. Was he a descendant of this squire of Vivianne's? Glancing up at her, François guessed that there was some sore point between her and the baron. He wasn't her father, but she'd lived most of her life thinking he was. That had to be rough, he thought. He glanced back at the lithograph of Vivianne and pointed to it.

"That's you?"

"Of course not!" she bit out. "I'm not dead."

"But it says—"

"Of course it's me!" She turned to glare at him with a loud exhale. "Yes...yes, it's me," she admitted peevishly. "But, obviously it also *isn't* me. Otherwise I wouldn't be here, right?"

"Right." He frowned. He was about to retort when Vincent brushed past him with a cup of tea for Vivianne.

"Ah, I see you've found it, Vianne," he said.

At first François didn't like Rouard using his new nickname for her. Then he'd decided that Rouard deserved it every bit as much as he did.

"My fa—" She swallowed convulsively then resumed in a wavering voice, "The baron didn't design a field cannon or invent mustard gas. That was Mortameur's doing. He's responsible for the Teutonic Order's victory ..." She looked up at François with intense eyes. "And the success of your present *Reich*…in this world, anyway…"

She slammed the book shut and François blinked in bemusement.

"I now know what I was supposed to learn," she went on soberly. "And what I'm supposed to do." She dropped her gaze to the book on her lap. Darkness lingered in her pressed lips and veiled her eyes. A darkness that scared him. He felt her migrate away from him, like a wayward comet finding the new orbit of an entirely other world to circle. And, while he refused to admit it, an ache swelled inside him at the thought of losing her.

"What are you talking about?" he said peevishly.

"I need to go back and remake history."

"What?" he exclaimed. "Go back? You can't be serious," he mocked in an angry tone. How could he protect her if she left him?

"The Tear brought me here so I could make my choice. I was always meant to go back."

"I won't let you go back to where they'll burn you as a witch!" he shrilled.

"It's not up for debate, François!"

"You're an idiot!" He stomped his foot. "I won't allow it!"

She surged to her feet and planted fists at her sides. "And it's certainly not up to you to *allow* me to do anything!"

Through the corner of his eye François saw Vincent sidestep back, as if out of the line of fire. François knew he was on his own and in his heart he recognized that he wasn't going to win. Vivianne was mad, willful and far too honorable.

"No, I guess not," he retorted. "You're just such a little miss self-reliant, you can't accept anything from anyone, even if it's good advice!"

"I'm not—"

"Damn right, you aren't!"

"This isn't about you! You're such a spoiled baby!"

François stared at her, blinking hard. He stumbled back then stomped away. He went back to his own place. He didn't care if it wasn't safe.

He flopped on the bed and flipped through his old magazines.

✠

After some time, François felt her shadow at his doorway. He didn't look up.

"I need to explain," he heard her agitated broken voice. "And you need to understand."

"No you don't," he muttered, not looking up. "I understand."

"No, you don't," she insisted loudly in a voice now shattered with emotion.

"Yes, I—!" He looked up. His mouth stayed open but he didn't voice the rest of his retort. She'd been crying. He gestured for her to take a seat across from him on the bed. "Go ahead," he said in a softer voice.

She came forward and took the seat then cleared her throat. "Mortameur was greedy. He wanted it all: an eternal life with my mother in a world of his making. He meddled with a part of history he wasn't entitled to. He went into the past...a time prior to his emanation...to ensure that *his* world prevailed of the two split worlds from the Battle of Grunwald. Because only one can; there's only one of me. Mortameur wanted to live forever in a world of his own making, this one. That's why he came back to Grunwald for me. That's why he wanted to sway me to embrace this world, to stay here...with him and keep this world going." She focused away from François, into the past. "It explains those awful books on fascism Father Daniel was supposed to make me read..." Vivianne gave François a searching look, hoping for some understanding. "You still don't get it, do you?"

"I'm still coping with two alternate realities and you traveling through them like they're only doors," he sulked. He still found it unnerving that this fifteenth century girl was grasping and mastering concepts of quantum time-travel and paradox that he couldn't even understand. Vivianne glared at him. It was clear that she wanted him to get it. It was very important to her. He saw that she'd interpreted his inability as reluctance. Maybe she was right. Releasing a long sigh, he said wearily, "Maybe you can explain it to me...like you would a child."

She rose and walked a circle in the room then faced him, and began to speak with command, "François, you asked me before why I came..." He watched her steel herself, lips pressing with the effort of sharing a painful truth. When it came out, he thought he detected relief in her face, like a dam breaking. "And I said that I just ran away. I'd deluded myself that I was searching for a brave knight to help. As if I'd find a knight here, anyway," she added ruefully. François swallowed. She'd obviously ruled him out as a candidate. "I really just wanted to leave it all behind ..." Her gaze dropped to the ground in obvious shame. "I really *was* just running away. Father Daniel told me but I didn't listen: *je dois devenir ce que je cherche.*"

Gazing up through her dark lashes from her downturned face, she told François every painful detail of what had transpired up to her colliding into him; about the pending battle and Mortameur's arrival, how he turned everything and everyone upside down; about his rape of the servant girl and Vivianne's cowardly retreat; about her father's mortifying accusation of her illicit sexual deed when all she'd done was start her period and how they'd punished Wolfgang for something he hadn't done; how she'd nearly killed Mortameur and how her entire community had turned against her, accusing her of being a witch, and hunted her down to burn at the stake. Some of the details he'd already discerned or discovered, but much of what she'd said helped him put together the missing pieces.

"François," she continued, eyes now fully on him, "I'm an Aeon. I'm a being of light. Maybe they're right about me. Perhaps I am a witch. What is a witch, after all, but a woman not understood." She sighed. "I have a duty as an Aeon. I have to go back and ensure that the other world makes it; if I stay here, this one has already and will continue to lead to much more horror and massive destruction at the expense of the other. Not that the other world is much better; but it is. There is no world Nazi empire there now, although they almost did create one and that world has been equally devastated by world wars and a century of almost nonstop violence. It's still, from what I see here in comparison, a better world, one with a chance. But, by saving that other world, I condemn this one to its death...and all those who live in it." It had come out in a rush. She dropped into his chair and added miserably, "I'm sorry."

They remained quiet for some time as he fully digested the meaning of her words. He finally got it. And he hated it.

"Wait," he said. "Why can't the two worlds merge like Antoine said before? He said that these twin realities tend to merge after awhile when—"

"No," she snapped, losing her temper. "You haven't been listening. It's too late for that. The worlds have strayed too far apart. They're too different. And there's only one of me. I have no twin to join with. I can't possibly bring them back together on my own. I don't know how I could possibly do that."

"I don't get it. Why can't you travel back and forth and do whatever it is you do to keep a world going and..."

"*Lieber Gott*, François! I'm not *God!*"

"But you're an *Aeon!*" he retorted.

She stared at him with a look of plaintive defeat and he grudgingly reminded himself that beneath the ethereal Aeon robes she wore was the naked body of an ordinary fourteen year-old girl. Save those telltale marks on her back, she was just another girl with normal dreams like anyone else. "So, you're saying that I'm going to die, this whole world's going to die..."

"Worse, possibly. You might never exist, once I go. I'll wipe you right out of existence. I'm not entirely clear on how these realized or unrealized realities work. Maybe you'll linger in a dream..."

So, he was to die. Or linger in someone's dream. *Her*

dreams, maybe?...

"Think of it this way," she suggested with a hopeful smile. "There's another you out there in that other world. Maybe it's a happier world and you're in a happier place. Maybe your parents are still alive and Paris flourishes in a cultural renaissance. Maybe you're not a thief but an explorer fulfilling your dreams. An artist living in the Latin Quarter about to travel the world..." She didn't look like she believed it either, François thought, studying her face.

She abruptly stood up and gazed directly at him with new determination. "I need my accoutrements," she said stiffly. "Where are they?"

"Your *what*?"

"My equipment, my sword and mail and tunic," she said, looking a little annoyed. "The things I came with."

"Oh, that..."

His expression must have betrayed him because she gave him a painful sickened look. "You didn't ..."

"I did," he said with forced calm. "I hawked it all." He watched her lips tighten with his revelation and babbled on, "Even the fancy tunic with the dragon on it. Dragons are really popular right now—"

"We have to get it all back," she cut in. She planted her fists on her hips. He decided that where she'd come from in that castle of hers she was used to giving orders. And having them followed.

François stiffened. "Are you kidding? I sold it all to Jacques the fencer. It's long gone. Besides—"

"Give him back the money you got for it—"

"He surged to his feet, defensive anger boiling up inside. "What do you think we've been living on all this time? That meal you just enjoyed. How do you think I paid for it? Or did you expect me to steal everything? It's gone, Vivianne. All the money. I'm sorry. Besides, Jacques would have sold it all himself to who knows who. It would be an impossible task to find it all."

While he spoke his throat began to swell and his chest ached; he watched as the burning anger in her eyes quickly melted to desperation then finally to despair and she dropped onto his stained mattress and sat, hunched. She dropped her sad gaze to the ground then brought a hand up to cover her mouth and closed her eyes. He would have preferred her anger to this.

It was bad enough that she was going. François realized that the ache in his chest was his ache for her; he didn't want her to go. The stubborn annoying crazy girl who'd been nothing but a perilous nuisance to him since she'd literally fallen into his life, had wedged her way into his heart. And he didn't want to let go. She'd healed him. She'd reminded him that he had a soul. Shown him the power of honor, conviction and faith. Given him something to live—and die—for. He feared that the wound her loss would leave inside him would leak out everything he'd learned. Everything he'd become.

"I'm sorry," he murmured. Suddenly desperate to make things right for her, he added, "I'll find a way to get it all back, Vivianne. Maybe we can—"

She grabbed his hand and looked up with glistening eyes. He barely stifled a moan as she tenderly placed the palm of his hand against her cheek and closed her eyes for a moment. Her cheek was wet. When she looked up at him there was no anger in her eyes; what lay there swelled his throat.

"It's alright, François," she said softly. "I have to go. I'll be fine without them."

How could she say that! She was heading straight into a hornet's nest of treachery and war—

Vivianne gently pulled him down to face her directly. He squatted, trembling, before her until their faces were so close he could feel her warm breath on him and see the teardrops that clung to her eyelashes. Like two travelers returning home, they leaned into each other. He found his mouth on hers in a glancing kiss. Her lips tasted of dew on the morning grass and the innocent promise of a new day. He folded his arms around her and she responded with a wonderful embrace. It was she who opened to him, inviting him inside her mouth in a frisson of mutual tasting. They kissed hungrily and he raptly drank her in like a good wine.

In that single kiss he suddenly understood her fully. Despite all the other girls he'd had, she felt like his first. And his only. She tasted of home.

How long they remained that way, ardently kissing and clutched in each other's arms, François had no idea. It could have been for a minute or an hour. All he knew was that it was his glimpse of eternity. His glimpse of God.

Even though he desperately wanted to, he did not press her for more like he would have with any other girl. Even though he throbbed with lustful desire, he respected her too much for that. No, it was more than respect. He cared too much for her. And felt the overwhelming urge to envelope her in a protective mantle instead.

Despite that right-up in *Roget's l'Histoire*, François knew Vivianne hadn't made out with anyone before; perhaps never even kissed someone before him. In her time-period she could have had a baby by her age already, he reflected. François knew his history; girls in the Middle Ages were generally married through arrangement by twelve and pregnant by age fourteen. And dead from complications by twenty. They lived hard and earnest lives. Sex for them was utilitarian, for breeding purposes, not some casual tryst for a cheap thrill like it was for the girls today.

Vivianne deserved better. Better than a quick jaunt with a thief and a bastard like him; better than making out in a filthy shack with a no-good tramp. She deserved a chance to take it slow and find true love. To find her knight, her *ritter*. Not that she'd find true love when she returned home, where marriages among nobles were arranged for reasons other than love. She was still the Lady Vivianne von Grunwald, after all. An honorable and noble woman who, if she survived the witch-hunt and other castle treacheries aimed at her, was destined to wield power and wealth in her land and would eventually direct an entire age to enlightenment. It was only then that François realized he was crying.

As he opened his eyes to pull back from her he found her deep hazel eyes smiling at him as she clung to his neck.

Then, without letting go, she slowly leaned back on the mattress and pulled him down with her. He couldn't believe it. She was choosing *him! Now!*

She laid her hands on his clumsy shaking fingers over the buttons of his shirt, and helped him undress. Then he was sliding her top over her head, revealing her spread out breasts; those girlish breasts he'd mocked when he'd first seen her. They were the most beautiful breasts he'd ever seen. He traced their swell with trembling hands. Then, feeling like he was entering a cathedral, he leaned down to kiss the hollow between them and inhaled her wonderful scent. He drew out sighing breaths from her and she ran her fingers through his wild hair.

They helped each other peel off trousers and under-garments. Then François was straddling her naked legs with his knees and exalting in her innocent girl's figure, never touched by a man's hands. By contrast, he was far from innocent; he'd had relations with many ladies, mostly mature women with volup-tuous curved bodies, experienced in lovemaking and in pleasuring. Yet, Vivianne's earnest and naïve vulnerability stirred his heart with a flutter he'd never before experienced. Was it love?

"Vivianne…" he breathed out, his voice a caress.

He tasted her very slowly and memorized every inch of her beautiful body. He began by kissing her feet, lips trailing up her long legs, past her silky thighs, then lingering over the hallowed triangle where her legs met.

He buried his face there and inhaled her exotic scent. It was not the filthy unwashed odor of Sylvie or the fake perfume of Lizette, but the natural spice she was born with. His lips and tongue coaxed out a gasp of startled pleasure from her and she grew deliciously wet. She seized him by the hair and stirred beneath him with a low moan of yearning. He reverently traced his lips over her body and moved up the hollow of her beautiful neck and finally came to her face. The face of home. He met her devoted gaze through a film of tears. Her eyes sparkled like another universe. Infinitely deep, they defined the eternity of her love. And for an instant-made-eternity Heaven was his. They kissed.

He made gentle and tender love to her, piercing her finally when she was ready for him with every part of her yearning body. She cried out as he burst through her barrier; yes, he was her first. Unspeakable joy spilled out of him in a rush of exaltation and he climaxed with an explosive cry. Then he felt the shudder of her body, convulsing in sobs. She was crying. He pulled away in concern and found her staring at him in wondrous joy as she wept. Then she seized him in a passionate embrace and they kissed again.

She'd entrusted him with the greatest gift she could give: her vulnerability…and her love. Something he would cherish for the rest of his life.

✠

They remained together, entwined on his lumpy stained mattress, the rest of the night. Unlike any of the girls he'd known, Vivianne wanted to please him as much as be pleasured.

Eager to learn, she said, "Teach me. Show me."

He guided her hands and talked her through each delicious move. She learned quickly, when to be tender and when to be rough. That night he taught her everything he knew: "Like this?" she would say as he shuddered with a gasp. "Oh, yes!" he would moan. She learned fast.

"How did you learn all this?" she finally asked as they lay side-by-side, sweating, on their backs between sessions.

"Women I was with," he murmured with an embarrassed smile, keeping his eyes closed. "And men," he added. Then, as if compelled to balance his heartless sex with passion, he turned to her and burst out, "I love you!"

"I love you too," she responded, placing her hand over his. "I think I loved you from the first moment I saw you, hovering over me and about to snatch my necklace."

"More like love-hate!" He laughed softly to cover up his shame of that selfish moment and sank back into bed to look up at his corrugated ceiling.

"They're often one in the same, aren't they, my little thief?" she teased with a lopsided smile. They made wild love and she eagerly tried one of the less conventional positions he'd shown her, even though it made her laugh with embarrassment.

✠

# ...30

WHEN François sighed awake mid-morning, Vivianne was already dressed and sitting next to him with expectation. He rubbed the sleep out of his eyes and sat up.

She unfastened her necklace and removed it from her neck. "I want you to have this." Before he had a chance to react she'd clasped it around his neck. "There."

He glanced down at the jewel-studded cross that hung next to his own silver locket, overcome with emotion. Her *ritterkreuz*, she'd called it: her knight's cross. He knew what the cross meant to her. It had been a gift—the only gift—her father had given her. The cross symbolized her world, her beliefs, her faith and strength and finally everything about her. It moved him deeply that she'd chosen to give it to him.

"François, it was you all along," she said, eyes blazing. "You're the stable rock the tear directed me to. I thought it was Antoine or even Rue des Rosiers itself. But just like your namesake of six hundred years ago, whose writing never swerved from the truth no matter which reality it was thrust into, you have that same inner strength and voice, François."

François sat in stunned silence. He'd never seen himself that way before. In sudden inspiration, he removed his locket, untangled it from her necklace, and fastened it around

Vivianne's neck. "It's not worth nearly as much as what you've given me, but it's all I have. It was given to me by my mother and it's the only thing I have of my parents…"

She glanced down at the locket and opened it. When she saw the picture of him inside, tears filled her eyes and she smiled.

"You don't have to go, Vianne." He grabbed her arm.

"I do!" she said firmly. "You know I do. I won't do what my mother and Mortameur did. I'm trying to fix what they did. Let me go." She pulled away from him. "Don't make it harder for both of us, François."

Their intimate moment was over. She got up. Her gaze had returned to its former reserve, protecting her traveling soul.

After some moments, realizing that he was staring at her, she turned to him with a self-conscious look. "What?"

He grinned like a little boy. "It's just that, even in those clothes you really do look like…well…someone from another time and place…like an *angel*."

"That's because I *am*," she said with a teasing smile.

✠

He walked her to the place where they'd first collided into one another. Her tear energy was there, Vivianne explained. That was where she could best summon it again.

As they neared it, François let his steps falter. She slowed with him and turned to him with a look of inquiry. Wearing a sloping grin, he handed her a small parcel, "You might find these handy over there."

She looked inside and grinned at the toothbrush and toothpaste. Then she stared at the revolver and shells.

"So, maybe, after you've been around for about six hundred years, you could look me up in 2015, when I'm twenty," he went on. "In this other reality, of course … my other self, that is. *Everything comes in time to those who can wait*." His grin turned into a wincing smile. He knew what she thought of the idea. "Yeah, I know," he murmured. Dumb thought. Why, after six hundred years, would she be interested in a tramp like him? A lady who'd no doubt be courted by dozens of dukes, princes, possibly kings. "Better to forget me—"

She turned to him. "I will never forget you." Then she straightened and gave him a penetrating stare. "And I expect you to never forget me, François Rabelais."

He flashed a rogue smile at her. "How can I not? I'll never forget the girl who chastised me for stealing then went on to steal the thing most precious to me."

She laughed through her tears, then ruthlessly wiped them away. "Goodbye, François. God be with you."

"And with you," he echoed, knowing he really meant it this time.

She stepped away from him and he knew he was meant to go no further. He watched her advance to the exact location where they'd collided. At once, as if sensing her presence, but more importantly, her intent, a light appeared in front of her. Her head became a halo of brightness as the tear opened in front of her, streaming white light.

"Vianne!" he called out with sudden urgency.

She turned her head to gaze at him over her shoulder and their eyes met.

"*Vivre!*..." He blew her a kiss. "*Pour moi! Pour nous...*"

She beamed back at him.

"*I know you will make your world a better world,*" he quietly added to himself, knowing she couldn't hear him. She'd already turned her head toward the growing light. Then she was gone in a blinding flash and a sudden deep ache in the hollow of his chest. He heard her muffled gasp and his heart throbbed in his throat in momentary alarm. What disaster had she collided into? There was nothing he could do, except pray for her. He stood in the deep silence with his head bowed in reverent prayer. *Dear God, keep her safe. My Vivianne. My joy...my life. I'm a bastard, but she's sweet and kind and deserves the best....*

✠

"I learned something in the few years I've inhabited this Earth, l'Oncle." François leaned back in his chair. He and his uncle were seated at a table of an outdoor café in Saint-Michel Square. His uncle faced him with an enigmatic expression. "The universality of differences," François continued. "The irony of contradiction. I learned that just as there are Black Knights who aren't Black Knights—for whatever reason, they've broken or never followed their vows of celibacy or loyalty—there are also *Guardiens* who aren't *Guardiens*..." He was gazing intensely at Antoine as he spoke his last words.

Antoine's reaction told François everything; his uncle was guilty of betrayal as he'd surmised. François leaned forward. "It was you who told Mortameur where to find Vivianne, wasn't it? That fight was fake. You've known him and Vivianne's father for years. That's why Mortameur found us a second time at Boulanger's place. You never really left the Montmartre. No one kicked you out. That was all faked to get you in with the street people, the students, artists, trouble-makers and anarchists so you could spy on them—on *me*—more effectively. You've been living comfortably on the hill all these years, going home to your comfortable bed after visiting with me on the cold winter streets of the Latin Quarter and giving me the odd meal out of charity. You're Wasserman, aren't you? You're with the *Schutzstaffel*." He felt anger boil up in the rising tension of his limbs and realized that he badly wanted to strike his uncle. But he quickly summoned the image of Vivianne with her quiet strength and, drawing on it like a breath of fresh air, he kept his cool. "It was probably even you who told them about my parents."

Antoine's eyes betrayed the truth and it was all François could do not to reach over the table and beat him with his fists. His hands tightened into fists on his lap and he felt his face convulse with thoughts of furious revenge. *No*, he stopped himself. There was a better way...Vivianne's way.

"Why?" he asked, trying not to let the disgust he was feeling color his voice. "I thought you loved my mother..."

Antoine made a scoffing sound with his lips. "If *I* couldn't have her *no one* could, least of all my brother," he said with a scowl. His eyes faltered and he shook his head. "Don't look at me that way."

"You were never an anarchist," François challenged Antoine. "You joined the movement to spy. Hell, you probably even ratted on your friend at school." God! He was right, François realized, watching his uncle's guilty expression. "Then what? You met my mother?"

"And introduced her unwittingly to my kid brother. I could have eventually converted her. But he got to her first. The no good git didn't deserve her. He was a ruffian. Not intelligent, sophisticated or suave like me. But Angeline always preferred the scoundrels."

François straightened with a long exhale and he saw his uncle relax. Antoine had a right to fear him; François's temper was notoriously uncontrolled. But his uncle would never suspect him of doing what he intended next. François's reputation for being a passionate, unthinking jerk with no allegiances to the *SSLF* would work in his favor for once. "I should kill you now for what you did to my parents," François said, getting up. "But I won't. I have more important things to do right now…"

"Where are you going?"

"*Je m'en vais chercher un grand peut-être.* Good bye Uncle."

✠

François shivered with excited dread and stared at the *Zarathustra Plan* in his shaking hands. He threw fearful glances around him as he stood in front of von Eisenreich's open safe. But he was alone; Lizette remained in a euphoric 'coma' on the bed, where he'd left her and the Grand Marshal was at his all-night meeting.

François returned his gaze to the thick bound document. It contained the most heinous plan for "ethnic cleansing" — a term coined by von Eisenreich himself — and the establishment of a New World Order. François studied the red and black cover.

Beneath the flame-coloured title *"Zarathustra Planen: die 'dunkle Ursach' Für den deutscher Sonderweg und Lebensraum—Griff nach der Weltmacht"* lay the image of a truncated pyramid with the all-seeing eye as its apex. The motto below read: *novus ordo seclorum.* Below it, inside a white circle, was the familiar black swastika.

François flipped through the two hundred pages that contained detailed instructions for executing the cruelest and most inhumane elimination of whole ethnic groups: "to purify humanity to be its very best" according to von Eisenreich, a bully and arrogant follower of "Exceptionalism" and "Social Darwinism" who believed in a pan-Germany.

The nihilistic *Zarathustra Plan* meant to establish a Nazi world-supremacy and New World Order through a five step program of guerila activities and openly offensive tactics headed by the *Schutzstaffel.* They ranged from secret infiltration and subtle coercion to open violence and intimidation. Their objectives included: the purposeful and targeted reduction of the world's population; implemention of an aggressive eugenics program and ubiquitous surveillance program that not only tracked everyone's movements but virtually all their communications; the creation of an uncompromising educational program that rewarded conformity and obedience; establishment of a propaganda system that would infiltrate all levels of humanity from community to individual; and the use of strong incentives for creating paranoia and spreading fear. According to this document, the SS had already infiltrated the highest levels of government in North America, the rest of Europe the South Pacific and parts of Asia; they'd formed an influencial cabal and set up financial cartels, kept virtually everyone under their surveillance and had already Beta-tested several depopulation techniques.

Ground tactics included a monstrous range of activities such as murder, torture, arbitrary arrest and detention, extra-judicial executions, rape and sexual assaults, the confinement of groups in enclosed ghettos, forcible removal, displacement and deportation, deliberate military attacks or threats of attacks on certain areas, and wanton destruction of property.

François slipped the document into his backpack with still shaking hands. This would be a boon for the Résistance. He closed the safe he'd just picked open and left the room. He hesitated briefly at the door of the bedroom where Lizette lay still naked on her back under the influence of wild sex, rapture and liquor. In short, thought François, she'd passed out.

Her face looked peaceful now; saliva had drooled down the side of her slightly open mouth as she snored softly in the bliss of a drunken sleep. François refused to think of what was going to happen to her once the Grand Marshal discovered the missing document. For at least a year, he'd given her sexual favors whenever the Grand Marshal was in overnight meetings; now it was time for payback, François concluded with a flinch of guilt. No one deserved the Grand Marshal's wrath; not even Lizette. But this document in his hands was bigger than her or him. It represented an entire world. *We must all do our part to make this world a better world*, he thought.

François gave her a mock salut then left the apartment and sprinted down the stairs. He froze.

A Nazi Black Knight was slowly mounting the stairs. The Knight looked up and their eyes met. François forced himself to look casual.

They passed each other on the stairs and François was about to sigh with relief when the Black Knight called, "Halt! Boy!"

François froze, heart slamming, and slowly turned to face the Knight. The man approached him with cold curiosity. When he was close enough for François to feel his breath on him, the man reached out and fingered the ritterkreuz on François's neck. "Where did you get this, thief?"

"Maybe I killed a Black Knight for it," François said jeeringly. His eyes flickered to the man's rank-insignia on his shoulders. His chest tightened. The man was a high-ranking officer. One of the highest. *Merde!*

"More like you stole it off him while he slept after he buggered you, whore!"

His reputation had preceded him, François realized.

And on the tails of that realization came another: this was Lizette's husband. His all-night meeting must have been called short. And François knew that he was doomed. Wasn't this whole world doomed, anyway? So close, he thought, feeling the document burn a hole on his back. *I was so close....*

He could have used the gun he'd given Vivianne; then again, she likely needed it.

In a last bid for life, François kicked fiercely out, connecting with the Grand Marshal's groin. Von Eisenreich doubled over with pain and François ran full tilt down the stairs. Once at the bottom, he made the mistake of turning....

✠

Pain slammed him backward as a bullet pierced his chest. It tore the breath out of him and a sudden vision of that incredible dream blossomed...of a valorous knight on a quest—himself—wading through a shallow swamp, rippled with a heavenly glow that streamed down through a towering cathedral. It shone upon him God's light of forgiveness, strength and compassion.And he knew he was going to die.

Vivianne. Her voice was the sweet perfume of a flower and her smile the pure radiance of the sun that warmed his heart. Her laugh was the bracing effervescence of champagne that thrilled him to his core and sent his soul on a journey home. Vivianne. His inspiration. His love. Someone to live...or die for—

When the second bullet took him he was mid-way through a smile. It froze on his lips as he fell into the light of a better world.

✠

# Book Three: The Summoning

"I am the light of the world, those who follow Me shall not walk in darkness, but have the light of life."

—John 8:12

## ...31
*Von Grunwald Castle, Prussia, 1410*

VIVIANNE burst to the surface with a gasping breath. She thrashed blindly to the edge, and emerged like a crocodile from the water. She clamored up the shore, shaking but knowing she was safe. The light drizzle hissed through the trees and spattered her already soaked body. She inhaled the fresh sweetness of beach and oak trees, undercut by the organic scent of bog and swamp.

*I'm home*, she thought; She gave in to her tears and wept hard. She slowly sat up and rocked her body, sobbing loudly. At first she wept in mindless grief and exhaustion. Then her sobs calmed down as her mind returned to that soundless ache that promised to remain her companion until she died...which wouldn't be for a very very long time, she realized.

She'd just doomed François's world. She had a new one to nurture, to make better, if she could. History had shown her the way. It meant abandoning his world, which would spiral into a fatal spin and burn to a crashing death—François along with it...or not exist at all. The boy she'd fallen in love with no longer existed. He was just a dream in her mind and her heart.

She suddenly remembered what his Uncle Antoine had said: there was no time or space for an Aeon; only choices. She'd made hers: lose a man to save a world. The choice, once decided, was clear. But why was it she who had to make it?

✠

As Vivianne emerged from the flooded forest on the hill,

backpack hoisted over her shoulders, she had her first glimpse of the von Grunwald castle and felt her heart tugged with complex emotions. This was still decidedly home to her. And yet, it felt like she'd been away for years. In truth she'd only been gone for about a week. If she could trust François's uncle, no time should have transpired here in the meantime. In fact, she had meant to return prior to nexus moment, whenever that was. It was entirely conceivable that she would see her other self fleeing, Vivianne contemplated as she surveyed the hill. Seeing the cavalry horses, she wondered about Willy, her own horse. Had he—or would he—manage to clamor out and save himself from a murky death?

A swift glance to her left at the assembling army in the valley below and the immense canopy of the *Hochmeister*, told her she was probably right. She could just make out the standard of the Hospital *Großmeister* below. They hadn't gotten as far as they had when she'd left: she'd arrived before she escaped. It was the eve of the Battle of Grunwald. Then a thought crossed her mind; perhaps in this world, she didn't escape....

✠

It took her awhile to reach the castle on foot. Painfully aware of her odd attire, Vivianne ignored the stares she got from the soldiers as she skirted a few of the lances with hasty steps.

She passed the very outer walls easily and reached the fortified castle gate where Warren, the gatekeeper, stood, looking down at her from the battlements. The portcullis was down, preventing access into the castle. At first Warren simply stared at her in bewildered amazement. Perhaps he hadn't realized that she'd escaped. Now the 'witch' had returned, she thought cynically. He pointed to her excitedly and was about to raise the alarm, when Vivianne willed the metal portcullis to rise. Warren shrieked and ran away as she strode beneath the archway of the armoury into the castle courtyard. His warning shrieks rang through the courtyard and caused a stir among the others.

Vivianne barely had a chance to notice men stoking the raging fire before ducking into the stable. It was crowded with horses, several of which belonged to some of the Teutonic Knights who were still on the castle grounds. The tethered horses snorted and stomped at her sudden entry. To her delighted surprise, she saw her horse, alive and well.

"Willy!" she cried out, seizing his neck and rubbing her face against him. Willy responded with a low neigh and pawed the ground. "I'm so glad you made it out," she said. "Or did you ever leave?" she ended, eyeing the dry horse. Vivianne glanced swiftly behind her and dared not stay any longer.

From the stable, she had access to a small ill-used stairway that led to the open corridor and chambers above, including the doctor's. Vivianne bolted up the stairs. Mind nagging with morbid curiosity, she slipped inside the doctor's outer chamber. She wasn't sure what she was looking for but soon found something of interest, a locked wooden chest tucked beneath his writing desk. She picked the lock and there found a hidden treasure: parchments with her mother's handwriting! They were potion recipes, descriptions of natural remedies and medicines and chemical formulas for more complex substances; where to find the ingredients, how to create the substances and how to store them. The doctor's notes were scrawled beside hers. One of her last entries and the doctor's matching notes made her breath stutter. Vivianne surged to her feet, heart pounding with anger. She knew what the good doctor had done. And why. She shrugged off her backpack and pulled out the gun that François had given her. Then she seized the bundled parchments and placed them into her backpack. She rushed out of his chamber into the open hall, clutching François's gun, and headed for the stairs then froze.

"There's the witch!" someone shouted from below. "Burn her!"

Speak of the devil; there he was, pointing to her. Doctor Grien stood amidst an angry crowd that had assembled in the courtyard below. She was trapped.

"You shouldn't have come back, My Lady," Grien

snarled. "Because you'll get what you deserve." Then he turned to several of the baron's guards and shouted, "Take her! Burn her!"

Vivianne took aim and shot the doctor, shattering his hand. He shrieked like a woman and collapsed on his knees, shuddering and cradling what was left of his left hand with his right one.

Vivianne raised her hands to the shocked crowd, commanding them to silence. The guards wisely did not advance, staring at her weapon with open fear. Vivianne focused on the weeping physician. He was crumpled in a huddle of shocked pain and shuddered like a leaf in the wind.

"Perhaps you'll think twice the next time you knowingly inject a blood-thinner into a woman when she is hemorrhaging," Vivianne said frostily to Grien. "You knew exactly what you were doing that day fourteen years ago when you injected my mother with coumadin and purposefully killed her and my twin brother, sparing me only by order of the baron. I saw your notes. My mother kept a detailed diary of her alchemy. You spied on her and secretly copied everything. When she died you stole her material. Don't deny it; I saw it and I know my mother's writing. Uta thought you were ignorant; you even fooled my mother. In fact, you recognized her brilliance. You wanted her dead to use her knowledge as your own. So, you gave her coumadin 'by mistake'—out of ignorance—but secretly knowing what it would do to her."

The doctor stared at her in terror, probably expecting her to take another shot at him, this time to finish him off. But she lowered the gun and waved to Reinmar Vogt and Walther Meissen with terse instructions to come forward and drag the doctor inside so he could tend to himself. They took the shivering doctor away, leaving a bloody trail behind them. Vivianne turned back to the crowd. As she eyed them with a steely gaze, the crowd hushed. She recognized a few Teutonic Knights in the milling crowd of the castle household by their telltale white robes and black cross-paté. She spotted Sigmund Haupt, the young peasant village boy Grien had beaton. She recognized Nerdhart Burdach and young Gunter, one of the baron's pages. And there was Tancred Frosch, of course.

"I might indeed be a witch as Doctor Grien so kindly suggested," Vivianne said in a cold voice she hardly recognized as her own. "But I'm *your* witch. For better or for worse, you have me ... at least for now as Your Lady. My father is ill as is the chaplain and a few others who have eaten the contaminated rye bread of late. It will pass and they will recover. However, during their temporary sickness, I will command the household until they are healthy and fit to rule. Are there any who disagree?" Although she'd spoken in a calm voice, she'd clearly delivered the last as a challenge. No one responded. In fact, most averted their gaze when hers alighted upon them...as if they feared being struck down dead by her witchy eyes. So long as she had the gun in her hand and the power of fear in their hearts, Vivianne would have no trouble, she decided and relaxed enough to feel her shoulders finally drop.

She let out a long breath and continued, "A great battle will be fought at dawn tomorrow between the Teutonic Order and the Lithuanians and Polish armies and it will continue until well into the early evening. I will not interfere with that battle. But I promise to defend this castle and all those inside it from unfriendly Saracens and Tartans who wish to ransack it and injure us. And believe me, they will come. They will come and attempt to lay siege on the castle. They will not succeed!" The horde were meant to succeed in this world, Vivianne reflected, reviewing *Roget's l'Histoire* in her mind; according to it, they burned the castle to the ground and murdered most of the occupants inside. She intended that they would not succeed in this alternative world of her making. "I don't hold you obliged to stay. In fact, I suggest that any of the Teutonic Knights leave now and return to your lances." She paused and watched them dutifully worm their way through the crowd toward the stable. "The rest of you," she continued, "are all free to stay or leave, as you choose. If you decide to leave, I suggest you make your arrangements immediately and vacate these grounds by the end of the day. I know that some of you are not friends of the

Teutons who may have raided your parent village. But my castle is non-partisan; it will be a sanctuary from both Teuton and Polish soldiers and their barbaric allies. If you stay, I do expect you to do your part in defending the castle; I expect all of you capable of taking arms to do so and I will make the armory available for everyone to arm themselves. I will be there in the front lines with you."

No one cheered. Not that she expected anyone to. But she recognized a few faces of silent acceptance. Then she saw Tancred push his way through the crowd. He came up to her, eyes averted as usual and brandished a bunch of flowers that he thrust out at her.

"Welcome back, My Lady!"

Vivianne sighed, moved by his clumsy overture, and accepted the flowers from his shaking hands. "Thank you, Tancred."

✠

## ...32

Vivianne turned to the larger of the two cells, where Wolfgang had been held and handled the sturdy lock. It was unbreakable. Although François had taught her about picking open locks, she thought she could get into Wolfgang's cell more quickly through the secret passage and trap door. Vivianne pelted to the Wild Child tapestry and pulled it aside. The secret door was gone! There was only a solid wall there now. She pressed her hands against the cold stone wall in dismay then felt a sudden rush of severe anguish and turned—

✠

As if transported to another world, she saw herself running down the lower hall, the castle household in mad pursuit. She had a clear memory of Mortameur lying face up, blood flowing out of his mouth and eyes fixed in death. A huge pool of blood from the fatal wound she'd inflicted spread beneath him. The swords that had pierced clear through his chest, protruded out of him, dripping blood. In this world she hadn't changed her mind at the last second and had instead ruthlessly summoned his murder with the von Grunwald heraldic shield. It was certain that in this world, the Lithuanians and Polish would clearly win the battle. The question was: in this world what would become of *her*? She recalled Mortameur's words—

✠

The people storm at her from both sides, trapping her at her secret door. She pulls aside the tapestry and finds the door gone. Incredulous, Vivianne slams herself against the cold stone wall, madly pushing, as they seize her with gruff hands and haul her outside.

She sees Walther and Nerdhart struggling with her cat, Fritz. They throw him down the dry well and she hears his yelp as he lands from a fall that was even too high for a cat with agile feet. They then pitch a few stones down the well and she hears the cat cry. It is cruel beyond measure. There the cat will lie, broken from its fall, and slowly starve to death. The little creature that had done no one any harm will suffer an agonizing long death.

Vivianne is dragged across the dirt toward the roaring fire as faces she knows jeer and shout at her in twisted anger and fear. They tear her clothes off and beat her. Walther and Nerdhart lash her to the ladder beside the bonfire, their dirty hands mauling her naked thighs as their mouths gape open with churlish grins. She lies helpless on the ground, face up, rain pelting on her like a million missals. Someone spits on her. It is

Gertrude. *God! What did I ever do to you to warrant such hatred!* Vivianne thinks with wretched self-pity.

Then Walther and Nerdhart are raising the ladder. She loses any composure she might have still had and screams in terror as they swing her up. She totters, facing the crackling flames. She feels the heat of the blaze on her stricken face and struggles in sudden terror. The heat and smoke beat her face and hair like the hot breath of Hell. Then she is falling with a sharp inhale. She screams and meets the scorching flames. Breath torn out of her, she is consumed in a blossoming of unspeakable pain. For an instant made eternity, a molten white light envelopes her and the vision of her knight in the cathedral of light shines like a beacon—

✠

—Then she was shivering and sweating in a huddled heap on the cold stone floor beneath the tapestry. Fritz rubbed up against her leg, purring. Vivianne seized him in a crushing embrace, making him squeak in protest, and kissed his furry head.

"Oh, Fritz!" she cried and rocked with him in her arms. "My sweet cat..."

What had just happened? She then pieced together a sudden realization: she'd witnessed her own death in this world. She'd been burned in this world as well. And it would have happened exactly as she'd experienced it, if not for *this*....

She raised the gun that François had given her. She'd saved herself—François had saved her. She inhaled sharply: by saving herself, she'd already altered history! She'd created a third alternative. Then a wild unabashed thought struck her like lightening. Could she save all the others as well, then?

It then occurred to her that what she'd experienced was some kind of reabsorbtion of her alternative life in this world. And with it, she realized that she'd discovered the nexus moment. One thing she had never been clear on was when the schism would occur, when the nexus portal to the split worlds would appear for her and her absent twin brother. What determining moment in history. Now she knew. It was the moment she either killed Mortameur or didn't kill him in the Great Hall. In one world, François's world—the one she'd chosen—she didn't kill Mortameur and he shared his knowledge with her father. In this world—presumably her brother's chosen world—she apparently did kill Mortameur and his knowledge died with him. *She'd* orchestrated the schism; not her father, not von Jungingen or one of his betraying knights. The fate of the Battle of Grunwald had depended on her decision to kill or not to kill Mortameur in the Great Hall.

Vivianne surged to her feet, still shaky from the dreadful experience of being burned alive, and rearranged her backpack. Had she or had she not killed Mortameur in the Great Hall? Was she truly now in her brother's reality? Had the tear taken her to it? Judging from the inaccessible secret passageway, she guessed that this was her twin brother's world. And, if that was the case, then....

Vivianne tucked François's gun into the waistband of her jeans and pelted down the empty hall. She ran up the spiral stairway to the Great Hall then slid to a halt with panting breaths. There he lay, sprawled in obvious death, a dark pool spread below him and the heraldic von Grunwald blades, shining with blood, pierced through his chest.

Her hands flung to her mouth in dismay at the sight and she fell to her knees. *I did that!* Then she remembered her act of treachery in François's world. It seemed inevitable that she kill Mortameur, no matter which reality she was in.

She thought of the two versions of *Roget's l'Histoire Compréhensif à 2010*:

In one world, François's world—the reality she'd intuitively chosen—the Teutonic Knights win the Battle of Grunwald because Mortameur shares his knowledge with the baron; Wolfgang and her father live to help create the German Empire; Wolfgang's descendant, Jurgen von Eisenreich, fails to deter the impetuous Kaiser Wilhelm II in firing the cautious Bizmark or in his policy of aggressive *Weltpolitik* that culminates in war twenty-five years later and her father's descendant, Claus von Grunwald, advizes Hitler I, during World War II, to drive into the Middle East instead of directly to Russia, solidifying the 1st Reich until the inevitable destruction of the world in post-2010 as Wolfgang's last descendant Dietmar von Eisenreich launches Plan Zarathustra, unleashing certain planetary destruction. World War III. The end. The predicted Suntiela Aeon.

In the other version of *Roget's l'Histoire Compréhensif à 2010*—her brother's intended reality in which she killed Mortameur with the shield—the Lithuanians and Polish decimate the Teutonic Order, killing virtually all its knights, including her father, Wolfgang von Eisenreich and Siegried von Heidelberg. Both world wars still occur, but the First World War is prolonged as there is no descendant of Wolfgang von Eisenreich to advise Kaiser Wilhelm II to call an early armistice. With no Claus von Grunwald to advise him against it, Adolf Hitler blunders in War World II by invading Russia in 1941 and effectively puts an end to his third Reich. Although the world is saved from the domination of a German empire and no Dietmar von Eisenriech exists to launch Plan Zarathustra, the cycle of nonstop violence engendered by the two wars poise nevertheless to escalate into a massive planetary world war in the late 21st Century: World War III. A technical-space war that will likely annihilate the entire human population. The inevitable would just happen later.

It made sense that she'd myopically choose the world where those she loved survived, only for them to see-in a future world based on unending treachery and violence. Her brother would have seen-in a darker immediate future but a world with more sporadic violence. But, in the end, both worlds contained excessive violence and suffering with a dire far-future.

Vivianne stood up suddenly, face flushed with determination. She refused to accept either choice. In both worlds, it seemed, she was burned to death; yet, here she was, alive and well. She'd already altered her brother's world; surely, it was a sign.

"If I am really the *Demiurge* then let me truly be one and carve out a world of my own making...a third possibility," she murmured. Then, after a pause, "Not a world for me...or François...but a *better* world." A world not ruled by violence, fear and greed; but a world tempered by humility, tolerance and compassion. One that valued community, service and enlightenment. A world with hope. A world of faith. A world that celebrated beauty.

It hinged on the fate and destiny of several people right here in Grunwald, people she had to save—or not save. Those she'd put her faith in, whether they appeared to deserve it or not right now, including the baron, Wolfgang von Eisenreich, Siegfried von Heidelberg and even Baldung Grien. She had to let the battle take its regular course, let von Renys betray the Teutonic Knights during a critical moment in the battle and let Ulrich von Jungingen proceed with his faulty plan and blunder, leading to his death and subsequent slaughter of his knights. She would not interfere with the battle, except to prevent a certain few from dying alongside their *Hochmeister*. She needed to find her father and Siegfried von Heidelberg. And Wolfgang who had disappeared down the dungeon hole—at least in one reality.

She noticed Mortemeur's gun holster strapped to his thigh. It still carried his knight's revolver—no one had taken it during the ensuing maelstrom. She bent down and wrenched both holster and gun free from the dead man. Then, pulling out the other gun from her waistband, she stared at both weapons. They were the same gun: Mortameur's revolver. How could the same item exist in two places at the same time? Then manifest like split personalities of the same individual in the same place? She shook her head with an ironic smile, tucked the schitzophrenic gun and holster into her backpack and returned François's gun to the small of her back then rose to her feet.

She was about to turn then flinched at the sudden reverberating words to her left:

"Come back to the scene of the crime to gloat over your handy work, eh?..."

She turned.

The baron sat in a heap where everyone had left him in the chaos of chasing after Vivianne. He looked pathetic, sitting in a puddle of his own vomit, twitching face scowling at her with mad bloodshot eyes. He seemed to have sobered up at least, Vivianne thought. Perhaps he would see some reason, she considered. "I came to...well...to give myself in, Father," she said demurely. "If you please, you could take me to the dungeon to await punishment at your command, once your other responsibilities are fulfilled."

He took the bait. "Yes! You've come to your senses! Let us go then, daughter!" He tried to get up, shaky limbs sliding on blood and vomit. Vivianne rushed forward to help him up. He tried to shrug her off then reluctantly gave in to the logic of letting her assist him. They made their way slowly down the hall and struggled down the stairs. He was under the impression that he was taking her there; it was she, however, leading him, and bearing a considerable amount of his weight as she did. Vivianne was reminded of her struggle to bring Francois back to the Marais after he was wounded. The baron was a lot heavier than Francois was and several times his body shook so violently that Vivianne nearly dropped him. By the time they reached the dungeon, Vivianne was sweating and taking in labored breaths. The door to the smaller left cell was partially open. Vivianne kicked it open then practically dragged the shaky baron inside. When she let go of him, he collapsed onto the stone floor, trembling and moaning. He hardly noticed as Vivianne left him there then shut the thick door behind her with a clank and closed the padlock.

She turned to the door to the larger cell, where Wolfgang was being kept, and had disappeared—in her other reality, that is. Perhaps he was still inside in this reality, she thought. In any case, she needed to find out. After investigating the lock again, she turned briskly to find something to smash it, and collided into Berthold Kramer, the *seneschal.*

He seized her by her two arms in a victorious cry: "Op!" He glared down at her with menacing eyes of challenge. "Where are you going so fast, My Lady?"

"Berthold—*Herr Seneschel*—just the man I was looking for." She wasn't actually looking for him, but she decided that he could be helpful. "I desperately need your help—"

"Help!" he scoffed, closing an iron grip on her arms as she tried to squirm free. He gave her a hard shake. She bobbed like a rag doll under his considerable strength. "Why should a witch need my help?"

She bit back a smile of irony; she had two weapons, both out of reach and not visible. Was that why he was acting more aggressively with her? Staring him directly in the eyes, she said, "I know you love your master, the baron, and do not wish for any harm to come to him. I've locked him in this dungeon cell." She pointed to the smaller cell door.

"What?!" His grip tightened hurtfully and he glowered at her.

"Hear me out, *Herr* Kramer!" she said in a voice edged with command. "If he goes into battle, he will surely die— needlessly! Don't ask me, but I know this to be true. There are those who would say that I am bewitching you with lies. But I know you to be a man of reason. You know my character, *Herr* Kramer, and you know that I truly love my father. I beseech you, therefore, to help me. The baron is ill; he truly doesn't know what he's doing. You've witnessed his irrational behaviour. You know this in your heart. He suffers an ailment, like the chaplain, that he got from the bad brown bread. He should be infirmed and isolated until he is better. And I assure you that he *will* get better. But right now he is not fit for battle. He'll be safe from his own folly right where he is."

Berthold frowned in thought. That was always a good sign. Berthold was a thoughtful man, given to long consideration. He did not jump to conclusions nor was he given to impetuous decision. And, unlike his stern wife who had long ago discounted Vivianne as a personal failure, Vivianne judged Berthold as not having formulated quite such a deprecating idea of her yet. Already, his grip had loosened considerably; another good sign. Vivianne sighed inwardly and felt the circulation return to her arms.

He stared into her eyes in sincere inquiry. She met his burning gaze unflinchingly. Then he gave out a long breath and deflated himself, like he'd made a reluctant decision. "I do not know for certain why, but I believe you, Your Ladyship," he said finally. "I will help you. *Gott helfe mir*, for the baron will surely punish me for this insubordination, but I will help you confine him until the battle is ended tomorrow and he is better."

She seized his two hands in hers. "Thank you! Please see that no one removes him from the dungeon cell; can you please open this cell for me?"

"Very well," Berthold said gruffly and pulled out his keys to open the padlock. Vivianne uttered a silent prayer of thanks for his incredible intuitive logic, considering the highly unnatural events that had just occurred. "I do not pretend to understand what is transpiring here, My Lady. But I assure you that if any ill befalls my master on account of your actions, I will have to take my own action," he warned.

"I fully understand, *Herr* Kramer, and were such a thing to occur I would volunteer myself gladly to your ministering. Now, I must go!"

Berthold nodded and hastily left.

Vivianne was about to open the cell door when she heard the hasty rustling of feet and pulled out her revolver. Uta rushed around the corner and started. Both cried out in mutual surprise.

"My Lady!" "Uta!" they gasped out in surprised relief.

"Oh, child, I feared the worst when they didn't find you—that you'd left the castle for the forest and drowned in the swamp." She almost had, Vivianne reflected. "Now, here you are...giving speeches to the entire household and commanding us to arms with such..." She struggled with the right word. "...influence..." Uta looked her up and down in fascination. "You're so different, child...a...woman, I'd say..."

Vivianne took Uta's hands in hers. "I'm so glad to see you well too, Uta. But I must see if Wolfgang is here. I have reason to believe that he has disappeared!"

Uta glanced down at her basket of herbs and wet

poultices. "I was just coming here, myself, to try and sneak in and give him this."

"Let me," Vivianne said, gently taking the basket from Uta's trembling hands. Was the old woman afraid of her now? Now that she was a self-proclaimed witch? "Thank you, Uta!" she said as her old nursemaid bid her adieu and turned back to the cell door.

In the meantime, the baron had awoken from his stupor and mistook her for a guard. "You! Guard! Let me out of here! I'm the baron! You idiot!"

Ignoring his angry outbursts, Vivianne entered the dungeon cell. She hastened straight for the trap door and opened it; there, slumped against the wall, looking up at her with big round eyes, sat Wolfgang, as though he'd never disappeared. Vivianne realized that he'd somehow entered her twin brother's world—the world of the secret passage from her world—when she'd first dumped him down the trap door in her world. Now, both of them were in her twin's world, so here Wolfgang was. He looked a lot better than when she'd first seen him on the rack, Vivianne thought. Her mother's medicine had undoubtedly worked.

"Can you stand up?" she asked.

"I don't know," he said weakly and tried to get up then fell back with a grunt.

"Never mind," she said. "I'll come down and help you." She scrambled down the ladder, wrapped her arm around his waist, and they struggled up the ladder. Vivianne directed Wolfgang to the rack. When he saw where she was leading him, he recoiled and began to tremble.

"No one's going to put you back on the rack, Wolfgang," she reassured him. "It's just a place to lay you down and tend your wounds." He looked plaintively at her, wide eyes betraying fear. "The baron is in the cell beside you. I've taken charge," she added.

That wasn't very reassuring, she realized. Last he'd seen her she was a spoiled child who'd incriminated him in a selfish wish to escape her fate. That self seemed so long ago, she thought; only six hundred years and back, she mused. He stared in horrified disbelief. "You?....*You've* taken charge?" he stammered.

"The baron's ill and Mortameur is dead," she explained. "*Herr* Kramer has assured me that the baron will remain in his cell until he gets better." That seemed to mollify Wolfgang and he let her help him recline on the rack. As he stretched out on the long board he groaned loudly.

"You need to take off your clothes," Vivianne said tersely.

"What?" He shrank from her in embarrassment and glanced past himself to his hose. "Why?"

"Don't be a fool," she chided. Without giving him a chance, she abruptly snatched his hose and yanked it off, revealing his nude lower torso. Wolfgang blushed and his hands twitched to cover his crotch. "I need to apply my medicine to your joints..." she added, not in the least perturbed by the sight of his naked body. "*All* your joints."

Uta had prepared a hot poultice of rue and lovage, preserved with honey and mineral powder, and Vivianne now applied it gently to Wolfgang's main joints; his knees, elbows, shoulders, hips and finally his groin. After initially cringing, he began to relax and leaned his head back, closing his eyes. It was obvious that the hot poultice was easing his pain. "Vianne..." he murmured with a smile.

"Keep it on well after it cools," she said and made to turn.

He raised his head and stared after her. "Where are you going?" His voice was a weak whine of panic. She knew he wanted her to stay.

"I need to get some help," she explained. "You should be in a real bed. I'll get someone to take you to my quarters for now where you can rest on a proper bed."

He looked disappointed but nodded. "Will I see you?"

"I have some matters to consult with Uta and the seneschal," she stammered her excuse. "I'll come...later...once you've settled in my bed and see how you're doing."

His eyes lit up and he smiled gratefully. "I'd like that."

She gave him a small smile, hoping he wasn't taking it the wrong way, and turned again to go. She recalled only too vividly the awful events written up in *Roget's l'Histoire*: abuses of courtly love and a servant in her bed.

"Vianne!" he called after her. Vivianne glanced back over her shoulder. "Thank you," he said. "I'm eternally grateful for your help. You saved my life."

They weren't out of the forest yet; she still needed to immobilize a few dangerous elements. Vivianne nodded to Wolfgang with a half smile and was about to turn again then decided to wait a moment; it looked like he was mustering something yet more to say to her.

He began, "You look so different..."

She glanced down at the strange clothes she wore.

He responded to her look, "Not just your clothes...*you* look different somehow...so grown up." Vivianne lowered her gaze for a moment. François had done that, taught her about life. And love. Wolfgang blushed and she knew he was finally saying what he'd led up to: "Did you mean what you said in the Great Hall? About us?"

Vivianne swallowed involuntarily. That was so long ago. Yet for Wolfgang, only a few hours had passed since that calamity. She felt her nose flare with the effort of giving him the truth gently. "I...I was being selfish," she struggled. "I thought I meant it then, but—"

"It's all right, Vianne," he cut her off. "I might like it after all if you *did* mean it."

She saw in his eyes what she dreaded. Oh, *Lieber Gott*, what have I done, leading him on! she scolded herself. Her hand strayed, looking for her cross, and found the locket that hung about her neck instead. At most, it had been a girlish fanciful love, an infatuation of the Wolfgang of her imaginings—her *ritter*—not the real boy. She'd even recognized it then. Perhaps if time had permitted...and she'd never gone into the future—her hand stroked the smooth engraved locket—things between them might have kindled into something she could remotely call love.

"I'm sorry, Wolfgang...I can't." She hurried out of the dungeon.

"Can't what?" The plaintive echo of his voice chased her down the hall as she fled.

✠

"Under no circumstance are you to let Wolfgang out of my room or the baron out of the dungeon cell. No matter what they say or do, *Frau* Kramer. Do you understand?" Vivianne instructed Frieda.

"Yes, my Lady," Frieda said. Vivianne turned away to hide the ironic smile that twisted her face. Frieda had sounded like she actually meant it. Before Vivianne had visited François's world, no one, least of all Frieda, had regarded her as a "lady". Now, at a time when she considered herself least "lady-like", everyone treated her like one. It was truly ironic, Vivianne thought as she undressed and got into her mother's old bed in the solar. Tomorrow would be a historic day....

✠

## ...33

IT was half past seven.

Vivianne had watched for the better part of the day as the violent battle raged for twelve hours in the fields of Grunwald. Between six and half past seven, the *Hochmeister* finally succumbed to the hordes of Lithuanian, Polish, Bohemian, Tartar, Moravian, and Moldavian who had closed in upon the Teutons. They'd circled the knights and slaughtered them with lances, daggers, pikes, scythes, and poignards. The hoofbeat of horses and strangling force of maddened hands, all combined to crush the powerful Teutonic Knights who only the day before had so arrogantly boasted of their impregnable force.

Vivianne watched as the Poles and Lithuanians burned everything that belonged to the Teutons, poured the Teuton's wine on the ground and handcuffed the prisoners with their own handcuffs. Thousands of bodies lay on the ground.

Vivianne stood on the castle battlement of the outer bailey and watched the horde of Saracens and Tarters swarm across the killing field of scattered corpses toward Grunwald Castle. The Poles and Lithuanians had left the spoils of the castle to their barbarian allies, she concluded.

While they brought no siege engines or ox-bow machines, the Saracens had time and brutality on their side. She made out archers with incendiary arrows and many foot soldiers dressed in peasant clothes, brandishing spears and axes.

She had hastily knighted most of the young squires and servants and even a few courageous girls, who made themselves helpful by doing runs for food, water and other equipment. Vivianne glanced over at Tancred, brandishing his bow with a pride she had never before seen in him. He did not look terrified; only single-minded determination animated his sallow face.

The horde reached the castle within moments and tried to storm in at the entrance, casting spears and torched arrows over the outer castle battlements. Fortunately, the castle was well guarded by a deep and wide moat, draw bridge and portcullis. Vivianne considered that they might try to burn the entrance and pick off the the inexperienced warriors on the ramparts. She kept several men by the entrance, ready to dowse any fires the Saracens started if they managed to get the draw bridge down. She'd also stationed two boys at murder holes over the gateway. They were equipped with 'missiles' of heavy stones and pitch for anyone trying to storm the entrance.

Several of the boys with little training, took careless risks by leaning over the crenels of the castle curtain walls instead of the loopholes of the merlons to aim their spears and arrow shots. They were easy targets for the more experienced Saracens who picked them off one by one.

The Saracen Tartar horde finally settled in front of the

castle, thinking perhaps to starve them out, thought Vivianne. And kill them off one by one. She thought she made out grapplers and rope and feared they might attempt to swim the moat and climb the castle walls at night. She needed to put this siege to a halt before nightfall.

✠

As Vivianne hastened down the crenellation toward the bastion, she ran across a moaning heap on the ground, a young man who'd received a spear in his arm.

It was young Sigmund Haupt. The boy was bleeding to death! She pressed firmly down on the deep wound, feeling warm blood seep through her fingers and panic pump through her. Someone rushed to her side. It was Doctor Grien. He kneeled down with a cursory glance at her and quickly attended, using his one good hand with a deftness that impressed her.

This was the same little boy the physician had beaten earlier for straying into the castle grounds to beg for food. "Since when are you in the habit of helping—and not beating—lowly peasants?" she said sharply.

"Since a witch defends the castle of my domicile!" he shot back. "Help me get this around his arm," he commanded, having ripped off the boy's shirt. She helped him tie the tourniquet and noticed that they'd succeeded in staunching the flow. Grien turned to her with a look of reluctant admiration. "You have a steady hand, My Lady, and aren't bothered by the sight of blood. You'd make a good nurse; you attend without concern for yourself—or your finery," he added with a sharp glance at her blood-soaked dress.

After commanding two other servants to take young Sigmund to the infirmary, Grien stood up with her and aimed steely eyes into hers.

"Why did you spare me?" he demanded in a halting voice. "Back there, in the courtyard, when you…when you shot my hand? I thought you were going to…"

Vivianne studied his long drawn-out face with disdain.

"You do well to ask. It is not for love of you, I can assure you, Doctor."

"Why, then?" he said, glaring at her with equal disdain. He hardly looked repentant for the sin she'd called him on: the sin of killing her mother for ambition. But his face betrayed an agitated guilt that she knew would eventually worry through his heart like gout through flesh.

"Perhaps because you are a medical doctor," she responded solemnly. "And I expect you will eventually become a very good one. Armed with my mother's alchemical knowledge, you have it in your power to do wonderful things for humanity—for *all* of humanity," she added, glancing at the peasant boy. "To revolutionize how we treat sickness and truly help others in need. That is all I care about now, Doctor Grien: for the possibility of your repentant good works in medicine. For that I spared you."

"But I killed your mother!" he spat out in angry challenge. "I vilified you; shouted for your death by fire."

She met his wild gaze with a calm stare. "I prefer to wager that you have enough strength of character to redeem yourself than languish in ineffectual guilt for the atrocities you've admitted to." She glanced down at his mangled hand. "Perhaps over the years, whenever you look at that hand you will remember this moment," she said with a pointed look at the moaning boy being carried away, "the moment when you became a good man and decided to make your world a better world." Then she curtsied in demure politeness. "Now, if you'll excuse me, I have a castle to defend, Doctor. Please continue your good work. You are much appreciated!"

It was clear to her that he hadn't expected such an answer. He stared, wide eyed with incredulous wonder, as she bid him farewell, took her long and bloodied skirt in her hands, and left him standing there.

She heard him mumble his acknowledgement, "Yes, My Lady," and saw him bow respectfully to her through the corner of her eyes.

✠

Close to sunset one particularly large Saracen came forward and called gruffly, "Give us the Baron von Grunwald and we'll let you alone! We only want that bastard Knight!"

Vivianne leaned over the parapet and called down, "I am his daughter the Baroness von Grunwald and I am in charge here. Know this; we will not release the baron to you! You have done what you came to Grunwald to do; you have defeated the Teutonic Order, you've rendered them extinct. The few left do not concern you any longer. Go home now!"

"*You* are in charge of defending this castle?" the brute said then let out a belly laugh. "A child defends this castle!"

The horde jeered. Vivianne saw Tancred's look of defensive anger. He cued up an arrow in his bow and aimed at the speaker. Vivianne waved him down. With a conspiratorial grin and wink at him, she pulled out her gun and held it at her side. He grinned back.

"Yes, I am the witch of Grunwald Castle and I have lost patience with you. If you don't clear off now, you will receive the wrath from my magic tube."

The barbarians laughed again.

Vivianne pulled out her weapon, aimed carefully and shot the brute in the leg. The shot thundered in her ear and sent her recoiling back. The Saracen screamed and fell, writhing on the ground. The others ran to his side and scrambled away with him, glancing fearfully back.

"Leave now and you will be spared," Vivianne called down as they tended to the howling Saracen. "I have no quarrel with you. But if you persist, I will take action. I repeat, you have done your duty with the Order. Now go and gloat in your victory. You have enough spoils from your fight. You have the finest armor and weapons enough from the dead Knights of the Order. Leave this castle and go home victorious and alive; or stay here and die. Choose carefully." She then stepped back out of sight and waited for something to happen.

Nothing did.

Eventually, Tancred hastened to her side. "M-m-milady!" he said excitedly. "They are retreating!"

She peered around one of the merlons and saw the horde retreat up the slope looting the scattered corpses as they made their way toward the main road.

Vivianne sighed. Her bluff had worked. Now it was time to release her father and Siegfried, the Templar Knight, from their jail cells. The day of battling wasn't over yet, she thought with a sigh. She'd managed to save the lives of key players in the 'history' of her world, but felt heartache for those she had not prevented from dying; over two hundred Teutonic Knights lay on the fields of Grunwald because of her.

✠

## ...34

"GET out of my way! Out of my way!" the baron stormed toward Vivianne in the main corridor leading to the Great Hall; he obviously did not mean to stop. His eyes glanced over her in anger. He had reason to be furious with her; not only had she locked him up in the dungeon, but no doubt he blamed her for the destruction of the entire Teutonic Order and the death of its *Hochmeister.*He must have felt shame in not having taken part in the battle, never mind that it would have ensured his death.

"I know you're not my real father," she said quietly with sudden calm, "but you brought me up like your own daughter. I'll always think of you as my father—"

"*Don't*! You're no daughter of mine!" he belched out and she winced at his cruel words. "Not after what you did. I'm ruined. I might as well be dead. I'm worse than dead. I disown you. I have no daughter!" With that final spitting fulmination he wheeled around, coat flying behind him, and stomped away. He shouted to the walls, not bothering to turn his head, "And get yourself out of here before I throw you out!"

Vivianne swallowed down her wounded pride and slowly wiped the baron's spittle off her cheek. Then, in a sudden welling of compassion, she cried, "Father!"

To her surprise he stopped then turned only his head to glare at her over his shoulder.

He let her approach him and she touched his shoulder. He winced then trembled at her touch but didn't recoil from her.

"I love you," she said. "I'll always love you, Father."

His eyes briefly spoke of a painful tenderness then they flamed with desire and he shuddered. "Go! Before I—"

*Violate me*, she finished his choking words in her mind.

He gruffly knocked her hand off his shoulder, flung his arms up in disgust and blustered off angrily. *He'll forgive me...eventually*, she decided with a long intake of air and straightened herself. *My father will forgive me...my father...*Her gaze dropped to the stone floor of the dark hall and Vivianne throught briefly of her real father, whom she'd barely met before he was shot dead by her mother's lover and twin brother...Like the twin brother Vivianne had never known...would they too have become lovers? Her real father had thought so. Vivianne looked up to gaze down the empty hall where the baron had disappeared. It would be years...perhaps decades...before he forgave her...if he ever did. *I'll just have to hope and wait*, she decided. Besides Uta, who was like an aunt to her, the baron was the closest thing she had to a relative. In the meantime, she needed to leave; she didn't for a moment doubt the genuineness of the baron's threat.

✠

Within a few short hours the entire household was alerted to Vivianne's imminent banishment. The baron ordered Frieda to provide Vivianne with anything she needed for a long journey, though where she would go, he wanted no part of deciding or knowing. He instructed *Père* Daniel to find a boy they could spare to accompany her wherever she journeyed and Theobald provided young Georg Sachsenhausen, one of his scullions. When *Père* Daniel informed her of her small entourage, she protested.

"It's hard enough that I must take care of myself on the road; now I must take care of this young boy too!"

He laughed. "He is supposed to help take care of you, mon enfant!"

Vivianne asked Tancred to help her prepare Willy for the journey.

When they were done, she seized his hand before he had a chance to bolt and, feeling his sweaty hand trembling inside her firm clasp, she pulled him close and gave him a light kiss on the cheek. He reddened then burst into a beaming smile, shaking with pleasure.

"Tancred," she said softly, still holding his hand, and forcing him to look up at her, "I must say this, that I don't love you." He stared at her with large calf-eyes that were neither sad nor disappointed, but caught up with every word she uttered. "But some girl will," she added emphatically. "She'll see how brave and honorable and selfless you are. And she'll be so fortunate to have you for her tender lover and the father of her children."

He blushed fiercely and trembled anew.

"Keep your head high, Tancred. You're worth a dozen Doctor Griens."

He grinned at that and she smiled back.

"W-w-where will you g-g-go?" Tancred asked the question on everyone else's mind.

Vivianne gave him a sighing smile. "Tancred, my father has given me a wonderful gift: to embark on a great adventure. I look forward to exploring our blessed land."

⊕

"Ah, petite!" *Père* Daniel approached from the

courtyard.

Vivianne thanked Tancred again and let *Père* take her hand in his. "Where will you go?"

She laughed lightly and sighed. "Truly, I don't know, *Père*. But don't worry on my account." She looked up at his homely face and into his tender blue-grey eyes with a sloping smile of assurance. "I can take care of myself."

"Ahh…" he nodded, eyes twinkling like sapphires. "It's not you I'd worry about!" Then he squeezed her hand. "*Petite*, I have an opportunity for you to consider. If nothing else, it would provide you with a wonderful destination in your travels. Marriage with a good man—" She was about to retort when he raised his hand and rested a finger on her lips. "Hear me out first. His name is *Compte* Jean d'Anjou. He has never married and has no heirs. He is old and ailing and despairs of his estate and name. He's eighty-two years old, *ma petite*. There would be no chance for amorous pursuits with him, for better or worse. And no need to consummate the marriage. He is not even looking for companionship, though, I dare say, he would welcome it, especially with you. Whatever else, it makes things simpler for you. You would be assured safe lodgings for the rest of your life. He is a wealthy noble who lives in the south of France. In Provence, not far from Toulon on the sea. They're an old vintner family. D'Anjou is a bit of a loner and an eccentric, though not queer or odious. He's a good man. All he wants is to have someone kind and true to carry on his estate and name. I have vouched for you in this letter." Père passed a folded and sealed parchment to her and without thinking she accepted it. "You would be the *Comtesse* d'Anjou, with lands and wealth for the rest of your living days and the freedom to do as you liked; to travel the world, carry on the work of your mother." He smiled suddenly at her. "*Become that which you seek…Make this world a better world.*" Then he looked deeply into her eyes. "Your mother was a good woman, *mon ange*. She helped people. She tried to make the world a better place; like you will succeed in doing."

Vivianne nodded in silence. She had taken the

parchment reluctantly and by doing so, she realized that she'd implicitly agreed. She looked up from the parchment into *Père* Daniel's kind eyes. "But he doesn't know me!" she objected.

"Ahh...but *I* know you and the count trusts my judgment totally. D'Anjou is a gentle and impeccable man, *ma petite*. I would not send you to him otherwise. I assure you that you will be content there, if not happy. And so will he be for his remaining years."

Vivianne studied the stone floor at her feet. What other choice did she have? When she met his eyes, she said quietly, "I will go."

The priest gave her a warm smile and rested his hands on her shoulders. "You have chosen wisely. I will worry no more, then."

"I'll miss you, *Père*!" She seized him in an embrace.

He hugged her back. "As I will you. You better go now. I will send a fast messenger to the *Compte* with word to expect you. Follow the main roads; they go mainly along the main rivers; the Vistula, the Rhine, Moselle, and Rhone. Mostly old Roman roads — they're good roads. Travel only by day and speak to no one. A woman traveling alone with just a young page is always a curiosity. There are far too many armed brigands and robber knights, looking for easy prey. But I know you can look after yourself well enough." He flashed a smile. He was probably thinking of her strange weapon from the future and how she hadn't hesitated to use it. "You will get there safely. I know you will."

✠

As Vivianne heaved the last of her travel packs on Willy and secured it, she heard a loud rustle and shuffling gait and looked up.

"My Lady!" It was Wolfgang. "A word, if you please."

Vivianne forced a smile as he approached her, walking in a limp. She curtsied and bowed her head slightly as he drew near. He responded instinctively to her formality with a bow in response. He was still panting from his obvious run.

"You should be resting," she said softly just as he opened his mouth to speak.

"I heard a rumor that you are leaving us," he said, refusing to be unbalanced by her interruption. "Surely it is just that…a rumor."

"It is no rumor, *Herr* von Eisenreich. I leave within the hour at my father's bidding."

"Why so formal, Vianne? Where would you go? You know nothing of the world; you have nowhere to go. You've never been out of your father's castle, except to the local villages." Just to Paris, France, six hundred years in the future, she added to herself. Wolfgang had obviously not heard the whole of it; that she was traveling to France to marry *le Compte* d'Anjou. Before she had a chance to retract her hand, he rushed forward and clasped it fast in his. "Stay with *me*…as my wife!" He stunned her by dropping to one knee and kept her hand gripped tightly in his. "Oh, Vianne! I don't care what they all say. I never did. They called your mother a witch; I still played with you. Now they call *you* a witch. I don't care. Perhaps you've bewitched me. I care for you and I would be honoured to have you as my bride. We could learn to love one another, surely! Marry me and stay here as my wife!"

She felt his heart pumping through his damp grip. He was trying so hard, she considered, recognizing how difficult it was for him to break out of the mould of convention. She acknowledged his courage and fear in this reckless move to save her. One, she reflected he might eventually regret. He would stifle her and she would drive him into bitterness. Besides, her path lay in a different direction from his.

Her hand slithered out of his. "I'm so sorry, Wolfgang. Everything's changed for us. Perhaps in another world, another time we might have … But, I have a journey that I must travel on my own. Where I go no one can follow…" No mortal, that is, she added silently to herself. "You will find another, someone more suited to you, a woman you will love deeply and have wonderful children with. Children who will change the world in marvelous ways," she ended with a sad smile. "Good bye, Wolfgang. God be with you."

He stood up and watched her mount her horse astride without aid. Vivianne reached down to take his hand. "Truly, Wolfgang, you will sire children who will make this world better. A world of peace and prosperity. I wish you and your coming family well."

"And you, Vivianne," he said and let her go, staring at her with amazement.

With a nod to Georg on his horse, Vivianne coaxed Willy out of the stable only to halt at the sight of Uta standing at the entrance. She held a cage that contained Vivianne's not too happy, snarling cat inside. Several people had gathered behind Uta with horses and packs. Vivianne blinked, bridling in suspicion. Uta did not look angry or desperate, nor did the others. Nevertheless, Vivianne found her hand straying to the sword sheathed at her side; both her guns were stashed in her backpack.

"The roads to France are no place for a lady traveling alone—even one who wields a sword like you, my lady," Uta said to Vivianne. So, the news *had* traveled to some. "I—we all...." She threw a glance back to the small party assembled behind her. "We wish to accompany you in service to your new destination. Once there, we wish to continue our service as your loyal servants, if it so please Your Ladyship." She bowed and the others followed. "We are yours to command."

Stunned, Vivianne scanned the party. She saw Tancred. Yes, he might as well come along. Flowers grew well where she was going. Then she saw Doctor Grien, bowed low behind Uta.

"You, too!" the words slipped out before she was able to stop herself.

Still bowing, he glanced up sharply to meet her eyes with a glower. "I recognize my destiny when I see it and—for good or for ill—it is bound up with yours, My Lady. I would be honored to accompany you and continue to serve you and your lord, the count, in my capacity as physician."

"Indeed!" she said with a bemused nod. In truth, he

would be most useful to her and her ailing husband-to-be, Vivianne decided. She scanned the rest of the party and recognized the two guards who had, in another world, eagerly stripped her, beat her and lashed her to the burning ladder to be burned alive. Vivianne felt an inward shudder at that too vivid memory and swallowed down her conflicting emotions. Perhaps this was serendipitous, she finally decided. She was on a path to seek redemption; why not this rag tag group as well for acts they'd committed in this or some other unrealized world? In truth, she'd welcome their company on the long road, particularly that of Uta, her old nursemaid and old companion since she was a child. And she would not come totally empty-handed to her new benefactor. She had these fine servants to offer as resources to his estate, the doctor particularly. Vivianne smiled with sudden warmth. "It would please me greatly if you would accompany me. I, too, would be honored by your company and very capable service. But what of your responsibilities here, to my father and his castle?"

The doctor surprised her with his ready answer, "The baron has given us his blessing, My Lady. *Père* Daniel already approached him in this matter and His Lordship has conceded that you require a proper entourage as well as our continued service to you at your new home."

Vivianne felt her throat close. Perhaps the baron forgave her already. She felt a small smile tug her lips. "Well, then let us depart," she said, feeling far more cheerful than she had only moments ago.

Warren scrambled to the rope and swiftly opened the portcullis, drawing an amused smile from Vivianne. She nodded to Berthold and Frieda, standing on the battlements above the gate. On the farthest of the battlements, she glimpsed a distant figure silhouetted against the sun. Her father. *Good-bye, father…*

✠

# ...35
*Wasserschloss Mespelbrunn, Northern Bavaria, 1447*

VIVIANNE nervously paced the parkay floor of the outer drawing room to her father's bedroom. On one of her turns she caught the eye of Konrad Frankl, the baron's austere Jewish lawyer. He watched her with steely unemotional eyes of haughty reserve. He stood, leaning by the outer door with his arms crossed. A very tall and lanky man of about Doctor Grien's age, Frankl resembled a wolf; outwardly calm yet ready to spring at his prey at a moment's notice. After a cursory glance at him, Vivianne continued to pace and eyed the heavy wooden door through which Doctor Baldung Grien had disappeared twenty minutes ago.

When Vivianne had received the baron's overly brief message to come—the first communication she'd received from him since their disastrous parting of thirty-seven years ago—she'd asked the sixty-eight year old doctor to accompany her, guessing that her father was terribly ill. When she and Grien had arrived at the castle by the water, the baron's head servant ushered them in, vindicating her intuition with a brief explanation of her dying father's wish to see his only daughter. They agreed to let Doctor Grien see her father but showed no optimism that he would make a difference; the baron's personal physician had already made the pronouncement.

The door snapped open and Vivianne jerked, nerves frayed. Baldung quietly closed the door behind him then met her inquiring eyes with a hard gaze. Then his eyes softened. "I'm sorry, My Lady. There's nothing I can do to help him. He is dying from cancer of the liver. I gave him some morphine to ease the pain, but he will likely not last the night." He glanced at Frankl, who nodded. Her father's physician had already given them the same prognosis. Then Grien turned to Vivianne with a nod. "Your father wishes very much to see you, My Lady."

Vivianne nodded to both men then proceeded to the

door and entered. Her father lay beneath a heap of covers on a large four-poster bed, looking very old and frail. His eyes looked closed and she could hear his labored breaths. She steeled herself to approach his bedside and gently touched his wrinkled hand.

His eyes shot open and she quickly retracted her hand. He stared at her as though she was a vision. "Dianne!" he cried out.

"No, Father. It's me...Vivianne, your daughter." To his dumbfounded stare, she added, "You sent for me. I came right away."

He seemed to come round from his hallucinatory reverie. "Ah! Daughter, I am dying," he wheezed out.

"I know, Father."

He kept staring at her in a kind of fearful fascination. "You are so like her ... so like Dianne ..." He began to weep. "I missed her so much, daughter. Oh, God, how I missed her all these years!" he wailed unabated and put his gnarled hands up to his convulsing face.

Vivianne placed her hands on his. "Dear Father...I know you did."

He looked up at her as if seeing her for the first time. "You *are* a witch! You look no older than a young maid, yet you're in your middle years." Fifty-one years to be exact, thought Vivianne. "You've bewitched the world!"

"That I have," she agreed with a sloping smile, thinking of the deeds she'd already accomplished to change her world.

"Are you well?" he inspected her with shrewd critical eyes. "Do you have a man, daughter? A family?"

She blinked at his blunt question. Unable to answer right away, she gazed down for a moment before replying, "No family, but I married *le Compte* d'Anjou...." She didn't bother to tell him that the *Compte* had long passed away, being her senior by many decades.

"Ahh, you married a Frenchman, after all! Yes, that's where they said you were to be found when I inquired for you. I am glad that you found yourself a husband, daughter. I trust he is a nice man, not like that ogre, Leduc." He seemed genuinely happy on her behalf and Vivianne swallowed convulsively. She had wondered why he'd called for her; perhaps he had forgiven her after all.

The baron's eyes suddenly glazed with delirious desire and he pulled her toward him with surprising strength for a dying man. She let him kiss her on the mouth. Vivianne instinctively firmed her lips tight, but he thrust his tongue between her pressed lips. Initially she recoiled with revulsion and made to pull away, then she forced herself to relax, embraced him and gave him the gift of her humbleness. To him, she was his beloved Dianne. Let it be so. Let him dream one last time of the woman he truly loved with all his heart and soul.

It was the last thing he did. Within several heartbeats he shuddered then exhaled a long sigh, letting her go and slumping back limp. Vivianne drew back and realized that her father had died in her arms, kissing her. She brushed his still-open eyes shut with her fingers then straightened and stared with complex emotions at the man she'd never quite known.

As two attendants rushed past her to the bed, Frankl, standing at the door waiting, cleared his throat. "A word, *Comptesse*," he said in a basso voice that reverberated in her gut. "There is some unfinished business to discuss."

✠

"With the exception of his knight's accoutrements, he's left you everything, my lady," Frankl said as they walked the grounds of the moated 13th Century castle. "This estate and associated territories including the Spessart Forest, and, of course, Grunwald Castle in Prussia…"

Vivianne had heard that shortly after she'd left Grunwald Castle, the baron had also gone to travel the world. He'd left the castle and its land to be tended by his competent seneschal, Bertold and his stern wife, Frieda. The baron never returned and instead settled in the Rhine in Bavaria where he met *Fechtmeister* Sigmund Ringeck and became good friends with Albrecht, Count Palantine of the Rhine and Duke of

Bavaria. Apparently, they'd gotten on famously together and her father had unofficially collaborated with Ringeck on his to-become famous *Fechtbuch*. Vivianne felt her throat swell with thoughts of her father's gruff and silent love. He'd loved her after all.

Vivianne paused beneath the archway that faced the leaf-littered large pond in front of the castle and turned to Frankl. He stood like a statue, neither patient nor impatient. She cocked her head with a thought. "I have a proposal for you Herr Frankl."

He remained exactly as he was before except for a single raised brow.

"I shall, after all, be needing a law practitioner of astute abilities and impeccable integrity...I think you may fit the bill, *Herr* Frankl." It was hard to tell if he was pleased but Vivianne imagined the slightest glimmer in his dark eyes.

✠

## ...36
*Château de Gruyéres, Western Switzerland, 1779*

VIVIANNE sat at her desk by the large window of the *Salle des Chevaliers* and looked up from her writings. The bottle-bottom window overlooked the adjacent hilltop village of Gruyéres and the fertile valley below it. Beyond lay the magnificent Préalpe Massifs of *Moléson, Dent du Broc, du Chamois* and *du Bourgoz*. Last night's snowfall had left a fine white dust like sugar powder on the landscape.

Vivianne gazed behind her to the wall tapestries and paintings that depicted the pastoral history of this castle and region. Gruyéres took its name and its coat of arms from the thirty thousand cranes that flew a migratory path every fall and spring through this area as part of a longer trek between Scandanavia and North Africa. The crane was a symbol of vigilance, long life and eternity—something she could relate to.

She mused on her own history. She'd been amassing wealth and connections among her peers, looking for nexus points, and preparing for changes in the world. She'd become extremely wealthy. Time had a way of doing that; so long as she managed her assets well and invested wisely. And hindsight had its advantages too; she'd studied the magical books her mother had left her, and took lessons from the subtle changes in their narrative from their previous iterations. They became her friends, her conspirators in a new vision for the world.

But she was otherwise alone. She'd outlived her family and friends. She'd outlived them all. Jean went first, only two years after they'd married. In that short time, they'd formed a bond of friendship that left her genuinely mourning his passing and grieving his companionship. As Père had assured her, the count had been a kind and gentle soul. Père hadn't told Vivianne of the count's keen sense of humor and his passion for literature. "Ma petite fille," he used to call her. It fit; she'd felt more like a daughter than a wife.

Shortly after, Uta, who'd been battling consumption with the doctor's help, had finally passed on. Then Vivianne's cat, Fritz, died after having lived a healthy twenty-seven years. He'd been her loyal companion when she'd had none in Grunwald. All the others had followed. Her father died in her arms at eighty-eight. Then the doctor passed on, leaving behind a family of six grown children with their own families. Much to her surprise, Grien had married and Vivianne found that it had mellowed him greatly and added to his joy of life.

Then Tancred and all his family passed on. She saw them all go. Père Daniel, who she'd managed to visit a few times, and Berthold and Frieda Kramer passed on. She'd even received an invitation to Wolfgang's funeral from the eldest of three boys and one girl; but she dared not attend, given that she could not pass for an eighty-four year old woman. Everyone she'd known from Grunwald was dead. Then it was time for her to move on to diffuse suspicion of a lady who never seemed to age beyond twenty-five. So, she found a respectable banker, continued with Frankl's discreet law firm to look after her estates, and moved elsewhere.

She spent many years at Mespelbrunn, her father's old estate in Bavaria. She roamed the pleasant grounds and hiked the surrounding Spessart Forest of the Elsava Valley. The 13th Century castle, with its distinctive watchtower and rust-coloured stucco manor-style buildings and courtyard, suited her quiet lifestyle of reading and writing. She wrote several books in the study, overlooking the quiet pond to the West. And studied history.

It was important to keep moving.

Vivianne had lived in Italy and Vienna and finally came here, to this peaceful castle in the 15th century village of Gruyères that overlooked the verdant Gruyere Valley. Her daily walks took her first through the upper borough, past the St. Germain Gate into the lower borough of the village, where she often enjoyed a good meal of roesti and raclette with the villagers.

And every night, without fail, she dreamt of her *ritter* in that heavenly cathedral. Whether it was she, herself, or whether it was François, she never knew; they seemed to be one and the same, merged into one personality, one entity, one energy. It didn't matter. Without fail, each morning she woke sighing for him then began her day with thoughts of gratitude and doing good deeds to make his loss worthwhile.

✠

## ...37
*Unter den Linden, Berlin, 1861*

THE oak door snapped open to the loud piercing cry of Princess

Victoria. The lanky Crown Prince Friedrich Wilhelm burst through the doorway, eyes wildly searching the anti-chamber. Servants, including Vivianne, who'd milled about the door since shortly after midnight, surged to their feet. Vivianne caught a glimpse through the open doorway of the Crown Princess, supported by *Fräulein* Stahl and Countess Blücher as she hunched over a table under a massive labor pain. Also in the room, attending her, were Doctor Wegner, another doctor, and the Countess Perponcher. Once her attack had subsided, the eighteen-year old Crown Princess excused her weakness and outburst in a shaky moan. In the short time Vivianne had been here, she had come to like the young English Princess, whose generous nature, clever wit and gifted artistic skills were truly warming.

"Someone, there! Lackey!" the Crown Prince glared out from the doorway. Vivianne pushed in front of Alfred and the pale Prince spotted her; she'd made herself visible for just this moment. "You, *fräulein*! Come and fetch this!" He shakily stuffed a letter of blue stationary into an address-marked envelope as if intended for posting.

Vivianne rushed forward and took the letter from the prince's sweaty hand. "Deliver this to Doctor Eduard Albert Martin at his residence on Dorotheenstrasse! Go!" he said in an agitated voice, then disappeared inside the room and slammed the door shut, muffling the Crown Princess's renewed wails.

Alfred touched Vivianne's shoulder. "I'll do it," he said authoritatively. Alfred was the footman who'd bungled the delivery in another world, Vivianne reflected. In another reality Alfred would have mailed the note to Doctor Martin instead of hand delivering it with the disastrous result of it not reaching him until late the next morning. Too late to prevent a mis-managed birth. In that reality, Doctor Martin would arrive over four hours after the Princess's water had broken, just in time to deliver the baby but too late to turn the breeched Wilhelm to a normal position.

"That's alright," Vivianne said, twitching the letter away from Albert's aggressive reach. Perhaps he fancied himself more important for doing this special task. She stared him down and brushed past him to find her friend, Oskar, one of the coachmen. It was imperative that Doctor Martin, the chief of obstetrics at the University of Berlin, arrive expediently to prevent what would otherwise nearly cost the lives of mother and child and end in a handicap that would later play a decisive role in the narcissist behavior of the future Kaiser. In that alternative reality, Doctor Martin would arrive well after 10 am the next morning to find Doctor Wegner and his German colleagues huddled in defeat in a corner of the room while the distraught Crown Prince Friedrich held his semi-conscious wife in his arms, having put a handkerchief into her mouth to prevent her from biting herself. Through Doctor Martin's grim determination the mother and future emperor of Germany lived; albeit, he would prove deformed and possibly brain-damaged.

Fiercely adamant that this particular scenario would not occur in *her* world, Vivianne threw on her coat and found Oskar waiting for her in stables in the back courtyard. He held out his hand to help her climb up top with him and she showed him the address on the letter. "Hurry!" she shrilled.

Oskar brashly kissed her on the cheek then whipped the horses into a charging gallop into the brisk January wind. Vivianne seized Oskar's waist to keep from flying back as the coach surged forward onto Unter den Linden toward the University, behind which the gynecologist lived. Thankfully, the roads were empty at this hour and he had free reign to go as fast as the streets would let him. They whipped past several Baroque and Neo-Classical buildings: the *Zeughaus, Neue Wache* to the north and the *Staatsoper* and *Bebelplatz* to the south. Oskar laughed with an excited glance at her. "We're saving the world, Vianne!" he yelled, remembering the romantic tale she told him about this night. "Aren't we?"

"Yes!" she said, thinking of the consequences that a normal birth—and arm—would have on Wilhelm II and how he would ultimately run his empire. "Yes, we are!" She gathered her long thick hair into one hand to keep it from flying in the wind and studied Oskar's typical Prussian profile. In contrast to her diminutive French features, the twenty year old had a ruggedly wide face, long nose and thick mouth; features softened by his thick blond hair and large brown eyes. Vivianne considered Oskar to be a bit dim and he reminded her of young Tancred at Grunwald. Like Tancred, he was an honorable young man who showed immense loyalty. Unlike Tancred, he was far from shy and had openly courted Vivianne since she'd established herself as a chambermaid in the Crown Prince's household at the *Kronprinzenpalais* on Unter den Linden a year ago. She'd coyly encouraged Oskar to ensure his total allegiance for this day.

They reached the doctor's residence within minutes and woke him. When he came down, still in his night dress, Vivianne gave him the note and urged him to come at once, providing him with more information than was in the note. He stared at her for a moment then hastily left them there to dress. Vivianne allowed herself to hope. They would get the good doctor there in time to possibly avert a disaster. As she and Oskar waited, a light snow began to fall then swiftly became a heavy snow that blanketed the streets and houses. Doctor Martin returned with his medical bag. He let himself into the coach as Vivianne and Oskar climbed up top. Oskar set the horses immediately into a full tilt gallop that sent the carriage sliding in the wet snow and Vivianne grasping him to keep herself from sliding off the bench. Vivianne felt the wet onslaught on her face and shivered in the bitter cold wind as Oskar sent the carriage hurtling in the direction of *Bebelplatz*, the site of the *Alte Bibliothek*, where Albert Einstein would later teach, and, in another world, where Nazi propaganda minister Joseph Goebbels organized the burning of over 20,000 books by Jews, Communists and Pacifists.

Sensing her trepidation, Oskar laughed in exhilaration then carelessly clasped his arms around her, letting the reins relax. He recklessly planted his lips on hers, even as she struggled, and squeezed her in a firm embrace. The carriage careered around a corner onto Unter den Linden and skidded toward the boulevard of bare Linden trees. Suddenly spooked by the trees, the horses reared and balked. The carriage slid uncontrollably in the snow. Oskar reacted too late. The carriage swung headlong into the stone wall of the Universität. Vivianne had an instant to contemplate the irony of her misplaced seduction before they smashed into the wall on Oskar's side—

Vivianne found herself on the snow-covered ground, looking up in a daze of pain at the carriage wreck, now on its side. She must have been thrown off with the impact. Luckily for her, she'd somehow landed clear of the rebounded carriage. There was no sign of stirring from the doctor inside. Oskar lay in an unnatural position beside her, clearly unconscious. She saw to her horror that the snow settling on his blond hair grew instantly dark. Then she saw the darkness spreading beneath his head. *Oh, dear God!* She tried to move and an intense pain in her leg surged up, grasping her breath in a strangle hold. She felt her vision dim and knew she was passing out. God! To have come so close! Before the darkness took her, Vivianne realized she'd failed to avert the coming Kaiser's defected birth and withered arm. Either the doctor was dead or seriously hurt and he might not even make it to the *kronprinzenpalais* at all; she'd only made matters worse....

✠

# ...38
*Charlottenburg Race Course, Berlin, 1889*

VIVIANNE pulled up the collar and hood of her fur coat to ward off the November chill as she walked next to Jurgen von Eisenreich in Berlin's Charlottenburg Race Course. The coat barely kept the winter wind from cutting through her cream-colored evening gown. Fastened at the back, it had no bustle and signaled the upcoming style. They were here to watch Europe's latest touring attraction from America: Buffalo Bill's *Wild West*

*Show*. Steering her by the elbow, von Eisenreich guided her up the rafter stairs toward the Royal Box, where the new Emperor was already seated with his retinue of several statesmen, including his aides-de-camp, and two imperial guards. Vivianne recognized the odious and obsequious Count Alfred von Waldersee, seated beside the Emperor. Twenty-seven years the Kaiser's senior, the Count was a power-mongering anti-Semite, who would prove to mould the weak-minded Crown Prince into the bigoted warlord Kaiser Wilhelm II was becoming.

Vivianne stole a long glance to the Reich's young ruler. It had been just a year since the Crown Prince had ascended to the imperial thrown and he had already stirred up trouble with his insulting behavior of his mother, the dowager Empress, and his uncompassionate handling of his father's funeral; then his shabby treatment of England's Queen and her son, the Prince of Wales.

Vivianne furtively studied the dashing thirty-year old ruler with deep interest. Dressed impeccably in uniform, he was rakishly handsome, she decided, with sharp intelligent eyes, a long aristocratic nose and well-waxed handle-bar mustache. She found herself staring at his withered left arm, which he rested on his lap. Though she could not make it out, it was a good six inches shorter than the other arm and partially lifeless. He'd been a breech birth and both he and his mother were lucky to be alive.

Vivianne reflected on that eventful day when she'd botched her attempt to save the last Emperor of Germany from an unnatural birth. While Oskar had been instantly killed, the doctor had survived the carriage accident with only a severe concussion; he'd still only managed to get to Unter den Linden by early afternoon, having lain unconscious and unattended for most of the morning then having awoken at Humboldt Hospital where he'd ironically been scheduled to speak that day and had then foolishly insisted on tending to Vivianne first, who'd suffered a nasty head wound that she hadn't even been aware of receiving.

The Emperor—like Vivianne—was here, in the District

of Charlottenburg in West Berlin, to see the show's star attraction, Annie Oakley, who acquired world fame for her skills with a Colt .45. The young sharpshooter had been invited by the Kaiser for a private performance for the Union-Club. Vivianne found her breaths escalate at the thought of what the impetuous Kaiser was about to do; and what she intended to do, as a result. Was it an ironic twist of history that only months ago Adolf Hitler was born this year? Vivianne glanced down at the program in her gloved hand:

*Programme of Miss Annie Oakley's Private Performance Before the Members and Their Friends of the Union-Club, Berlin, on November 13, 1889, at Charlottenburg Race Course.*

There followed a list of up to seventeen feats she would perform, beginning with her exhibition of rifle shooting, followed by clay-pigeon sharp-shooting then various feats involving trapping and agility in weapon handling. She was not fated to get very far in her program before calamity of sorts would strike, Vivianne thought cynically.

"He's alone...without his family?" she asked von Eisenreich. That would make it much easier, she concluded with an inward sigh.

"Dona prefers the comfort and warmth of the royal palace in Potsdam, and the company of her children," he responded. "She's not interested in this sort of thing. She has few interests other than church service, I'm afraid." Then he leaned his head close to hers to confide. "Ten years ago, Wilhelm was smitten by his beautiful cousin, Victoria Elizabeth, the second eldest daughter of the Grand Duke and Duchess of Hesse and the Rhine. But Ella wouldn't have him." Then von Eisenreich surveyed Vivianne with an appraising look and smiled enigmatically. "In fact, she looked a lot like you."

Vivianne swallowed down a sudden discomfort, not sure of its source. Von Eisenreich went on, "Poor Wilhelm became very self-conscious about his arm and thought himself unattractive. That might be why he chose a plain and simple, but pious woman."

More like narrow-minded, anti-Semitic and bigoted

against Jews and Roman Catholics, Vivianne thought. Unfortunately the Empress fit in too well with the Kaiser's own bigoted views and apparently her nature only served to exacerbate the Kaiser's arrogance and insufferable nature.

Von Eisenreich chuckled to himself. "I heard that the Empress Dona was called unimaginative and prejudiced by the Emperor's own mother. Dona hates the English. But don't we all!" He laughed.

Vivianne thought of the cutting words of the gossiping socialite, Daisy, Princess of Pless: *for a woman in that position I have never met anyone so devoid of any individual thought or agility of brain and understanding. She is just like a good, quiet, soft cow that has calves and eats grass slowly then lies down and ruminates.*

"Apart from that homosexual, Count Philipp von Eulenburg, I'm the Emperor's only real friend," von Eisenreich confided rather smugly to Vivianne as they approached the Royal Box.

As if he felt her stealthy glance, the Kaiser turned to look directly at her. After an unabashedly long appraisal, he let his eyes drift away and leaned out, looking past his aide to focus on von Eisenreich. "Ah, Jurgen! So that's why you dallied and missed my retinue!" The Kaiser yelled in a coarse Potsdam accent, eyes flitting back critically to Vivianne like she was merchandize. He stood up and clapped von Eisenreich hard on the back, clearly happy to see him. Vivianne got a clear view of his short left arm with dark brown mole on his shriveled hand. She noted that he was rather short in stature for a man, about her height or less, with a squat and slightly lopsided neck—owing to his left arm being shorter than the other. Eisenreich drew Vivianne forward.

"This is the *Comptesse* d'Anjou," von Eisenreich said.

She pulled down her hood and curtsied slightly, eyes downcast. "I'm honored and humbled, your Imperial Majesty," she said.

"No doubt you are!" he responded, swiftly tucking his left hand in his pocket. When she raised her eyes to meet his, Vivianne caught the brief instant as his eyes grew wide and deep with hidden intensity.

Jurgen caught it too. "I thought so, also," he said with amusement to the Emperor. He was, no doubt referring to her likeness to the Princess Ella.

The Kaiser sucked in a breath and straightened with an imperceptible tremble, as if to shake off an old memory. Then he gave Vivianne a cold smile and extended his good hand to her in greeting. She accepted and instantly winced with excruciating pain. He barked out a cruel laugh and said, "The French are, I'm afraid, just like the English when it comes to my German mailed fist!"

Vivianne had heard of his sadistic handshake: he was in the habit of turning his many rings inward prior to clasping one's hand with a vice-like grip. Somehow, she hadn't expected him to inflict her with it. Perhaps it was his way of punishing his cousin for not accepting his marriage proposal, she concluded, regretful of her resemblance. The Kaiser hung on to her hand much longer than he needed to, Vivianne decided, squirming and attempting to retract it from his painful grasp. His grip was too strong.

Their eyes locked. And to her frustrated anger, her eyes teared up with the stinging pain through her glove.

In that moment she saw the hurt little boy in that bigoted, arrogant and angry face. She instantly knew that she'd misjudged one of his critical nexuses. Her mission this day might have been prevented. If she'd intersected with his life earlier, and somehow convinced his beloved Ella to accept his proposal, the single-minded but compassionate princess might have softened him, completed him, inspired him to be the great man he could have become instead of the bitter and insecure bully he now was.

Something passed between them and he abruptly let go of her hand with a sudden intake of air. "I beg pardon," he said, voice softening from that harsh Potsdam accent. "You reminded me of someone I once knew..." In a flush of solicitous emotion, he pulled off her glove to inspect the damage he'd inflicted on her hand. Several red welts had surfaced on the inside of her lower palm where his rings had gouged into her flesh. "Ahh...such dear soft and warm hands..." he cooed in near reverence. "How remarkable...the soft insides of your hands..."

Vivianne slowly pulled her hand away.

They both looked awkward for a moment. Then the Kaiser broke out into a blustery laugh and turned to von Eisenreich.

"So, where's your good wife, von Eisenreich?"

"Like you, I left her at home with my dear children, where she should be, your Majesty," von Eisenreich responded cheerfully. "They're no fun at these sorts of things."

"Ah, but I wager the *Comptesse* is," said the Emperor brashly and took the opportunity to rake her over with appreciativce eyes.

Von Eisenreich let loose a conspiratorial laugh, as if to ratify the Kaiser's innuendo. He then leaned into Vivianne beside him with a chuckle until his shoulder collided into hers. "I brought my lovely companion, the charming *Comptesse* d'Anjou, to improve my demeanor and make me interesting."

The Kaiser threw his head back and shouted an open-mouthed laugh of abandon then stomped his foot. "Indeed, she has managed that!" He surveyed Vivianne with critical eyes that flashed with approval. When she'd first been introduced to him, she'd felt the Kaiser's burning gaze roam over her like the eager hands of a lover. "Good choice," Wilhelm said.

He'd clearly deduced that she was von Eisenreich's mistress and Jurgen had as much as confirmed it. The Kaiser had several mistresses of his own and Vivianne had the impression he wouldn't have minded another.

As Uta had predicted, Vivianne had indeed filled out into what most men commonly considered a woman of striking beauty. And she'd had many years to cultivate it into an irresistible package. She was now over four hundred years old, yet she looked no more than in her early twenties. That arcane quality alone, she knew, was enough to drive men to distraction.

Vivianne had only met von Eisenreich last week at a masked ball and, knowing his weakness for beautiful women, she'd shamelessly flirted with him; within short order she'd seduced his keen interest in her and ensured for herself an invitation to this event.

The Kaiser let his gaze stray to Vivianne as he spoke to von Eisenreich. Then he finally let his eyes rest openly on her with a cool smile. "You speak German very well for a French woman, *Comptesse*," he said to her. "I detected no accent when we were first introduced."

She smiled demurely and didn't bother to correct him on her German lineage.

Then the show began and their attention was diverted to the ring below. Vivianne's heart raced when Annie Oakley finally emerged. The diminutive woman stood facing the royal box in a smartly collared buckskin dress, bedecked with glittering metals from contests she'd won, cowboy hat, and holding her Colt .45.

Von Eisenreich leaned his head close to hers. "Chief Sitting Bull gave her the nickname of 'Little Sure Shot' because of her dead shot with a pistol, rifle and shotgun. Did you know that she began handling firearms at the tender age of nine to supply her widowed mother with game and eventually paid off the mortgage on her mother's house."

Vivianne let her brows rise in impressed surprise. In truth she knew. She knew everything about the American sharp-shooter. At 90 feet Annie could shoot a dime tossed in the air. With the thin edge of a playing card facing her at 90 feet, she could hit the card and puncture it with five or six more shots as it settled to the ground.

Vivianne felt her mouth go dry; she knew what came next.

With a flourishing turn, Annie faced the royal box and announced, "For my final act, I will attempt to shoot the ashes from the cigar of a lady or gentleman in the audience. "Who will volunteer to hold the cigar?" she asked the audience. Vivianne's heart pounded. She knew that the little sharpshooter from Cincinnati expected no one to volunteer; Annie had simply asked for laughs. Her attentive manager-husband, Frank Butler, always stepped forward and offered himself. Not this time —

Just as laughter bubbled up in the crowd, Kaiser Wilhelm leapt out of the royal box and strutted into the arena to a stunned audience. Laughter turned to gasps as the Kaiser approached the sharpshooter. Annie Oakley visibly stiffened. In horror, Vivianne thought. The two guards scrambled forward from the rafters but the Kaiser gruffly waved them off. Vivianne marveled at Annie's cool resolve; after handing the cigar to Wilhelm, the performer paced off her usual distance and the Kaiser lit the cigar with flourish.

Several German policemen rushed into the arena in a panicked attempt to preempt the stunt, but the Kaiser brusquely waved them off too. Then he lifted his head and placed the cigar to his mouth in a pose of a statue.

"No," Annie said. "In your hand, please, Your Majesty," she instructed. He looked disappointed but did as she'd asked.

Annie raised her Colt and took aim.

Vivianne swallowed the gorge in her throat. This was the moment she'd waited for; the moment for which she'd come. If this volatile and ambitious ruler were removed from the scene, one of the key reasons for World War I would also vanish. An entire world war would likely be averted. She only had to redirect the bullet; it was made of metal, after all. Kill a bully and incriminate and ruin the life of an innocent young woman … in exchange for over two million lives and the prevention of an age of non-stop violence—

Annie fired.

And blew away Wilhelm's ashes. The audience uttered a collective sigh. Wilhelm waved at the crowd with a self-pleased grin. Vivianne fell back in a faint in desperate relief and disappointment.

✠

She came to in a moving carriage that rocked and swayed to the rhythmic clopping of the horses. Her fur coat had been removed and was laid loosely over her instead. Suddenly realizing that her head was resting not on a pillow but on von

Eisenreich's lap, Vivianne jerked up into a sitting position and blinked at the older man, instinctively pulling the coat up to her neck as if she were otherwise exposed.

"Are you all right?" he asked with genuine concern. He didn't seem to think that having her head on his lap was a matter if indecency. Someone had carried her here; was it him? "The Kaiser was quite taken that you thought so much for his welfare," von Eisenreich went on. "He gave you this as a token." Von Eisenreich handed her a bag of fancy rock candy made in America with a drawing of the Wild West Show.

"Yes, I'm fine," she responded, taking the bag of candy then leaning back and closing her eyes for a moment to recollect herself. She'd missed her best opportunity to avert the rising tide of war. But at the final moment she just couldn't do it, couldn't be the cause of a man's murder and the ruin of a good woman's life. She'd had two chances and had failed both times to change the course of history; it seemed history had its own agenda, she concluded miserably. "I'm just not cut out for this," she muttered before she realized it.

"I'm sorry. I didn't realize you were so sensitive, My Lady," von Eisenreich said solicitously, mistaking her comment. "I hadn't figured you for the kind to collapse at such things, somehow..."

She finally opened her eyes and gazed at him. "I hadn't either."

He studied her for a moment then turned to look at the scenery. After a long silence, Vivianne asked, "Where are we going?...My coachman?"

"I sent your coachman away for a few hours with instructions to pick you up at my estate. You will have some refreshment first, My Lady," he insisted.

Vivianne nodded gratefully, still feeling lightheaded with thoughts of failure.

When they reached his estate in the countryside, von Eisenreich guided her to a solarium. He helped remove her coat and laid it over a chair then sat down across from her at a small table as one of the maids served them some tea and hot biscuits.

Vivianne gratefully sipped the refreshing drink, and studied the opulent room in silence, keenly aware of von Eisenreich's gaze upon her. Feeling herself again, she turned to face him with a look of inquiry. "Where is your family?"

"Ah, Georg informed me that my wife and my two elder children are in town, shopping. Only my youngest, Wolfgang, is home. I've instructed Georg to fetch him."

Within moments a small boy with curly long locks of dusty-brown hair came bounding into the solarium and rushed to his father.

"This is Wolfgang, my youngest son," von Eisenreich said, rising to seize the boy in a loving embrace. "He's five years old. Say hello to the *Comptess* d'Anjou, Wolfgang."

The boy held out his little hand to Vivianne, who also stood to take his hand and shook it. "Hello, *Comptesse*," he said, offering her a shy smile.

"Hello, Wolfgang," Vivianne answered, smiling back. She crouched down to face little Wolfgang directly and asked, "Do you like candy?"

His eyes lit up and he let his gaze stray to the package in her other hand. Vivianne smiled with a glance up at von Eisenreich. "Oh, yes!" the boy chimed in. "It's my favorite thing!"

"Then this is for you to share with your brother and sister," she said, handing the ecstatic boy the bag. "It's from Buffalo Bill's Wild West Show in America."

"Really?" Wolfgang said in amazement. He took the bag and unabashedly stared at Vivianne, who stood up and laughed self-consciously.

"Stop staring at the *Comptesse*, Wolfgang!" von Eisenreich chided his son. "Now, off you go with your candy; and share with your brother and sister like the *Comptesse* instructed you!"

The boy bolted down the corridor, gleefully clutching his prize. Von Eisenreich turned to Vivianne, whose gaze still followed the boy until he disappeared into the house. "Come, some fresh air will be good for you, put some color back into your beautiful cheeks," he said, taking her fur coat and offering it to her. "Little Wolfgang has a good eye, just like his papa," von Eisenreich continued with a chuckle as they strolled outside into the biting chill. He led Vivianne along a path into their orchard and they walked along a line of gnarly bare apple trees. "It's clear that you've captivated my little son—as you have captivated me—with your beauty, *Comptesse*." He clasped her hand in his with the fervor of a lover.

"I'm too old for you," Vivianne practically gasped at his passionate overture and threw flickering glances through the trees for prying eyes. She was four hundred years old. And he was a married man!

Von Eisenreich shouted out a guffaw. "That's choice! What? You'd have me rob the cradle instead, lass? You're no more than twenty-one, I'd wager." She thought she looked about twenty-five, but didn't argue with von Eisenreich. "And I'm an old man who's been in the sac a few times more than you. I think I might be able to show you a few tricks yet."

"No doubt." She smiled demurely, hand deftly sliding out of his. She'd had time to regain control. "But what would your good wife have to say of that?"

He made an exasperated scoffing sound. "You would bring her up. She is truly the love of my life and has sired three beautiful children by me."

"As it should be, My Lord." She turned and let him come beside her as they continued down the orchard path. "Might I ask how successful you've been in swaying the Kaiser from dismissing the chancellor?"

"I'm afraid, the Kaiser remains entrenched in his current policies," von Eisenreich said to her. "And von Bismark is not part of them."

"You must present him with an equally seductive alternative, then. You must do something, or his aggressive policy of *Weltpolitik* will escalate unchecked. Fueled by his war-mongering military staff, it will eventually lead to a world war from which we may all never recover. You must make him more aware of the consequences of his impulsive actions. Sometimes words are more dangerous than actions. We all know he's a bit of a buffoon; but despite his bombast, the Kaiser's careless words have the power to incite a needless and disastrous war, Jurgen."

"A more seductive alternative, eh...Perhaps I should give *you* to him!" He laughed sharply. "You would keep him nicely distracted."

She turned to him with earnest intensity and aggressively seized his arm. "Jurgen, you *must* give him an alternative. It is the only way to avert a world catastrophe. You must stay close to the Emperor; council him to be more attentive to his chancellors, von Bizmark and later von Bethmann-Hollweg—"

"How do you know he—"

"...You must help prevent any scandal with Eulenburg," she continued in a rush of words. She knew she was revealing too much but she felt compelled to convince him. "It will not only hurt the Kaiser but he will lose an important voice for pacifist restraint. And, as a result, those sabre-rattling military chiefs will tighten their grip on your sovereign. He is weak-minded, you know that. It is not by his will that he will unleash a war, but by his weakness. Council the Kaiser against war, Jurgen, and stand by him; give him the strength to endure those who will taunt him with accusations of cowardice. Council him against speaking of war and arming for it with that blasted navy of his...or war will happen and a dreadful thing it will prove to be for us all."

He glanced down where she'd grabbed his arm then flashed his eyes at her, barely suppressing an open grin. "My God, woman, you arouse me with your passion in politics! You make it sound as though you actually knew the future. You are far too serious about all this than is natural for a woman of your age and stature, *Comptesse*."

"I am no more serious than you should be in your position as one of the Kaiser's closest counselors, *Herr* von Eisenreich," she replied tartly.

"Well," he said, hand closing over the one she'd laid on his arm. "I liked it better when you called me Jurgen, *Comptesse* d'Anjou. I would do the same only you haven't yet given me your Christian name. But perhaps that would be repaired with a kiss...."

Vivianne saw her coach draw up at the entrance. "Ah, here is my coachman," she announced with a demure smile, sliding her hand out of his and easing away from him. "I do thank you for your kindness. I must go." She hastened down the path, hardly waiting for von Eisenreich to catch up, and soon saw the coachman step down and open the door for her. "Good bye, Jurgen," she said, turning to him and offering him her hand.

He took it eagerly and bent down to give it a gentle kiss then reluctantly let go. "When will I see you again?" She didn't reply right away and he added, "Soon, I hope?"

"*Adieu*, my friend," she said.

As she stepped into the coach, glancing back at von Eisenreich, Vivianne realized that any attempts to prevent a war based on Jurgen's abilities to influence the Kaiser were doomed. Jurgen was not sufficiently convinced that entering a war with England and her allies would be tragic for everyone, including Germany. He was a typical Prussian. He was not a pacifist; part of the reason why he was so close to his sovereign. As the coach drew away and Vivianne waved to Jurgen, she knew that this was likely the last time she'd see him. She'd tried twice and both times she'd failed to prevent a war; it seemed that History willed the war to happen. If she continued on this path with Jurgen, she would have to devote a great deal of time, convincing and nurturing, not to mention expending considerable effort to keep him from bedding her; Jurgen was neither talented enough nor disposed enough to sway the Kaiser from listening to his war-mongering generals and admirals or from his own reckless blustering, which would all inevitably lead to war. There were simply far too many variables to deal with at this stage. If she stayed, she'd nullify any other potential efforts. She had one last chance to prevent the full scale devastation of a long drawn-out war and that depended on an Englishman and another von Eisenreich. For now, she needed to disappear again.

✠

## ...39
*New York, 1905*

VIVIANNE straightened when she glimpsed the elegantly dressed Serbian as he entered Bryant Park. From her bench in the shade of a sycamore tree, she watched him saunter to his favorite bench then sit down and cross his legs. He emitted a somber sigh, pulled out a small notebook from his jacket pocket and began to write. Vivianne studied his long face, straight nose and well groomed mustache. It was an intense face, though worn with reserve. He quelled the fire that burned inside him beneath a shell of enigmatic reflection. He brushed a hand over his thick hair, then set his mouth in a thin line of determined concentration as he hastily sketched something inside the notebook. He didn't look terribly heartbroken for a man who had just lost his dream, she reflected. But she did recognize disappointment on his furrowed brow. He was used to that, she decided, reviewing his personal history, which had been plagued by rivalry and betrayal for nearly all his life. A visionary of his genius quality was easy fodder for bullying, whether it was schoolmates or the scientific community.

After adjusting her brimmed hat and flowing blue lace gown, Vivianne rose and approached the forty-eight year old Serbian visionary, musing how he would later be called the "Father of the 20th Century".

She was barely a metre away from him before he looked up, ready to express annoyance at being interrupted. She took pleasure in seeing his expression change from a glower to a startled look of curiosity. She knew she was beautiful, but it was rather delightful to see that she could divert this intense scientist.

"Hello, Mister Tesla," Vivianne greeted him with a

curtsy. "I am the *Comptesse* d'Anjou at your service. May I join you and sit down?"

He frowned at first then nodded politely with not quite a smile. He was not known for his smiles, she recalled. Tesla rose to his feet and bowed to her but did not offer his hand. She did not press him, knowing of his particular compulsion for avoiding human contact. "Of course you may," he said with a mild accent and nodded to her in invitation. They both sat down in unison and he added, "To what do I owe this pleasure, *Comptesse*? Do I know you?"

"No, Mister Tesla." She smiled with irony. "We have never met—not in person, anyway. But I believe you may be interested in what I have to say." She paused to take in his curiosity and continued, "Pardon me for what I am about to reveal of your affairs, but I represent the interests of *La Banque Internationale du Monde* in Geneva, Switzerland—perhaps you know of us—and the law offices of Frankl & Frankl. We are one of the five largest investment banks in the world, dating back to the late 1400s with offices in Amsterdam and Hamburg. We are a private bank who screen for altruistic and environmentally conscious investors. In short, we help finance only those projects that will help *make the world a better world*." She paused.

Tesla studied her inquisitively but said nothing.

She smiled internally at his puzzled expression then continued, "We are very interested in your Wardenclyffe Tower in Shoreham, Long Island, and associated global wireless power transmission."

Tesla slid his notebook back into his jacket pocket and now gave her his full attention. She knew that he'd been trying for years to gain backing for his enigmatic projects with little to no success.

She continued, "You theorized that electrical energy can be transmitted through the earth and the atmosphere...without power lines."

"Yes, I can light lamps at moderate distances and can detect the transmitted energy at much greater distances. The Wardenclyffe Tower uses a rapidly alternating electrostatic field and was a proof-of-concept for global wireless power transmission."

"Yes, I know."

He frowned. "But my funding—"

"Yes, I know. Your backers don't like the idea of unmetered power consumption."

His face hardened with dark thoughts. "Free electricity isn't profitable."

"Least of all to greedy bankers with no vision or faith like J.P. Morgan or John Jacob Astor," she added. "I know you've been in financial trouble with high construction costs since Morgan pulled out last year and encouraged other investors to do the same."

Her last remark made him stiffen. She was hitting a painful nerve.

"I know about your expired patents and the resulting lack of royalty payments," she continued. "Within another five to ten years your projects will all be defunk and you will be totally broke. And no one will listen to the ideas that come to you fully formed through visions and dreams."

He straightened and looked her directly in the eyes. "What do you want of me, *Comptesse*? Who *are* you?"

"An ally," she answered. "I am well aware of your humanitarian pursuits and altruistic nature. I know that you wish simply to make the world a better world. That is my wish also. Energy is and will continue to be one of the most important forces on this earth. Like water, it should be free and available to each and everyone of us. I think you can provide us with that gift and would be happy to as well. Mister Tesla, I want to offer you financial backing at zero percent interest."

He let loose a humorless laugh. He had finally learned to be cynical about bankers, she thought.

"Make no mistake, Mister Tesla; I expect to become one of the wealthiest people on this planet because of you. But I will gain that wealth only as you gain yours, through a partnership, and not at the expense of others; rather, for the benefit of others. Your wireless technology will help in areas you have yet to imagine: instant global communications and the personal computer; clean energy for homes and industry; laser medicine; robotics; interstellar travel; instant matter transference; even time travel and so much more."

He was staring at her now. "Who are you, really?"

*An angel*, she thought to herself. "I'm part of the future, Mister Tesla. A future of your making." Then without thinking, she held out her hand. "You can call me Vivianne."

To her delighted surprise, he smiled for the first time. He took her hand then lightly kissed it, as was the custom of most eastern Europeans. "And you can call me Nikola."

✠

# ...40
*Weimar, November 1914*

WHEN she'd first met and seduced him in Potsdam, Wolfgang had cocked his head to one side and studied Vivianne with close to a frown. "Didn't you know my father?" he'd blurted out. "I thought he knew a *Comptesse* d'Anjou when I was five...."

She blinked at him in enigmatic silence, letting him figure out the illogic of his question. She looked a good five years younger than him; she'd have been just born when he was five. Wolfgang laughed with sudden embarrassment. "Of course it couldn't be you. She was in her twenties when I was five. She'd be in her fifties now." He shook his head. "It's just that..." he trailed, unable to let it go. "It's just that you remind me so much of her. I only met her once or twice but I remember that she was beautiful. And kind; she gave me a bag of rock candy made in America once. The bag had a drawing of Buffalo Bill's *Wild West Show* on it. I ate the candy right away but I kept the bag; I might still have it." He chuckled. Then he tore his gaze from hers and pursed his lips in thoughts of the past. "I heard the rumors; everyone thought she was my father's mistress."

She leaned forward until she almost touched him but didn't. "What did *you* think?"

Drawn into her gaze his eyes reflected her almost plaintive look. "I thought she was an angel," he responded honestly. Then he straightened and gave her a crooked smile. "I knew my father was a womanizer. But I wanted to think she was innocent and virtuous. I'm not sure why…"

Now, lying in a hotel bed in Weimar, she stroked his bared leg. He sighed and pulled her up close to him.

"You are the most elegant, bright and refined young lady I've met…" She'd had a few years to finally get the lady-like thing down right, Vivianne reflected with an inward smile. "…yet you make love like a harlot," Wolfgang went on. "Where did you learn all that?"

From a fifteen-year old French boy in a future that wasn't going to happen, she thought and absently pressed her lips together. He'd taught her everything she knew of love, Vivianne reflected, and let her hand stray to the locket that hung off her neck.

Wolfgang misunderstood. "I'm sorry. I didn't mean to pry. I was just curious. You present somewhat of a paradox to me, that's all. So worldly and wise yet so young and innocent. You are at best intriguing."

"No one is ever what they seem," she murmured into his hair. "We are all more than our projected selves. Always more…"

"You're right, there's always more," Wolfgang said, drawing back to eye her with an enigmatic smile. "Take you, for instance. There's always something you're holding back, something you keep deep inside you. Something for a special person…the person in there, perhaps?" He pointed to her locket.

She blinked at him with the weight of the truth, unable to reply—certainly not willing to share—and resisted the urge to finger the locket again. Instead she leaned into him again and probed his ear with her tongue. She knew he'd forgotten his questions when he inhaled sharply in deep arousal and she felt him harden against her. She opened to him and he seized her passionately. As she guided him inside her all his questions were suspended in the ecstasy of the moment.

✠

Wolfgang snorted himself awake from having drifted briefly into a doze. Taking advantage of his loosened grip over her breast, and without glancing back at him, Vivianne pulled off the covers and swung her legs over the side of the bed. She rose, avoiding his hand as he reached a lazy arm out to touch the slope of her naked back, fingers alighting on her dark purple markings.

As she stepped out of his reach, he drawled lazily, "Those markings on your back...I've never seen anything like that before..." Nor would he again, Vivianne thought. She took the long hobble skirt in her hands and fumbled with it, rearranging her thoughts and making a point of not looking back at Wolfgang.

They'd become lovers shortly after she'd met him. They'd met secretly in Potsdam and Berlin, London, Vienna and other cities across Europe for the better part of a year as she subtly coached him in political matters. She'd first captured his attention with her feminine beauty, then intrigued him with her intellect and reason and finally swayed him with her passion, both physical and mental. She knew he was a little in love with her. And she'd ruthlessly used that love to compel him to meet his destiny as one of the finest statesmen history would recognize. He had, after all, just orchestrated the armistice of the Great War and averted a World War. After the disaster of Ypres, Wolfgang had cajoled the fearful Chancellor Bethmann-Hollweg to listen to Chief of Staff Falkenhayn's entreaty for a settlement and had persuaded the stubborn Kaiser Wilhelm II to agree. Bethmann-Hollweg presented a fair case to the Russians and the French as well as Great Britain, who, after dallying, had finally considered entering the war in earnest. They'd all seen the logic of this action, weighted against a long drawn out relentless war and they'd chosen peace.

Wolfgang was the world's silent hero. He would never know just how much he'd averted: millions of casualties and a whole other world war and century of violence. It was a moment of victory for the entire planet, Vivianne thought.

Wolfgang raised himself on his elbow and audibly sighed; a brash signal to her that he was regarding her appreciatively. She gave him a fleeting glance and smiled faintly and coquettishly slid her long skirt over her rump in a slow purposeful way to let him enjoy her fully. She was leaving and he knew it. He blurted out, "When will I see you again?" His voice was mildly pleading.

She suspended her action of dressing and her eyes met his briefly before she let her gaze stray to the door.

He understood and his face darkened. "I'm not going to, am I?" He'd seen it coming. She'd given him enough hints.

Vivianne pulled on her lampshade tunic in a long pause of silence before settling her eyes back on him with an enigmatic look. "My work is done here, Wolfgang. You've done a great service for humankind but your work has just begun. You saved us from a terrible legacy of violence and constant war. You are a great statesman and your skills will be very important in the next little while. I predict that you will be indispensible to the Kaiser. Germany and the rest of the world have much mending and building to do. And you'll be a large part of it, Wolfgang. As for me..." She smiled wistfully. "I must disappear until I'm needed again."

He frowned. "Who *are* you, *Comptesse* d'Anjou?" he murmured in half-frustration and half-wonder. "An *angel*?"

She looked demurely down and let the side of her mouth curl in a coy smile, one she learned drove men crazy with desire.

"Who is he?" He added, "Some young lad from the past..."

Not from the past, she thought.

"Someone who broke your heart..."

More like *filled* it, she reflected.

"You've let me bed you and you've given me your tender love for two years, but not your soul or your heart—*that* you've locked away for *him*."

Yes, she thought, feeling a sudden stinging heat behind her eyes. It was so long ago—about four hundred years ago— that her adolescent self had returned from a future France to her father's castle, having championed a world and lost the boy of her dreams. Yet, in some ways it seemed like only yesterday.

Wolfgang threw off the covers and leapt up naked from the bed, muscular body rushing forward to seize her by her hands. "Stay, Vivianne! I love you. Marry me!"

She gently pulled away from him and gave him a sad pleading look. They'd discussed this before and had agreed on a compromise. Now, he was breaking their covenant of not discussing the topic of marriage. "Wolfgang, I *can't* stay," she said sternly. "That was our agreement: not to hold on to one another."

"I know it was, but—"

She placed a finger over his lips and whispered, " '*He who binds himself to a joy does the winged life destroy*'—"

" '*He who kisses the joy as it flies lives in eternity's sunrise*'," Wolfgang finished for her in a slightly peevish voice after clutching and moving her hand from his mouth.

She kissed him, a long deep kiss that swelled with her genuine love for him.

As he swam in the passion she'd evoked, Vivianne coquettishly slithered out of his embrace. He might have thought she was heading back for the bed; instead she fled out the door of the hotel room. In his state of undress, he was hardly fit to give chase and she knew she'd once more escaped from a fate she longed for.

✠

## ...41
*Paris, August 2025*

VIVIANNE passed the security door and entered the spacious lobby of *Aeonic Visions*. Its Paris office was housed in a solar and wind-powered hemp-building near le Jardin des Tuileries in the 1ère Arrondissment. It contained a biomimetically engineered heating, circulatory and waste system, hemp-made furniture and a living roof.

Directly above her, in a color-changing holo, she read:

*You are enlightened from the very beginning. Enlightenment is your nature. Enlightenment is not something that has to be achieved. It is not a goal. It is your source. It is your very energy*—Osho.

Vivianne gazed for some moments at the Impressionist art work on the walls and the forty-foot high sycamore trees. Then with a quiet smile of contentment, she took the moving stairway to Rouard's office on the top floor.

After a hasty rap at his door, she let herself into his atrium-style office.

Her forty year old CEO sat behind his desk in a dark Armani suit. As she stepped through the door, he sprang to his feet with a wide grin and closed the space between them in a loping stride. "*Comptesse*! You look splendid! I'm so happy to see you again in person!"

Rouard gave her a warm hug.

They kissed on both cheeks as was the French custom and as he stepped back he took the liberty of admiring her coifed dark hair and her slylish medium heels and everything in-between. Vivianne smiled demurely. She had chosen this smart charcoal gray 40's style business skirt, silk green top and form-fitting jacket for Rouard's benefit, knowing fully well that he appreciated her form; her slim tall legs, flat narrow waist and well-formed hips and breasts. She knew that he was just a little in love with her. And perhaps the feeling was mutual, she decided with a slanted smile.

"It's so nice to see you again, Vincent," she said, taking in how his physique fit well in that Armani suit. He was a tall full-bodied man, ruggedly handsome with slicked back longish hair and one day-old facial hair that made him look more Italian than French. She glanced admiringly at his Reuental VC entertainment system sprawled below the full sized marble statue of David and sat down in the chair by his desk. He crossed over to the credenza and poured her a 2010 *Grand Cru Chasselas* by Alain Emery from Aigle, Switzerland. One of her favorite haunts.

He showed her the bottle and she laughed. "I brought that for *you*, Vincent!"

"And I saved it for when you next came. A pity the Swiss don't export their wine," he mused. "Of course, they barely have enough for themselves, I suppose!"

Vivianne nodded with an unlady-like grin as Rouard handed her a glass of the elegant white wine. "So, when was it we last saw one another? Geneva?"

He sat at his desk and took a long appreciative sip. "I think so. It's nice to see you face to face instead of via the internet. We really must meet more often, *Comptesse*!"

She crossed her legs and leaned back, pondering with inner sadness that they would in fact soon meet in person less often—he would eventually become suspicious of her eternal youth. The internet had become a good friend to her for that sort of thing, she decided. Avatars were so ambiguous. "Yes, we must, Vincent," she simply said. "So, how are we doing?"

"Well, this is more a review for you. You've been so attentive in all aspects of *Aeonic Visions...*" He trailed.

"The lady of the house must know everything, so she can effectively oversee her staff. Otherwise she is a fool and will be taken for it," Vivianne said with a slanted smile. She thought of her long-dead head housekeeper.

Rouard flipped open a large dossier and pretended to study it; Vivianne knew he had all the information in his head. "First of all, congratulations on having so many of your companies recognized by the *Earth Foundation...*"

...Also hers, Vivianne thought slyly. She'd established

that non-profit altruism-based organization close to a century ago under an alter-ego. Of course, those who currently ran the organization had no idea of her connection.

She'd also created the *New World Syndicate*, in the 16th Century and found champions to promote altruistic syndicalism as an alternative to capitalism and state socialism: an economic and ecological model in which all participants in an organized trade internally shared equal ownership of its services and production. It was a bold and all-trusting movement organized from the bottom-up and based on direct democracy, confederation and a decentralized socialism. A system that celebrated the best of humankind; not its worst. Her vindication was to see commensalistic syndicalism replace the souless greed of capitalism in many parts of the world. She'd witnessed the retention of monasteries and 'the commons'; support of the locality; fair distribution of assets; and the practice of charity.

Rouard went on, "The foundation released its top ranked 'World's Most Ethical and Altruistic Organizations' last week and several of your companies made the top one hundred." He briefly consulted his file and read, "like *La Banque Internationale du Monde*; your Geneva and New York-based *Earth Magazine*; the *First Response & Relief Foundation*; *Tesla Energy & Wind Limited, Worldwide Classroom, Nature's Renaissance,* and even *Aeon Visions*. Congratulations!" He leaned back, obviously pleased with himself. Those were just the companies that she was currently connected with; there were at least two dozen more that she'd had a hand in forming, anonymously and under pseudonymous identities.

Vivianne leaned forward. "Of course *Aeon Visions* is on the list; it has the best CEO in the world." She winked at him and smiled demurely. "And speaking of, how are our daughter organizations doing?"

He grinned and flipped a page. "Well, let's start with the Educational Arm: Helena opened the new virtual and physical campus in Prague last week with great success. The Dalai Lama attended the ceremony. Helena told me that he asked for you, *Comptesse*."

Vivianne smiled at Rouard with genuine appreciation and nodded her approval. The *Worldwide Classroom of the Extraordinary* was a unique educational project she had initiated in the early 40s. After achieving accreditation, the open teaching institute expanded its unique curriculum into areas particularly aimed at teachers and mentors. And it was far from ordinary in every way. While it offered courses in the hard sciences, engineering, commerce and the liberal arts through Metatron University, the global school's teaching mantra was far from traditional. Instructors were encouraged to take students out of the classroom, on field trips via *Tesla Travel* or on virtual trips all over the world. As part of a holistic and comprehensive liberal arts and science program, Worldwide Classroom offered mixed degrees in compassion and meditation; altruistic ecology and economics; social studies & compassion; writing & wellness; whole nutrition studies; philosophy & education.

Helena Heidelberg, the Head of Metatron University, had also initiated the *Meaning Through Creation Institute*, aimed specifically at empowering older women to share their intuitive wisdom through creative pursuits. Only fitting that she carried on the work of her ancestor and Vivianne's good friend who fought so well in the 1500s for women's rights.

"The Environmental Arm happily reports that our associate the David Suzuki Foundation has convinced the provincial school board to extend the ecology stream starting from primary through secondary grades in all public schools in British Columbia and Ontario, Canada. The new programs will commence in the fall semester of most public schools this year. It is a beginning, *Comptesse!*"

Vivianne clapped her hands in delight. This had been one of her personal missions: to educate youth in the principles of ecology, a science of relationships and consequence. She had for many years been an avid supporter of economics based on ecological principals such as creative cooperation and niche partitioning.

"Canadian limnologist Nina Munteanu also reports that Masaru Emoto's Water Course will make a world tour with the

World Science Academy next month. And—I've saved the best for last—" He grinned like a boy, showing perfect teeth in a maverick smile. "Your latest book, *A Return to Nature's Elixors* is currently the number one New York Bestseller and its associated Elixor Line is making huge profits! The Plantain tinctures and oils are particularly popular."

Vivianne smiled. Uta would be proud of her.

Victor continued his report on their Justice and Compassion Arm, the Science & Engineering Arm—affectionately called the Tesla Arm, their World Relief & Rescue Arm, and several others.

Many hours and an ordered pizza later, Vivianne left to wander the city that had once captured her heart.

"Don't be a stranger!" Rouard called after her at the door as the sun dipped toward the horizon, painting the city in shades of gold.

Vivianne waved back from the moving stairway. That was just what she would soon be: a stranger. She had a few years yet before Rouard saw her no more. Youth-giving nutrients aside, she could not disguise her eternal youth for much longer. Soon it would be time for self-induced seclusion; when she would contact Frankl & Frankl—the only people who knew and kept her secret. She would leave them with instructions on her various estates and assets as she languished like a hermit until she was needed again.

✠

Rue des Rosiers looked far from the slum of hovels and garbage she'd experienced when she'd fallen into it so long ago. Francois's hut, of course wasn't there. Although in some ways it was very much the same as she'd remembered it, Rue des Rosiers now flourished as part of the lively Jewish sector of the Marais in the 4ème Arrondisement. This was a new world, she reflected; one in which the Jewish people had not suffered the oppression and humiliation of antizionism

She absently took herself across the Seine to the Latin

Quarter and west along the river toward Saint-Michel Square.

It was different, yet the same. *Everything* was different, yet the same, she conceded, as she sat down on a bench with a view of the fountain at Saint-Michel Square.

She looked down and smiled with irony; she'd changed into an outfit almost exactly like the one she'd worn when she was here six hundred years ago: jeans with a dark olive tank top.

Vivianne contemplated her world, the world of her making. She felt good about it. One of her greatest accomplishments was the prevention of a long drawn out First World War. Wolfgang von Eisenreich's negotiated "armistice of desperation" had averted the tragedy of brutal trench warfare, with its mass killings. It generated a renewed sense of community as the world breathed a great sigh of relief. Over two million lives had been spared. With the German Kaiser's prestige diminished, a genuine parliamentary government finally prevailed, again as a result of Wolfgang's skillful navigations. Russia, never having suffered the drain of 1914-1915, continued its economic and political development, unscathed, and developed a limited monarchy with a parliamentary government; the revolution never happened. Wolfgang von Eisenreich's armistice had prevented the devastation of the world's soul and the planet skipped a more sinister legacy that would have otherwise scarred all of humanity: World War II and the ensuing never-ending violence in the world.

World War II didn't happen. Instead, Vladimir Lenin died an exile in Switzerland. Adolf Hitler enjoyed notoriety in Munich's bohemian circles; and his sons became artists of repute in the modernist movement. Picasso never painted *Guernica* and Hemingway never wrote *Farewell to Arms*. Albert Einstein flourished as a physicist and philanthropist and there was no devastation in Hiroshima or Nagasaki. Europe had become a community of tolerance and creative endeavor. And the entire world had flourished as a result. Tesla's free energy and wireless communications had enabled the planetary community to exist free of oppression and hardship. Even the environment had benefited; global warming, the major bane of her alternative world never amounted to much here, where scientific efforts of a world community, not diverted by war-efforts, had addressed "greenhouse" emissions and other kinds of pollution in both the air and in the water. She saw evidence of this difference in the lush and healthy trees of Paris compared with the struggling vegetation of François's world.

Of a certainty, she had not cured the world of all its ills. So long as there were people in the world—indeed life of any kind—there would be poverty, treachery and misfortune. Millions of quiet personal tragedies would continue, invisible beneath the veil of the world's grandness. Helpless victims of ill-chance or ill-intent would suffer quietly: the despair of an old man who'd lost his wife to disease; a cat trapped and starving to death in a dry well; the muffled cries of a woman ravaged in some back room by a spurned suitor. Nature's apparent cruelty would endure.

It was, however, she decided, a better world. She smiled briefly.

Tesla's free energy and other inventions had prevented many potential ailments of a growing world population. The planet and all its life thrived in a healthy environment of clean air, water and soil and a mindset based on generosity and altruism—something her other worlds could not believe possible or embrace with faith.

As for her…she'd acquired a great deal of wealth over the years. Wise management of her estates and holdings had given her a lot of opportunities to do good work. She'd formed several corporations devoted to charity, scientific research, humanitarian pursuits and education and had hired men and women of integrity, like Rouard, to run them while she, who eventually outlived them all, remained in the background.

She'd let herself get close to the men she'd influenced. She'd enjoyed their company for a brief time, even slept with some of them. Each had loved her in his own way. There'd been the elegant old Jurgen von Eisenreich with whom she'd had lively sparring discussions and who'd openly lusted for her despite being married with three children. Then there was

Wolfgang von Eisenreich, Jurgen's son, who reminded Vivianne of her childhood friend and his namesake. Wolfgang had been her lover and a gentle friend. And there were women too. Great friends like Vivian von Heidelberg, Seigfried's brilliant grand-daughter, who had spearheaded a movement for equality for women and identified minorities. The movement in the United Kingdom had spread worldwide thanks to the Comptesse's powerful contacts.

She'd loved them all. And left them all. Just like her first and only true love…Vivianne bent forward and leaned her arms on her lap, turning her hands palm upward to study them. They were young hands, smooth and soft; not the hands of a six hundred year old person. Before she realized it, she'd clasped them with a deep exhale, closed her eyes and began to pray.

…*Dear Lord, I've been your willing instrument all these years, and you've used me well. You've placed me on the path of several great men of war and helped me convince them that peace was achievable. I've traveled the world for six centuries, doing your good work. Now you've delivered me here. To a place I've avoided all these years. A place that lives only in my memory. A place of incredible joy…and great anguish.…*

"Oh, why am I here!" she ended in a whisper to herself and felt tears she hadn't shed in a very long time scald her eyes. God hadn't sent her here. She'd come to fulfill…or put an end to …her foolish dream. The dream that haunted her nightly still. Her dream of a noble knight, not of noble birth, but of noble intent; her *ritter*. Francois.

She heard the music of *La Mer* waft over with the warm breeze from one of the open cafés and absently watched the fountain of water spill out of the sea cherubim at the center. "…*Et d'une chanson d'amour…la mer…a bercé mon coeur pour la vie…*"

Life flowed like water, Vivianne reflected, ever cycling, and history with it. She thought it uncanny how events 'wanted' to occur; there were times when they appeared to have a life of their own in the march of time. As if God's all-knowing hand was orchestrating it. Of course God was. Whatever happened was meant to happen one way or another. She'd seen it; she'd participated in its dance, reeling from partner to partner as the music changed yet remained the same—

"May I have this dance?"

Her heart thundered. She knew that voice! Vivianne looked up and stared at François. His double, that is. He was older, in his twenties; he'd lost that boyish teenage look and had matured in both physique and in stature. She noticed that his hands were clean and manicured and he was well dressed. And his leather shoes were fairly new and buffed; he obviously wasn't living in the streets.

"Hello, I'm François Rabelais," he introduced himself with a rakish smile.

"I'm Vivianne Schoen," she replied, standing up to face him. Then she recognized her *ritterkreuz* around his neck. He'd found it! Where? Did that mean that the worlds had joined?…

He followed her gaze to the cross that hung off his neck and gave her a sloping smile of inquiry.

"It's just that cross…" she explained in a shaky voice. "I was wondering how you'd gotten it." She felt herself trembling.

He grinned. "I found it five years ago in a pawn shop and it spoke to me—I just had to have it. Funny," he added with a wistful smile. "Right after that I began to have strange dreams." He was gazing at her with eyes of intense wonder. "*You* were in them." She held back a sharp inhale and brought her hands to her mouth. "Well, someone very like you, that is," he ended with a loose smile, noticing her reaction. "It's as though I summoned you."

She held his gaze for a long moment as her mind traveled to that short week in another place and time that had changed her life. She said softly, "Perhaps you did."

"May I sit?" he asked, and to her nod took the seat beside her on the bench.

"Do…you come here often?" she asked, feeling like she'd entered her own dream.

He nodded. "Every day since I've been having those dreams. It's as though a ghost kept telling me to come here; that

I'd find something…" He flashed another lopsided grin.

They fell into a easeful conversation about all sorts of things. He shared that he had recently moved out of his parent's home and found an apartment in the Latin Quarter; he was a musician, studying at the Sorbonne and did gigs at The Café Marie and other places in the Latin Quarter. His smile warmed her like the bright flame of a hearth's fire. She felt like she'd come home at last.

His eyes penetrated hers. "It's been my dream to travel the world…"

*Yes, I know,* Vivianne almost said.

"Would you like to join me?"

She gave him a startled grin, unleashing a joy she hadn't even realized she had. "But we've only just met," she objected mildly. "You don't know me."

His eyes, always a deep shade of blue, sparkled like the ocean on a summer day. "Traveling with someone is one of the best ways to get to know them. Besides, I feel like I *do* know you…if only because of my dreams," he ended with a slanted smile. Then he grew serious and explained, "I was going to go with my girlfriend, Lizette, but she wasn't really interested and then we broke up just a few days ago. She left me with two tickets and a dream…"

✠

# Epilogue
*Atlantic Ocean, September 2025*

FRANÇOIS and Vivianne lounged on deck chairs on the upper aft deck of the Saint Lucia, sipping orange juleps. He'd just finished sharing his dream about how his namesake had saved the world from a madman's genocidal plan called Plan Zarathustra.

"You know what I think…I'm that knight. I've been walking through a dark swamp-forest, littered with the debris and decay of a dark conflict. And I stumble into a cathedral, shimmering with a light like I've never before seen…it's *you*."

"What?"

"The cathedral of light is you, Vianne…"

She drew in a sharp breath with her own startling realization: in her dream *she* was the *ritter*; and *François* was the cathedral of light into whose heart she'd entered. They'd both dreamed of journeying into the other's heart.

"Oh, my God…" she breathed out the words.

"Yeah, that's what I thought too." He grinned.

"François, I had exactly the same dream, only I was the *ritter*—I mean, the knight. We shared the same dream, the same…journey."

"I know," he said calmly. "It's the only way it could be. The *me* in my dream did it all for you." François gave her a wry appreciative smile. "You really do look like someone from another time and place…like an *angel*…"

"That's because I *am*," she said with a teasing smile.

388

"And you really did summon me, didn't you?" he teased back.

And it would be the last summoning she would do, thought Vivianne. She brought her hands to cup his face and leaned forward to kiss him, intending not to let go for a long time. "François," she breathed his name in a sigh then lost herself in his kiss. He'd been her first....And he'd be her last.

*Gott sei Dank.*

✠

# Glossary

**Aeon**    'Life'; also 'age', 'eternity', 'eternal life'; a being of light and spirit capable of summoning and manipulating the world of matter. Angels. In Gnosticism, aeons correspond to the various emanations of God. Aeons belong to the pleroma and come in paired twins, who the Gnostics call syzygies. According to Plato, an aeon relates to the eternal world of ideas, which he conceived was "behind" the perceived world.

**Alber**    'Fool'; in the Fool's Guard, the point of the sword is lowered to the ground, appearing to "foolishly" expose the upper parts of the body and inviting an attack. Although the Fool's Guard exposes the upper openings it provides excellent protection to the lower openings. From the Fool's Guard an attack or displacement can be made with the false edge of the sword or the hilt of the sword can be quickly raised into a hanging parry (German).

**Backsteingotik**    Gothic-style architecture of Teutonic Knights in Baltic Region (German).

**Balderich**    Baldric; a belt, usually of ornamented leather, worn across the chest to support a sword (German).

**Barbolle**    Old English (medieval) slang word relating to the fishy smelling discharge from the vagina from a bacterial infection.

**Bascinet**    Bassinet or basinet; a medieval European open-faced military helmet, typically fitted with an aventail and hinged visor.

**Bauernlümmel**    Peasant oaf; dumb farmer (German)

**Bloßfechten**    Unarmoured fencing with the longsword; also called "bare fighting" or foot combat (German) Unarmored combat in the *Fechtschulen* as distinguished from armored fighting.

**Boulangerie**   Bakery; a place where bread is sold (French).

**Bouquinist**   Riverside vendor (e.g., along the Seine in Paris); used-book seller (French).

**Butterfly Effect**   The sensitive dependence on initial conditions, where a small change at one place in a nonlinear system can result in large differences to a later state. Coined by Edward Lorenz as part of chaos theory.

**Cassis**   A black current liquor (French).

**Charcouterie**   A shop that sells prepared meats (e.g., sausage, hams, patés; French).

**Cockspurs**   Narrow-leaved green herbage: grown as lawns; used as pasture for grazing animals; cut and dried as hay, used in medieval times to help in labor.

**Commensal Syndicalism**   Commensalism is an ecological term that describes a relationship between two organisms in which one benefits and the other is neutrally affected. See "Syndicalism".

**Connard**   Jerk ('prick'; French).

**Creative cooperation**   The synergistic interaction or communication that kindles new ideas through the exploration of differences and the creation of a third alternative, better than either single previous one.

**Crenel**   An open space or notch between two merlons in a battlement or crenelated wall.

**Cross Pattée**   Also *tatzenkreuz*; known also as cross patty or cross formée; a type of cross with arms narrow at the centre and broader at the perimeter; the form appeared very early in medieval art as in metal work; one of its variant forms is the iron cross.

**Coumadin**   Brand name for warfarin, used as an anticoagulant normally used in the prevention of thrombosis and thromboembolism, the formation of blood clots in the blood vessels and their migration elsewhere in the body respecttively. Also used as a pesticide.

**Cuxham**   Spice prepared from salted fermented unripe grapes and apples, used in cooking; acidic and gives a sharp savoury flavour to food (English)

**Demiurge**    A concept from the platonic, Neopythagorean, Middle Platonic, and Neoplatonic schools of philosophy for an artisan-like figure responsible for the fashioning and maintenance of the physical universe. The term was adopted by the Gnostics; creator of the universe; fashioner of ideas and the perceptable world.

**Drang nach Osten**    'Yearning for the East', 'thrust toward the East', 'push eastward', 'drive toward the East'; a term used to designate German expansion into Slavic lands (e.g., *Ostsiedlung*), it became a motto of the German nationalist movement in the late nineteenth century. Some historical discourses combine historical German settlement in Eastern Europe, medieval military expeditions like the ones of the Teutonic Knights, and Germanisation policies and warfare like the lebensraum concept openly embraced by the Nazis. One of the core elements of German nationalism, it became part of Nazi ideology.

**Dropsy**    An old term for the swelling of soft tissues due to the accumulation of excess water; edema (English).

**Dwale**    An herbal mixture used to dull pain; a medieval herbal anaesthetic and likely mixture of opium, henbane, mulberry juice, lettuce, hemlock, mandragora, and ivy.

**Eclampsia**    An acute and life-threatening complication of pregnancy, characterized by the appearance of tonic-clonic seizures, usually in a patient who had developed pre-eclampsia. (Preeclampsia and eclampsia are collectively called *Hypertensive disorder of pregnancy* and *toxemia of pregnancy*).

**Exceptionalism**    The perception that a country, society, institution, movement, or time period is "exceptional" (i.e., unusual or extraordinary) in some way and therefore does not need to conform to normal rules or general principles; a theme of uniqueness that

German romantic philosopher-historians, particularly Johann Gottfried Herder and Johann Gottlieb Fichte promoted in the late 18th century. They emphasized the unique 'national spirit' and 'soul' of the *Volk (Volksgeist)*, as a cultural entity with its own distinctive history. This notion strongly influenced the growth of nationalism in 19th-century Europe — especially those ruled by elites. See "Sonderweg"

**Edelzinn**     Relief pewter (German).

**Ergotism**     The effect of long-term ergot poisoning, traditionally due to the ingestion of alkaloids produced by the *Claviceps purpurea* fungus, which infects rye and other cereals. Also known as ergotoxicosis, ergot poisoning and Saint Anthony's Fire. Ergot poisoning is a proposed explanation of bewitchment.

**Fechtbuch**     'Fight book' or 'fencing book' (German); a German manual on fighting techniques and methods, particularly swordsmanship, among the more famous are those by the masters Johannes Liechtenauer's of 1389, Sigmund Ringneck of c. 1440, Hans Talhoffer of 1443, Peter von Danzig of 1452, Paulus Kal of c.1460, Johannes Leckuechner ("Lebkomer") of 1482, Peter Falkner of 1490, H. von Speyer of 1491, Joerg Wilhalm of 1523, Andre Pauerfeindts of 1516, and Gregor Erhart from the early 1500's.

**Fechtmeister**     'Fight master' (German); a German Master of defence or martial arts expert.

**Flagon**     A large vessel, usually with a handle and spout and lid to hold liquor, for serving at the table (English).

**Flic**     Policeman; cop (French).

**Fromagerie**     Cheese shop (French).

**Frumenty**     A thick wheat porridge that was traditionally served with venison and a popular dish in Western European medieval cuisine.

**Fylfot**     Also 'fylfot cross' or 'swastika'; the swastika is a type of 'solar cross', with arms bent at right angles, suggesting a whirling or turning motion. Long before the symbol was co-opted as an emblem of Hitler's Nazi party, it was a sacred symbol to Hindu, Jain, and Buddhist religions, as well as in Norse, Basque, Baltic, and Celtic Paganism. The name *Swastika* derives from from "su," meaning "good," and "vasti"," meaning "being" (together; well being in Sanskrit) In India, it is used as a fertility and good luck charm. The right turning Indian swastika symbolizes the sun and positive energy, and is most commonly associated with the deity Ganesh, a God of prosperity and wealth. Some Indians regard an anti-clockwise swastika (used by the Nazis) as an opposing, dark force, a symbol of the goddess Kali. Together, the two can be regarded as symbolically similar to the Yin Yang symbol of Taoism, or the two Pillars of Kabbalah.

| | |
|---|---|
| **Garderobe** | A medieval toilet. |
| **Glaßmalerei** | Painted-glass (German). |
| **Glaßmaler** | Glass-painter (German). |
| **Guter Gott** | Good God (German). |
| **Gott helfe mir** | God help me |
| **"Gott Mit Uns!"** | "God is with us!" (Teutonic battle cry) (German). |
| **"Gott sei Dank"** | "Thank God" (German). |
| **Großkomtur** | Grand commander of the Teutonic Knights (German). |
| **Großmeister** | Grand master (German) of a military order of knighthood other than the Teutonic Order (which uses *Hochmeister*). |
| **Grunwald Coat of Arms** | A sable field with broad green oak tree and a golden unicorn, *salient reguardant* to the sinister, in front of the tree |
| **Hanseatic League** | Also 'Hansa' (low German); an economic alliance of trading cities and their merchant guilds that dominated trade along the coast of Northern Europe. |

|  |  |
|---|---|
|  | Greatest seaports for the northern trade of amber, herring, salt and grain was Elbing. |
| **Hase** | Rabbit (German); used as an endearment usually by a mother to her child. |
| **Halbschwert** | Half-swording; using both hands, one on the hilt and one on the blade, to better control the weapon in thrusts and jabs (German);'half-sword' techniques of gripping the middle of the blade itself with the second hand or typically left hand (often by gloves or armored gauntlets); also called *Halt-Schwert* or *Kurzen Schwert*, they allow a wide range of offensive and defensive striking and deflecting actions as well as thrusts. It is used for the more powerful and more accurate stabs. The term comes from the pose of the left hand on the blade cutting the sword in half. |
| **Harnisch-fechten** | Armoured fighting; fighting in protective gear, most specifically plate armour (German); also known as harness fighting. |
| **Haubergeon** | A knight's long chain mail and leather tunic, usually long sleeved. |
| **Hochmeister** | High master; Grand Master (German) of the Teutonic Order and only used for this order; holder of the supreme office of the Teutonic Order. |
| **Holy Fire** | Also called *ignis sacer* (Latin) or St. Anthony's fire; refers to one of the following diseases: ergotism (in France and Germany); erysipelas (England and the USA); Herpes zoster. See ergotism. |
| **Ignis sacer** | See "Holy Fire" and "ergotism". |
| **Kir** | A favorite aperitif of the French, made with cassis topped with white wine (French). |
| **Klappuizier** | Vizor of a helmet (German). |
| **Klugscheißer** | A 'big mouth'; 'smart ass'; 'smart aleck' (German) |
| **Knechten** | Hired knight (if recruited from Prussia) (German) |
| **Komtur** | Commander (Teutonic Knight) of the Order within a specific region (German). |

| | |
|---|---|
| **Krzyzacy** | Black Cross, 'the crossed knights' (Polish); Polish term for the Teutonic Knights. |
| **Kunst des Fechten** | The art of fighting (German); a German Medieval martial art practiced in the 14th and 15th Centuries; taught by the 14th century fencing master Johannes Liechtenauer using the longsword. |
| **la Nouvelle Vac** | The new wave (French). |
| **Lebensraum (German)** | 'Living space'; the intention and desire to expand into other countries to provide living space for the growing German race. The idea of a Germanic people without sufficient space dates back to long before Adolf Hitler brought it to prominence. Through the Middle Ages, German population pressures led to settlement in Eastern Europe, a practice called *Ostsiedlung* and coined 'Drang nach Osten'. |
| **l'Ordre régne** | The reigning order (French). |
| **Lieber Gott** | Dear God (German). |
| **Lizard League** | Also Lizard Union; an organization of Prussian nobles and knights established in Culmerland (Chelmno Land) in 1397. Its goal was to combat lawlessness, although it discreetly sought the transfer of Culmerland from the Teutonic Knights to Poland. Nicholas von Renys, Komtur of Kulm, was one of its founding members. |
| **Lümmel** | Lout; boor, insolent oaf; rascal; rogue; ruffian; penis (e.g., "think with your head; not with your lümmel") (German) |
| **Merlon** | The vertical solid part of a battlement or crenellated parapet. |
| **Minnelied** | Love poem (German). |
| **Minnesäng** | Courtly love poetry (German). |
| **Minnesänger** | Someone who writes and performs courtly love poetry (German). |
| **Mormal** | A bad sore, cancer or gangrene (French); 'a deadly |

sore' and associated with ergotism (*ignis sacer* or the Holy Fire).

**Music of the Spheres**

The Music of the Spheres incorporates meta-physiccal principle that mathematical relationships express qualities or 'tones' of energy which manifest in numbers, visual angles, shapes and sounds – all connected within a pattern of proportion. In his *Harmonicies Mundi* Kepler describeed how the particular tone in a planet's 'song' depends on the ratio of its orbit, just as the realtionship of a keynote to its octave. According to Kepler, the connection between sacred geometry, cosmology, astrology, harmonics, and music is through *musica universalis.*

**New World Order**

Refers to the emergence of a totalitarian one-world government, through the actions of a powerful elite (e.g., Nazi Party) with a globalist agenda to rule the world through an authoritarian world government that would replace sovereign nation-states and use an aggressive propaganda campaign that idolizes its establishment as the culmination of history's progress and the natural evolution of humanity.

**Niche Partitioning**

An ecological (and economic) term that describes how two species (companies) can co-exist by allocating resources (niche means "job"); the process allows two species to partition certain resources so that one species does not monopolize the resource and out-compete the other to its exclusion.

**Noblewoman's Guard**

Also 'Upward Proud Woman's guard'; Fiore Dei Liberi's term for a position with the blade held over or on the right shoulder. In one version it is held horizontal almost resting on the shoulder. In another it is held at a 45-degree angle as if in a shoulder-level "high" guard, but with the opposite shoulder turned more forward. The Women's guard seems related to horizontal cut, as the posture can be assumed both preliminary to such a blow and as a result of such a blow. Yet it is more likely this guard is actually a shoulder-level *Vom Dach* (high guard).

**Ochs**

Ox; a guard position with the sword held to either

side of the head, with the point (as a horn) aiming at the opponent's face. (German).

**Ordensbug** Castle (state) (German).

**Ordensburgen** Pertaining to castle (state) (German).

**Orpo** Abbreviation commonly used for *Ordnungspolizei*, a *Schutzstaffel*–run German police force (German). See "Schutzstaffel".

**Pal** A smart communication device / computer the size of an iphone

**Pastis** Milky yellowish strong apéritif that tastes of liquorice (French)

**Pepin** Also Pippin; nickname given to someone short, named after Pepin the Short (Pepin le Bref) from the 8th Century.

**Pflug** 'Plough', low (middle) guard in medieval swordsmanship; a position with the sword held to either side of the body with the pommel near the back hip, with the point aiming at the opponent's chest or face. Some historical manuals state that when this guard is held on the right side of the body that the short edge should be facing up and when held on the left side of the body the short edge should be facing down with the thumb on the flat of the blade (German).

**Pleroma** 'Fullness'; Gnostic concept referring to the totality of divine powers or 'ideal realm' wherin Aeons are expressed as the thoughts of God (Greek); according to Jung it is both nothing and everything; the non-living world that is undifferentiated by subjectivity according to Gregory Bateson.

**Poissonerie** Fish shop (French).

**Putain** Whore (French).

**Quartier** Neighbourhood (French).

**Reichsfürst** Prince of the empire (German).

**Reliquary** 'Shrine'; a container, usually jeweled and gilded, to house sacred religious relics.

**Rette**    Save; rescue (German)

**Ringen am Schwert**    Close combat fighting technigues that include striking with the pommel or using *halb-schwert* techniques of grabbing the sword's blade with her hands and striking, thrusting, or deflecting; or trapping his forearms with her other arm and disarming him by tripping, kicking and grappling moves. Described in *Fechtmeister* Johannes Leichtenauer's *Fechtsbuch*. ("Wrestling at the sword").

**Ritter**    Knight (German).

**Ritterkreuz**    Knight's cross (German); The Knight's Cross of the Iron Cross was the highest award of Germany to recognize extreme battlefield bravery or successful military leadership.

**Rossfechten**    Mounted combat (German).

**Scriptorium**    A place for writing, commonly used to refer to a room in medieval European monastery devoted to the copying of manuscripts by monastic scribes.

**Schadenfruede**    Taking malicious pleasure in somebody else's misfortune (German).

**Schlacht**    Battle (German).

**Schutzstaffel**    'Protection Squadron'(German); a major paramilitary organization under Adolf Hitler and the Nazi Party; An elite guard of the Nazi Orpo, (knicknamed the SS) and run by the Black Knights in François's world.

**Social Darwinism**    An ideology of society that applies biological concepts of Darwinism and evolutionary theory to sociology and politics, often with the assumption that conflict between groups in society leads to social progress as superior groups outcompete inferior ones. An example of applied Social Darwinism is the competition between individuals in a model of laissez-fair capitalism; the ideology has motivated and been used to justify notions of eugenics scientific racism, imperialism, fascism, and Nazism.

**Sonderweg**     "Special path"(German); a notion that considers the German-speaking lands or country to follow a unique and 'exceptional' course, distinct from others; used to explain German foreign policy and ideology prior and during WWI, characterized by trying to find a "third way" to be implemented for the world, other than western 'vulgar' democracy or eastern Czaristic autocracy;  Germany's Sonderweg began in the Enlightenment and would ultimately lead to the killing fields of the Holocaust through Nazi application of Neitzsche, Treitschke, Bernharadi and vulgarized versions of Kant, Fichte, and Hegel; promoted by German historians and journalists, notably Friedrich Meinecke, Ernst Troeltsch and Thomas Mann; historian Fritz Fischer argues that the Nationalist Socialism movement in Germany arose long before 1914 (and the Treaty of Versailles) and resulted from long-standing ambitions of the German power elite supported by the pro-socialistic teachings of the Lutheran church in an expansionist philosophy;  in Francois's world it represents a nihilistic fascist philosophy promoted by the current Nazi Regime of Europe and promulgated in the *Zarathustra Plan* for world domination. See "Exceptionalism", "Social Darwinism", "Lebensraum", and "Drang nash Osten".

**Soteltes**     An elaborate sugar sculpture.

**Stundenbuch**     Book of Hours (German); a devotional illuminated manuscript popular in the Middle Ages.

**Sturmhaupt-**     A captain within the ranks of the *Schutzstaffel*
**führer**     (German).

**Subtlety**     Edible statue of brightly coloured marzipan (English)

**Syndicalism**     An economic guild-like system proposed as a replacement for capitalism and state socialism; a 'collective' model that advocates interest aggregation of multiple non-competative units to nego-tiate and manage an economy; a bottom-up system in which all participants share equal ownership of its services and production. A current version of syndicalism can be found in the "collective creati-vity" practiced by some silicon valley companies (e.g., Pixar) in which all members of the creative team are recognized.

**Tagelied**  A particular form of medieval German language lyric; dawnsong (German).

**Tankard**  A large one-handed drinking vessel, usually of silver or pewter, with a cover (English)

**Truppführer**  A sergeant within the ranks of the *Schutzstaffel* (German).

**Überlauffen**  A move in close hand-to-hand combat in which attacks are outreached by diving into or out of another's action.

**Verjuice**  A 'green' juice made from unripe grapes; 'vertjus'; very acidic juice made from pressing unripe grapes, crabapples ; or other sour fruit; widely used in the Middle Ages as an ingredient in sauces, as a condi-ment or to deglaze preparations.

**Viper's Dance**  'dancing mania'; victims suffered from ergot poi-soning, which was known as St Anthony's Fire in the Middle Ages.

**Völkisch Movement**  'Völkische Bewegung '(German); German inter-pretation of the populist movement, with a romantic focus on folklore and the "organic". The term *völkisch*, meaning 'ethnic', derives from the German word Volk (cognate with the English "folk"), corresponding to 'people', with connotations in German of 'people-powered', 'folksy' and 'folkloric'. According to the historian James Webb, the word also has "overtones of 'nation', 'race' and 'tribe'.

**Vom tag**  'From the roof', a high guard; in the German school of fencing, a basic position with the sword held either on the right shoulder or above the head. The blade can be held vertically or at roughly 45-degrees.

**Weltpolitik**  Refers to the foreign policy advanced by Kaiser Wilhelm II of Germany in the late 1800s (German), replacing the earlier 'Realpolitik' approach. Up until Wilhelm's dismissal of Chancellor Otto von Bismarck, Germany had concentrated its efforts on eliminating the possibility of a two-front in Europe. It was content with being the leading power on the Continent by means of its army and subtle diplomacy. Wilhelm was far more ambitious. Frustrated with the limits of Germany's geographical position in the centre of Europe, his aim was to transform the country into a global power by means of aggressive diplomacy and a large navy. Weltpolitik was thus primarily a naval policy.

# Selected Bibliography

Brown, Sarah and David O'Conner. 1991. "Medieval Craftsmen: Glass-Painters". The British Museum Press. London, England.

Coldstream, Nicola. 1991. "Medieval Craftsmen: Masons and Sculptors". The British Museum Press. London, England.

Cowley, Robert (ed). 1999. "What If? Military Historians Imagine What Might Have Been". Pan Books, London, England.

DeHamel, Christopher. 1992. "Medieval Craftsmen: Scribes and Illuminators". The British Museum Press. London, England.

Tobler, Christian Henry. 2004. "Fighting with the German Longsword". The Chivalry Bookshelf, Highland Village, Texas.

Turnbull, Stephen. 2005. "Tannenberg 1410: disaster for the teutonic knights". Praeger,Westport, CT.

Van der Kist, John. 2001. "Kaiser Wilhelm II: Germany's Last Emperor". The History Press.

Willmott, I I.P. 2003. "World War I". DK, London, England.

✠

 **Nina Munteanu** is a Canadian ecologist and novelist. In addition to eight published novels, she has authored award-winning short stories, articles and non-fiction books, which have been translated into several languages throughout the world. Recognition for her work includes the *Midwest Book Review Reader's Choice Award*, finalist for *Foreword Magazine's Book of the Year Award*, the *SLF Fountain Award*, and the *Aurora Award*, Canada's top prize in science fiction.

Nina served as assistant editor-in-chief of *Imagikon*, a Romanian speculative magazine. She regularly publishes reviews and essays in magazines such as *The New York Review of Science Fiction* and *Strange Horizons*, and serves as staff writer for several online and print magazines.

Nina lectured for over twenty years at colleges and universities, where she taught ecology, limnology & environmental education and published papers in scientific journals. She has been providing personal coaching and group workshops on writing and publishing for over twenty years. Her guidebook, The Fiction Writer: Get Published, Write Now! is being used by schools and universities across North America and was published in Romania by *Editura Paralela 45*. Nina's award-winning blog *The Alien Next Door* hosts lively discussion on science, travel, pop culture, writing and movies. Visit www.ninamunteanu.com to find her teaching DVDs, other teaching materials and to sign on for personal coaching.

✠

CPSIA information can be obtained at www.ICGtesting.com
Printed in the USA
LVOW081903090413

328363LV00006B/714/P